The Ernesto "Che" Guevara School for Wayward Girls

Also by William F. Gavin
One Hell of a Candidate

The Ernesto "Che" Guevara
School for Wayward Girls

★

WILLIAM F. GAVIN

THOMAS DUNNE BOOKS ☙ ST. MARTIN'S PRESS
NEW YORK

THOMAS DUNNE BOOKS.
An imprint of St. Martin's Press.

www.stmartins.com

Book design by Jonathan Bennett

Library of Congress Cataloging-in-Publication Data

Gavin, William F.
    The Ernesto "Che" Guevara School for Wayward Girls : a novel of politics / William F. Gavin.—1st ed.
        p.   cm.
    ISBN 0-312-33889-9
    EAN 978-0-312-33889-3
    1. Speechwriters—Fiction.   2. Washington (D.C.)—Fiction.   3. Prostitutes—Rehabilitation—Fiction.   4. Women college teachers—Fiction.   5. Montana—Fiction. I. Title.

PS3607.A985E76 2006
813'.5—dc22

                                                          2005051886

First Edition: January 2006

10   9   8   7   6   5   4   3   2   1

To Nina Graybill and Sean Desmond

"Che cosa faccio? Scrivo.
E come vivo? Vivo!"
("What do I do here? I write.
And how do I live? I live!")

Rodolfo, in *La Boheme*

PART ONE

Saying A

ONE

Peter Holmes Dickinson, thirty-four, of the Main Line Dickinsons—a branch of the, alas, no longer superwealthy but still insufferably arrogant Philadelphia Dickinsons—lay naked and supine on his bed. He groaned as only a suddenly awakened hangover victim can groan, piteously, from the fathomless depths of his thirsty heart. His long blond hair had only recently begun its inexorable journey northward into baldness, and his once lean, muscled body (he had been the almost star of the Penn swimming team) was now beginning to show faint but discernible signs of mid-thirties male belly bulge and general softness. But all things considered, he was still as handsome, and proud, as the devil.

Something or someone was shaking him. He rolled onto his side. In the semidarkness of the room, illuminated only by the light coming from the bathroom, he discovered (1) his left wrist was handcuffed to a bedpost and (2) there was a tall blond woman dressed in a Fairfax County, Virginia, Police Department uniform standing by the bed, smiling down at him. There was only one problem: Pete couldn't remember why a police officer was in his bedroom, or why he was handcuffed.

"You pooped out on me toward the end, honey," the officer said in a low voice, with a pleasant, warm, down-home Virginia drawl. "I think you had too much of that Italian vino. Well, it's late—or early, I guess, two-thirty—and I really got to get home."

Pete, his brain just beginning to function, now realized they were in his 1,400-square-foot, two-bedroom, two-bath, tenth-floor condo in the new, exciting, expensive Lynhill South high-rise (doorman, underground parking, concierge, gym, all the amenities, the works) in Arlington, Virginia.

"I'll take my cuffs back, honey," she said softly, "and then I'm out of here. If I ever lose these things, I'll be in *big* trouble."

He felt her remove the cuffs.

"Now, you take care," she whispered, bending over him. "Remember we got that date to go swimming. You can show me some new strokes."

She stuck her tongue in his ear, giggled, and, closing the door quietly, with early-in-the-morning courtesy, was gone. Brief fragments of memories flickered in and out of Pete's brain. Two bottles of Chianti . . . the super-size pizzas . . . her whoops and snorts, and that annoying whinnying sound she made as she bounced about his bed. *Marcie*. That was her name. No. Marlie. It was *Marlie*. Police Officer First Class Marlie Rae Perkins. How could he, of all people, a Dickinson and a former speechwriter for President Tyler ("Ty the Guy") Ferguson, ever forget a hick name like that? The Dickinsons simply did not know or want to know people with names like Marlie Rae. But this was the Washington area, and one met all kinds, in often very surprising ways.

Two weeks ago, at one in the morning, Pete had been driving his black-onyx-colored Lexus SC430 hardtop convertible (top down, of course) on Chain Bridge Road in McLean, just before the junction with Old Dominion Road. He was on his way home from a quickie with the bored, lonely wife of a Uruguayan—or was it Paraguayan?—embassy official who lived in Oakton. Smoking a joint and debriefing himself on the night's events, he had forgotten to check his speedometer. The flashing light of the police cruiser appeared out of nowhere and he pulled over, flipping the joint out the window. Trying to charm his way out of the ticket, he flirted a bit—Pete flirted the way birds fly, instinctively and well—with the rather large but very attractive officer. But then, damn it, she saw the *other* joint, on the seat beside him. *Goddamn it, in his reveries, he had forgotten the damned other one!* She looked at the joint, looked at Pete, and then picked it up. She held it between two fingers, stared into his blue eyes, went back to her car, and a few minutes later came back and gave him a speeding ticket.

"Drive carefully, Mr. Dickinson," she said. "You can't be too careful."

She called him two nights later—he assumed police officers had their ways of finding out telephone numbers—and said she wanted to talk to him. He agreed to meet her in a country-music bar in Arlington. By this time he had concluded she wasn't going to press the marijuana charge, but he was curious as to what she had in mind. Blackmail? Worse, a lecture on the evils of drugs? He was also intrigued by the outside possibility of making love with a police-woman. In matters of sex, if little else, Peter Holmes Dickinson was egalitarian.

So he met Marlie Rae in the Arlington beer joint. There was recorded country music playing. The whining nasal bleats of let's-pretend cowboys, singing of cheating, drinking, God, and the flag, pained him, but what could one expect from a girl named Marlie Rae (who, thank God, was in civvies, a plaid shirt and jeans)? Pete quickly discovered they had little in common, surprise, surprise. At one point she said, delightedly, "That's a Hank Williams record playing now. A golden oldie. 'Hey, Good Lookin'.' Don't you think he was the greatest? Hank Senior, I mean?"

Pete wasn't all too clear about the identity of Hank Williams, senior or otherwise, but under the circumstances he thought it best to grunt and nod assent. There was something about Marlie Rae Perkins—an animal vitality? an unashamedly frank sexual interest in him? the Brünnhilde-like splendor of her healthy, blond-beast good looks (Pete's father had turned him on to Wagner years ago)—that kept him sitting in the booth for two more pitchers of cheap, watery, tasteless domestic beer; innumerable awful buffalo wings; and dead-end discussions of almost every topic that came to mind. Finally she downed a beer, smacked her lips, and said to him, "Look, honey, let's be honest. Like you said, you used to be a speechwriter for the president himself, and you lived on that rich Main Line—even I heard of that place. And I'm just a Fairfax County police officer, although I was born in Patrick County, Virginia. But I'm not dumb."

"Oh, I don't think you're—"

"Oh hell, honey, yes, you do. I can tell from what you said, and how you listened. I'm a cop, remember? Trained to listen. Most men think all women are dumb anyway. That's okay. You and me come from two different worlds, like they say. But unless I'm missing something, you aren't staying here just for my real interesting conversation, right?"

"Well, er—"

"Then why don't we just agree that as soon as we can, we're going to, you know, get to know each other much better. That's what I want, and I figure that's what you want."

To his surprise, last evening Marlie had showed up at his apartment door, in uniform, right after completing her shift. She was carrying two bottles of Chianti and two extra-large sausage pizzas. They chatted about this and that (Pete, while telling her about his swimming prowess, casually, and of course without for a moment meaning it, said they should go swimming sometime) and finished one bottle of wine. Pete, fascinated by the coarse, peasant effrontery of the Chianti (and of Marlie), drank most of the cheap wine out of sheer perversity. They ate one of the pizzas. Then they stopped talking and started kissing—she made the first move, which amused and pleased Pete. For the next twenty-three minutes and forty-two seconds, counting initial tentative moves, Pete found that Marlie Rae Perkins, of the Patrick County, Virginia, Perkinses, was energetic, cooperative, imaginative, and indefatigable. She was generously built, not exactly Pete's style, but he liked the way she moved, quickly and with purpose, like an NBA power forward who could drive to the hoop. Finally she gave forth a strangled yodel (damn near smothering him with an embrace of steel), and Pete offered his usual muffled "Uh!" (Dickinsons rarely gave anything away, especially in bed).

They rested for a bit and then drank the other bottle of wine—Pete drank most of it again, this time beguiled by the brash charm of its blatant, if transparent, desire to please (again, like Marlie herself)—and split the other, no longer hot, pizza. Pete, his stomach queasy, began to feel he had perhaps overindulged. Then Marlie got the cuffs and they started in again, but this time it wasn't quite the same. Pete, quite drunk by now, wasn't up to it and he could tell after a while that she was going through the motions. Eventually he fell asleep, frustrated, limp, drunk, and exhausted. The next thing he knew, there she was, standing by the bed, smiling down at him. And here he was now, still in bed, suffering the various spiritual, psychic, nervous, gastric, and depressive manifestations of a hangover from cheap wine. If that wasn't enough, he couldn't sleep, because he was worried. He was deeply in debt, with no quick way of getting out.

His speechwriting/consulting business wasn't doing well. Except for union chief Tim Flaherty and one or two others, the blue-chip clients he had expected to be knocking down his door had not appeared. (Did President Ty the Guy, his former boss—they were now estranged—have something to do with this? Was Pete blacklisted?) Pete had gone in way over his head when he bought the Lexus convertible, and then the condominium. Now he was having trouble meeting payments on both. He had a drawerful of unpaid bills, and he was getting increasingly less polite "have a bad day" telephone calls and letters from those he owed money. He had long since given up the high-rent office on K Street and now worked out of his second bedroom, made into a makeshift office.

Then there was his little gambling, er, *gaming*, problem. It began when he made some stupid bets on NFL games and then tried to recoup his losses by doubling the amount he wagered. (The goddamn Eagles couldn't beat the spread if they were playing Saint Joe's Prep!) He was now $10,680 in debt to a large, jolly, gregarious, back-slapping, coke-snorting, red-haired northern Virginia construction mogul named Jeb Hammerford (Jeb Stuart Hammerford, University of Virginia, University of Virginia Law School, rich, with a very rich and well-connected-in-Richmond daddy who had gone to VMI, the Virginia business equivalent of being a made man in New Jersey). Pete had met Jeb one night at GameDaze, a popular Washington sports bar. They talked and drank, bullshitted each other, and made a friendly two-hundred-dollar wager on Sunday's Eagles-Redskins game. The 'Skins managed to beat the spread. Pete doubled the bet the next time he met Jeb, and things began to slide after that. The last time they talked, in fact, Jeb had not been as jolly as usual.

"At the University, a man pays what he owes, Pete. It's what gentlemen do. Edgar Allan Poe was asked to leave the University because of a gambling debt problem."

"That must have made Poe ravin' mad," Pete said, but Jeb just looked at him, puzzled.

Things were so bad that Pete had even begun thinking of taking the last desperate measure: asking—begging—his father for money. The thought of the smug look on Trevor Dickinson's face as he listened to his son's plea was disheartening. But things might come to that, and he had to steel himself for the humiliation.

And finally, there was the little problem of cocaine. Pete, of course, had dabbled in the drug at prep school. He used it sparingly in college and then dropped it—he wasn't hooked, after all—while he was working for the Guy. But since he left the White House, he had resumed his participation in one of young, affluent America's favorite recreational pastimes. He now found himself in debt to a small, skinny, blond, evil-tempered, acne-ridden, tattooed young white dude named Dean—Pete did not know his last name—from somewhere in Loudon County, Virginia. Dean was, somehow or other, an acquaintance of Jeb's. (Jeb was one of those indolent, wealthy young men who liked to walk on the dark side of town and did not feel manly unless somehow involved with low-life scum.) Dean wasn't exactly a skinhead, but he shaved his skull pretty close. He had done some time in jail—he boasted of it—and had a backwoods white-guy's totally macho Aryan attitude. Dean also had a big gun that, the last time Pete had met him, in the men's room at GameDaze, to consummate a cocaine/money-transfer business deal, he had displayed as he made firm suggestions that the debt be cleared, and soon. Considering where they were at the time, and what Pete had heard about the sexual predilections of primitive white Southern males (he had, after all, seen *Deliverance*), Pete was thankful that was *all* Dean displayed.

So here he was, in bed, unable to sleep, hungover, his stomach in rebellion.

He got up—with all deliberate speed—and stumbled to the bathroom. He gazed at his reflection in the bathroom mirror. Puffy-faced, unshaven, eyes red-rimmed, a real charmer. Young Mr. Dickinson, enjoying a typically civilized, leisurely morning at home.

How did I get into this mess?

Oh, for Christ's sake, Dickinson, stop whining, be a man.

He brushed his teeth, gargled (he was a no-flavoring, hard-line original Listerine man), and made his way back to bed. Eventually he fell asleep. He dreamed he was back on the swim team at Penn, doing laps, the perfect union of his body and the water, suspended between earth and sky, away from his father, away from his problems, away from his periodic attacks of self-loathing, himself alone, lap after lap. . . . As he swam, someone was playing music. . . . Baroque? . . . Bach? The clock radio had sounded: 6:22. Time to get up. This morning he had to start writing the speech for the executive director of the Institute for the Promotion of Acquisitive Values, a libertarian think tank dedicated to fighting bias and insensitivity against greedy people. He somehow managed to shower, shave, dress, and make a pot of coffee. Barefoot, he padded to his office. He sat in front of his iMac and stared at the screen as it went through its start-up ritual. His brain wasn't working after last night's semi-orgy. He had no energy.

There were only two remedies for creative sluggishness—the music of Richard Wagner and a little short of cocaine. He searched through his CDs, pulled out the Georg Solti–Vienna Philharmonic version of Wagner's greatest hits from the Ring Cycle, and placed the disc in his white Bose CD player. He hit the remote. The music from "The Entrance of the Gods into Valhalla" began to play. Sublime. His father considered it a sacrilege to play great music as background noise while one is writing or reading. But Pete had learned that Wagner's music, played full blast, could break through any kind of fog, especially when enhanced by coke. As the music played, he got the coke from a shoe box in the closet, a small mirror from his dresser, and an old-fashioned single-edge razor blade from the medicine cabinet. He carried them to the kitchen table, recalling, as he always did when he performed this ritual, the beginning of *Ulysses* (he had been an English major, after all) in which stately, plump Buck Mulligan, carrying his mirror and razor (but no coke), mockingly intones the words of the start of the Roman Catholic Mass, back in the days when they still used Latin:

Introibo ad altare dei . . .

Pete was not religious (Dickinsons believed in a slim, well-dressed Episcopal God, a gentleman, like them, who had a balanced portfolio and the courtesy not to bother them) but knew the need for ritual. Carefully—*carefully*—he poured two small, thin lines of the white powder (let's not be greedy, let's make it last) on the smooth surface of the mirror. He used the razor blade to chop the cocaine and make the lines even. He reached into his wallet, took out a ten-dollar bill (in the old days he used a hundred, the mark of a coke sophisticate), rolled it expertly into a straw, and leaned his head over the mirror so that his head was close to the white lines. With a finger pressing on one nostril, he quickly snorted one line. Wait. Wait. Wait. Patience. Now the second snort. Wait. Wait. Tingling in the nose. White cold bliss. Start of a society high. Ah, yes. He moistened his finger, rubbed it over the residue of the coke on the mirror, and massaged his gums with his dream-laden finger. Here he was, a good multiculturalist, in solidarity with all those good Andean folks who have been chewing cocoa leaves for a thousand years. Long live diversity.

Now wait. Smoking hits sooner, but snorting lasts longer. He had learned that in St. Elwalds, his (and his father's and his father's father's) prep school, where he and his childhood pal Gooch Curruthers used to experiment with recreational drug usage. Gooch, after the suicide of his father—caught dipping into the till of his brokerage house, Mr. Curruthers had pulled a Hemingway, putting a shotgun in his mouth—had dropped out and was now a drug-free, New Age, semi-wannabe Deadhead, going to the Rainbow gathering every year, atoning for what the white man did to the Indians. The last time—five years ago—Pete had seen him, Gooch babbled about the Earth Mother. Poor Gooch.

Beginning to feel good—calm, serene, filled with boundless energy—Pete went back to his office and looked up at the framed picture of Stan Laurel and Oliver Hardy above his computer table. Fat Ollie looking, as usual, exasperated; skinny Stan looking beatifically dopey. Pete smiled. He did not love many people or many things, but he loved Stan and Ollie, always had, and in graduate school he had written a well-received paper on them. He looked back at the iMac screen. The cursor was waiting, blinking for action. Pete himself was ready for action. The problem was, there was no action. Even surfing along the top of the cocaine high, Pete wasn't getting any ideas. He found himself listening to the Wagner instead of concentrating on the speech. The music reminded him: tonight he was going to a charity gala performance at the Kennedy Center, black-tie, a tribute not to Wagner, more's the pity, but to the Golden Age of American Music. His date had gotten two tickets from a lobbyist. Pete wondered if he would have to sit through "Climb Ev'ry Mountain" or "You'll Never Walk Alone," two saccharine sins against music for which Rodgers and Hammerstein were no doubt suffering in hell.

He had to get the "Greed Is Good" speech out of the way because he had also contracted to write remarks for the head of some group called the National Association of Developmental Ecologists, whatever the hell that was, and he would have to read through the background material and then write a speech to be delivered to a bunch of . . . of . . . a bunch of what? He didn't know what developmental ecologists did. But a good speechwriter should be able to write a speech about anything, as long as he's provided with background material. Pete was proud of his craftsmanship and was always on the hunt for what he had come to think of as the Ted Sorensen Moment, when you write a sentence or phrase that will be remembered.

"Ask not what your country can do for you; ask what you can do for your country."

Write one good line—even an obviously forced, artificial inversion—and it would be remembered forever. Oh, sure, most speechwriters affected a cynical view of their craft, but there wasn't one among them who didn't want his stuff to be quoted in the media and, better, be remembered. The line did not have to be beautiful or even make sense, it just had to have that magic quality of being memorable. Pete knew that he couldn't force a Sorensen Moment. It would have to come in its own time. But he also knew every speechwriter wanted three things: the speaker to deliver his speech as written, a lot of speech excerpts in the media the next day, and one good line by which he would be remembered. How many speechwriters are known to the public? A handful— Ted Sorensen, Peggy Noonan, a few others. To escape the anonymity, to step from behind the curtain . . . ah, well, someday he'd find the Moment.

The CD was now playing "The Ride of the Valkyries." That made him think of Marlie Rae. Well, she was cheaper than cocaine and he didn't owe her money, so the night had not been a total loss. He grinned as he fantasized about bringing Marlie, Miss Virginia Storm Trooper, in her gray blouse, dark pants uniform, to the family manse back in Bryn Mawr, Pennsylvania, and introducing her to Dad.

Back to work. *How can I turn greed into a virtue? You're a speechwriter; just do it. If you can't do it, then fake it.* He began to type:

Acquisition is at the heart of the American dream: a house, a job, an education, a car, labor-saving devices for the household—we all want to acquire. Americans are often called go-getters—we go in order to get, because getters is what we are. So why are ordinary Americans criticized as being "greedy" when we acquire things that make our lives better? Getting things, owning things, and wanting more things isn't greed—it's the American dream in action. . . .

There. At last. A beginning. It wasn't good. It wasn't true. But it was a start.

TWO

That evening, in the Grand Foyer of the Kennedy Center, standing next to the huge, craggy bronze bust of John F. Kennedy, Pete was waiting for his date, a Hill staffer for a New York congressman, to come back from the ladies' room, that great dark star from whose gravitational pull no woman returns in less than fifteen minutes. He was in the midst of a slight post-cocaine downer. The music in the first part of the gala—he thought of it as Sinatra music, *la-da this, la-da that, I lo-ove you, you don't lo-ove me, boo-hoo*—sounded all the same to Peter and bored him to no end. Aside from periodic doses of Wagner, served hot and loud and long, he preferred punk, early heavy metal, Nirvana, music that *moved*, classics such as Echo and the Bunnymen and Sonic Youth (in their transitional phase, of course). He was trying to distract himself from troublesome thoughts of debt. Earlier that afternoon he had called his father in Bryn Mawr. *Peter, what a surprise, how good to hear from you.* Pete didn't tell Trevor exactly why he'd be paying him a visit *(Oh, it's been a long time, Dad, I just thought it would be good to catch up)*, but they each agreed it was time they got together again. God, what an awful, humiliating hour or so it would be as he groveled before his father, asking for a loan.

Wait a minute. I don't have to ask for the money on the first visit. I'll use this trip to put him in a nice paternal mood. I'll make my move later on, only if I'm really desperate. This time, I'll just play the attentive son, listen to him boast about his latest girlfriend or talk interminably about the biography of Thomas Love Peacock he's been working on since the fourth century BCE. There's no need to rush things. Not yet.

To distract himself from thoughts of money problems, Pete glanced up at the bronze Kennedy bust. He considered it the stupidest, ugliest piece of public art ever created. He made a point to bring out-of-town visitors to the Grand Foyer just to laugh at this piece of pretentious kitsch. It made Kennedy look as if he had some loathsome skin disease—which, now that Pete came to think of it, he may have had, given the parlous state of his health and his documented excesses in the skin trade. Pete turned his head and saw a beautiful young woman staring in his direction, in fact, right at him, although as soon as he made eye contact she looked at the Kennedy head.

It's Che Che. My God, it's Che Che Hart.

She was across the foyer, by the Opera House steps, wearing a simple, ruinously expensive simple black dress—Pete knew about such things—and a single strand of pearls. He instantly recalled how it had been, less than three years ago, when he and Che Che had been *the* Washington young couple. A photo of them had appeared in *Washingtonian* magazine, with an accompanying text:

> Peter Dickinson, this season's golden boy, a world-class (just ask him) speechwriter for President Ty Ferguson, and Ernestina "Che Che" Hart (named after the legendary charismatic communist leader Ernesto "Che" Guevara), gorgeous daughter of wealthy left-wing activist Donna Hart Lyons, are positively *scorching up the place*. Ballet or opera or theater at the Kennedy Center? You'll probably see Pete 'n' Che there, holding hands and making wickedly funny but knowledgeable comments about the shows. Go to one of those fun sports occurrences, a Wizards victory, at the MCI Center, and there's our Pete with gorgeous (did we say that?) Che Che.

But one night, at a Democratic fund-raiser hosted by Che Che's mother in the Hyatt Regency on Capitol Hill, Che Che caught Pete, in a stairwell of all places, lip-wrestling with a cute, tiny, ambitious blond lobbyist for some environmental group, Green Something or Other. Che Che tried to slug Pete, but overswung. He ducked; Che Che hit the blonde in the side of the head and hurt her own hand. Che Che 'n' Pete was, immediately, so over. Two weeks later she moved to New York City, to work for her mother's foundation, Lion-Heart. At first, Pete just blew it off. All right, she left him. Things like that had happened to him since prep school. But for the next few months he was afflicted with a strange, troubling, and to him unique sensation—he missed Che Che, badly. He had never missed anyone in his life.

But now, here she was, directly across the foyer, pretending not to notice him. Her perfect face (*People* magazine had once said she was "part Nefertiti mystery, part Lena Horne sass," and provided pictures of Nefertiti and Lena for those who might not get the reference), her flawless light brown skin, those light green eyes, the very way she stood there, at ease with herself and the world, radiated a confident, unforced, and therefore devastating sexiness. Pete smiled as he saw middle-aged men in tuxes walk past her with their wives and give Che Che that quick, discreet, impossible-to-resist-at-any-age, instinctive male second glance. He had to decide quickly, before his date returned—should he walk across the foyer and say hello? But how to begin? He suffered from the speechwriter's *deformation professionelle,* a tendency to see life in terms of rhetoric. The introduction, usually the least-reported part of a speech, was very important. A politician gifted with the silver eloquence of Demosthenes and the lung power of William Jennings Bryan delivering the Cross of Gold speech might give an oration that thrilled the audience, but if in his introductory remarks he forgot the name of some third-rate hack at the dais or called the local football team by the wrong name, he was doomed. It was the same with meeting women—the intro should be a grabber, giving you the advantage. Pete thought for a few seconds, but couldn't come up with any introductory words that would get him over the initial hurdle with Che Che. He had read in the *Post* that she was back in town, teaching at Georgetown. But should he tell her he knew? It might make him seem needy. He didn't want to start the conversation by admitting he had been thinking of her. But what intro would work? To hell with it, I'll do what I warn my clients not to do—ad-lib. He walked toward her.

"Hello, Che," he said in his smooth, buttery baritone voice. "You're the most beautiful girl in the room, as always."

"You're looking well yourself, Peter. Very James Bondish in your black tie."

"I noticed you looking at the bust of Kennedy," he said. "What do you think?"

"I think it's wonderful."

"Amazing. I was thinking the very same thing."

"That's odd. In bed one night, you once told me the Kennedy bust was the stupidest piece of public art ever produced."

"Did I really say that? You have a great memory."

"Well, as I said, we were in bed, and you hadn't impressed me with anything else, so your aesthetic criticism stuck in my mind."

"Che, I'm disappointed. You're still doing that 1940s Roz Russell schtick from *His Girl Friday*. Banter. Badinage. But Roz had much better timing."

"She was playing opposite Cary Grant. I'm not that lucky."

"Are you still in New York?"

"In fact, I've back at the Volta Place house in Georgetown. I'm teaching history at Georgetown."

"Oh, *yes*, I forgot. I think I saw the piece in the *Post*. How do you like teaching?"

"Oh, I can't make cultural references to anything outside of current pop music, because they don't get it. But aside from that, I'm getting along fine."

"I've been following your mother's feud with Ezra Tyne. Why the hell is she even bothering with him? He's a right-wing nutcake."

"My mom never feels comfortable unless she's fighting someone. She's been fighting all her life. Now she's thinking of running against President Ferguson next year."

"Good for her. Ask her if she needs a good, if very expensive, speechwriter."

"Wouldn't that be interesting? The Guy's former speechwriter, writing for his worst enemy."

"I have my own writing and consulting shop now."

"By the way, I was impressed by that op-ed piece you did in the *Post* telling why you left the White House. If I didn't know you better, I would have believed every word."

Out of the corner of his eye, Pete saw his date making her way through the crowd.

"Well, it's nice to see you again, Che. I had forgotten that feeling."

"What feeling?"

"How great it was during those rare intervals when you weren't breaking my balls."

Three days later he called her, at her university office. Why don't we have lunch, just catch up on things? They ate at a Vietnamese place on M Street. They talked for a long time, about her teaching job (kids these days knew nothing), the book she was working on (coming along), his speechwriting firm (well, not a *firm*—a one-man boutique shop, the way he described it). Things couldn't be better, Pete said. I'm turning away business. Che Che asked about his father.

"Nothing new with Trevor," Pete said. "He has a new girlfriend, or maybe he's had another one since the last one I met. We're like nations that have had certain difficulties with each other—our relations are not cordial, but correct."

"I bet he's proud of you."

"Why would my father be proud of me?"

"Well, for one thing, you are—or were—a speechwriter for the president."

Pete laughed.

"Trevor considers politics beneath contempt. To him, being a speechwriter, even for a president, is the equivalent of playing piano in a whorehouse."

"Are you still devoted to Stan and Ollie?"

"Why, certainly," he said, pronouncing it *soit-en-leh*, as Georgia-born-and-bred Ollie had.

"I used to think you liked them more than you liked me."

"I have to be frank—it was a damned close call, Che. Stan and Ollie are *very* yin and yang. Exasperation and acceptance. Scheming and believing. You should have read my Annenberg School paper on them: 'Transgendering, Sexual Confusion and Ur-Hegemonic Feminism in *Sons of the Desert.*' "

"I'd forgotten how much you know about so many inconsequential things."

"It's a gift."

A week after that, they had dinner at Chez François in Great Falls in Virginia. In Washington, lunch is a business or political opportunity, but going to Chez François for dinner is an event. The wooded, affluent Great Falls area, plus the French country-inn Alsatian charm and the great food and the warm, personal but not overbearing service, made it worthwhile to drive all the way out there. Not that Pete drove—he hired a limousine for the evening so that he and Che Che could drink wine without having to drive home half-drunk. After their meal, they went to the limo, holding hands, and Pete asked the driver to drive through the Virginia countryside for a while. Pete and Che Che, just ever so slightly drunk, started kissing. When they got back to her place on Volta Place, in Georgetown, Che Che gave Pete the key, he fumbled around in the lock, and they went inside. They never said a word, started kissing in the dark, and made love on the couch in the living room. Afterward, as they lay on the living-room rug in postcoital afterglow, Pete wondered what it would be like—just fantasizing, of course—to be married to Che Che. *All that money.* There would be a prenup—Donna Hart Lyons wouldn't let her daughter fritter away all that money—but in the meantime, before the marriage ended—and this was all fantasy, mind you—in the meantime, as Che Che's husband, he could certainly settle all his debts, expand his business, do a lot of other good things, travel . . . of course, all of this was fantasizing. But just suppose. Che Che was worth thinking about.

* * *

When Che Che Hart was nine years old, a shy, plump child with skin just half a shade darker than café au lait, with light green eyes and black hair worn in a semi-Afro, her blond, beautiful mother, Donna Hart, who was just beginning to be noticed as an actress in New York, had decided it was a good time to take her daughter to the Metropolitan Opera. There was only one problem: Che Che did not want to go. She had heard operatic music on the radio and on albums at their apartment and didn't like it. To Che Che, opera was just screeching, and, besides, the screeching was in foreign languages. But her mother had insisted they go to the Met and see *La Bohème*. And so, dressed to within an inch of her life, subdued, sullen, silent, and fiercely determined, as only a nine-year-old can be, not to have good time, Che Che sat stiffly in her seat, waiting, grim-faced, part of her Operation Spite Job. As the opera began, two men were singing. One of them caught her eye, not to mention her ear. He was very handsome and had a thrilling voice. Later on in the act, the handsome man sang with a nice-looking lady. By this time, Che Che had fallen hopelessly in love with the man. As the first act ended, Che Che said to her mother, "Momma, in the story, who is that man, the one who just sang with the lady?"

"Rodolfo. He's the tenor."

"What does he do, in the opera? The other man is a painter. Why were they in that big room with the stove?"

Donna explained that Rodolfo was a poet, and his poems did not sell very well, so he was very poor but happy, along with his friends.

A poet. Che Che had, of course, read poems in school, but she had never before seen, let alone met, a poet or anyone playing a poet onstage. So this is what they looked like: tall, handsome and . . . and what? She didn't have the words to capture what she felt about Rodolfo. When the curtain rose for act two and Che Che saw the set, an outdoor café, she gasped. It was . . . well, it was the greatest, most magical, most fascinating thing she had ever seen or heard. All those people, dressed in colorful costumes, singing happily, strolling back and forth past the café as the orchestra played—it was wonderful. It was too much to take in at a glance. She looked for the poet. There he was, at the café, sitting next to the lady from the first act. Che Che didn't much like the lady and was in fact a bit jealous of her. Imagine being able to sit and sing with someone who actually wrote poems.

And then came the magic. A beautiful, slender, blond lady in a red dress—Che Che could pick her out immediately in the big crowd—strolled across the big stage on the arm of a funny old man. They sat at a table at the outdoor café. There were a few snatches of singing between the lady and one of those men from the first act. Then the lady stood and faced the audience. For the slightest moment there was no sound and then she began to sing:

Quando me n'vò,
Quando me n'vò soletta . . .

Che Che had no idea what the lady was singing or why, but her eyes brimmed with tears, not of sadness but of a kind of happiness she had never before known, a sweet, sad glory whose source was a great mystery to her. It was not just that the lady was slim and blond and beautiful, just like Mom, or that her voice was thrilling or that the music was so beautiful. It was that as she sang, the lady was the center of everything, not just of the opera house but, to Che Che, of the whole world. The way the lady smiled and the way she moved and the strong, confident sound of her thrilling voice showed that she knew she deserved to be the center of the world. Che Che marveled that there could be anything like this, that anyone could feel the way the lady most obviously did, that anyone could be so beautiful and white, and not overweight and dark, like Che Che Hart herself. More than anything else in the whole world Che Che wanted to be that lady in the red dress. To Che Che, the blond lady was lovely, an unattainable dream of perfection and power.

In between acts two and three, Che Che was excited.

"Does the poet love the lady in the red dress?"

"No, dear, that's Musetta. She loves Rodolfo's friend, the painter. Rodolfo loves Mimi."

"If I wrote the opera, I'd have the poet and Musetta love each other and marry each other. They belong together."

"P... I... should have had you as a librettist, darling."

For the rest of her life, Che Che would remember that afternoon: the music, Rodolfo, Musetta, and the sad fact that although—to Che Che—they were clearly meant for each other, they never got together, and—

"Che Che, where the hell's your head at?"

Che Che blinked, still half caught in her daydream. There, standing in front of her, was all five foot eight, 156 dynamic pounds of Sammy "I Am Da" Yuan, part Irish, part Chinese, all American and, yes, all badass, a former member of the feared, elite Tiger Squad of the ultrasecret Omega Special Forces Group. He was also a former world-class protection specialist to the stars, a former world freestyle martial arts champion for three consecutive years, and self-described as "the toughest man in Georgetown, which ain't saying much." Sammy was wearing (aside from his frown) a gray T-shirt, black gym shorts, and what Che Che had learned were called focus mitts, big pads Sammy used while Che Che practiced her technique. He was Che Che's self-defense instructor, her part-time, unofficial guru, and occasional escort. But when they were practicing, he was all business. They were standing on a mat in his private gym, a room lined with mirrors. He was staring at her, not at all pleased.

"Sorry, Sammy, I guess I wasn't concentrating," Che Che said, head down.

"You *guess*, missy? Let me tell you something—you *never*, ever come to Sammy's House of Kicks and daydream. You understand that?"

"Yes, Sammy, I'm sorry."

"Let me tell you only three things—I could give you ten—you've done wrong in the last three minutes. One, your stance is sloppy, too wide. I could have kicked your leg and you would have fallen on your ass. *Focus.* Two, your offensive front kick is bad—bad chambering, no force to the thrust, and you don't quickly rechamber the kick to the starting position. Three, did you ever hear of combinations? A jab, then a cross? The old one-two? Girl, where the *hell's* your head at?"

"Guilty as charged, Sammy. I'm really sorry."

"Let me show you," Sammy said. He assumed the boxing stance, chin down, left hand out. He threw a jab and then a cross, full speed, but with his great reflexes pulled each punch before it landed.

"That's a one-two, Che Che," he said gruffly, staring at her.

His voice then softened a bit.

"Tell me again, Che Che—why are you coming to the House of Kicks?"

"To learn self-defense and—"

"No. You're here to become your own woman. You're beautiful, you're smart, you're rich, but all that doesn't mean anything because of your relationship with your mom."

"I love my mother."

"I know you do. But you're angry with yourself because you let her manipulate you."

"Mom's a very strong woman. She manipulates everyone."

"I know, it's tough being the daughter of an assertive, successful—"

"Try bossy."

"—woman like your mother, true, but there's a lot you could learn from her. What we do here can help you, make you depend on yourself alone. But only if you do it right. Now, go take your shower. Next time, bring your head with you."

He walked away, with that lazy, feline grace of his, and then turned back and said, "Are we still on for dinner Friday night?"

"Oh, damn it, Sammy, I forgot. My mother is doing the Dave McNair show. She's coming down from New York and—"

"That's okay," Sammy said. "I understand. But remember—she can be manipulative only if you let her."

In the shower, as the needles of hot water pounded her, Che Che, ashamed of her performance, vowed to become more disciplined. But she knew why she had lost focus. She knew why she couldn't concentrate. She smiled.

Peter Dickinson. He may not be a poet, honey, but he'll have to do, until the real thing comes along.

She was still smiling as she left the House of Kicks and walked along M Street, turned right at the gold-domed bank building at the corner of Wisconsin, and walked up Wisconsin toward her home on Volta Place (the very street where Soviet agent Alger Hiss had once lived, her mother had reminded her when she purchased the building for Che Che), in the heart of Georgetown. As male passersby did variations on the freestyle second glance, she strolled past the quaint restaurants, small art galleries, cobblestone streets and trolley tracks, relics of an older, slower, more gentle (and, she reminded herself, racially segregated) Washington. The tree-lined quiet streets and the expensive row houses made Georgetown special to her, aside from the fact she was living so close to the university. When she arrived home she took out her key and opened the forest green door with its gleaming brass knocker and kick plate (her mother: "When are you getting a home-security system, dear?" Che Che: "Mom, I train with Sammy Yuan—I *am* a home-security system"), and avoiding the well-stocked kitchen where caloric temptation awaited, she ran directly upstairs to her second-floor office. Small and cozy, it was her favorite room in the house, filled with books and old, comfortable secondhand furniture she had picked up at yard sales and auctions, the kind of furniture she could have afforded if all she had was an associate professor's salary. On or near the sills of the windows looking out on Volta Place, she had placed what she called the Che Che Hart Home for Growth-Challenged Plants, a dozen or so green (and brown and yellow) growing things (Che Che had no idea what their names were) that had been given to her as presents or that she had offered to take care of when friends had given up on them.

She sat at her computer and tried to hammer out chapter three of her book about the life and times of her grandfather, Abe Steinberg, the last of the commie diehards. After half an hour or so, she sighed, got up from the desk, and did some stretching exercises to see if she could jump-start her mind by moving her body. But nothing was working today. Her mind was a million miles away. Ideas that had seemed so brilliant when she had jotted them down a week ago looked flat and dead on the computer screen. She desperately wanted to finish the book. It would make her name—*her* name, not the name of Donna Hart Lyons's daughter. Che Che had not published enough, she knew that, and she knew her department chairman knew that. This was the book that would turn it all around, a scholarly, objective but passionate recounting of her old bolshie grampa's ideological adventures on the Left. Maybe she was too close to Grampa to do him justice in a book, but she was going to try. But not today. The writing juices weren't flowing. Giving up, she went downstairs, opened the refrigerator, took out a bottle of water, and sat at the kitchen table, thinking of how she and Peter had made love, on the couch in the living room. It was as if they had never been apart. The rightness, the naturalness, was still there, after all that time apart.

But can I trust him? He said he'd changed, gotten mature, learned from his mistakes. *But has he?* After all, Peter was a speechwriter. Writing glib phrases for politicians about "getting beyond this" and "moving on" and "putting the past behind us" was part of his business. It was good to know he had a highly successful speechwriting business and was making a lot of money. Some men Che Che dated wanted nothing but her money, she knew, but with Peter it was different.

Che Che wondered what her mother would say when she found out her daughter was once again involved with Peter Dickinson. But then again, Che Che had spent her entire life wondering what her mother thought, or had thought, or would think. Like Musetta in *La Bohème,* Donna always seized center stage, held it, and gloried in it. Mom could be a royal pain, but to Che Che she was, like Musetta, still an unattainable ideal of power and perfection.

THREE

DAVE: Here we are, nuanced and fair, as always, with Donna Hart Lyons, former star of the long-running soap, or as we say today, daytime drama *Today We Love*. She played Leslie Hunter, the rich witch you loved to hate. As you can see, she is as gorgeous as ever. And she won a lot of Emmies. How many, Donna?

DONNA: Three, Dave. It should have been four. And earlier in my career I was nominated for two Obies but did not win. But let's not dwell on what might have been, darling.

DAVE: Good advice. Anyhow, our guest has retired from showbiz, but she is still what *Time* magazine once called her, "the Godmother of the American Left." She is chairman of LionCo Industries. And she's the founder and very active president of the left-liberal LionHeart Foundation. Although we disagree on just about everything politically, she is our favorite self-confessed, big-time, left-wing activist guest. Is that a fair description, Donna?

DONNA: I prefer honored actress, devoted mother, and American patriot. But I just *love* being described as "big-time."

DAVE: Donna, you're making news these days on two fronts. First, you're in a feud with Ezra Tyne, the right-wing radio-talk-show host. He's having a great time making fun of your school to help teenage prostitutes, the Ernesto Che Guevara School for Wayward Girls. How is that venture going so far?

DONNA: The Che School is even now holding classes on its site at LionWest, my ranch in Montana. The school offers an educational program through which teenage prostitutes can learn feminist and progressive values that will enable them to rebuild their lives.

DAVE: A lot of people are saying you may have stumbled badly on this idea. The country isn't ready for it.

DONNA: The country wasn't ready for civil rights, child-labor laws, and women's reproductive freedom, either.

DAVE: What about that crazy name for the school? Guevara was a communist. He helped your pal Fidel install a totalitarian regime down there. What does Che Guevara have to do with prostitutes?

DONNA: The Cuban Revolution, acting on socialist principles, cleansed Cuba of the prostitution that demeaned Cuban women who sold themselves for the Yankee dollar. Under socialism, former Cuban prostitutes were trained and got jobs that helped the greater community.

DAVE: Are you trying to tell me there have been no hookers in Havana since Fidel took over? C'mon, get real, Donna.

DONNA: There will always be unfortunate women, especially in patriarchal cultures, who have bought the male myth about the worthlessness of women. But I believe we can end prostitution in our own country through rehabilitation along progressive lines, and the place to begin is with teenagers.

DAVE: I'm looking here at the fact sheet your foundation put out about the school. Let me read some of the courses that will be offered: Women's Role Models, from Medea to Madonna; International Corporate Greed and Male Dominance: Their Balls, Our Globe; "Carry Me Back to Ol' Vagina": The Racial Politics of Anatomy. Donna, it all sounds crazy to me.

DONNA: Dave, you vote for conservative Republicans, so who are you to call *me* crazy?

DAVE: What's the deal with *wayward?* It's a word your feminist sisters don't like.

DONNA: I deliberately chose the word. It connotes having lost one's way. That's what these teenage girls have done. They got into the life because they were provided with the wrong role models in a society that systematically demeans and exploits the powerless, especially young girls. In the Che School they will learn about great progressive women whose names never appear in American high school textbooks, like Emma Goldman and Rosa Luxemburg and Dolores Ibárruri, or, as she was known, La Pasionaria, of Spanish Civil War fame.

DAVE: Radio call-in host Ezra Tyne is getting an awful lot of publicity making fun of all this. His ratings are way up.

DONNA: Ezra Tyne is a fascistic, bigoted, cruel, ignorant, dangerous, and irresponsible man, without a shred of human decency or compassion. His fan club, Ezra's Raiders, is a frightening group of thugs and sociopaths in a paramilitary organization modeled on the SS.

DAVE: Don't hold back, Donna—tell us what you really think. But let's turn to the second and more important reason you're in the news. You have been a stalwart Democratic Party fund-raiser and left-wing activist for many years. But recently you've gone out of your way to criticize President Tyler Ferguson, of your own party. There are rumors you plan to take over the American Advance Party created by billionaire Calvin Quincy in his losing third-party bid some years ago. But the AAP is a hollow shell these days. Cal is holed up in his fortress out there in Puget Sound and nobody's heard from him in quite a while. The party's annual national committee meeting is to be held in August, right here in Washington. You'll be speaking to them. Is this the beginning of your takeover, hostile or friendly, of the AAP, to set you up for their nomination next year?

DONNA: The American Advance Party is certainly in need of rejuvenation. But I haven't made up my mind yet in that direction. I'm just going to the meeting to share my views with AAP committeemen and -women.

DAVE: I bet. Well, are you going to challenge President Ferguson next year in any way? Yes or no?

DONNA: Whatever I do, I won't run against him in the primaries. The Democratic Party is dead from the neck up, so why bother? The party has no ideas, no excitement. It has stopped caring about the poor and working people. I blame much of this on President Ferguson and his so-called centrist approach. In a circle, the center is farthest away from the perimeter. In politics, if you stay in the center, you're out of touch with the majority who live and work away from the center. I mean, of course, women, the poor, the black, the workers, the—

DAVE: Yeah, sure, but a lot of folks would say, let's be frank, Donna, you're very wealthy, you know nothing about the poor and working people.

DONNA: That's nonsense. My father owned a delicatessen in the Bronx. I'm proud to say that I worked there as a child. I could make a great pastrami sandwich for you, if I could find good rye bread here in Washington.

DAVE: Maybe that's why you come down here from New York so rarely, the great rye bread shortage in D.C. Get some of your lefty friends in Congress to get government subsidies for good Jewish rye bread, or air-lift it to us from New York. Even I'll support that. You spoke of your father, Abe Steinberg, a man the Left admires—they call him the Deli Lama. He was a card-carrying member of the American Communist Party, am I right?

DONNA: My mother also. Premature antifascists, I call them. They wanted to improve the life of the poor, black Americans, women, and exploited working people, at a time when such views were not fashionable. Because my father stood up to Senator Joe McCarthy's bullying, he barely escaped unjust imprisonment. I'm very proud of him. My mother has been dead for many years, but my father is still with us, I'm glad to say. He's eighty-six—in August he'll be eighty-seven. He is as feisty and stubborn as ever. He doesn't apologize for his life. In fact, my daughter—

DAVE: Ernestina Hart, but she's called Che Che, after Che Guevara—

DONNA: That's right. Che Che is a history professor, right here in Washington, at Georgetown University, and she is writing a book about my father. But let me get back to your point about my working-class street creds, as they say. Yes, my late husband, Gar Lyons, left me a lot of money. But I'm not apologizing for that. I've paid my dues. Early in my career, when Che Che was a baby and my first husband deserted me, I knew what it is to be hungry and powerless and afraid. I waited on tables, I—

DAVE: Okay, Donna, we get the picture. You're a real proletarian babe. But let me ask you again: Yes or no, are you, a longtime Democrat, one of the richest and most powerful women in the country, going to run as a third-party candidate against President Ty Ferguson next year?

DONNA: Let's say I am taking a look at my options. My father has a saying: He who says A has to say B.

DAVE: Very intriguing. But what does it mean?

DONNA: It means that if you want to do something difficult but necessary, you have to take all steps to do it, even if that means being called ruthless and doing things weaker people frown upon. As we would say today, if you want to talk the talk, be willing to walk the walk, no matter where it takes you or what it costs. If I run for president, I'll do it for the good of the Democratic Party, and of the country.

Tim Flaherty, president of the Union of Work-Challenged Employees, pressed the power button on the TV remote and said to his wife of thirty years, "Donna's going to run, Margaret Mary, mark my words."

"I'll pray she comes back to her senses," Margaret Mary said. "There's power in prayer, Tim, even if Donna Lyons doesn't know it."

They sat before the seventy-inch hi-res TV set in their tastefully appointed (they had hired an interior decorator) living room of their six-bedroom home in Potomac, Maryland, just outside Washington. It was the kind of house and the kind of community neither of them, in their younger days, would have ever dared dream of. But with patience, shrewdness, and a certain amount of ruthlessness, Tim had slowly but inexorably risen from the tough streets of South Boston through the ranks of the Union of Work-Challenged Employees. He had transformed the union from a weak, unimportant, fringe member of the labor coalition into one of the most ideologically progressive, politically active, militant unions in America.

Tim, in his mid-sixties, had a full head of hair that was not entirely gray but no longer black, a soft, plump, well-fed body, bright blue eyes, and pink cheeks. He looked in fact like a character out of a children's book about Farmer Jones and his wife and their merry days on the farm, not that Tim had ever lived on a farm. His impoverished, exploited, beaten, starved, and conquered Irish ancestors had done enough farming, and had little enough to show for it, God knows, to last the Flaherty family for eternity.

"There's power in television, too," Tim said. "Do you see how great Donna looks on TV? The camera loves her. She ain't young anymore, but that don't matter. You want to keep on looking at her, no matter what she's saying. If she runs, she'll blast Ty Ferguson off the screen. She'll be splitting the left-liberal vote and handing the election over to the Republicans. Just a few votes in a few states can make the difference. Don't she see that?"

"Maybe it's God's will, Tim," Margaret Mary replied. She came from a long line of Catholic women who believed suffering was a burden to be borne in patience and humility—no cross, no Christ. Tim believed that in her blessed simplicity she had little understanding, unlike him, of the different but no less demanding pieties of the Age of Embittered, Entitled, Eternal Victimhood. He knew Margaret Mary was still, in many ways, innocent, in the old-fashioned sense of being ignorant of what the world is all about.

Margaret Mary, dressed conservatively as always (tonight she was wearing a dark blue pleated skirt and a starched white blouse buttoned almost to the neck, her idea of leisurewear), at fifty-six was petite and still trim and, yes, even pretty, with hair that was just turning gray. But there was something . . . Tim could never put his finger on it . . . *holy* about her. *Holy* wasn't exactly the word. Maybe *otherworldly* was better. Whatever the quality, it gave her what Tim had long since thought of as her "vestal virgin" look. She looked like a nun who had cast the habit aside but still had the scrubbed, pure, plain, shiny, never-been-touched look about her. Margaret Mary had turned away from sex years ago. (Tim felt she had never been all that interested anyhow.) These days she slept in her own bedroom (which had so many crucifixes and holy pictures, it looked like a shrine). But the Flahertys were Catholics of the old school, and there was never talk about a divorce. Besides, Tim found her useful because a lot of his money was in her name, and she signed a lot of papers she never looked at, for purposes Tim never disclosed to her.

Margaret Mary got up from the couch, kissed Tim chastely on the brow, and went to her bedroom, leaving him to brood upon Donna Hart Lyons's treachery.

He was at the peak of his powers, with thousands of unskilled, undermotivated, angry, bitter, lazy, frustrated, envious, incompetent, and disgruntled men and women at his disposal, all fighting for the principles he had annunciated in his inaugural address as union president:

"Just because a worker hates his job or does it badly every single day or doesn't show up every day or is always late or shows disrespect for his superiors and fights with his or her colleagues in the workplace is no reason to deny him or her pay raises and more benefits. In fact, the work-challenged and differently job-motivated are the biggest group left in American society who are victims of discrimination, but their rights are ignored by the government. They should get more money for doing the same job as non-challenged workers because being work-challenged means that even more faith must be shown in you by your employer. And they should get government help because of their disability. Decades ago, the work-challenged sang 'Take This Job and Shove It,' but in this new century we say: to hell with the work ethic—give us our rights, and give them to us now!"

One Republican critic said the UWCE was made up of "those who work in the linty pockets of the economy—video-rental stores, one-hour photo booths, fast-food restaurants, and Kinko's." Strictly speaking, this elitist smear was not true. Yes, many UWCE members worked in dead-end jobs, but the aversion to hard work and the detestation of the work ethic at the heart of the UWCE ethos cut across economic lines. White-collar wage slaves chained to their computers, public safety officers sick of risking their lives for taxpayer ingrates, and adjunct professors of English fifty miles off the tenure track and running out of gas shared Tim's vision of bitching and moaning as not only the right of freeborn Americans but a virtue deserving monetary compensation and government entitlements.

On his way to the top, as Tim sacrificed his time and energy for the good of the union, he had also helped himself. He had amassed a tidy little fortune by shrewd and secretive under-the-table deals with employers, embezzlement of union funds, and manipulation of stocks in union insurance companies. With union money and some of his own, he had helped finance many liberal politicians before they became powerful, so he had many influential friends. Loyal son of the Church that he was, Tim was a friend and confidant of politically liberal Roman Catholic bishops and their national staff in Washington, most of whom devoutly believed, as he and Margaret Mary did, that the beatitudes found their economic equivalent in the quadrennial platform of the Democratic Party.

Denied conjugal rights at home, Tim over the years had had many mistresses (in fact, he had had mistresses *before* being denied his conjugal rights, but he tended to forget that), including his current one, Connie Erickson, a sexy thirty-six-year-old labor lawyer. So now, with his big salary, a practically unlimited expense account, the limo and the condo in Florida, and a young mistress who introduced him to sexual activities he had never read about or even heard of, let alone practiced, he was doing very well. He was assiduously courted by Democratic politicians, including the president. Approaching his golden years, Tim Flaherty was living in style and in comfort, and the UWCE was gaining more and more political influence within the Democratic Party as the work-challenged became aware that they were victims and were entitled to . . . well, entitled to entitlements. President Ferguson would be addressing the upcoming UWCE annual convention in Florida. Tim would be making a speech at the same meeting. He made a mental note to get in touch with Pete Dickinson, who had been writing very good speeches for him. Tim wanted the UWCE speech to be the best.

So, everywhere Tim looked, life was good—but now this, the threat of a split in the Democratic Party by one of the wealthiest and most powerful women in America, a woman Tim had always looked upon as a friend and ally. Morose, wounded, Tim sighed and stared at the triptych of photographs, ornately framed, that graced the wall facing the picture window. Franklin D. Roosevelt. John F. Kennedy. Robert F. Kennedy. To Tim, they were the holy political trinity. Yes, maybe he was old-fashioned—out of touch, as the younger types in the union headquarters liked to remind him. But the example of these three great men had been a source of lasting strength to him. Decades ago, as a young man, he had been part of the ultimately failed movement within the Church to get the two assassinated Kennedy brothers canonized. Martyrs, that's what they were, victims of right-wing hate. They gave up their lives for us. Greater love hath no man. FDR was nominally a Protestant, but Tim believed that the great president was the victim of invincible ignorance, which, if Tim remembered his pre–Vatican II catechism correctly, took FDR off the hook. Anyhow, these days, Protestants or Catholics—who cared?

In the Galway crystal vase (the Flahertys were from Athenry, County Galway) beneath the photographs, there were three fresh roses, replaced daily by Raúl, the Flahertys' young Salvadorean all-purpose handyman. (And, yes, Tim liked to remind visitors, Raúl has his green card, and his Social Security is all paid up.) The roses, graced with a glistening sheen of moisture, seemed to Tim to be weeping, and as sad as he himself was.

If the Democrats were weakened by a primary fight, the Republicans would take back the White House. Tim winced as he thought about what that would mean for him if a Republican-led Justice Department started looking into certain deals he had made, especially the insurance scam. It was hopeless, hopeless. If Donna Hart Lyons, with all her money and all her influence, split the party on the left, the Democrats could lose the White House. But she was obstinate, and it looked as if she had made up her mind and—

No!

No, by God, he thought. *No, I'm a fighter and I'm not giving up*. He walked to the photographs and touched each in turn. Blessed Jack never gave up. Saint Bobby never gave up. Venerable FDR never gave up. And neither would Tim Flaherty. For the good of the party, he would go to see the Godmother.

Donna Hart Lyons sat in the backseat of her armored limousine as it made its way along the Dulles Access Road toward Dulles Airport. Frank Sinatra's

"You Go to My Head," Donna's absolute favorite work of the master's, was on the CD player. Donna was, as Dave McNair had said, still gorgeous. At fifty, she was still blond (in a manner of speaking) and blue-eyed. Those fabulous legs, the left one now crossed over the right, showing a discreet amount of toned, sexy, shapely thigh, still went on forever.

Donna had just speed-dialed Dr. Arthur Kalitch, one of the three psychological counselors available to her by phone, 24/7. The other two—Martha Tuttle Nussleman, a sharp young cognitive specialist, and Jana Bilstocki, a housewife from Queens who had watched every *Oprah Winfrey Show* ever televised and was therefore something of a lay expert on the psychological healing arts—were working the day shift today. Dr. Kalitch, a Freudian of the old hard-line school (he had a couch and, imitating the master, pieces of Egyptian bric-a-brac in his office), tended to talk too much, one of those rare analysts who babble more than their patients do. But Donna felt that she needed some reassurance after the TV interview with Dave McNair. She could never tell how good she was in such situations—no script, bad lighting, no direction, and sharing the screen with McNair made her uncomfortable. She knew, as the public did not, that beyond the small, colorful image that appeared on the television, a TV studio is drab, almost grim in its utilitarian spareness. Of course, she had worked in soaps for many years and was used to the factory-like atmosphere. But in the soaps, at least there was a script, a story, some continuity. You were making magic on the factory floors. But on a talk show, the tacky feeling was magnified, and Donna could never be quite certain she was coming across as she should. It was as if the workaday, shabby reality of the talk-show studio robbed her of that inner glow that had made her a star.

Dr. Kalitch, now on the phone, told her that her superego had transcended her id's predilection for dominance—or something like that; Donna tended not to listen, wanting only the sound of his gentle voice. Kalitch babbled in Freud-speak for a while, and then Donna ended the call. She closed her eyes, leaned back, and listened to Frank sing about "Nancy, with the laughing face," which made her think of her own daughter, Che Che, and the pleasant time they had had that afternoon.

Che Che was the only good thing left of Donna's marriage—at eighteen—to Johnnie Hart, a good-looking, two-timing, jive-talking, drug-taking, drug-dealing black trumpet player who tried to disguise his lack of chops by telling people he was an artistic heir to Miles Davis. Miles, Johnnie said, didn't need to play in the high register or use a lot of notes like Dizzy or Roy, and neither did Johnnie Hart. Jazz musicians smiled condescendingly. They knew Johnnie's approach could be traced not to aesthetic choices or an artistic vision but to a lack of technical mastery and no feeling for the music, or as one sly old bass player said, "Hart got no heart—and no chops." But Johnnie got his share of paying gigs because he had stage presence, was good-looking, and could play the kind of jazz enjoyed by people who don't know anything about jazz but think they ought to like it.

Donna had loved music, especially jazz, ever since childhood visits with her father to jazz concerts. Those forays into Greenwich Village and Harlem were only to show solidarity with black people; Abe Steinberg thought that music, except " L'Internationale," the great revolutionary anthem, had no ideological reason for being. What was it that Lenin had said? Listening to Beethoven made you want to pat people on the head.

The first time she heard Johnnie play, Donna had quickly realized his level of competence was suited to gigs in Las Vegas lounges, but she was crazy about him. In fact, it was in Las Vegas (where Johnnie and Donna had gone when Donna, pregnant, left home with the curses of her mother ringing in her ears) that Che Che was born. And it was in Las Vegas that one morning Donna awoke to discover that Johnnie had abandoned her, taking the small amount of money left in their checking account. (Two years later his horribly mutilated remains were found stuffed in a refrigerator in a dump outside Chicago. Police believed he was the victim of a disagreement with certain Jamaican businessmen who dealt in illicit pharmaceuticals.) When Johnnie deserted her, Donna, with a new baby, had suffered greatly, but she had triumphed. She had overcome every obstacle that life and fate could throw at her and . . .

Donna smiled. She was beginning to think in the clichéd concepts familiar to the soaps in which she reigned for so many years. *Triumph! Overcome obstacles! Life and fate!* In fact, life had taught her that there is no fate. You make your own life. And she had, all in all, made a good life, for herself and Che Che. Things had been going along so well until Ezra Tyne had stepped into the picture. Donna looked at the digital clock on the dashboard. Just in time.

"James," she said to the driver, "please turn on the Tyne show."

She listened to Ezra Tyne's radio show as a form of discipline, attempting to examine objectively what he said, trying to figure out why a slimeball had such a passionately devoted audience. Were there really that many demented people in the United States? *Know your enemy,* she thought.

At first there was a commercial for a local car dealer. And then there was that voice:

"Have no fear," it said, "Unca *Ezra's* here! This is the Ezra Tyne show, on RRA—Radio Real America—dedicated to family, working, friendship, and patriotism of the old-fashioned kind. Since I'm the one talkin', I guess I must be Ezra. Here's my story: I don't want to be no billionaire. I don't have the head for money, never did. I can't *be* good-lookin'—the good Lord didn't favor me with movie-star looks, unless Bela Lugosi comes to mind. I just want to get our country back from the greedy Hollywood and New York types whose only god is the almighty dollar. If your brain's been washed, dried, ironed, folded, and put in the drawer by the media big boys and the lefty liberals, call me and I'll straighten you out. If you think President Ty the Lie Ferguson would have to take graduate courses to rise to the level of village idiot, I'm your man. If you think giving whores a degree in nuclear physics is a bit too much, I'm your boy. Let me hear what they been spoon-feeding you—Unca Ezra'll set you straight."

Ezra Tyne's voice had a thin, raspy, irritating, and irritable sound, with a slight, rough, cheap-rye-whiskey undertone. It was an insinuating voice, a night-time voice with a touch of battery acid in it, an instrument made for whining about bad luck, for bringing up ancient grudges, for rubbing raw psychic wounds. It was the wised-up voice of embittered, defeated, white working people listening out there in the dark, men (mostly) who had been tricked too many times by the big boys, the bastards who ran things, the elite—in government, in education, in unions, in the media, and all over the goddamn country—those New York and Hollywood and Washington phonies in their three-thousand-dollar suits. Ezra's was the voice of quick-tempered, hungover, drinking-rotgut-whiskey-in-the-morning white men with names like Earle and Doc and Lefty and Red. They couldn't be called Forgotten Americans because no one had ever remembered them in the first place. But now they had a voice, and it was Ezra Tyne's.

"If you're not the right *kind* of minority, if you ain't received the liberal establishment's seal of approval, if you can't pull the old *victim* scam, if you can't get the bought-and-paid-for politicians like President Ty the Stye in My Eye Ferguson to feel sorry for you and give you OPM—other people's money— well, this is the show for you. This is the place for the *other* dissidents, the *other* exploited folks, the *other* dispossessed, the *other* poor bastards who are getting screwed, shampooed, and tattooed by big government, big business, labor bosses, officially designated perpetual victims and full-time whiners and anti-discrimination professional moaners who demand deformative faction—oops, I mean affirmative action—this is the show for you. Well, what's new tonight? Lessee, I got a call today from Buck Torrence, out there in Bakersfield, he's head of Ezra's Raiders in California. For you folks new to the show, probably tuned in by mistake, Ezra's Raiders is a national group of real American patriots, despite what the left media says about them. The Raiders believe in true Americanism of the old-fashioned kind. A lot of them drive hogs—Harley-Davidsons to you, buddy—and they also drive the sissy Left crazy. They don't have much use for the tree huggers and the penis enviers of both sexes. Of course, the people who control the media—no need to mention names—hate the Raiders because Raiders stand up for their rights, with their fists if they have to. They don't take no nonsense from left-wing pansies or dykes or folks like that. Anyhow, ol' Buck tells me there's gonna be a Raiders' general meeting in Sacramento in two weeks or so. I'll try to be out there, Buck, schedule permitting. It does ol' Unca Ezra's heart good to know there are thousands of folks like Buck who are willing to stand up for America. Lots of luck to you, Buck, and if you see one of those tree huggers, teach them what real Americans think. What else is in the news? Oh, yeah, Donna Tart Liar—oops, 'scuse me, folks, my diction's bad, I guess I have to take another ebonics course—Donna Hart Lyons, the Godmother of the Left, the dean of the School of Female Oral Studies, is putting us all on notice she might run for president. Now, for God's sakes, folks, don't *panic*. Don't call nine-one-one. Before you start grabbing your weapons and going into the survival mode and sending the family to your shelter in the basement, just remember: Donna was a TV actress. She played a rich bitch. For you dumbbells out there, that is what is known in Holly-weird as typecasting. Actresses lie for a living. They pretend to be other people. They make up emotions they don't feel. So maybe Donna wasn't serious about running for president. Of course, ol' Unca Ezra respects Donna for what she's doing for hookers. Just to show how much I care about getting every American whore a Harvard degree, I promise to pay tuition for the first ten floozies who call and tell me why they want to read the great books—in comic book form, of course. But, anyhow, Ms. Liar, if you're listening, you've been against ordinary American families and the real America all your life, ever since you were born, a real red-diaper baby, ever since you sliced salami and pastrami in the Deli Lama's delicatessen in the Bronx all those years ago. Your name was Donna Steinberg back then and—"

"Shut it off, James," Donna snapped. Despite every effort to remain cool and objective and try to analyze this maniac's jabbering, she could feel herself getting angry. She could not be objective about Ezra Tyne. He always got to her, infuriated her.

I'm going on the attack against Tyne. I'm going to destroy the son of a bitch. And I know just the man who can tell me how to do it. My father. I'll go to see the Deli Lama.

FOUR

Donna, waiting for her father, sat on the floral-print sofa she had chosen, along with all the other homey, comfortable furniture; soothing earth-tone landscape paintings; and brightly colored drapes for the sitting room of the Abe Steinberg Suite of the LionHeart Residence for Progressive Seniors in Westchester, New York. Seniordale, a subsidiary of LionCo, had purchased and renovated the property, a large Victorian mansion and extensive grounds once owned by John Timmons Mosley, the legendary Wall Street lawyer and, later, Supreme Court justice. Donna had bought it to provide Abe with a residence of his own, since he adamantly refused to live with her. ("What, I'm going to live with my own daughter? Abe Steinberg, a charity case? Never!") The Abe Steinberg Suite took up the top floor of the building. Abe insisted on paying his own way—two hundred dollars a month. Donna didn't tell him that the going rate for such a luxurious place was closer to ten thousand a month.

The residence had all the amenities to make a progressive senior's golden years comfortable: the Abraham Lincoln Brigade Dining Facility, the Big Bill Haywood Fitness Center, the W. E. B. du Bois Library, containing, according to a brochure, "the largest collection of progressive literature in Westchester County, including an almost complete file of *The Nation* magazine, 1928–1950," and the Sacco and Vanzetti Progressive Values Auditorium, in which once a week the fifty or so (at the residence, seniors came and seniors, er, went) residents gathered to debate the issues in the vituperative, often savage manner that characterizes left-wing factionalism, even among eighty-year-olds. After abusing one another, reading one another out of one progressive faction or another, and reciting key passages from scripture (works of Marx, Engels, Lenin, Che Guevara, and brief, inspirational excerpts from the political utterances of Barbra Streisand), they would become exhausted and have to be taken to their rooms for a nap. Two hours later they'd return, refreshed, to pass resolutions, make blanket condemnations of Republicans, and sign petitions protesting various national and global injustices. Abe rarely mingled with the other residents, calling them "a bunch of droolers, real idiots, liberals—they play cards all day, and when they debate, there's no scientific critique of the economy, nothing."

Donna, restless and just a bit irritated at having to wait for her father (she usually did not have to wait for anyone or anything), stood up from the couch and walked to the windows looking out on the acres of lush, well-tended green lawn, with big maples and oaks, and the various early-spring flower gardens around the grounds. She knew her father was not happy there, but then again she could not remember a time when he had ever been happy. Happiness, in Abe's view, was for the liberals, the idiots, the ones without a scientific critique of society and history. For a true Red, he argued, there's no time for personal happiness. The time and effort that had gone into restoring the grounds of the old mansion were, in Abe's view, a waste of money.

He had made his suite into a museum of leftist iconography. By the doorway there was a marble pedestal, eight feet high, on top of which stood a three-times-larger-than-life-size bronze bust of Al Gunn, once Abe's best friend in the party and a martyr to the McCarthyite witch hunts of the fifties. Donna had commissioned the bust and presented it to Abe as a birthday present ten years ago. It was the only time she had ever seen tears come to the old man's eyes. The huge bust of Al Gunn, his gaunt, haggard face reflecting not only his suffering but that of the toiling masses from whom Abe and he had come, dominated the room.

On the open fall front of a bookcase near the window, there were a few items Abe also prized: a framed photograph, autographed, of Lazar Kaganovich, who played a key role in the state-imposed famine that had starved to death millions in Ukraine and elsewhere—some scholars said six million—in the 1930s, Abe's ancient, cheap, battered personal copy of Lenin's *What Is to Be Done?*, with its split binding, dog-eared pages, and scribbling in the margins of almost every page; a few old Soviet coins; and, in a cheap metal holder bearing a hammer and sickle, an especially prized item in the Abe Steinberg Great Red Oldies Collection: a mass-produced Soviet-era letter opener with an icon-like portrait of Lenin on the handle. Abe was more proud of the letter opener, given to him as a gift in Moscow by some Cominform bureaucrat, than any gift he had ever received, except, of course, the Kaganovich photo. In a silver frame next to the letter opener there was a photograph of Abe, taken in 1948, standing, stiff and unsmiling in a cheap, ill-fitting suit, before a doorway to a room in some Moscow government building. Abe, then part of the American delegation to the Second Annual World Socialist Peace Through Worker Solidarity conference, had been told that this room, yes, this very room in front of which you are standing—it is forbidden to enter—is one of the many rooms in which Stalin himself, the great Stalin, had worked and slept as he moved from one secure place to another as his great mind gave forth the victorious strategy during the Great Patriotic War against the imperialist, capitalist, fascist aggressor.

Donna smiled as she thought of the situation: the building in which she now stood, with this lovely room with its gorgeous view, had been purchased with the money of Garwood Hill Lyons, a man who, while he had never been a fascist or an imperialist, had spent his life as a capitalist aggressor. Gar, her late husband, former special presidential envoy to the Geneva Talks on World Poverty, former ambassador to the Court of St. James's, former assistant secretary of state for international political/economic affairs, Democratic Party fund-raiser extraordinaire, unofficial political adviser to three presidents, and, when she married him, one of the most influential, oldest, richest, and by far randiest Democrat power brokers in America.

The Lyons family fortune had begun in the eighteenth century when Jeremiah Lyons, an upstanding Massachusetts merchant, became a secret partner with a slave trader. Jeremiah's descendants joined forces with the Delano brothers (Franklin Roosevelt's mother was a Delano) in the opium trade in China and sold patent medicine with John D. Rockefeller's father. Gar's father, Abner, had been a silent partner of Joe Kennedy and worked behind the scenes with Lucky Luciano and Frank Costello during and just after Prohibition. By the time Gar was born, the family had amassed so much money that, under the tutelage of educators at the Bertrand Russell School for Progressive Tots in New York City, the Eugene V. Debs Experimental School in Vermont, and then Harvard University, Gar learned to feel guilty about his wealth, although not quite guilty enough to give it away. Gar was, if nothing else, a pragmatic young man and he learned to live quite happily with both his guilt and his money. His guilt led him to do good; his money allowed him to live well. On his twenty-first birthday, he registered as a Democrat, in expiation for the sins of his greedy, blood-sucking Republican ancestors. To show solidarity with the working class, Gar one day walked a picket line while his valet, cunningly disguised as a worker, carried a placard. Gar thoroughly enjoyed the experience, but he had to leave after five minutes or so because—how best to put this?—the workers had an offensive odor; besides, he was to attend the theater that night and needed his rest.

As he grew older he became wealthier and, through gifts to progressive causes, managed to keep his guilty feelings in check. When Gar was eighty-one, he attended a charity fund-raiser and put his spotted, gnarled right hand on Donna's lovely ass as she walked by him in one of her gorgeous red gowns. She stopped walking, looked at him, smiled, and said, "Gar, darling, perhaps we should talk." They talked. That night she slept with him (quite literally; it had been a long day for Gar, and when they got in bed, he fell asleep instantly). They were married within a month. Gar died less than six months later, a beatific smile on his face, after a particularly vigorous display of senior sexuality with his wife (no male-enhancement products needed for Gar when he was on his game, thank you). At the funeral service in the packed National Cathedral, the bishop said that Gar, a great philanthropist, "died as he lived, *giving, giving, giving.*" There were many among the celebrity-filled mourners who, knowing the true story (Donna had confided in some friends), stifled laughter.

Gar, besotted by his bride, had modified the prenup and left most of his fortune to Donna, outraging his two surviving children from his first and third
marriages, who challenged the will. Donna mounted a strong counteroffensive
in the media and with the best (i.e., the most ruthless and pitiless) lawyers in
America, the universally feared New York firm of Harrigan Shapiro. To the
surprise of many, but not to Donna, who always accurately judged the character of her enemies, the Lyons children gave up the fight in six months, settling
for a relatively piddling sum in the scores of millions. Donna now had everything that a militant-left activist could want: a progressive's conscience and a
billionaire's money. Now if only she could solve the Tyne problem. If only—

"So, a big visit from the TV queen. My lucky day."

Donna turned and there was her father, wielding his walker in a stomping,
aggressive manner, slowly making his way into the room. Wearing an old,
faded blue shirt buttoned to the neck, a pair of worn khakis bunched around his
skinny waist, clomping around on cheap sandals, Abe Steinberg looked like a
biblical patriarch who bought his clothes at Kmart. With his full head of long
white hair, his wizened, wrinkled, white-stubbled face, and that great, proud
beak of a nose, he also looked something like an old, angry turtle. He shuffled
toward Donna, his small body bent, his wheezing emphasizing every move of
the walker. The feisty, argumentative, irritable, indomitable Abe of old, the
Abe Steinberg of a thousand party disputes, the Abe who was once held by two
grinning Alabama highway patrolmen and beaten bloody by two others, the
Abe who saw his best friend, Al Gunn, die in jail during the McCarthy witch
hunt, the Abe whose belief in the party had survived the Hitler-Stalin pact
and even Stalin's brutal postwar murders of the Jews ("All right, goddamn it,
Stalin was *wrong*, may he rot in hell, but the *party* is always right!"), and the fall
of the Soviet Union—that Abe, the Abe Donna loved and revered, was still inside that frail, decrepit body. Donna could see the old Abe in those ancient,
knowing turtle's eyes, which, she guessed, had seen things she could never even
imagine.

Abe Steinberg, the Deli Lama, the progressive patriarch, the eternal Red, slowly, carefully eased himself into position to sit—his back facing the couch—and slowly sank until he was sitting, wheezing and huffing. Donna sat by him and kissed him on the forehead. Irritated, he waved her away.

"Stop with the kissing. Better you should give me a laxative. A kiss I can get anyplace, but a bowel movement—that's a real gift. So, why do you bother to come and see an old man like me, living in this place, the middle of nowhere, nobody here worth talking to, a man can't find a decent pickle?"

"I have a problem, Daddy. I need your advice."

"*You* got a problem? No, you got *money*. *I* got a problem. My kidneys are shot. I got gas all day, I wouldn't wish this condition on Herbert Hoover. On Nixon yes, but not on Hoover. My body is making sounds I never heard before, my eyes don't work good, and the food here, who can eat it? Did these people ever really see a good piece of corned beef in their life? So what's your big problem, Miss Big TV Star?"

Donna recited the Ezra Tyne–Che School story.

"And I don't know what to do," she said in conclusion. "I'm . . . it's like I'm paralyzed. Every time I open my mouth, Tyne just laughs. My idea for the Che School is a good one, Dad, it really is. We can help these girls. But I'm becoming a laughingstock because of Tyne. I know—the smart thing is to ignore him. But I can't. I won't. But I don't know what to do."

She sat there looking at Abe, waiting for wise counsel. Abe blinked, wheezed, scratched his crotch, and squinted at her. Then he said, softly, "Boo-hoo."

Donna stared at him in puzzlement.

"Boo-hoo," Abe said again, his face suddenly contorted into a mask of mock grief. "Boo-hoo, *oy vey*, look at me, everybody, such troubles I got, poor little Donna Steinberg from Melrose in the Bronx, everybody's mean on me. I got—what?—five billions dollars? I got my health, I can go to the bathroom and it ain't like I'm ripping my guts out. I got a nice daughter. But still, I'm poor little Donna, boo-hoo. I got all the prizes these TV people give to each other. So you think I'm happy because I got enough money I could feed the population of Asia five times over? No! This idiot Tyne made *fun* of me, so I run to my father. My father—a man who didn't give me the courtesy of a phone call when I married that colored musician. So like I said, boo-hoo."

Abe reached across the couch, and for a moment Donna thought he was going to embrace or caress her. But instead he slapped her in the face. It was not a stinging slap, he didn't have the strength for that. It felt, in fact, something like an exaggerated pat on the face, but Donna knew it was a slap. She leaped back.

"Daddy! What—"

"Shut up for once in your life and listen to me," Abe Steinberg said, his voice suddenly transformed from the wheeze of a doddering old man to the threatening whisper of the Deli Lama, someone who meant business, an operative, his eyes alive, years younger than his body. "I'm ashamed of you. You're Abe Steinberg's *daughter*. Act like it."

He pointed a shaky, bony finger at the bust of Al Gunn.

"See that man? He never complained. He worked. Remember that. Don't disgrace me in front of Al Gunn. Stop with the *kvetching*. Stop with the hurt feelings. Nobody likes a whiner. Go *after* this son of a bitch Tyne. Attack him. Destroy him."

"How can I attack?" Donna said, now recovered from the surprise of the slap. "LionClaw—my security people—are investigating him, looking for something, a scandal, anything, but we have nothing on him yet. I can't sue him. Tyne won't debate. Every time I try to make my position clear, he ridicules it."

Abe held his head with both hands and rocked back and forth.

"Position? Debate?" he said. "Don't be stupid. *Think* for a minute. What do you do best?"

"Best? What do you mean?"

"What, am I speaking Yiddish here, a language, by the way, now that I bring it up, you never learned, even though I begged you? Your mother was against it, but I wanted you to learn. But not you. You knew everything. . . . Where was I? What was I talking about?"

"About my problem with Ezra Tyne. You were saying I should do what I do best."

"Oh yeah, so I'm asking you—what's your strength, what's the thing you're best at?"

"Politics, I suppose. I—"

Abe pointed at her and cackled loudly, ending his laugh in a fit of wet hacking.

"Politics? Politics my *ass*," he said when he had at last recovered. "You *dabble* in politics. Not much better than the goddamn liberals. You got no science. No discipline. You never read Marx. I asked you, I begged you when you were a girl, read *Das Kapital*. But not you. I read that book when I was fifteen. It changed my life. I did things for the party. I did a lot of things."

Abe stopped talking and stared into space for a few moments.

"Daddy," Donna said, "is there anything wrong?"

"Where was I?" Abe responded. "What the hell are we talking about?"

"About how I never read Karl Marx. But I did, years later. I found it very, very dull."

"Dull to you. Everything to me. You need a scientific method to do true class analysis, the way we had in my day. A bunch of phony revolutionaries, that's who you people are today. *Liberals*. A disgrace. So you demonstrate. You protest. Big deal. You're a political baby, that's why you cry when they attack you. You—"

"All right, Daddy, I get the picture. But get back to the point. How do I fight against Ezra Tyne?"

"Your strength is, you're an *actress*, idiot, *an entertainer*. Pretty good, so they tell me. I was never interested in make-believe. TV should have been used to educate the workers, not to sell toilet paper—not that I need much of that the way I'm constipated. You know show business, you know entertaining people; in fact, that's *all* you know. Am I right? Or am I right?"

"I guess so."

"You guess so. I know so. Well, that's good, because politics in this country is already about ninety percent entertainment. Entertain the idiots and you'll get this Tyne off your back. Don't offer to debate the schmuck. Eisenstein, in that movie *Potemkin*, did he debate? No, he *showed*. He knew the value of agit-prop. Show, don't tell, give the idiots razzmatazz. Now, that's all I got to say. I got to get back to reading Engels and wait for my bowels to move."

"Dad, you need to rest."

"I'll be resting permanent, soon enough. How is my Che Che?"

"She sends her love and says she'll be coming to see you soon, to ask you questions about the book she's writing."

"Miss Smarty-Pants College Professor, that's my Che Che," Abe said proudly. "You should have gone to college, Donna. You broke your mother's heart, marrying that colored musician. You didn't go to college, you ran away with him. Later you married that old man, a regular bloodsucking boss. I'm too tired to talk anymore. I'm exhausted. Talking to you, it wears me out. Here, help me up."

Donna took him under the arms—he was as light as a child, but his body was all bones, without a child's vibrant feel of life—and he got his hands on his walker. He began his wheezing, stomping way across the floor. He paused at the bust of Al Gunn.

"See that man? Al Gunn was a *mensch*."

Then the Deli Lama was gone. Donna sat there, thinking. She looked at the bust of Al Gunn.

Marvin, she thought. *I have to talk this over with Al's son, Marvin. He'll know what to do.*

FIVE

One rainy day in April of 1968, when bespectacled, bearded, and stoned Marvin Gunn was a sophomore at Columbia University, he made his radical bones by urinating on a National Guardsman's shiny boots at an antiwar demonstration near the Pentagon. When the infuriated soldier punched him, the news photo taken of Marvin, blood streaming from his nose, his mouth open in a barbaric yawp of shock and rage, made him instantly famous. The photograph—which would ultimately win a Pulitzer Prize—was cropped to protect the sensibilities of those who might be disillusioned to see that Marvin had been exposing more than his detestation of imperialist aggression. The cropped photo was reproduced on thousands of posters. In every college dorm and underground press office in the country, there was a poster of Marvin Gunn, the embodiment of the sixties' idealistic youth, of leftist rebellion and dissent, and of righteous, sincere rage, the true guarantor of radical integrity. A bootleg copy of the uncropped photo was a staple of women's dorms and the nascent gay liberation movement.

Short, skinny, studious-looking, lacking natural charisma, a bit of a whiner, Marvin was an unlikely icon of the Left. But the photo and his pedigree as a red-diaper baby—"See that guy? He's Al Gunn's kid."—quickly made him an antiwar leader. He was in the front row of every demonstration unless he was in bed with young women sexually inflamed by that most potent of erotic mixtures: left-wing ideological frenzy, media celebrity, and progressive lust between the politically righteous. For a young man whose irritating voice, lack of good looks, and what later would be called galloping nerdiness had severely limited his sexual experience, Marvin became a thrivin', jivin', pile-drivin' sex machine.

But then suddenly it all ended. One day in 1970, at a safe house of Students for American Ideals (SAI), he was on the second floor, balling some black bourgeois chick who was ashamed that she spoke good English, when the infamous West Forty-first Street Baltimore Massacre broke out. Three members of the SAI and one Baltimore policeman were shot to death in a forty-five-minute gun battle. The safe house, in a white working-class enclave of Baltimore, was burned to the ground, along with most homes on that side of the street. The police said they had been fired upon first; the SAI said that the police had, unprovoked, opened fire and that the SAI had fired only in self-defense. Marvin, quickly jumping off the girl and into his pants and T-shirt, escaped by jumping out the back second-story window and landing in a hedge as the house filled with tear gas and the pigs fired away. He made his way, from safe house to safe house, to Canada, and then to Cuba and then, after two years, came home to face trial on charges stemming from the shooting of the policeman. After his acquittal, he surprised just about everyone who knew him only as a celebrity activist by going back to college and getting his degree in education. He moved to Miami, got married, then divorced. He returned to New York and taught poor black and Hispanic children in the toughest New York City public schools. Then, six years ago, Donna, who had known Marvin practically all her life—her father and his had, after all, been best friends—gave him a LionHeart grant (renewed without scrutiny every year since) to study his father's case. He was now a fixture at the foundation, always at work in his windowless basement office, buried in documents from the 1940s and 1950s.

Although in the years since his days of glory Marvin's hair had gone gray and he had put on a few extra pounds around the middle, he was somewhat attractive in a middle-aged, bookish, public-intellectual kind of way. In fact, with his thick glasses and his graying goatee, he looked a bit like Trotsky, and what could be hotter than that to left-wing women of a certain age? Marvin was now Donna's confidant, escort, and, when the mood struck her, lover. But there was no misunderstanding, on Donna's part at least, that their relationship was rooted more in a past they shared rather than a future they might build together. Marvin, dazzled by Donna's all-devouring personality, had a slightly more hopeful view.

Tonight, having driven in from Queens at Donna's command, Marvin was sitting with her in the hideaway on the top floor of one of the brownstones that served as the LionHeart Foundation headquarters in New York. Next door was the gleaming glass-and-steel fifteen-story building that housed most of the foundation administrative, financial, and public relations staff. The brownstone combination—where the foundation had originally been located before Donna had the office building erected—now was home to the resident scholars, fellows, some grantees, and some people about whom no one was quite certain as to what they did or who they were, most of them relics from the progressive political past.

Donna and Marvin sat in the two beige Early Georgian (*not* Queen Anne, darling, as Donna liked to point out) walnut wing armchairs flanking the fireplace (which had real logs aglow). The room was eclectically furnished and decorated: a gold Savonnerie rug with rococo garlands; a mahogany lowboy (good for *you*, darling, this one *is* a Queen Anne) on which, ten minutes ago, an aide had placed an exquisite Harden-Krofts silver tea set; a nineteenth-century cherrywood Biedermeier sofa; and Donna's favorite piece, the massive pediment-topped, mahogany bureau bookcase, a masterpiece of many compartments, drawers, and two molded panel doors. In other places in the large room were tables and chairs named after centuries, kings, or queens. Over the fireplace hung one small, perfect Klee. On the other walls were two Kandinskys, and one Piet Mondrian. The mix-and-match, clash-and-clatter, name-your-century, wildly loose-leaf look of the room reflected Donna's First Principle of Decorative Aesthetics, which was, if you're rich enough to buy it, and if you like looking at it, buy it, darling, and then look at it as often as you can. Forget about clashing styles. Life is too short. This room was Donna's refuge from the world, her place to just *be*, to read, to greet very special visitors, or to just sit and talk.

"Marvin," she said, "a couple of things. First, I want you to fly out to the Che School. Snoop around. Find out what's going on. Ask any questions you want, of the girls, the staff, the administration. Then come back and report personally to me. I'd go myself but I'm very busy."

"How are the local Montana residents taking all this, Donna? I mean, all those working girls in one place?"

"Unsurprisingly, many of them are upset. Reactionaries of the worst sort, cowboys, gun owners, the kind with American flags on their pickup trucks. You know what that state needs? Diversity. Montana is probably the whitest state in the Union. I'm thinking of starting a community of African Americans out there, as a LionHeart project, to give those people an idea of what American diversity is all about. Now, let me switch subjects. I saw my father today."

"How is he?"

"Cranky, demanding, ill-humored, the man we all know and love. But it was a good visit. My father is still very shrewd about politics."

"Who knows more than the Deli Lama? He's a national resource."

"We discussed the Tyne situation. I think what he was trying to tell me— in so many words—is that rhetoric and argument and attempts at reasoned discourse have seen their best days. No one knows how to argue or debate anymore. Americans can't follow arguments. They need action and images— movies, TV, ads, anything visual, not words. The only thing is, I'm not quite certain how to implement his idea. I need something different, something good, for the Che School fund-raiser, and that's coming up soon."

For a few moments they sat in silence. Then Donna, rising from her chair, said, "Marvin, follow me."

They walked out of the room and a few steps down the red-carpeted hallway, to her private elevator. Three floors below they stepped out into a hallway connected to the administrative building and went into the foyer of the Lion-Heart Foundation Hollywood Ten Memorial Theater. Donna turned on some lights and walked down the side aisle to the door leading backstage. In a minute she was onstage, looking out at the dimly lit rows of empty seats. Marvin had an aisle seat in the second row.

"I always feel good on a stage," Donna said. "I think better."

She took a few steps downstage and said to Marvin, "I have to come up with some dramatic way of getting Tyne to stop attacking me."

"Donna, forget about him. You could—"

"No, damn it, everybody tells me to ignore him, but I will *not*. That's the trouble with progressives today. We laugh at the primitives. We chuckle at reactionary stupidity. And then we wake up one day and discover that they've won another victory. Well, I'm not making that mistake with Tyne. He's been sniping away at me for years, and I'm fed up. I want to destroy him, Marvin. End of argument. But I have to think *theater*. Maybe I should do a one-woman show. I could play a kind of Everywoman. I could do a lot of characters, each of them somehow a victim of the kind of philosophy Tyne espouses. I could play, say, an old woman hurt by Medicare cuts, and then a working mom and—"

"Too preachy, Donna," Marvin said.

"Maybe you're right. Besides, let's face it—do I still have the acting chops to pull off a one-woman, multicharacter show?"

"You've been away for a few years, you have to consider that."

Donna frowned, turned, and walked upstage, then faced Marvin.

"How about this: I'll stage a mock debate: just a bare stage with few props—two lecterns, maybe a moderator. I'll play myself and I'll get some good actor to play Tyne, and we'll debate the issues, poverty, the environment, big business, and—"

"Donna, I'm falling asleep already just thinking about it," Marvin whined. "It's too intellectual. No pizzazz. Can I make a little suggestion here?"

"Of course, Marvin, I want you to."

Marvin walked down the aisle until he was standing just below Donna.

"One word, Donna: *fun*. Did you ever think that maybe instead of all this high-mindedness, you might need something that will grab the audience right away? Like a clown with his pants on fire? Something loud and brash and, excuse the expression, funny?"

"Funny? But this is serious."

"But that's the point, Donna. Tyne *isn't* serious. He's a joke, a bad joke, but still a joke. Why take him seriously? You only build him up."

Donna sat on the apron of the stage, her legs dangling.

"That's pretty much what my father was trying to tell me, I suppose. In politics, ridicule is better than a syllogism. If I can pull it off at the fund-raiser, I'll be on the offensive. I'll give myself a whole new political image, just when I need it. Why didn't I think of this weeks ago?"

"Because you hadn't talked to the Deli Lama and me. Look, Donna, forgive me, but I'm calling it a night. Che Che wants to interview me for her book. I have to get prepared for her questions. She knows more than I do about Abe, even though I know more about my father."

Donna jumped down from the stage and embraced him.

"Do a good job for me at the Che School, Marvin. I'm counting on you. I want to know how things are going."

Donna hurried back to her hideaway. High on a rush of new energy, she began to doodle, make little notes, sketching out a plan for some kind of skit to be done at the upcoming Che School fund-raising dinner. She would importune showbiz friends—*sympatico* politically—in New York and Hollywood to become part of her skit. Now she was ready to begin the great counterattack at her fund-raiser. Ezra Tyne would never know what hit him.

And once I get Tyne out of the way, the next target is Ty Ferguson.

"This won't do, Harry," said President Tyler Ferguson, pointing to the speech draft on his desk. "I want a great speech for Tim Flaherty's union people, a rip-roaring, rousing speech that's going to put me back on top by appealing to the work-challenged. But what I'm getting from my writers is pap, gruel, nothing I can sink my teeth into."

The first thing people noticed about Ty the Guy, aside from his craggy good looks and smooth, masculine voice, was that nothing in his personal appearance was out of place, nothing overdone, nothing wanting. Even after a long, tiring day, like this one, his blue shirt was crisp (he made a full change of clothes at least three times a day) and his pressed blue suit showed just the right amount of cuff, disclosing discreet, expensive monogrammed gold cuff links. His trademark red-white-and-blue-striped tie (known as "the Guy Tie") had, as always, a small, perfect knot beneath the eyelet collar and the gold tiepin. Every hair on his large head—and he had a lot of hair, still brown (oh, well, some distinguished gray along the temples) and thick—was in place, parted down the middle in the old-fashioned way.

Seated behind his desk in the Oval Office, he had on the rimless eyeglasses he never wore in public. They gave him what he thought was an objective, cool, professorial look. But when the Guy put on these glasses, to most of his staff he resembled those Aryan-looking actors who played cultivated but cruel SS men in old movies about World War II, the kind one saw on the cable channels. He looked as if he were about to say that while he personally abhorred violence and loved Shakespeare and Schubert *lieder,* he had no alternative (*ach, what can one do, mein Herr?*) but to proceed with the torture.

"No, this just won't do," he snapped at Harry Gottlieb, his White House chief of staff. "No places where I introduce work-challenged people in the audience and ask them to stand up. People who stand up in the audience always get applause."

Harry, in his early fifties, a balding, bespectacled, rumpled, pudgy apple dumpling of a man—in short (and he was short), a nebbish, but with eyes that behind his glasses radiated intelligence—sat across the desk from the Guy, sweating as he feverishly took notes. Harry was not one of those celebrity chiefs of staff whose photos are on the cover of newsmagazines. He rarely spoke to the media. He was not part of the Guy's inner circle and, in fact, had worked for Governor Kevin Stanley of New York ("the Liberal's Liberal"), one of the Guy's opponents during the Democratic primary elections. But Harry, a lawyer with experience as a top-level congressional aide on the House Ways and

Means Committee and then in private practice at Jennings Grace Caulfield, the Beltway insiders' law firm, knew Washington inside out (the Washington of power, not the actual city itself—like most bureaucrats and government-dependent white people, in the unlikely event he ever found himself in Anacostia, he never would have been able to find his way home). Harry knew policy and he knew politics, and because he was a born networker as well as an ideological idealist, he knew and was trusted by many useful people in high, middle, and low places in various Washington bureaucracies and on the Hill. He was a good manager, but he was not—to his disappointment—a policy maker. Originally he had thought he would be able to influence the president in left-liberal directions, but such was not the case. The Guy needed someone to run things, not run the Guy. But Harry was a problem solver, a good traffic cop, keeping the paperwork moving along, making certain everyone was on message, ensuring that the president was at the right place at the right time with the right set of prepared remarks.

It was 10:47 P.M. Harry was bone-weary, but he knew the Guy liked to hold these little end-of-the day sessions to tidy up things, since he hated loose ends. The offending speech draft was in the exact center of the Guy's desk. Using a meticulously sharpened pencil, the Guy pushed the draft one inch toward Harry.

"This thing is brain-dead. There's no *life* in it," the Guy said, smoothing down his tie with his left hand in a characteristic gesture *(neat, neat)*. "May I remind you, my reelection is less than two years away? Forty-three percent of *Democrats* say I don't understand the problems of working people. *Me*. A lifelong Democrat whose father knew what the inside of a coal mine looked like."

The Guy's father had indeed at one time been in a coal mine, that much was accurate. But accuracy is not synonymous with truth, especially in politics, and the Guy, early in his political career, tended to leave out relevant data about his background. His father, the son of a prosperous hardware store owner in Pittsburgh, had worked *at*, not *in*, a coal mine for only two months, between his junior and senior years at Pitt. He had been underground twice during that time, not to dig coal but to bring his boss lunch. Ty himself had grown up in the Pittsburgh suburbs and, before he entered politics, had never come within miles of a coal mine in his life. As far back as Ty could remember, his father had been a certified public accountant.

The media had long since uncovered and reported these facts, so the Guy had to drop the "a miner's son" slogan he used in his first race for the House and adopt the more accurate but less satisfying "inside of a coal mine" fudge. But the coal-miner's-son myth had a strong hold on the Guy's psyche, and every now and then he would refer to himself as a coal miner's son.

"You're right, it's unfair, and wrong. And disgraceful, Mr. President," Harry responded.

"I need a speech that shows I'm sensitive to the work-challenged. But I won't go off the deep end for Tim Flaherty. I won't bash business. Flaherty wants me on the attack all the time. And he's peeved because he thinks I haven't made up my mind about the bill to give benefits to work-challenged Americans."

"Have you made up your mind, Mr. President?"

"No, damn it, but that's irrelevant. I don't want Flaherty going around *saying* I haven't made up my mind. It makes me look indecisive. I may go one way or the other, but I'm not tipping my hand until the speech. His union is important and it's growing. The fact is, a hell of a lot of American workers don't like their jobs or their bosses. Flaherty speaks for people like that. And he's got a point. Why shouldn't they get benefits to help them compensate for being work-challenged and being, er, disgruntled, or whatever it is? The work-challenged are coming out of the closet, Harry, and they're our people. I can't afford to alienate Flaherty. He even wants me to hire some of his work-challenged folks for my staff. Maybe I will."

"You're right, Mr. President," Harry said as he scribbled on a yellow legal pad. "I'll tell the writers to take another shot at the speech. As you know, they've been working hard and—"

"Damn it, Harry, you're not *listening*," the Guy said, his face taking on that cold, deadly, get-out-the-electrodes look. "I've had it with those pampered speechwriters. I want you to take away their White House mess privileges. Let them brown-bag it. They don't deserve the honor. Writer types are all the same, prima donnas, disloyal and treacherous. I wish to God I could get rid of the whole crew. Besides, *I'm sick of rhetoric.* Where is it written that a president had to be so damned entertaining and scintillating and inspiring and eloquent all the time? Can't I just do my job and let others babble? If I had my way, all I'd do is go places and introduce people from the audience. Let them stand up. People like to see real people stand up. But do my precious geniuses know that?"

"You're right, sir. Writers are very difficult people, Mr. President. Very temperamental."

"That's *it!* Temperamental. *Artistes,* very sensitive, 'Oh please don't change one word or I'll cry' types. And they can't be trusted. They leave you to pursue their own ambitions, like Pete Dickinson did. But between you and me, at least Dickinson could write, after a fashion. I'll give him that much."

"You're right, Mr. President. Pete is a very good writer."

"But he was never a team player, never. Selfish and arrogant. I'm glad he's gone."

"I couldn't agree more, sir. And that article he wrote about you in the *Post* was unforgivable."

"Yes, but if I have to give these damned speeches, I want someone who writes the way Dickinson wrote, that ungrateful turncoat."

The Guy, again using the pencil, pushed the speech draft a few inches more toward Harry, who picked it up from the desk.

"Don't bother returning that to the writers. Just throw it away," the Guy said. "*Find me a writer,* Harry, a writer who can give me a speech that will knock their socks off at the UWCE meeting. And remember—I want a speech with passages that allow me to point to people in the audience and ask them to stand up. And use the word *links.*"

"*Links,* sir?"

"Links. The Internet and all that. I don't know what it is or they are, exactly, links. But I keep on hearing and seeing the word. People want to believe their president knows about computers. So put in something about links."

"Yes, sir. Links."

The Guy removed his glasses and rubbed them with a tissue. He rolled the tissue into a tight ball and dropped it in the exact center of the wastepaper basket. He replaced his glasses, and said to Harry, "There's one other thing. I want you to meet, soon, with Donna Hart Lyons. Secretly, of course. I don't want that woman running against me next time. I have enough troubles without her. Find out what she wants. Don't beg. But don't attack. Be firm. But be flexible. Don't give up an inch. But seek compromise. I do not want that woman to take over the AAP. Do you understand what I'm saying?"

"Yes, sir."

An hour and a half later, Harry sat alone in the den of his large, sprawling, expensive Great Falls home, nursing the one scotch on the rocks he allowed himself every night. His wife of twenty-three years (they were childless by choice) had divorced him a year ago, complaining bitterly of his workaholic habits and devotion to the Guy.

"You're almost never home," she had shouted at him, "and when you're home, you're thinking of work. We hardly ever make love, we don't go out, you barely speak to me. When I say something, you get mad because it interrupts your thoughts about the Guy. To hell with you, you bastard, and to hell with the Guy!"

Harry knew that what she had yelled was all too true. So there he was, rattling around in this big, empty, if beautiful, house—lonely, wondering if the sacrifices he had made for the Guy were worth it all.

All right, admit it. You have a guilty conscience. You ran Kevin Stanley's race. You did it right—no compromises. All right, some compromises. But not on the big things. And for a while it looked as if Kevin would win because he appealed to the purists. But it all fell apart in the primaries. We couldn't expand beyond our base. Kevin lost, and it broke your heart. But when the Guy asked you to be his chief of staff—where were your damn purity and ideals then? You jumped at the chance. Oh sure, you kidded yourself you would influence things, serve as the conscience of the Oval Office. All you are is a paper pusher. But you love being chief of staff, don't you? If the Guy sacks you, it's back to the law firm. Big money, but no reason to get up in the morning. You can't stay on as chief of staff much beyond this year, you'll have a heart attack or burn out. Then what? All right, stop bitching. Now you have to meet with Donna Hart Lyons and persuade her not to run. But first you have to solve this goddamn speechwriter problem. But where do I find a speechwriter who can write like Pete Dickinson without actually being *Pete Dickinson?*

He took the last sip of scotch and put the glass on the night table. The place to begin with the speechwriter problem was with Pete Dickinson. Without Pete, nothing could be done. There was one little problem: the Guy hated Pete, and Pete hated the Guy.

I wonder what Pete is up to these days? I think I'll give him a call tomorrow.

Pete Dickinson swam in long, easy strokes, making almost perfect turns, but after eight laps he could begin to feel his technique slowly disintegrate through small but cumulatively deadly imperfections. By the twelfth lap he was winded. His kick lacked power, his arm strokes were sloppy, his rhythm was choppy. When, breathing heavily, he reached one end of the pool, he turned to see Marlie Rae coming toward him, still swimming.

They were in the pool at the Fairfax County Spring Hill Recreation Center in McLean. Marlie Rae, a Fairfax County resident (although not in McLean—too expensive for a poor cop like Marlie Rae), had a season pass, and Pete had condescended to swim in a public pool because, given his finances, he had recently dropped membership to his private club.

Marlie Rae wasn't a good swimmer. She was in fact a splash-making pool plodder who inexpertly, and with wasted motion, pushed the water out of her way. She had no sense of style, but her form, if clumsy, had utilitarian merit, and Pete could detect no sign of weariness in her movements. It bothered him that he, a former collegiate swimmer, a star (almost), was out of shape, short of breath, and aching all over, while she, untrained and innocent of technique, was still going strong. Whatever she did—sex, swimming, talking—she radiated a kind of oblivious, natural happiness, a state of nirvana-like bliss he knew he could never achieve, except when he was stoned. He was now too winded and tired to swim anymore, but he didn't want her to know how out of shape he was, so he decided to take desperate measures—he would talk with her. When she reached him, he grabbed her around the waist and pulled her to him, put his arm around her waist, and kissed her.

"That's enough," he said, "I don't want the Fairfax police saying I caused one of their finest to have a heart attack."

"Honey, I was going strong," she said, puffing and taking off her swimming goggles. "Not as good as you in the water, but I could do this all day."

"Isn't that what you said to me in bed the other night?"

"Maybe I did, honey, but remember: I wasn't under oath, so it don't necessarily count."

Pete had a gift for small talk with women, although he didn't always choose to exercise it. More than a few women had succumbed to him after being softened up by mindless chatter about this and that. He was adept at the kind of conversation that ostensibly demonstrates that a man is sensitive and willing and even eager to have real relationship, not just one based on sex, and is really, *really* eager to know what the woman thinks about this and how she feels about that. Now, with the echoing pool sounds of other swimmers as background noise, their desultory conversation wandered in and out and above and below many topics—movies, TV—and, somehow, alit upon Vacations I Have Enjoyed. Marlie Rae had just told him about the Perkins family visit to Orlando and the fabulous time they had in Disney World.

"What was your favorite vacation?" she said.

"When I was a boy my father took us—my mother and me, this was before they were divorced—to Rio. It was some kind of USIA cultural-exchange thing and he lectured on literature in universities down there. I was fourteen. Walking around the beaches and seeing those perfect girls wearing almost nothing was just about the greatest thing ever. But it wasn't just the girls. Even at that age I could tell Rio was special. They know how to live down there. Since then I've been to other great places. Prague, when I was there, was wonderful, unspoiled. San Francisco and Quebec, two of my favorite cities in the world. Tuscany and—"

"You really been to all those places?"

"And, of course, France. The French are a very strange people, but France itself is wonderful. Have you ever been there?"

"I never even been out of this country."

"Maybe someday I'll show you the France I know," he said, looking directly into her eyes (the oldest trick in the world, but it works almost every time). "Just the two of us."

"Paris? France? Oh, my Gawd, I always wanted to see Paris."

"Paris is great, but Paris isn't the real France. Provence used to be the place, but no one I know goes there anymore, it's become overrun by tourists."

"Oh, I wouldn't mind going anyplace in France. You read so much about it. The Eiffel Tower they got there. That big museum. Those bike races. Do you really mean it? About going to France? You and me? That would be real fun, going to France and seeing all those things with you."

"Why not? After all, I'm your guest at the pool. Why shouldn't you be my guest in Brittany or Burgundy?"

Later, in the locker room, Marlie Rae thought, *He's real nice. He's not a snob, like I thought. He's just different. And wouldn't it be something if we really went all the way to France together? I mean, anything's possible.*

Three hours later Pete, sitting before his computer, trying to figure out a new way to praise greed, picked up the ringing phone.

"Pete? It's Harry."

"Harry? What—"

"Meet me, tomorrow, around noon, at Great Falls Park. I want to talk with you. It's important. You know how to get there?"

"Great Falls Park? All the way out there?"

"Right, all the way out here, in the depths of the Fairfax County wilderness. Lewis and Clark territory. Do you need a trusty Indian guide? Er, Native American."

"I know Great Falls. I can find it. But what's this all about?"

"Just meet me there at the visitors center, you can't miss it."

"Can't you tell me what it's about?"

"The future. Yours and mine."

Pete put down the phone and wondered what Harry Gottlieb wanted. They had never been particularly close, but at least Harry hadn't joined the wolf pack when Pete was driven from the White House. Pete knew that in Washington, when you get a telephone call from someone you haven't seen in a long time, it means either one of two things: he wants something from you or he wants to pass on bad news about you.

But that could wait for tomorrow. Right now he had to finish the greed speech. And then, first thing tomorrow morning, before he went to see Harry, he had to start on that UWCE speech for union boss Tim Flaherty. Busy, busy, busy—but not quite busy enough to make headway paying off those debts.

SIX

There was a time, Pete's grandfather had once told him, when the Irish in America knew their place, when maids named Bridget curtsied and gardeners named Paddy pinched the peak of their workingman's caps in reverence when a Dickinson walked by. What would Grandfather say if he knew his grandson was writing a speech for an Irish union boss?

Tim Flaherty had an in-house union speechwriter, but things weren't working out (he had given Pete no specifics of the situation), so he had turned to Pete a few months ago. Writing speeches for a man who was head of a labor union dedicated to rewarding and glorifying sloth, incompetence, and indifference was difficult. The usual appeals to the work ethic, union solidarity, and improved working conditions didn't mean anything to people who had no work ethic, bitched and griped about their own union, and really didn't care if work conditions improved, because it was work itself they didn't like. Pete was having a hard time getting started with the speech. He was in no need of Wagner—or coke—to jolt him into activity, but still, he couldn't think of anything to write.

To jump-start the draft, he did his finger exercise, typing out variations of what he thought of as the all-purpose political speech line, a sentence that contained words such as *America, people, spirit, freedom, vision, strength, destiny,* and *dream:*

> Sacrifice is the spirit of the American dream of liberty, and freedom is the strength of our vision of destiny.

The strength of the American people is the dream of destiny, and the spirit of freedom and sacrifice is the vision of liberty.

The vision of destiny is the spirit of liberty and strength of the American people, and the dream of freedom and sacrifice.

No matter how you juggled and mixed and matched the evocative words, they had a certain lilt but meant absolutely nothing, the very model of what inspirational political prose should be. Now that he had finger exercises out of the way, he really had to get to work. But nothing came.

Speechwriting. It isn't an art, and not much of a craft, he thought. Certainly not a calling. It certainly wasn't a career. Good political speechwriters tended to burn out young, and Pete felt he was reaching that point. Over the years he had written national convention speeches, Rose Garden remarks, commencement-speaker drool, campaign hype, one-liners, slogans, brief remarks for the floor of the House, and winding, windy, wearying speeches for the Senate floor. And for every speech he had written, he had heard fifty more. And what was the use of it all? Write a speech with vision, and critics will say it lacks specifics. Write a speech that lists the facts, and the critics say it lacks vision. Write the best speech in the world, but if there's one single error of fact in it or, worse, a "gaffe," some unintended offense against an ethnic or religious or gender group, the press and the opposition will concentrate on that and forget the rest. *Speechwriting*. Many people who knew Pete often asked how he, of all people, had stumbled or fallen into that most unlikely of jobs for a Main Line snob? It was, Pete admitted to himself as he stared at his iMac, a strange, labyrinthine tale.

He had never had strongly held political views, and found ideological passions—left, right, ecological, or feminist—too silly for words. He considered himself a liberal Democrat only because his father was, nominally, an aristocratic liberal of the 1950s Adlai Stevenson noblesse oblige school. Trevor Dickinson felt that politics was vulgar, but if people must have politics, they may as well have liberal, humane, learned, financially well-off, aristocratic leaders. In the social and academic environment in which Pete came of age, it had been easier for him to go along with the prevailing—indeed, all but universal—ideologically left-liberal views of academia.

Pete, although an English major, knew he would never follow his father into academia. So, after his graduation from Penn's Annenberg School for Communication, he halfheartedly accepted a position on the Washington staff of a suburban Philadelphia Democratic congressman, Templeton "Tony" Garret, a pleasant, unassuming, wealthy, dim-witted man whose political philosophy was to offend as few people as possible and to follow the broad path of political moderation in all things. Pete's father warned him against getting mixed up in politics, but despite (or was it because of?) these's objections, Pete took the job. After a few boring (Pete was easily bored) months of answering constituent letters, he was promoted to—or, at least, told to assume—the position of press aide/speechwriter. He quickly attracted attention for an ability (a knack? a gift? a freakish party trick, like being able to wiggle one's ears?) he had never known he possessed: he could write effective speeches in someone else's voice. As he wrote floor remarks and speeches for Congressman Garret, it was, to Pete, as if Garret were dictating the lines, in the patrician, civil, contented, high-pitched tone of a stupid man with old money, a young (second) wife, and a safe congressional seat.

Pete learned quickly how to write speeches for the House floor: speak in headlines, argue in slogans, and never waste precious time putting forth an opponent's argument in order to refute it. In the Senate there was unlimited time for debate, but in the House bills came to the floor with rules limiting debate time. Debate in the Senate was something like a nineteenth-century novel, with lots of room to spread out; in the House, debate was more like an exchange of haiku—swift, spare, and often puzzling. Denunciation (but with civility), proclamation, and self-assertion were the three keys to successful floor remarks. Many evenings Pete sat on the floor of the House, weary, waiting for the drawn-out debate to end, listening to some inarticulate lunkhead quote Winston Churchill (or, far worse, Yogi Berra), as if no one had ever quoted him before, or misquote what Santayana had said about learning from history or what Lord Acton had said about the corrupting influence of power. Pete's work eventually came to the attention of the junior senator from Pennsylvania, Tyler Ferguson. The Guy, up for reelection, positioning himself for his run for the presidential nomination, was buying the best talent he could find, and he made Pete an offer. Pete, although he knew the Guy's reputation as a less-than-inspiring public speaker, immediately accepted because the Guy was being named, by those who named, as a potential presidential candidate.

None of this impressed Pete's father. Main Line mandarins, having seen it all—or having owned it all—are not easily impressed.

"Politicians are all scoundrels, my boy," Trevor Dickinson said condescendingly. "There is something deeply, psychologically warped, ontologically *evil*, in fact, about human beings who *need* to be elected to public office. I am a liberal, of course—all decent, intelligent people are—but I have no illusions about politics. Ferguson in particular is disturbing. I have watched him on television. The man has no animating principle. I believe he is some kind of construct, an automaton, a golem, cleverly devised by political consultants to appear human."

"But, Dad, I'm writing for the man who might be the next president. Doesn't that mean anything?"

"Peter, Peter, speechwriting isn't *real* writing. What a speechwriter does is salvage a slogan here, find some mindless or sentimentally patriotic drivel there, throw in political truisms and crowd-pleasing clichés from the rubbish bin of past speeches, recast them, and then fit them together. Voilà, a speech! A speechwriter isn't a writer—he's a *wright*, like a wheelwright or a boatwright, a hireling paid a wage to fit separate parts together to make something utilitarian. I'm happy for your success. But as I've said so many times, Washington is a place where clear thinking goes to die, like those great beasts in the legend of the elephant's graveyard."

Pete remembered his father's words as he sat in his home office, trying desperately to cobble together something for Tim Flaherty to say to his rank and file. He put the Wagner into the Bose. "Forest Murmurs." Good, soothing. The loveliness of the music somehow reminded him of Che Che. He didn't know what to do about her. It would be nice to have access to all that money.

Still, nothing on the screen. In the immortal words of Oliver Hardy, this was a fine kettle of fish. Was it time for the jolt that refreshed? Maybe. But he wanted to see what happened. He reached over to his worktable and grabbed some material that Flaherty's press secretary had sent. Maybe something in the fact sheets might inspire him. He read for a few minutes and dropped the propaganda back on the table. Nothing.

The Wagner disc had arrived at the last scene of *Götterdämmerung*. The world of illusion going, going, and with the last glowing chords, gone. That resolution, that completeness, that tragic inevitability, that reminder of the uselessness of all striving, penetrated Pete's mind and gave him a sense of serenity. He typed:

> The work-challenged are at the heart of the American experience. To be challenged by the very idea of work, and to despise your job and your boss, is part of the American dream. To be work-challenged is to tell the corporate greed merchants who want to run our lives: I am an individual. I am not a cog in your corporate machine. I am not a replaceable part, to be thrown away because I refuse to believe in your so called work ethic. I am not a cheerleader for big business. And I won't allow myself to become a victim of prejudice and bigotry because of what I believe about work.

It wasn't much. It wasn't true. It wasn't good. But it was a start. He had to get something written this morning because this afternoon he was going to met Harry Gottlieb at Great Falls Park, whatever that was all about.

Project: "LEFT ALONE: One American's Journey in the Radical Left"

Taped interview between Che Che Hart and Abe Steinberg, at the Abe Steinberg Suite of the LionHeart Residence for Progressive Seniors, Westchester, New York.

—Grampa, we're going to pick it up at—

—Pick what up? What are you talkin'? Pick up what?

—What I mean is, we'll resume your story. Last time we were talking about—

—I know what we were talkin' about, Miss Smarty Pants Professor. I'm friggin' old, excuse my French, but I'm not dead yet. Even though they try to kill me here with the food. I wouldn't feed it to Roy Cohn. Yes, I would.

—The last time we were talking about the McCarthy days and the investigations.

—My wife, your grandma Sadie, you don't remember her, left me after that. For what? I ask you.

—Well, we can talk about that if you like. . . .

—Like? I'm too old to like anything. Too old to like girls. Too old to like food. Maybe a custard. And I don't even like custard. What I wouldn't give to be able to eat pastrami. They don't make custard the right way here.

—Maybe we should get back to the McCarthy days.

—What's to get back to? They ruined me. I almost lost my deli, people stopped coming. In our neighborhood, Melrose in the Bronx, everybody was some kind of left-winger, liberal, whatever. Communists organized rent strikes in the Bronx. They didn't just talk. The Bronx in those days was class-conscious, people didn't believe the bullshit of the landlords and the Hearst press. To us, the Bronx wasn't just the Grand Concourse or Yankee Stadium or the zoo or all those colleges we had up there. The Bronx was working people who fought the exploiters. But not all of them, not even the communists, could say A, and then say B. If you're a real revolutionary, if you say A, then you *have* to say B. The liberals said they wanted to reform the system. *Reform.* Did the iceberg reform the *Titanic?* No. It sunk it. Before your time, the *Titanic.* They made a movie. I didn't see it. I don't like the movies anymore. I used to like John Garfield. His real name was Jules Garfinkle or whatever, he changed his name. A lot of Jews had to change their names in those days. . . . Where was I? Oh yeah. Did you know Roy Cohn, that bastard, was a Jew? Besides being queer?

—Gay, Grampa, these days we say "gay." Can you remember what it felt like, sitting there, with Joe McCarthy screaming at you?

—A Jew, and he treated me like that. He was a Jew but he hated the Jews.

—McCarthy wasn't a Jew.

—No, idiot. Roy Cohn. We were talking about Roy Cohn.

—Now we're talking about the McCarthy hearing where you said, and I'm quoting from *The New York Times,* "You want names? I'll give you names of Americans who believe what I believe. Here's a list. Write them down, here they are, my fellow spies and traitors and dupes. George Washington, a revolutionary, a real subversive. Thomas Jefferson, he was a big Red, believed in inalienable rights. Tom Paine, another one, an atheist, so put him in jail. Sam Adams, agitator, he got his orders straight from Moscow." What was it like, sitting there and publicly confronting them, knowing you risked prison? A few years before that, one of your best friends, Al Gunn—

—That's his bust up there. Al Gunn. A great man.

—He went to prison on perjury charges, denying he was a communist spy, and died there, leaving a wife and child. His wife committed suicide. Grampa? [Silence.] Grampa, we can end here if this is too much for you.

—All right, so I cry a little bit. Poor Al Gunn. He was a *mensch*.

—I know, Grampa. I've been interviewing his son, Marvin. You remember Marvin. He works for LionHeart, for Mom. He lives in Queens.

—Queens? You call that living?

—Marvin's proud of his father. He told me he even once thought of changing his name back to the original, Guinsberg, with a *u*.

—Like I said, a lot of Jews did that in those days, change their names. A Jewish name, it didn't get you too far. And then the party would give us fake names sometimes, for different things we'd be doing. When we went down South, helped the colored people, it was better not to have a Jew name. I took different names: Jack Gordon, Bill Davis. Once I used Joseph Rogers, real American-sounding. Joseph Rogers. It was easy to remember. See, it rhymed with Dodgers. In '47 they won the pennant. The Dodgers signed Jackie Robinson in 1946—I could see they were a progressive baseball club, so I rooted for them, even though I didn't like baseball.

—Is everything ideological?

—Everything is part of the class struggle. So I rooted for the Dodgers. The Yanks were the luckiest team ever. Like a big business, who could root for them? In the series, Al Gionfriddo made the great catch on DiMaggio. I was there! In Yankee Stadium. I can remember all that, but I can't remember when I had my last bowel movement. Old age is hell. You can't remember what you want to remember, and you can't forget what you want to forget. . . . Where was I?

—Using aliases. For party work.

—Yeah. The rednecks would beat you up or kill you, Jewish name or no Jewish name, if you even talked about colored people voting. Those bastards, highway patrolmen down there in Alabama, they beat me up good, broke my ribs, knocked out my teeth, broke my nose, like it needed to get bigger with a bump. So what difference did it make, if your name was Joseph Rogers or Abe Steinberg? Which reminds me—why aren't you a communist?

—I was never interested in politics in that way, Grampa, you know that.

—Not interested? You know what Trotsky—that bastard—said? He said, "You may not be interested in politics, but politics is interested in you." True, even if he was a bastard.

—That's all over, Grampa. Those were the old days.

—We knew what the hell a revolution was back then. It ain't child's play, believe me. You got to make tough decisions. For the good of the party, you do things. [Silence.] I told them off, didn't I? Thomas Jefferson, a real Red. Sam Adams. A hero. Now Sam Adams is a beer. That was a good one. Wasn't it? I did the right thing, didn't I?

—Yes, Grampa, you did a marvelous thing, very brave. I don't agree with what you believed then, most people don't, but I admire you for telling the truth and standing up for what you believe in. I'm proud of you for standing up to people who were bullying you. Mom always tried to follow your example.

—Your mother married that colored musician, what's-his-name.

—Johnnie Hart. He was my father.

—Yeah, him. A *schwartze* musician, no offense, who would have thought our Donna would do that? Where was I? When things were going bad, a lot of people were losing faith in the party—not me, but Al Gunn—that's his bust over there on that big pedestal, weighs a ton—Al would say, Abe, being in the party under a capitalist system is like working for the sanitation department— we're up to our ears in horseshit but we got to keep on shoveling. It's sacrifice, all the time. Tom Paine, a real Red. I told them off, didn't I?

—You sure did, Grampa.

—I don't want to talk about it no more. I'm tired. I'm sick. I'm an old man. Get out of here, leave me alone.

SEVEN

After roughing out a first draft of the Flaherty speech, Pete drove north along Old Dominion Drive in McLean, on his way to Great Falls Park to meet Harry Gottlieb. Thinking of Harry reminded Pete of his brief career and bitter departure as a White House speechwriter.

After being hired by Senator Ty Ferguson, Pete soon became his number one speechwriter; and when Ty announced his candidacy for the presidency, Pete churned out punchy preconvention stuff at a rapid pace. He wrote most of the Guy's acceptance speech at the convention in San Francisco and became adept at acceptance-ese, the special language of acceptance speeches:

> I see an America that is filled with promise—and where every promise shall be fulfilled.
>
> I see an America where we can protect national freedom, without losing civil liberties.

Pete wrote a section of the acceptance speech in which the Guy paid tribute to his grandmother, who was sitting on the convention floor, near the great prowlike podium. In the event, the passage did not go quite as planned:

> Now, I have heard it said that folks of Scottish heritage know the virtue of thrift, a-ha, a-ha. My grandmother, an immigrant from Scotland, instilled that virtue in me. Gumma—that's what we call her—used to save string. Still does, I guess. One day I asked her why she bothered to save little pieces

of string. Gumma said to me, "Laddie"—I am always Laddie to her—
"Laddie, wherever ye go, save what ye can and pay your way, boy, pay your
way. Work hard and save harder."

Gumma, tonight I want you to know that your Laddie remembers. And I
want you to just stand up, so all these good folks can honor you as I have all
these years. Stand up there, Gumma. There she is, my ninety-eight-year-old
Gumma. Wave, Gumma, wave. There she is—just stand up, Gumma. Somebody down there please help Gumma stand. There you go. Steady. Oops, almost fell there. Hold her now. Hold her! A little unsteady, my Gumma, but
she knows my administration won't be unsteady, a-ha, a-ha. She knows—
there you go, Gumma, wave to your Laddie. . . . I'm up here, darling. . . .
Good, good, that is America in that wave, right there. That is the dream.
Stop waving now, Gumma. There you go. No, stop waving. Sit down,
Gumma. It's all right, Gumma, just sit, dear.

Despite Gumma, the Guy won the presidency and Pete became a White House
speechwriter. In all administrations, the speechwriters' shop is made up of two
factions: the True Believers, usually the most fanatically loyal group on the White
House staff, and the Mercenaries, those shrewd and ambitious young men and
women who are going to use the job as a launching pad to lucrative careers in media, lobbying, or consulting. Pete, most definitely in the second camp, swiftly became a star (Young Up-and-Coming Division) in Celebrity Washington, a small,
imaginary city populated by a few news-media types, some lobbyists, lawyers
with a talent for getting their name in the newspaper, political consultants who
have by diligence and the care and feeding of media contacts achieved guru sta-
tus, some high-level administration appointees, congressmen and senators with
important leadership posts or committee assignments, and, every now and then, a
small handful of what are called "key" congressional staffers and high-profile
presidential speechwriters.

High-profile speechwriters? Surely an oxymoron, *mon ami?* But, alas,
anonymity, once a presidential speechwriter's prime virtue, had long since been

abandoned, as speechwriters tattled to the media about their contribution to major speeches. But even in this tell-all world of supposedly behind-the-scenes work, Pete stood out for blatant self-promotion, and his romance with high-profile Che Che didn't help matters. His name was in the newspapers almost as often as the Guy's, or so it seemed. Pete's fellow speechwriters, harmless drudges without his charisma (or *chutzpah*), became jealous and then bitter and then downright nasty as Pete's photo appeared in the Style section of the *Post* over and over. And then, six months after the inauguration, one of Pete's contacts in the press, in a thumb-sucker piece ("Whither the Administration? Six Months and Counting"), quoted Pete by name as having said, just after the inaugural address: "With the possible exception of William Henry Harrison's fatal stem-winder, the Guy's was the most boring and idiotic inaugural address in history. Harrison was lucky—he died soon after."

Pete tried to dance his way out of it. He did the "out of context" shuffle, and then the "I was misquoted" mambo, and finally the "If anyone was offended by what I said, I apologize" boogie, but things began to deteriorate very quickly. Staff members—not including Harry Gottlieb, who tolerated Pete, up to a point—spread the word to reporters that Pete Dickinson was not a team player. They used other derogatory clichés (e.g., "not on the same page"), all suggesting Pete was a self-centered, self-aggrandizing, egomaniacal skunk—which Pete knew was essentially true, if a trifle harsh, but it hurt that his own colleagues thought so. After a few more months of being abused, ignored, and rejected, Pete finally resigned, after fourteen months on the job. Three weeks later, in an op-ed piece in *The Washington Post*, "A Promise Unfulfilled," Pete wrote:

> "I see an America that is filled with promise—and where every promise shall be fulfilled." Of all the words I wrote for President Tyler Ferguson, these from his acceptance speech are the saddest of all because President Ferguson has not yet fulfilled the promises he made to the American people. I will leave to others to question the opportunities missed and the hopes dashed

in foreign policy and domestic policy. The health bill, the farm bill, the crisis in Peru, the situation in east Africa—these and other opportunities for presidential leadership were missed. I speak here of the president's refusal to enlist the English language on behalf of his causes, to offer a vision that matches his patriotism, his passion for politics, and his superb political skills. I speak of his well-known dislike of what he calls "mere rhetoric," as if rhetoric were something added to presidential power, a kind of frosting on the cake. But for a president, rhetoric *is* substance, rhetoric *is* vision. In the Oval Office strong, moving, passionately felt words are often the most effective form of presidential action. But President Ferguson is the anti-rhetoric president.

For a week or or so, Pete was in the news. He was on television. He was getting clients. And then, gradually, it all stopped. So, in debt, his business on the ropes, here he was at Great Falls Park, wondering what Harry had on his mind. He paid the entry fee and drove about a hundred yards to the large parking area, parked the car, checked his cell phone (no messages, as usual), and walked to the visitors center, a large wooden building in the rustic style, with a concrete ramp leading up to a hall of exhibits. Near the building there were a few young mothers in sweat suits pushing baby strollers, and some joggers. Not a very big crowd, but more than he had expected on a weekday. He was about to walk up the incline to the visitors center's exhibit area when he heard:

"Pete."

Standing alone, his back against the visitors center wall was Harry Gottlieb, wearing a green and white Philadelphia Eagles jacket and baseball hat, and sunglasses. They walked in silence to the first overlook. They stared at the tumbling waters of the Potomac River below, cascading, bashing and crashing and splashing against and over and around the primeval outcropping of enormous, jagged gray boulders, the broken water swirling about in eddies, in swiftly changing blurs of green and white, water and foam, leaping in the air and falling and leaping again.

"I always bring visitors here," Harry said. "Most beautiful natural sight in the area. But not too many tourists get to see it. After some good rainfalls, like we had last week, the water is high and you get the full effect. You ever been out here before?"

"No. I hate nature. It reminds me of all those stupid environmental speeches I've written. Why are we here, Harry?"

"Calm down, we'll get to that. Just enjoy the sight. At least you can say you've seen Great Falls. People I bring out here sometimes expect something like Niagara Falls and they're disappointed. But this is better. At Niagara Falls the water just . . . well, it just *falls* . . . *boom*. Spectacular, but dumb. But here you can see the Potomac rushing down, after all those miles of traveling, in a bad mood, running into the rocks and beating the living hell out of them, all day, every day. You see some action. The river's going to win in the long run, but I always root for the rocks. Rocks can take it."

Two minutes later they were walking through the trees, Harry in the lead, on a narrow, barely defined path, strewn with last year's fallen leaves. The river, unseen, rushed into the Mather Gorge far below them, to their left. No one else was on the path, in either direction. Harry stopped by a fallen, rotted-out tree and sat on it, brushing off a broken branch.

"Out here we have a chance to talk. I don't trust buildings of any kind anymore. Too much sophisticated surveillance stuff out there these days. I didn't think it would be good—for either of us—to be seen together," he said. "The president is out of town, doing some fund-raising for the party up in Michigan today, so I got a little time to myself. Anyhow, let me get down to business. What would you think of writing the Guy's speech to Tim Flaherty's union people?"

Pete was just about to say he was already writing Flaherty's speech at the same meeting. But Flaherty, for some intra-union reason, didn't want it known he wasn't using his in-house speechwriter. So Pete said, "I'm waiting for the punch line, Harry. Where's the zinger?"

"No punch line, no zinger. Just a straightforward business proposition."

"Harry, you brought me out here, in the middle of the *woods,* for this?"

Harry told Pete about the Guy's dissatisfaction with recent speech drafts.

"Oh, hell, he's always bitching about something," Pete said. "But what does all this have to do with me? I quit working for him, remember?"

"Yeah, yeah, but ever since you left him, as I said, quite frankly, the big speeches haven't been that good. They're flat. You know how he is. He has great feelings of inadequacy when he speaks."

"For good reason."

"The writers try, but they don't have your touch."

"The Guy had my touch, at his beck and call, but then he turned on me."

"You turned on him first. Anyhow, I massage the drafts as much as I can. I can even imitate your stuff a little. In fact, I'm not so bad at it. But it doesn't work all the time. So, my question is this. If I can fix it so you get paid, will you write some speeches for the Guy?"

"Harry, even if I agreed to do that—and I'd have to be out of my mind—why would the Guy take me back on staff?"

"Well, see, you wouldn't exactly be on staff. You'd stay where you are, in your own business."

"But how—"

"Don't worry about any of it. I'll take care of the whole thing. All you have to do is write speeches when I ask you. I'm talking about the big speeches. The other writers can handle the usual crap."

"Harry, after that op-ed piece I did—"

"That doesn't matter. As I said, the Guy is never going to know you're writing the speeches."

"I'm going to write for the Guy. But he's not going to know about it. Do I have that right?"

"You have it right."

"Harry, I have to tell you I'm really pissed off you brought me all the way out here for this, goddamn it. I thought it was about something serious."

With that, Pete shook his head, wheeled about, and began walking back to the parking lot, leaving Harry sitting alone on the fallen tree trunk.

* * *

Two days later Pete was working away on the Flaherty speech when the phone rang. It was his CPA.

"Pete, I got something I thought you'd want to know right away. Prepare yourself, because it's not too good."

"What are you talking about?"

"A guy in know in the IRS called me at home last night, unofficially, back channel. Your name has come up—I don't know how—and there's going to be a full-scale audit. He said they're coming after you, guns blazing. Is there anything about your taxes you've been keeping from me? Tell me the truth, Pete."

"Don't be ridiculous. Of course not. Maybe there might have been a few little things, minor things like—"

"*Hold it right there*. Just hold that thought. At this point I don't want to know any more than I should. But let me just say one thing. There *aren't* any little things for the IRS."

"How the hell do I know if every penny is accounted for? I made a good-faith effort, that's all I know."

"You better know more than that if they come after you. Let me give you a piece of advice—free. If you still have any friends in the administration, which I doubt, maybe you should give them a call, because it looks to me as if they're going to lower the boom on you."

Later that afternoon Pete's phone rang again.

"Pete? Harry."

"I figured you'd call. You son of a bitch."

"Meet me tomorrow, same time, same place."

Pete spent the first five minutes of the second meeting at Great Falls Park cursing out Harry, scaring some birds, and alarming a female senior citizen who was backpacking through the woods. When she was far enough away down the trail, Harry, unperturbed, said, "Calm down, Pete. Take a deep breath."

"You bastard. You sicced the goddamn IRS on me."

"Did I?"

"You *bastard*."

They walked along in silence.

"Looks like rain," Harry said. "When we were here the other day, it was beautiful. But I like this place even when the weather—"

"Skip the Weather Channel talk, Harry. Get to the point."

"Do you want this IRS problem you mentioned—and I'm not saying I know anything about it—to ease up?"

"No, of course not. I *enjoy* paying my CPA money I don't have. I enjoy the thought of IRS goons looking at all my records. It's the Dickinson streak of masochism in me."

"Then use your brains. You and I reach a private agreement, who gets hurt? You get the IRS off your back and I get your inestimable services. I can arrange it so you get paid for these speeches by an outside source, top dollar. I know how your business is going and I know you need the money."

"You've been spying on me."

"No, I don't have to spy. People gossip. So?"

"This is crazy. I'd be writing speeches for a man who hates me, a man I don't like and I don't believe in."

"You didn't like him or believe in him when you worked for him. You used him for prestige and he used you to make him sound halfway human. So there's no big change there."

"The Guy will recognize my style."

"I have ways of dealing with that. So, is it yes or no?"

"Give me some time—"

"There is no time. I need to get this thing settled now."

"You're not kidding about the taxes?"

"You have my word."

"And I'll get paid?"

"You can count on it."

Pete turned away and walked a few steps along the path. Finally he turned and came back to Harry.

"All right, damn it, I'll do it," he said. "But one thing—nobody can ever find out about my doing this. After what I wrote about the Guy, I'd look like a fool."

"Do you think I'm going to call the *Post* and tell them? I can't let it be known you're writing the speeches because I'd be fired. You can't let it be known because you'd look bad, working for a man you deserted and turned on. We both have too much to lose."

Pete didn't say anything. Somewhere amid the trees, birds called to one another. It had started to rain, softly but persistently.

"All right, then, if you can pull it off," Pete said finally, putting up the collar of his jacket against the rain. "But how do we do this?"

"I'll send you the background material for each speech, the deadlines, the general themes he wants to hit. You send the stuff to me by messenger, to my home. Give me anecdotes, warmth, and a lot of places where the Guy introduces people from the audience so they can stand up and be acknowledged. He likes that."

"Tell me about it. Someday he'll perfect the stand-up gimmick to the point where he doesn't say anything, he just introduces people."

"Don't give him any ideas. And do something with the word *links*, as in links on a Web site. He likes the word. Don't ask me why, I don't know. So we're clear on this, right?"

"And no one will be any the wiser, Stanley."

"What?"

"That's what Ollie says to Stan in *Sons of the Desert*."

"Is that the one they're in the Foreign Legion?"

"No, that's *Flying Deuces*. A lot of people make that mistake. But in *Sons of the Desert* their scheme blows up in their faces."

"Well, we're not Laurel and Hardy."

"Don't bet on it, Ollie," Peter said, doing a not-so-bad Stan Laurel.

"Very funny. Oh yeah, one more thing. Of course, the Guy needs a lot of stuff praising stupid, incompetent, and indolent people who don't want to work."

"The American way," Pete said, and shaking his head in disbelief, began walking back to his car.

A week later the Guy, making a curious discordant humming sound, skimmed the last page of the speech draft Harry had given him a few minutes before. He looked up from the draft and squinted at Harry through the Himmler eyeglasses. Then he put the draft on the desk in front of him. He touched it with a pencil to square it away.

"This is not . . . half bad," the Guy said cautiously, removing his glasses and placing them in a black case. He placed the case in the inside pocket of his suit jacket. He touched his lapel and smoothed his tie.

"It needs work, of course," the Guy said. "But it has places where I can introduce people, I like that. It has a good thing about being anti-work-challenged as the new American bigotry. I like the way it deals with federal aid for the work-challenged. I like that links reference. And it's punchy. Who did this?"

Here goes, thought Harry, his heart pounding. *Just say it.*

"Well, as a matter of fact, uh, I did, Mr. President."

"*You?* You wrote this?"

"Yes, sir."

"I don't believe it. You?"

"Yes, sir. I'm glad you like it."

"Since when have you been a speechwriter?"

"Oh, I used to do a lot of writing when I was on the committee staff on the Hill. And at the law firm I churned out a lot of, uh, stuff. And I massage the speeches when they come over from the writers."

"Not enough, obviously. You surprise me, Harry. In fact, some of this sounds almost like the stuff Dickinson used to do."

"I'm glad you noticed that, Mr. President. I tried to use some of his, er, style, anecdotes, little stories."

"I see. Harry, why the hell didn't you tell me you could write?"

"It never came up until now, Mr. President. But given your, er, very under-standable discontent, your unhappiness—quite justified—with the writers, I just took the plunge and hoped you'd like it."

The Guy stared at Harry for a few moments.

"Ummmm. Not bad," he said finally. "Not great. But I'll work on it, make it better. I like the way this was handled, Harry."

"Thank you, sir."

That night at home, lying in bed, sipping his daily scotch, and watching *My Fair Lady* on TV, Harry did something wholly uncharacteristic—he congratulated himself. It was not his practice to indulge in self-praise. There were always too many problems demanding his attention for him to allow himself the luxury of enjoying his few unqualified successes. But now he relaxed and enjoyed every moment of what he had accomplished. He sipped the scotch, savoring the smoky aroma, the iodine taste, the slight burn on the tongue.

Ahhhh.

As he luxuriated in the decadent, pagan comfort of lying alone in a king-size bed, he realized there were some questions left unanswered about his Great Speechwriting Coup, as he had come to think of it. But there were so many good things. For one thing, in a relatively short time he had solved a problem that had seemed hopeless. A fact here, a half-truth there, a lie placed just so, a favor called in from an old friend from the Hill who was now in just the right place in the IRS, a little bit of bluff, sufficient amounts of *chutzpah*, a little pinch of method acting, a readiness to risk, an ability to take all these conflicting and problematic parts together, hammer them, saw off parts, glue here, staple there, and make something useful and workable out of them—that was an accomplishment worth drinking to.

Harry was particularly proud of his bluff about the IRS. There had never been an IRS investigation of Pete Dickinson, at least none that Harry knew of. But he knew that Pete, like everyone else, believed a presidential chief of staff could just pick up a telephone and get somebody audited at any time, on a whim, an idea Pete had probably picked up from a lot of bad Washington movies. But Harry Gottlieb would never attempt anything so blatantly stupid, not to mention crooked. He had simply asked his old friend at the IRS, a former congressional aide like Harry, to make one phone call in which Pete's CPA was told—falsely—that an audit was in the works.

Pete's imagination did the rest. The hardest part had come when Harry had to look the Guy straight in the eye and say he had written the speech. But he had pulled it off. Now, in bed, relaxed, content, watching Eliza at the ball, Harry took another sip of scotch. Eliza, a thing of beauty, danced; Higgins smirked contentedly; and then came the scene where Higgins is praised by his household staff.

Harry held up his glass and toasted himself.

Congratulations, Professor Gottlieb! On your glorious vic-tor-eeeee!

One critic of Ezra Tyne's had written:

> Tyne's thoughts, if one may call them that, are the detritus of a lifetime of undisciplined, unshaped reading, an autodidact's grab bag of half-understood myths, irrelevant factoids, misremembered statistics, pointless anecdotes, scraps of doggerel, non-sequitur aphorisms, barroom wisdom, bad jokes, conspiracy theories (and often conspiracy theories about conspiracy theories), blatant prejudices, jailhouse cynicism, scenes from old movies, the sum total of a thousand lonely rainy nights in small towns, waiting for the bus to the next small town, trying to read a much-thumbed porno paperback by the light of a drugstore window while you wait for it to stop raining so you can continue your journey to Noplace, USA. Tyne's mind reflects this kind of rootless, nomadic existence—of the body and the mind.

This night Ezra was in a good mood because some of the callers were hostile, and that always gave him a nice little edge. He could feel the power flowing his way when some lefty idiot attacked him:

CALLER: This is Susan from New York City.

░░░░ I ░░░ ░░░ ░░ ░░░░ ░░░░ ░░░░░░░ ░░░░░░ ░░░'░ ░░░░░ ░░░'░░ ░░░░, honey. No need for identification.

CALLER: I'm not one of your sycophantic fans, and I want—

EZRA: Whoa. Hold up, sweet Sue. Calm down. Sick-o what? You can't use words like that on Unca Ezra's show. Calling my fans sick-os. A lot of them are a little soft in the brain, just like me, but we can't help that. That's not Christian, what you said, if you'll excuse the word *Christian*, you probably being an ACLU type from New York City and all, that word might offend you. Now let me guess. You're one of those radical feminists they still got up there, right?

CALLER: I'm an American woman who finds your woman-bashing, race-baiting, and anti-Semitism offensive. I believe in treating all human beings fairly and helping the needy, so I guess in your book I'm a feminist. But let me—

EZRA: Now, tell me something, Suzie Q. Why do you call poor Unca Ezra an anti-Semite?

CALLER: Why? Your shameless, undocumented attacks on Israel, your

EZRA: Now hold on, Miss Civil Liberties of 1972. Folks like you and your relatives got most of the media and Hollyweird tied up, but on this show, real Americans get a chance to talk and I'm a real American. In foreign policy, I follow the rules of George Washington's Farewell Address. You know what that great man said? You probably don't, because, after all, he was a man and you probably hate men.

CALLER: That is not true, I—

EZRA: Let me speak, sugar cakes. George Washington warned us against what he called "inveterate antipathies" and "passionate attachments" to other nations. Any nation. That means the good ol' USA had no permanent friends, no permanent enemies, and—this the important part—no permanent clients. But there's folks who think some nations have a right to be on our payroll forever. I just don't think that's right. That's what you folks call anti-Semitism. But if that makes me an anti-Semite, so was George Washington. Give my regards to your significant other, whoever she or it may be. Next victim.

CALLER: Unca Ezra, Donna Tart Liar is going to have her big fund-raiser tomorrow night, in Washington, for her school of happy hookers. She's been saying she'll have a big surprise for you. You know what she's talking about?

EZRA: No, I never know what that woman is talking about, but, hell, neither does she. She's mad at Unca Ezra. But why? All I've been saying is I agree with her. I think every bimbo, hooker, pross, and lady of the evening in America, Mexico, Denmark, and parts of Outer Mongolia should get tuition-free education at the university of their choice. I don't know what Mizz Liar has in mind tomorrow night but I won't be paying attention, because I just enrolled in a black community program, Take a Harvard Ho to Lunch. Next batter, step up to the plate.

CALLER: Unca Ezra, this is Joe from Topeka.

EZRA: I was in and out of Topeka a few times, years back, Joe. Riding the rails, hitching rides. I can't remember a damned thing about the place. I must have been drunk or stoned. What's on your mind?

CALLER: Unca Ezra, here's the thing—why don't you run for president next time?

EZRA: Why, thank you, Joe. Kind of you. The funny thing is, speaking of national politics, I got a call the other day, you know, from a very high ranking official of the American Advance Party, can't mention his name, and you know what he said to me? He said, Unca Ezra, we gotta have you come to our annual meeting in August, right there in Washington, to set our folks straight, talk common sense about where this country is headed. Well, I thanked him but I said, son, Unca Ezra don't make no speeches. Don't do stand-up comedy, bar mitzvahs, weddings, or funerals, either. It's my way of stopping noise pollution, I'm a big environmentalist. But who can tell? One of these days, Unca Ezra just might decide to make one of those big speeches, let people know what's on his alleged mind. Yessir, Unca Ezra is thinking seriously about this one.

When the show was over, Ezra smiled. It is said of some men that their smiles never reach their eyes. In Ezra's case, his smile barely reached his lips. His lean face—"weathered" to his admirers, "creased" or "wrinkled" to his critics—was framed by shoulder-length brown-gray hair. He may have been in his late forties or maybe his fifties or maybe his early sixties, it was hard to tell. In public or at work, he wore a baseball cap (peak forward, no rapper he) bearing the word EZRA on it. His eyes were hidden by dark blue aviator glasses, his trademark. His upper lip was covered with a big, sprawling 1960s hippie mustache. It was the kind of face you might see on a drifter getting off an interstate bus at six-thirty on a cold, gray, mean, rainy Thursday morning in November after a long, sleepless ride from Oklahoma City to Memphis. Ezra always waited until the show was over to light a cigarette. He inhaled, sucked it in, deep, deep, deep, held it—*Jesus that was good, worth dying for. I'd give up one lung for that any day. Let it out, slow*. He sat there, smoking, coming down from the high of doing the show.

He looked around the studio. The state-of-the-art microphone, his greatest friend, was the only thing of value in the dingy little room, cluttered with half-empty coffee containers, ashtrays filled with cigarette butts (Ezra smoked, goddamn it, and to hell with the health-nut secret police), and a mess of clipped newspapers, well-thumbed men's magazines, and, on the far wall, a picture of Nixon greeting Elvis. Ezra sometimes wondered whether or not his show, which thundered the truth and gave regular folks a fighting chance, shouldn't originate from a more, well, not exactly palatial, that wouldn't be right for the champion of ordinary folks, but certainly a little more upscale environment. Ah, to hell with it, nobody cared what this place looked like. All they cared about was his voice, which, in a way, if you believed in those things, and Ezra wasn't fully convinced, came straight from heaven, because God, if he was up there, sang the same tune as Ezra.

Things are lookin' up for ol' Unca Ezra. Damned right, Elmer! My show is doing well in the ratings. I got Donna Liar on the run. People asking me if I want to run for president. Hmmmmmm . . . why the hell not? Can't be worse than the bozos they've been getting. And wouldn't it be sweet to just take that AAP nomination away from Lyin' Tart?

The light on his special private phone flashed. There was only one person in the world who knew that number. Ezra frowned but didn't pick up the phone. He continued smoking and after ten seconds or so—let her wait—he said into the phone, "What now?"

"You out of your *mind?*"

That old, familiar sound. Part whine, part screech.

"Nice to hear your sweet voice again, Lorna."

"You got bats in your belfry? I been telling you, don't make no appearances. I been telling you, don't get your photograph taken, stay mysterious. But more and more I'm seeing your picture in the paper and magazines. Now you're getting suckered into making a *speech?* Are you crazy?"

"Thanks for the encouragement, as usual."

"I'm only telling you the truth. Nobody else will, all your stupid fans swelling your big head some more."

"Tell me one thing, Lorna. Why in hell do you call? To make me feel better, is that it?"

"Maybe 'cause I want you to keep the show goin', keep on makin' money, although goddamn you, you send little enough to me and Johnnie. You ever think of that? You ever think, for one damned minute, you could be sending us a little more, and a little more often? You're living like a damn king out in your place in Leesburg, with all your whores, and we're living out here outside Roanoke, like dirt. I ought to—"

"Johnnie asleep?" Ezra said, eager to change the subject away from money.

"Hell no, he's watching the damn TV, some cartoon or such."

"Which one is he watching?"

"Sylvester the goddamn pussycat chasing that damned canary bird."

"I don't mind Sylvester, never did, he's all right, he tries to do his job, but I never could stand that bird, talks like a big fairy. Don't bother Johnnie, don't call him to the phone, let him watch his toons. Always great to hear your sweet voice, Lorna, like getting hit in the nuts with a hockey stick."

"Goddamn you, you better think twice before you start making speeches. And one more thing—"

Ezra put down the phone and lit another cigarette. He glanced at the morning newspapers, just to the left of the microphone, and thought:

Every damn time I make a little progress, Lorna wants to drag me back.

Then why the hell do you have this special phone here, just for her, like she wants?

I don't know.

Yes, you do. You're used to her. Even when she pisses you off, she's still Lorna. She knows you, Ezra. Hell, she knew you before you was called Ezra. And she knows things about you, secret things. She's kinda like a toothache you've had for so long, you wouldn't know what to do without it. And then there's Johnnie. . . .

I'm going to have to do something about that woman, sooner or later. I got plans and she don't fit into them.

EIGHT

Imperially slim. When young Peter Dickinson, in St. Elwald's prep school, first came across Edwin Arlington Robinson's poem "Richard Corey" and saw those words, he immediately thought of his father. The description was perfect, because it captured not only the way Trevor Dickinson looked but what he was: attractive, aristocratic, distant, always looking ever so slightly bored, but too much of a Dickinson to say so. And, of course, when Pete read *The Great Gatsby*, he knew immediately what Fitzgerald meant when he wrote that Daisy had a voice "full of money," because Pete had heard that voice all his life.

"It's good to see you, Peter," Trevor said in his smooth, languid manner, standing in the doorway of the Dickinson family fieldstone home in Bryn Mawr. Trevor, dressed in a dark blue double-breasted blazer (with his flat stomach, he could get away with it), a light blue button-down shirt open at the collar, khaki pants, and black loafers, looked like a senior male model in an advertisement for a new luxury car or old double-malt scotch.

"Good to see you, too, Dad. You're looking great."

"My boy, never say that to a man over sixty. What it sounds like is, you're looking well for a doddering old man with one foot in the grave. But these days I take compliments where I can get them. Come in, come in."

They walked from the foyer to the living room, with its Oriental rug and Oriental antiques and bric-a-brac, purchased on around-the-world cruises by four generations of the family. The room was also filled with family heirlooms, good, solid, no-nonsense furniture, and portraits of Dickinson ancestors on the walls. Contrary to widespread belief (which Trevor did nothing to dispute), the Dickinsons were *not* related to the John Dickinson who signed the Constitution. But their branch of the family was in its own way illustrious, claiming over two and a half centuries successful Philadelphia merchants, many judges, two Episcopal bishops, a few nationally known scholars, and enough high-priced, high-toned Philadelphia lawyers to successfully sue the devil himself or keep him out of jail. The big room looked the same as always to Pete, except that there was something drab about it, as if it hadn't been properly cleaned. There was dust, quite noticeable, on the tables.

"I've made martinis," Trevor said. "I know they're out of fashion, but so am I. Martinis are the only civilized drink, symbols of a golden age when people took drinking seriously."

"Shaken, not stirred?"

"That dreadful James Bond nonsense has besmirched a noble drink. A true martini is neither shaken nor stirred—it simply *is*. Sean Connery always reminded me of some kind of semiliterate Scottish stevedore dressed up in an ill-fitting rented tuxedo. I know you don't like martinis—your health-obssensed generation doesn't know what it's missing—but drink one for me. How's that, my boy?"

Pete sipped. Colder than a long bad winter in northern Minnesota, immediately bracing.

"Not bad."

"I'll take that as a compliment, Peter. Now let me look at you. You've put on a pound or two. Watch your diet. At twenty, one can eat a whole side of beef and not gain a pound. At forty the mere appearance of a piece of chocolate cake can give you a pound you don't need. But otherwise, you look fairly acceptable. Your hairline is, shall we say, not what it once was, but I'd say you have a few years before the general retreat begins. How was your trip?"

"Awful, as usual. Typical I-95 backups."

"Too many cars, too many stupid people going places, the curse of prosperity. So much for the trickle-down theory. Have you heard from your mother recently?"

"A while ago. She was going on a cruise."

"Not the *Love Boat*, I assume. Actually, I'm glad she remarried. What is it that her new husband does? Sells used cars in Kansas or one of those dreadful flat states?"

"Missouri. He has four auto dealerships in and around St. Louis, in fact. He does quite well."

"I have no doubt he does. A car salesman. I can picture cozy nights around the fireplace as they discuss transmissions. Ah, well, so long as she's happy. She *is* happy, isn't she?"

"I guess. So how is, uh, Jane? Is that her name?"

"Oh, my boy, you must learn to keep up with things. Jane and I have long since gone our separate ways. She somehow got the preposterous idea that we were going to get married. You might be surprised to learn I've been going out with Ruth Curruthers—"

"Gooch's mother? You're going out with *her?*"

"Nothing serious, old man, just quiet dinners or maybe a trip to hear the orchestra at its dreadfully up-to-date new digs. Since Ormandy left, it's been all downhill. When they play Wagner, they bellow and—"

"I just can't believe you're dating Mrs. Curruthers."

"Why are you surprised?"

"Well, for one thing, you always said she was stupid."

"True enough, but she's pleasant, affectionate, and reasonably attractive."

"I just never thought of Gooch's mother as—"

"As a woman? Let me assure you, Ruth Curruthers is very much a woman. After Brent Curruthers shot himself I became friendly with her. It's been rather nice, going out with someone—"

"Your own age?"

"That *wasn't* what I was going to say. I was about to say someone of one's own background. But your point is well taken. Perhaps since the divorce, I have been a bit too . . . unselective in my choice of female companions."

Peter wanted to say, *Yes, but then again you were unselective in your choice of other women companions* before *the divorce*. But this was not the time to attack. This was, after all, the charm offensive.

"I am acutely aware that a man my age," Trevor said, "can very quickly become an object of ridicule if he chases younger women. I think part of the reason your mother divorced me was not that I cheated on her but that I had done it with women half her age."

"I think you're telling me more than I want to know about you and Mom."

"Point taken. Well, then, how is your business?"

"Booming. Couldn't be better."

"Bravo for you."

"More work than I can handle, actually. I'm thinking of taking on help."

"How marvelous. Here, let me just pour you another."

"No, I'm fine."

"Well, I'm glad to hear you're doing so well."

"You never thought much of speechwriting, as I recall."

"Success is success after all, no matter what the work."

On the terrace, after a leisurely lunch, they spoke about Trevor's book ("Coming along, my boy"). Pete, who long ago, at his father's insistence, had read Peacock's *Nightmare Abbey* and *Crotchet Castle*, tried to remember bits and pieces so he could ask his father questions that he was only too glad to answer at length. As Trevor pontificated about Peacock's civilized, urbane, and sly satiric wit, Pete noticed that the silver wasn't looking its best—tarnished, in fact—uncharacteristic of the Dickinson table.

"Where's Rosa?" Pete asked, referring to the Dickinsons' longtime cook, maid, and nanny.

"In Guatemala, visiting her two hundred relatives."

Rosa's absence would account for the run-down look of the house. Pete promised Trevor that next time it would not be so long between visits.

"That sounds fine. Peter, let me say I'm proud of you," Trevor said as he stretched out his long legs in a terrace chair.

"I never thought you were proud of me."

"Dickinsons are not demonstrative. You know that. But do stay in touch."

On the drive back to Washington, Pete thought: *Operation Dear Old Dad, Part One. At just the right time, maybe in a few weeks, I'll suggest that a little loan might be in order.*

LionWest, Donna's little weekend retreat in Montana, was a stone-and-log mansion, with two wings off a huge central glass-enclosed greeting hall, designed according to western frontier taste (the logs) and modern aesthetic sensibilities (the bold, stark stone and the glass), complete with twenty-four-hour security guards from LionClaw; a small theater with stage machinery and a roomful of props and costumes, just in case Donna got the urge to act; an indoor Olympic-size pool; a state-of-the-abs gym; live-in servants; up-to-the-second security systems (motion and heat detectors, discreetly hidden cameras); and, a mile away from the building, private cabins for special guests and a helicopter landing pad.

As the SUV, driven by a LionClaw guard, pulled away from the circular driveway near the front porch, Marvin Gunn, in the backseat, turned to look at the ruggedly beautiful house (Donna did not like to use the word *mansion*) and shook his head in wonder. Marvin had visited LionWest before, but he could never get over the sheer size and scope of the place. The Che School was about three miles away from the house, so as the SUV drove north Marvin used the time to acquaint himself with the facts and figures of Donna's latest social experiment.

There were fifty-six girls in the first class. They were of all races and came from across the country, to ensure diversity. Most of them had undergone extensive interviews with teams of social scientists and psychologists before being accepted as students, but a few had been chosen at random so that no one could say Donna had loaded the dice by selecting girls who were already motivated to get out of the life. Each girl had her own room, and the girls received a stipend of two thousands dollars a month, which was automatically deposited into banks of their choice. The catch was that in order to get the money, a girl had to stay at the Che School for at least one year. Every human need—food, clothing, health care, physical fitness, leisure-time activities—was provided for them. There was no contact with the outside word, television viewing was carefully monitored, and, of course, illicit drugs, alcohol, and sex were forbidden. Donna intended the Che School to be a working model of socialist/feminist progress: individual happiness achieved through service to the greater community, all under the guidance of brilliant, dedicated, ideologically motivated leaders who knew what was best and did all in their power to help the girls understand that everything at the school was designed to help wayward girls become progressive women.

As the SUV approached the school, Marvin noted that workmen were building a chain-link fence around the school site. *What's that all about? Donna never mentioned a fence.* He then saw the two-story, rather nondescript main school building, designed and constructed along purely utilitarian—in fact, rather ugly—lines. The only thing remarkable about the structure was its very existence, in the natural surroundings of the empty land. Isolated and alien-looking in its stark angularity, the Che School building, in its own strange way, made a statement: human reason in the pursuit of progress has its own demands, and Nature, even Big Sky Montana Nature, must bow to the power of human progress through education. Donna had ordered the architect to avoid making an aesthetic statement when he created the school building. She wanted the very existence of the building, here in the open country of western Montana, to let visitors know that at LionWest, Donna's wishes for a better world were all that mattered. The school banner, designed to look like the Cuban flag—six alternating blue and white horizontal stripes, with a red triangle on the left and a gold star within the triangle—unfurled in the breeze atop the school building. The difference in the Che School banner was that instead of a gold star, there was an idealized portrait of Che, copied from the "Blessed Che" picture that was a left-wing icon around the world. Behind the main building was a dormitory for the girls and two buildings housing faculty and staff. These buildings were constructed with the stone-and-glass attractive modernism of the Lion-West house itself. Donna felt that while it was all right for the school itself to be stark and businesslike, the living quarters should be beautiful, in the austere, no-frills architectural sense she admired.

At the school entrance, a LionClaw security guard opened the door of the SUV and Marvin emerged to be greeted by an energetic, muscular, short, stocky, middle-aged woman with a butch haircut. She wore a sweat suit with the words SAPPHIC LUST across the chest. This was the dean of the Che School, Dr. Babette "Babs" (or "the Babster") Battaglia, senior fellow in Progressive Women's Studies of the LionHeart Foundation. Twenty years ago Babs had gained notoriety with her prize-winning study "Was Lincoln a Pansy? The Proposition Abe Was *Really* Dedicated To." One of her right-wing clergymen critics said Babs herself was dedicated to "the vile abominations, detestable vices, and loathsome degeneracies of Sapphic lust in its most sordid forms." Babs had adopted the phrase and now used it on her letterhead and T-shirts.

"Marvin! How the hell are ya," she shouted, embracing him and slapping him on the back. "You're looking great, kid. Love that goatee, love it. Glad to have you out here at LionWest, where even the deer and the antelope have to think progressive before we let them play."

"Donna wants me to just check on how things are going," Marvin said. He gestured to the workmen. "What's the fence all about?"

"Well, to be honest, we have a few problems. A few of the girls got bored and sneaked off campus. They somehow got a ride into Missoula and got arrested for soliciting. We expelled them, of course. But I think it might be best to build a fence, just to remind the girls that this thing isn't going to work if people start wandering off, looking for johns."

"Won't the fence make the girls feel like prisoners?"

"I don't see it that way. We're not keeping the girls in—we're keeping societal pressures out, just the way Donna wants it. Anyhow, that's not the big problem. We have a bit of a class struggle going on, you know, economic and social classes against each other."

"But Donna wants the school to teach them a sense of solidarity and community."

"Jesus, Marvin, spare me the ideological bullshit, I got enough problems. These chicks come from all different kinds of backgrounds. You're bound to have problems when you put them all in one place, isolate them, cut them off from everything, and all they see is each other, all day every day twenty-four/seven. So we got this class thing. The girls who worked the streets, a lot of them black or Hispanic, are looked down on by girls, mostly white, who did more upscale whoring. Girls with pimps think they're better than freelancers. Girls from the city think small-town whores are dumb. Things like that. They're forming cliques. We got one tough nut to handle, named Monique. She appeared in some porno flicks for a while but then turned pro and worked upscale. She's smart, her damn IQ is off the charts, but she's a real ball-breaker, always asking wiseass questions in class, bitching about the restrictions. I tell her, Monique, this is for your own good, and she's like, I know what my own good is, not you. She's a rotten apple. You should talk to her."

"I will. Thanks for telling me the truth, Babs. But Donna's not going to be pleased. She can't have it known that she has class divisions at this school, of all places, or that you need a fence. Her critics would eat her alive. Crazy Ezra Tyne is already on her ass."

For the next three hours, Marvin went from classroom to classroom, sitting in the back of the room, listening, and taking notes. On the walls of each classroom were reproductions of great lefty art: Picasso's *Guernica*, the Ben Shahn paintings honoring Sacco and Vanzetti, copies of murals by David Siqueiros and Diego Rivera, and other revered masterpieces of the class struggle. Over the blackboard in each room a poster, in red letters on a white background, proclaimed some sacred slogan from the all-time leftist hit parade:

I WOULD RATHER DIE ON MY FEET THAN LIVE ON MY KNEES

ERASE THE INFAMY!

YOU HAVE NOTHING TO LOSE BUT YOUR CHAINS

The girls wore a school uniform: white T-shirts with the words THE ERNESTO CHE GUEVARA SCHOOL FOR WAYWARD GIRLS in red across the front, classic early Fidel Castro fatigues (baggy, not quite chic, really), a red Che beret (quite chic), and army boots. As Marvin sat in the back of the classes and listened, he noticed the glassy-eyed stares, barely stifled yawns, and droopy eyelids of the girls as environmental/geopolitical activists, geopolitical/ economic/direct-actioners, young bearded anarchists with attitude, old bald socialists with ponytails, and feminists of every description lectured on the joys of progressive thought or rhapsodized about the poetry of Pablo Neruda. It seemed to Marvin as if the entire activist intellectual Left had been gathered in one place to give the girls the undiluted, pure, potent message of progressivism. But the girls didn't seem to be listening. Later, Marvin interviewed some of the girls to get their views on how things were going.

Most of them were fairly attractive (they were young, and attractiveness had, after all, been a prerequisite for their former jobs) and intelligent, if not brilliant, shrewd about what they wanted. Almost all of them said they found the course of study to be irrelevant to their need to learn new skills but were willing to give the school a chance because they really did want to leave the life, and they wanted to collect the stipend, in one lump sum. If Donna said that listening to all of this progressive bullshit helped them, they were prepared, if not happy, to listen.

Monique, the troublemaker—Marvin saw her last—was tall and good-looking; even in the Che School sack-suit uniform, she radiated a direct, provocative sexuality.

"Let me get right to the point, Monique," Marvin said. "I've been told you're a troublemaker."

"Your little goatee is cute."

"What's wrong with the school?"

"Oh, it's not *that* bad. The food is pretty good. We read all these books and things. But I get bored. There's nothing to do out here."

"Then why did you come here?"

"It sounded like a good idea at the time. They're paying us to stay here, and there's all the fresh air and exercise and all, if you like that kind of thing. It didn't sound too bad. Besides, my pimp was beating me. Not on my face, he wasn't dumb, but he was hitting me. So I figured, you need a break, what the hell, take a chance. What did I have to lose?"

"I talked to the girls and they look up to you. You're a natural leader. If you show the way, they'll follow. The whole point of the school is for all of you to feel part of something larger, a community."

"The girls don't give a damn about that stuff. We all thought we'd get some job training or something. But all we get is this political bullshit, all day long. In fact, I have to go back to my room and read some book by a guy named Upton Sinclair. I heard of him, but I never read anything by him. *The Jungle*. It's disgusting, about slaughterhouses. What's that got to do with whores?"

When she left the room, a wispy but powerful scent of something, some perfume, lingered. Monique, Marvin felt, was the key. If they could get her to become an enthusiastic supporter of the school, it would be success. If not . . .

Marvin did not relish the long trip back to New York, especially with the news he'd have to tell Donna. Already there was trouble in this progressive eden. Human nature, recalcitrant, stupid, selfish, reactionary, shortsighted, not knowing what was best for it, human nature, that old bugaboo of progressives since the French Revolution, was up to its old tricks. Human nature, which a thousand books and studies and articles had proved did not exist, and which revolutions had try to stamp out again and again, was still there: dumb, hungry, grinning, idiotic human nature, standing in the way of the orderly, logical organization of the best human instincts, led by the best leaders, whose minds were illuminated by the best ideas.

NINE

Nuanced and Fair with Dave McNair. Fox News Channel.

DAVE: . . . and we're back, nuanced and fair, as always, with Kate Hepple-white, author of the controversial bestseller whose title says it all: *Left-wingers Should Be Shot Dead on Sight!* Kate, a lot of people—not yours truly, but even some conservatives—are saying that you are a little too harsh on the left wing. What do you say to that?

KATE: I only regret that I didn't make the book tougher. The Left has been on a century-long assault against American values. They deserve everything I give them—and more.

DAVE: Well, let me play devil's advocate for a minute. Take my friendly spar-ring partner, Donna Hart Lyons. I disagree with her, strongly, but I don't think she's a criminal. You have an entire chapter devoted to her and you really lace into her.

KATE: Donna Hart Lyons is undoubtedly the most dangerous woman in Amer-ica. She uses her late husband's money, made in the capitalist system, to destroy that system.

DAVE: Tonight here in Washington—as we speak, as matter of fact—she is holding a fund-raiser for her Che School. All the left-wing and liberal big-money people from New York and Hollywood and Washington will be there, all applauding Donna.

KATE: Which proves my point. Those people talk about diversity, but this is the least diverse group in America. Think of it: all those people live in similar suburban or prestigious urban neighborhoods. Their children all attend the same elite private schools, and then go on to the same prestigious universities, where they mingle with students exactly like themselves, or with token blacks and Hispanics and gender-challenged midgets. All of these people read the same newspapers, magazines, and books. They all vote the same. Where's the diversity?

Che Che, in her elegant dark green evening gown, sat at a table near the dais in the hotel ballroom, packed with more than four hundred celebrity guests, waiting for the Che School fund-raising dinner to begin. She watched with pride as Donna, looking her radiant, star-quality best in a devastating red gown (her exclusive color; every other woman knew better than to wear a red dress when Donna was around), made a triumphal procession along the dais as the fifteen-piece band played a medley of Sinatra favorites (except, at Donna's order, "The Lady Is a Tramp"). Donna, shaking hands, air-kissing, hugging, touching, blowing kisses, and waving, made her way past a long row of adoring show-business activists, political activists, and progressive media celebrities. When she reached her seat, she waved to the crowd. The ballroom erupted into cheers and applause for the Godmother. Behind the dais was a makeshift stage, complete with curtain, where the night's festivities would be presented. At the top of the proscenium was a sign covered by drapes.

Che Che, at her request, was seated, with Marvin and Pete, at table twelve, reserved for TV writer activists. Pete, sitting across the table from her, looked very handsome in his tux. Che Che had asked him to write some remarks for Donna tonight, and Che Che could tell he was a bit nervous, awaiting the reception his words would get from this hard-to-please crowd of showbiz sophisticates. Earlier in the evening some of the writers at the table had received the Lenny Bruce First Amendment Award for Expanding the Boundaries of Artistic TV Expression. To Che Che's left was Sam Goniff, bald, ponytailed, fat, and fifty, legendary in the world of TV sitcom writers for being the first to write a script in which the TV sitcom wife shouts at her husband, "You left up the toilet seat again!" the first toilet-seat-up joke ever in prime time. Seated next to Sam was Audrey Holtz Hirsch, looking scrumptious in her fancy spaghetti-strap dark blue gown. Audrey was the first writer to use an approving *ahhhhh* sound on the laugh track in a tender scene of sitcom reconciliation. Following Sam's artistic lead, Audrey used the word *pee,* as in "I gotta pee," in a sitcom script, a breakthrough that challenged the stodgy, reactionary, stupid attitudes of evangelical, religious-right would-be censors. Across the table from Sam was an even more revered TV writer, Sid Armann, a dour, skeletal, hollow-eyed man of sixty-six. Long out of the TV sitcom writing business (let's face it, it's a young man's game), Sid, when he was the head writer for the old cop show *Chicago Mopes,* wrote a groundbreaking scene in which the hero, Detective Stanley "Pooch" Pucinski, goes into the men's room and, while using a urinal (realistic sound effects provided), discusses a case with his partner, who is sitting in a stall (sound effects provided, but door closed—the goddamn right-wing censoring network bastards).

Che Che glanced across the table, past the centerpiece with its roses and tulips and hydrangeas, and tried to catch Pete's eye, but he was talking with Sid and seemed to be enjoying himself. Che Che was delighted because she had been afraid he would be bored or feel out of place with all these ideological types, even though they were writers like him. But not even Pete's presence could calm the butterflies in Che Che's stomach. A few days ago, her mother had told her what she was going to do tonight. Now, as the show was about to begin, Che Che tuned to Marvin for support.

"Marvin, suppose it doesn't come off?"

"Donna will make it come off. You just watch."

Throughout the dinner—lobster or steak, a vegetarian plate, or a Deli Lama special pastrami sandwich, with pickle air-lifted from New York—Che Che ate sparingly, nibbling at the greens of the salad. She could not rid herself of the feeling of foreboding. When she looked up from her plate, she saw that her mother was not at her seat on the dais. That meant she was backstage, preparing for the sketch. *So they're getting ready,* Che Che thought. *Now we'll see.*

Sam Goniff, now at the dais, acting as emcee, said: "I know that most of us here tonight came here for one noble, selfless reason—the great pastrami. [Cheers.] But seriously, folks, we are here because we know the Che School deserves our support, our faith—and our money. [Cheers.] We know our great friend Donna Hart Lyons has been attacked by a vicious half-wit thug who has the brains of a Republican and the social conscience of a rattlesnake, Ezra Tyne. [Loud, sustained boos, hisses.] Tyne has slithered out from under his rock and did what he does best—smear, ridicule, and savage a humanitarian ideal he doesn't understand."

The lights in the ballroom lowered and a spotlight illuminated Sam.

"And so, Donna has asked that we all think of Ezra Tyne as she and some friends introduce us to a new educational institution, a place they call . . ."

Sam paused and then shouted:

"The Dear Old Unca Ezra School for Fascist Girls!"

The spot went off, and the cover over the sign fell, showing the words Sam had just spoken, spelled out in blinking lights.

The band played a catchy, marchlike tune, and the curtain rose, disclosing a row of ten cots, on each of which lay a woman dressed in a modified SS uniform—black jacket, black shorts, and a cute little SS officer's cap. As the music swelled, the women, one by one—among them three Emmy winners (including Donna) and current movie sensation Mims Taylor, more widely known for her large breasts than for any discernible talent—leaped from the cots, formed a military line, and gave the audience a stiff-armed Nazi salute. They made a right face and, their arms extended, began marching about the stage, singing:

"At the Dear Old Unca Ezra
School for Fascist Girls
We all love Unca Ezra,
'Cuz we're little right-wing pearls!
A great big fat swastika
Each morning here unfurls,
At the Dear Old Unca Ezra School for Fascist Girls!

"At the Dear Old Unca Ezra
School for femme fay-tals
We're taught to be real racist thugs
We're Unca Ezra's pals!
We love ol' Ezra very much
About him we are nuts,
At the dear ol Unca Ezra
School . . . for . . . fascist . . . sluts!"

The women then linked arms and, in classic Rockette fashion, did a coordinated high-kicking step, to great applause. Then Diane Hecker, winner of two Academy Awards, addressed Donna:

DIANE. *When is Unca Ezra going to arrive?*

DONNA: *I think I see him now!*

A fat man in an SS uniform, leading a small pink piglet on a leash, came onstage.

"Ladies," he announced as he pointed to the piglet, "here is our great leader, Unca Ezra!"

The Unca Ezra gals made squealing sounds and then quickly gathered in a semicircle around the bewildered little animal, giving it the Nazi salute, as they sang, to the approximate tune of "It Happened in Sun Valley," a song from a 1940s movie:

"We love our Unca Ezra,
He's the pig we idolize!
He tells the biggest lies,
He teaches us to hate and to despise!
Like right-wing fanatics, we give you his sign. *[They gave the Nazi salute.]*
If you liked Adolf Hitler,
You're gonna love Tyne.
We love our
Unca Ezra!
He's the pig we idolize!"

At that moment, as the Ezra gals went into their high-kick routine, the crowd roared its approval as dozens of young men and women wearing T-shirts bearing the words THE DEAR OLD UNCA EZRA SCHOOL FOR FASCIST GIRLS and a cartoon drawing picture of a very small pig wearing blue-tinted aviator glasses ran through the audience, distributing similar T-shirts at every table. But suddenly everyone was staring at the stage where members of the cast were receiving T-shirts. As each actress received her new T-shirt, she removed the SS jacket and placed the Unca Ezra shirt over the white T-shirt beneath. But when Mims Taylor took off her SS jacket, there was no T-shirt beneath—just Mims, in all her zesty breasty glory.

Mims gave a bump and grind and then slithered downstage to the band's "take it off" music as the crowd stood, cheered, whistled, and stomped. She then slowly wriggled into the Unca Ezra T-shirt, which was—how unfortunate—just a size too small, so she had to do a lot of wriggling as mock groans and boos of dismay and shouts of "Take it off!" were heard from all sections of the ballroom. Now covered, Mims held up her hands and after thirty seconds or so, the happy crowd became quiet enough for her to shout, "Let me introduce the woman of the evening, of the decade, of the century, the Godmother—the next president of the United States—Donna Hart Lyons!"

Donna, wearing her Unca Ezra T-shirt, extended her arms and acknowledged the great, raw, animal-like roar that greeted her name. She walked downstage and hugged Mims. Mims embraced her as the crowd cheered wildly. Donna, holding up the palms of her hands for silence, got most of the crowd to sit. She said, "Are we having fun?"

Another delighted roar.

"Good. I think Mims gave Unca Ezra the only argument he understands. [Cheers.] Or maybe I should say Mims gave him the only *two* arguments he understands! [Bigger cheers.] Now just let me say two things. First, we are going to sell these piggy T-shirts all over the country and we are going to use the money to help fund the Che School. If Mr. Tyne wants to sue because we are using his name, I say: see you in court! [Cheers.] Second, all I can say is, I love you all and I thank you; thank you all from the bottom of my heart."

She began to walk offstage. But she knew she had them, and she wanted to take advantage of the moment. So she came downstage and held up her hand for silence. Then she said: "As you know, I am scheduled to make a speech to the American Advance Party in a few weeks. [Sustained cheers.] In that speech I will speak of the need for someone to stand up to the administration and offer the American people—working people, blacks, women, the poor, and the underprivileged—a truly progressive program that meets the needs of all those who have been left out. [Cheers.] My speech will be built on one idea: Government for the people and people for each other. [Cheers, applause.] And I want you all to know I will bring that message to the entire nation next year." [Louder cheers, whistles, applause.]

She waited for the exact moment. Then: "Some hate me for being a woman. Others hate me because I'm progressive. And still others hate me because I am a Jew. But I have news for them—I'm ready to fight. [Loud, sustained cheers.] I'm ready to fight like I've never fought before, fight for the ideals we share, fight for the millions and tens of millions who can't fight for themselves, fight for justice and peace and sane, decent government that treats the poor and the needy like people and not like things!" [Loud cheers.] Above the stage, a red, white, and blue banner dropped, bearing the words

GOVERNMENT FOR THE PEOPLE AND PEOPLE FOR EACH OTHER

Donna had planned to say a few words about the Che School, part of the speech Pete Dickinson had written for her, but with the instinct of a born actress, she knew when to get off. Pete's slogan about government and people had done the trick. Nothing she could say now could top this. She waved to the crowd and ran back to join her colleagues as they bowed and threw kisses to the adoring crowd that cheered and cheered and cheered. Che Che, tears in her eyes, knew her mother had done it again. Pete, across the table, applauded unenthusiastically, thinking, *Why in the hell didn't she use the whole speech? I worked my ass off on that.*

The *New York Post* (over a photo of high-kicking Donna):

DONNA KICKS! EZRA'S BUTT!

The *New York Daily News:*

SCORE: MIMS 2 — EZRA 0

The New York Times:

CHARITY FUND-RAISER SATIRIZES RADIO CELEBRITY

Jeb Hammerford, sitting in his usual booth in the rear of Gugliardi's Restaurant in the Galleria Mall in Tysons Corner, plowed into the spaghetti and meatballs.

"That tomato sauce is just loaded with garlic. And these meatballs? Damn good. Dean, be my guest, dig in, son, and see what good food is," Jeb said to Dean Mumphreys, seated across from him.

"I respect my body too much to eat crap like this," Dean said, with the superior, less-fat-than-thou sneer of the recently converted vegan.

Since almost everything Dean said—which wasn't much—was said with a sneer, Jeb did not take the rejection as a personal insult. To each his own, that was Jeb's motto. Jeb was in that precarious state where one or two more food orgies might push him from being merely heavy to borderline obese, but he was ready to accept the risks because the food at Goog's was succulent, positively evil, saturated with calories, and sinfully rich with intense, immediate pleasure. Goog's wasn't fancy. There were no snooty northern Italian dishes served. Goog's wasn't ashamed of tomato sauces. You came to Goog's to eat—and listen to the Sinatra recordings (Goog, when he had a place in New York, had been one of Frank's favorite chefs), not to show your great taste in fine cuisine. The place was close to Jeb's construction business headquarters on International Drive, and Jeb was a Goog's regular. He was wearing a dark blue Armani suit (his jacket covered by a large white napkin, which he had tucked into his shirt collar), tailored to make the most of his ample figure, a light blue shirt, an expensive dark blue tie with little white dots, and a pair of four-hundred-dollar Italian loafers.

Jeb did not feel comfortable sitting across from Dean, whose acne was bad today, on fire, and it almost turned Jeb off his food. But Dean had appeared out of nowhere—*has this lil' pissant sumbitch drug pusher been following me?* Jeb wondered—and plunked himself down, dressed in his usual T-shirt and jeans. Trying his best not to look at Dean's ravaged face, Jeb expertly twirled some pasta onto his fork and began to devour it. That poor damned pasta never had a chance. After doing some big damage to a meatball the size of a baseball, Jeb wiped his mouth and dabbed at his lips with the big white napkin.

"So how are you, youngblood?" he said, his words graced by that wonderfully soft, attractive Virginia lilt. "Please pass the garlic bread."

Dean didn't move. Jeb gave a little shrug and reached over to grab a piece of bread.

"So," he said to Dean, "what can I do for you this fine day?"

In his casual, almost sleepy way, Dean said, "That political bitch boy you put me with—"

"Whoa, hold on now, big fella, I'm not getting this. Who you talking about?"

"Bitch with the long blond hair, friend of yours. Knows the president or some damn thing or other."

"Oh yeah, Pete Dickinson. Not exactly a friend of mine. I *know* him. I figured the two of you could help each other. He had a demand, you had the supply. That's what makes this country great, supply and demand. Now you mention it, he owes me money, in fact. He makes some damn stupid bets, but when it comes time to pay, seems he's always short."

"Well, that bitch owes *me* money. So I'm telling you, now. He better pay me. Or you better pay me. Somebody better pay me."

"Get in line, Dean. Like I tol' ya, son, he owes me money, and I knew him first."

Dean looked over Jeb's right shoulder and sneered, just a little sneer, not much on it, no heat, just an ordinary "I ain't got time for this shit" sneer, dismissive and half amused.

"Look, I'd just as soon do you as him."

"Oh, I be *so* scared," Jeb said in a shaky tiny falsetto voice, as he began to lift a hunk of meatball northward. "I be pee in my pants."

"Nothing funny here, man. You put him onto me, and now it's on you, he don't pay up."

Jeb, in a unexpectedly swift, smooth motion for such a big man, placed a surprisingly strong hand on Dean's left hand and began to squeeze.

"You *touchin'* me?" Dean asked incredulously, wincing, trying to get free. "You touchin' me on my *hand?*"

"Sonny, will you do me a favor?" Jeb said, smiling, not raising his voice. "Pass the bread, like I asked you a while ago. Right now."

Dean passed the basket of bread to Jeb.

Jeb let go of Dean's hand. "Spotty," he said in a pleasant tone of voice, no fire at all, "don't *ever* threaten ol' Jeb, even in fun. I got some niggers who work for me, their combined IQ is about seventy-six, just a little above your level. I'll send them to your shack out there in Cootersville, whatever the hell it's called, and I'll have have them cut off your dick and make you eat it if you ever talk disrespectful to me again. You're an ex-con and stupid as a warthog, and I score some coke off you now and then, so I make allowances for you, but just mind your manners. And for God's sakes, boy, go see a dermatologist, you look like hell."

"If that bitch don't give me my money, I'm going to hurt him. Bad."

"That's your call, sonny boy. But don't kill him until he's paid me first."

TEN

Donna stood on the porch of LionWest, wearing a blue denim jacket over an Ezra piggy T-shirt and a new pair of snug-fitting jeans (she could still get away with it—well, just about) ingeniously and expensively designed to look old and faded. Sipping coffee from a white mug bearing the LionCo logo (an abstract roaring lion's head, in red), she looked west toward the Bitterroot Mountains and smiled. Her spoof of Ezra Tyne had created a media sensation, and she was back on top, the old Donna, confident and triumphant. When she had appeared on Jay Leno's show, the audience stood and cheered. Now, her smile increased as she watched Che Che, in the pleasant chill and blessed stillness of the spring morning, riding her horse outside the front gate. Che Che waved and the horse wheeled at her effortless command—she was an expert horsewoman—and galloped toward the grove of trees to the north. Donna sneaked a quick look at her wristwatch. Alarmed by Marvin's report, she had decided to pay a surprise visit to the Che School today and say a few words to students and faculty. But first it would soon be time to meet with Tim Flaherty, who had sounded mysterious over the phone but conveyed his urgent need to "talk to you, personal." Sighing—it was so peaceful just standing there—she reluctantly left the porch and walked quickly through the greeting hall, past the living room, past the dining room, to her office at the rear of the house.

Donna sat in an elaborately carved high-back mahogany chair at a nineteenth-century mahogany desk that had once belonged to Pat Coogan, a Montana copper baron, one of the tough Irishmen who had come to work the copper mines, lived long enough to beat the odds, and become rich. Behind her, the big picture window disclosed a glorious view of the Bitterroots. She punched in the sound system and Frank's voice sang: *"I'm a fool to love you. . . ."*

Donna listened to the rare glory of perfection, perhaps the greatest torch song ever, sung by the master at the height of his powers and the depth of his carrying-the-torch despair (did anyone carry a torch these days?). On the desk were two framed photographs: one of Che Che when she was six, dressed up like a cowgirl, and the other of two young women in waitress uniforms, smiling broadly as they stood in front of a large sign:

The Las Vegas Towers Presents:

Jerry Vale

Jack Carter

The Tower Girls "On Parade"

The photograph was signed "To Donna, Love and oooooxxxxs! Fawn, 4/18/77."

Donna typed in two passwords. An encrypted message appeared on the screen. She typed in another password and another encrypted message appeared. She typed in a letter-and-number series and on the screen appeared the words *Flaherty, Timothy*. Donna met with no one without first skimming such a file, compiled by a special investigative unit of LionClaw. Each visitor, in her main LionHeart Foundation New York office or, less frequently, here at the ranch, had to be scrutinized by LionClaw.

As she quickly glanced through Tim Flaherty's dossier, there was little to surprise her. She had known him for more than two decades. They had walked picket lines together. They had demonstrated together, arm in arm, for racial justice and against that simpleton Reagan's prowar policies in Central America and his desire to blow up the world. She knew about Tim's tawdry infidelities with young women. She knew he had stolen from the union over the years. She knew that his wife, Margaret Mary, was proud, docile, and clueless. What more was there to know about Tim Flaherty? He had a new mistress, but so what? Donna was fond of him. He was greedy, weak, hypocritical, and horny, like most men, but he had sound political instincts, a genuine concern for the needy, and a good heart, all of which made the coming meeting nothing she looked forward to. She knew why he had flown all the way out to the ranch, and it wasn't to discuss ideology. Tim wanted her to—

"Mom! What a great day. You should have been out riding with me. It's glorious."

Donna looked up to see Che Che stride into the office, wearing a checkered shirt and jeans, radiating outdoor vitality. Donna sat on the couch, with its view of the lovely, lonely mountains. As Che Che approached the couch she stopped at the desk and shouted in delight, "Mom, I haven't seen my cowgirl picture in *years*."

"Whoever would have thought when I took it that someday you'd be riding your own horses," Donna said.

"And here's your favorite picture, you and . . . what's her name?"

"Fawn. We were good friends in Las Vegas, when we were waitresses at the casino."

"She was pretty. Whatever happened to her?"

"I have no idea. Once I left Las Vegas, I had enough to do, taking care of you and trying to break into the business. I've kept the photo all these years because it reminds me of the tough times, when I—when we—didn't have anything. When you're young, as I was then, you're too dumb to know things are hopeless. So you just keep on living and fighting and one day things aren't hopeless anymore. But there were good times back then, too. Having you was one of those times. Come sit with me and talk."

Che Che put down the picture and sat on the couch.

"How is your book going?"

"Grampa's been helpful, after his fashion. I'll be talking to Marvin about his father."

"Dear Marvin, he's obsessed with his father's history, the poor dear."

"How are things here, Mom?"

"I'm going to have to straighten out some problems at the school later. But now I have a meeting with Tim Flaherty."

"Good or bad?"

"Bad, I'm sure, but I don't yet know why. Anything else happening with you?"

"Oh . . . not much. Sammy Yuan is mad at me because I'm not focusing."

"Darling, tell me again—why do you want to learn how to kick and punch people?"

"That's not it. It's finding yourself. Being yourself. Not just how to deliver a kick or a punch, but to try to make each kick and punch perfect. Sammy says it's the perfection—the quest for perfection—that counts."

"I have a feeling, based only on what you've told me about him, that Mr. Yuan has a crush on you."

"Oh, Mom, Sammy is just my teacher."

There was silence and then Che Che said, "I think I'm going to stay out here tomorrow, just do nothing. Then I'll go to New York for a few days and just spend some time up there, doing some research, do the interviews with Marvin, maybe go to some plays and visit some museums. And, oh yes, I almost forgot—when you're in Washington, will you just ask someone to check on my plants? I don't want the little babies dying on me while I'm away. I just need some time alone. I need time . . . to think."

Maternal instinct (a concept frowned upon by Donna's feminist friends) clicked on in Donna's heart when she heard the hesitation. There were three beats of silence—sometimes it's better to wait, Donna knew. Che Che didn't say anything, so Donna said casually, "Is it Peter Dickinson?"

"I didn't think it showed," Che Che said with a wistful little smile. "I think I'm in love with him. Again."

"Che Che, you've been burned once. Why go through it again? You can have any man you want."

"I don't want any man. And that's what drives me crazy. I'm guilty of the stupidest, most stereotypical woman's temptation—falling for the Bad Boy. That seems to run in the family."

"What's that supposed to mean?"

"Why did you get mixed up with my father? He hurt you."

"That was different."

"No, it wasn't. We're both attracted to the wrong kind of man."

"What's the right kind? Do you have any idea why, after all you know about him, you still feel this way?"

"I've been asking myself the same question. And I think—I know this is going to sound funny—there's something so *sad* about Peter."

"Sad? That's the last word I'd associate with Mr. Dickinson. Of course, I don't know him as well as you do, but he seems to me to be all surface—what you see is what you get. He's handsome, bright, egocentric, arrogant, and very talented. By the way, his slogan—"Government for the People and People for Each Other"—got great coverage. *CBS Evening News* did a segment on it. Your Mr. Dickinson does good work. I'll use him again. But I just don't associate all that ego with the word *sad*."

"I've tried to come up with a better word. But there's no other word for it. It's as if he's never really liked himself."

"Darling, let me tell you something I learned from bitter experience: never—*never*—try to play psychologist in a love affair. Most men simply aren't that deep."

"Maybe. Anyhow, I'm in love with Peter, so there it is. It's different this time, I can feel it. He's more attentive. He shares his feelings with me. I think he's finally grown up. But I don't know where the whole thing is going, or if it's going anywhere. You're right—I got burned once. I never want to go through that again."

"Then stop seeing him."

"I can't."

"Darling, I'm glad you want to discuss these things with me, but now I have to prepare for my meeting with Tim. You must be tired after all that riding. Take a nap. And don't make any rash decisions about Peter."

Ten minutes later, as Donna sat alone, there was a knock on the door.

"Come in."

"Mrs. Lyons, Mr. Flaherty," said Vince Ferrano, the head of LionClaw's personal-security team for Donna. Vince was a former prizefighter (a heavyweight with a good but not great right hand, no left hand to speak of), now a personal-protection specialist who had left his own agency to work for Donna. With his broken nose, square jaw, and military buzz cut, he looked like someone who had stepped out of the pages of an old *Soldier of Fortune* magazine. He held open the door and stepped aside as Tim bounded toward the desk with the chest-out, chin-up, take-charge stride of men of short stature but great power.

"Tim, darling!" Donna said, rising and walking to meet and embrace him. "It's so good to see you. Come sit with me on the couch by the window. The view of the mountains is lovely."

"Donna, I ain't out here to see the scenery. I won't bend your ear. I got to get back and prepare for the union meeting in Florida. President's coming."

"Please give him my regards, if he'll accept them."

"I doubt he will. You and I have known each other too long to beat around the bush, so I'll get right to the point. I got to ask you something right out, straight. Is this true what I read? Are you taking over the AAP to run against the Guy? Yes or no?"

"What I want is what you want—a presidential candidate who will speak for our values. I don't care who it is or where he—or she—comes from. But I'm not going to wait around until some other Democrat decides to put the president on notice."

"If you challenge the president in the general election next year, you'll take votes from him. The Republicans will win. My God, Donna, think what you're doing. Is that what you want?"

"Tim, dear, the Guy thinks he doesn't have to listen to progressives like us. He thinks we have nowhere else to go. Well, maybe I've found someplace to go."

"Donna, *listen to me*. You *can't* do it."

Donna stared at Tim, her eyes wide in mock surprise.

"Tim, *no* one tells me what I can and cannot do, not even a great old friend like you. That's one of the fringe benefits of having all this money. I do what I damn well please."

"The Republicans will turn the Justice Department loose on me. They'll make all kinds of accusations. Lies, all of it, but what can you do? You know the Republicans would love to put my head on a wall of the Oval Office, like a hunting trophy, any way they can. So I just can't stand still and see you split the Democratic vote. I'll come out against you, strong, if you run, Donna."

"Thanks for being candid with me, Tim. That's the trait I admire more than any other. Blunt honesty and integrity, just like my father."

Donna arose from her couch and graciously held out her hand in a gesture combining condescension and magnanimity. It was the same gesture she had used so many times when playing the reigning bitch on *Today We Love*. Then she said, in that Middle-Atlantic voice from which, after years of training, almost—*almost*—every last speck of the Bronx had been scrubbed clean: "Tim, I can't promise anything. True progressives may just have to think of other alternatives than supporting the Guy. At the moment he is quite unacceptable."

"I'm telling you, Donna, you can't do this. It's crazy. Think of the good of the party. Tell me you won't do it."

"I *am* thinking of the good of the party. It is not good for the party to have Ty Ferguson at its head. He believes in nothing. He's rolling over for big business in his rush toward the middle. But we can talk about these things some other time. Now that you've come all the way out here and told me what you think, why not enjoy the beautiful day? My daughter's been out riding. Would you like to go riding?"

"We didn't ride horses where I come from. We bet on them. Maybe sometimes we ate them in the old days without knowing it. But think what you're doing, Donna. Try to think of the consequences. For all of us."

"As always, Tim, I'll give what you say careful consideration. Give my love to Margaret Mary, she's so sweet," Donna said, taking Tim's arm gently and guiding him to the office door. "And try to understand—"

"Oh, I understand. I hope you understand when I do what I have to do."

Donna pressed a button on the desk, and Vince came in.

"Vince, please call the plane and tell them Mr. Flaherty will be flying to Washington."

When Tim left the room, Donna slumped into her desk chair. She was suddenly exhausted.

Maybe it's time to just relax, take some time off, just do nothing, I'm getting tired fast these days.

She walked across the room to the great window and looked at the mountains. Vince Ferrano came back to the office.

"Mr. Flaherty's on his way, Mrs. Lyons."

"Before you go I have a few things. First, have we found anything about Ezra Tyne's background?"

"No, ma'am. Nothing hard. There's a chance we might be able to—"

"I'm not interested in the specific aspects of how you get what you get. Just get it. Now here's one other thing. There's a young man named Peter Dickinson, a friend of my daughter's. He has a speechwriting business in Washington. I want a quick, discreet, but in-depth background check done on him. Get on it today. Have the information ready for me when we get to Washington."

"Will do. The driver is ready anytime you are, Mrs. Lyons, to drive you to the school."

Pete sat staring at the iMac screen. He had just finished reading all the background material on the National Association of Developmental Ecologists, excruciatingly boring stuff. A half hour earlier he had talked with Ned Davenport, the Washington rep of the association, who would be giving the speech. Ned wanted, in his words, "something warm, see, you have to put in the human touch for developmental ecologists, something light, with a few of those little anecdotes, like the president does."

Pete sighed. The allegedly humanizing anecdote drove out general principles, long-range views, objective analysis, and reasoned argument, all to be replaced by warm personal stories, little parables of gooey sentiment. When had it begun? As with most political evil, Pete thought, it had probably started with Nixon and his Checkers speech in 1952, and then his 1968 acceptance speech, in which he prattled about his boyhood, hearing a train whistle in the night. These days, no speaker could afford not to have a little homey anecdote in a speech, no matter what the topic. When he was working for the Guy, Pete, disgusted about having to shoehorn in little stories about one-armed bakers who lived on dog food, black teenagers who were forced by poverty to drink cheap soft drinks, and farmers who had accidentally planted corn instead of wheat, had written, for his own amusement, a parody of the Gettysburg Address, as it might have sounded if Ty the Guy had delivered it:

> . . . the brave men, living and dead, who struggled here have consecrated it far above our poor power to add or detract. I speak of men like Josh Chamberlain, a fighting hero from the great state of Maine. [Cheers.] Only a year ago he was teaching rhetoric at Bowdoin College, a great school [cheers], but what he did on Little Round Top was no rhetorical gesture, a-ha, a-ha. Just ask the rebels! [Cheers, standing o.] Today we have Josh and his great family in the audience, right by that big tombstone over there. I ask them to stand . . . stand up there, Josh, hero of Little Round Top!

Pete stared at the screen. Nothing. He knew what he needed.

He went to the closet, got the plastic bag and the mirror and the blade. Then, rolled ten-dollar bill at the ready, he performed the ritual. Waiting for it to kick in, he thought about Che Che. Her mother's fund-raiser had been one of the most successful political events in recent years. His slogan was a great success, although he had no idea what it was supposed to mean. He had been hoping a few in that affluent crowd would notice how good the remarks had been and ask Donna who wrote them. If that had happened, Pete would have new clients. But nothing had happened, except that Donna used his slogan. Yes, he had gotten a good fee for the remarks, but he had been counting on a lot of PR. And after the Che School dinner, maybe because of all the excitement, Che Che had been distant, and instead of going to his room in the hotel, she went to her own. Now she was at Donna's ranch. What the hell was wrong with her? One minute it seemed as if she were falling for him, and the next she reverted to her old wise-cracking ways.

Maybe he should tell her he loved her. A big step. Or maybe it was better to let her sulk. He could afford to refrain from sex with Che Che—he was getting more than he could handle with Marlie Rae. But he had to start getting serious. He had to decide whether to just do it, ask Che Che to marry him. His debts weren't getting any smaller. Writing a few speeches here and there didn't pay the bills. Of course, there was always dear old dad as the next-to-last resort. But he didn't really want to ask his father. Trevor would smile that condescending smile and . . .

Pete, beginning to feel the white bliss, stared at the blinking cursor. He looked up and saw Ollie, as exasperated as he himself was. He smiled. Stan and Ollie always made him feel better. The bliss remained.

Donna always remembered a story she had once heard about the British conductor Sir Thomas Beecham. When he planned to conduct a serious, modern piece that audiences would not like but that deserved a performance, he would also schedule on the same program an audience favorite—Tchaikovsky, Brahms, or Mozart. He called these old crowd-pleasers "lollipops." If the audience ate its spinach (Bartók, say) it would get a lollipop. As Babs and Donna entered the Che School building, Donna thought, *First the spinach, then the lollipop. Always leave them happy.*

The Babster shouted: "All right, people, listen up. We have with us today the founder of this great institution, Mrs. Lyons. She wants to say a few words to you."

Donna waited for a moment and then said, in a loud voice: "Although Babs has reported to me on the great progress most of you are making, she has also told me that some of you do not yet understand the mission of this institution. So let me make it clear. This is not a rest home. This is not a vacation resort. This is a battlefield. This is a place where the struggle between decency and progress on the one hand, and greed and exploitation on the other, will fight it out. And I don't expect to lose that fight. The Che School is the place where you—victims of a sexist, racist, exploitative society—can rebuild your lives according to the visions of a just, equitable society. But some of you have complained about various aspects of our work here, including the new fence. Let me say I commend Babs for building the chain-link fence. It reminds all of us that the Che School is a place set apart and—"

"The fence sucks."

Amid the gasps and oohs and aahs, a tall beautiful Che girl took two steps forward and stood there, hands brazenly on hips, her T-shirt perhaps just half a size too small.

So this is Monique. She's a knockout, just as Marvin reported. Well, bring it on, Monique. I've handled tougher ones than you.

"What did you say?" Donna said.

"The fence sucks. We don't need it. What are we, in prison?"

"What is your name?"

"Monique. And I thought—"

"You *thought?* You thought what, Monique?" Donna said, glaring at her. "You thought you could be rude to me, and that would intimidate me? My dear, I was in show business for many years, where rudeness is a way of life, and no one ever intimidated me."

"I thought you believed what they teach us here."

"What's that supposed to mean?"

"They teach us to speak out against injustice. Well, the fence is an injustice."

Donna sneaked a quick glance at Babs, who was red in the face.

"Let me be clear to you, Monique, and to all of you," Donna said. "I believe in dissent. Dissent is at the very heart of our vision. But I believe in *progressive* dissent, not dissent that seeks to stand in the way of progressive principles. I will not tolerate anarchy or the deliberate sabotage of progressive reform. If any of you cannot adjust to the Che School's necessary regulations, made for your own good, I will be glad to provide you with a one-way plane ticket out of here. I didn't build this school to see it destroyed by someone's mistaken idea of dissent. Are there any questions?"

Monique smiled, shrugged, and returned to her place with the other girls.

Lollipop time.

"Now that we have that out of the way, let me tell you the good news," Donna said. "I know that the school is very demanding. You need some kind of recreation, some way of meeting other people. From now on, certain Che girls will have an open invitation to meet, mix, and mingle with my guests at selected events here at LionWest. No one will know you are connected with the school. If by this time I can't trust you to meet outsiders, under supervision, I guess I can't trust you anywhere. But I know you will make me proud."

The girls applauded.

I've got them. Now, the lollipop supreme.

"There's some more good news," she said. "In a while, I will be speaking to the American Advance Party's annual meeting. I want you to come with me to Washington, where I will introduce you to the national media. You are going to become famous."

As the cheers and applause grew, Donna looked at Monique, who had joined in.

"One point, and it is a major one," Donna said, still looking at Monique. "Only those girls who from now on meet the high standards of the school will be granted the privilege of meeting my guests and coming to Washington. Girls, it is up to you."

She turned and walked away as Babs shouted, "Dis-*missed.*"

ELEVEN

Although Che Che Hart had been in the LionHeart Foundation's New York City brownstone headquarters (as opposed to the glass-and-steel administration building next door) innumerable times, she never got over the feeling that once she passed through the revolving doors of the main entrance, she entered a parallel universe, similar to but essentially different from the one she usually inhabited. On the first floor, ninety-five-year-old breakaway neo-semi-Trotskyites of the Pinsk persuasion, wearing raggedy, moth-eaten gray sweaters—winter or summer—stood at the openings of their cubicles and screeched maledictions at ninety-eight-year-old quasi-semi-Mensheviks of the Minsk persuasion, while former copy boys of the *Daily Worker* brandished canes at former labor union organizers who had been hit one too many times by police billy clubs at the Ford River Rouge plant strike in 1936. Mysterious, bedraggled, gray-haired women who chain-smoked foul-smelling cigarettes and never talked to anyone muttered to themselves in undecipherable Eastern European dialects as they pored over documents written in Cyrillic script.

On the second floor, bald, big-bellied former members of the 1960s radical groups, in their day the advance guard of anti-establishmentarianism, the hope of the disenfranchised and exploited, the young shining knights of progressivism, the scourge of the pigs and the fuzz, but now crippled by arthritis, gout, diminished libidos, and enlarged prostates, sipped herbal tea and debated the dynamics of participatory democracy with a now drug-free former Black Panther subminister of defense and a onetime assistant to an assistant to the midwest Grafton County advance man for Gene McCarthy's New Hampshire campaign in 1968.

On the third floor, on tables and desks and piled up in hallways, there were stacks and stacks of unread, unpublished foundation studies, scores of them, gathering dust. These were the result of projects that Donna had funded and then forgotten, including the Irish Guilt and Reparations Project, in which teams of social scientists, scholars in the new fields of reparations economics and guiltology, and spokespersons for various ethnic, religious, political, ideological, and national groups argued about degrees of guilt and types of reparations for atrocities, invasions, occupations, slights, insults, insensitivities, and other denials of human rights in Ireland, going back to antiquity. The Irish Guilt and Reparations Project was now in its twelfth year, with no prospect for a speedy conclusion, because on that small island there has always been a lot for which to feel guilty. The Celtic people came to Ireland in the second century B.C. and raped, enslaved, subjugated, and slaughtered the original inhabitants. Then Christianity, led by the notorious anti-religious-diversity bigot, so-called Saint Patrick, overthrew the Druidism of the Celts, a clear case of religious hegemonic imperialism. Then the Vikings raped, pillaged, and plundered until they were exhausted. Then the Anglo-Normans invaded and took Celtic lands by brutal force, building castles as they went. Then the British created plantations in what is now Northern Ireland and drove the Celtic Irish out of their own lands to starve and die. Then Cromwell massacred the Irish and drove them "to Hell or Connaught" to starve and die. Then the potato famine came, in which the entire majesty and glory of the British Empire, at the peak of its power, stood by and watched as the dispossessed went off to exile and more than a million starved and died. Then came the rebellion of 1916, the first revolution of the twentieth century.

Then there was a division of Ireland and the subsequent civil war in the Free State, bloodier and more savage than the war against the British. Then there was Bloody Sunday, 1969. Then the IRA, the Protestant hit teams, and the British imprisonment and interrogation horrors. All of this—and much more—on one small island on the periphery of Europe. According to the Irish Guilt and Reparations Project, descendants of each guilty group had to make monetary reparations to the offended group, according to a complicated schedule of payments. Donna hoped to expand the project to the entire world, as far back as the Israelite invasion of Canaan, in which every man, woman, and child was either enslaved or killed, as recorded in the Book of Joshua.

But no place in the old building better typified the loose-leaf, anarchic nature of LionHeart than Marvin Gunn's basement office. Only two people, including Marvin, could sit in the room at a time because every other part of it, floor to ceiling, was used to store government documents; history books; video- and audiocassettes; ancient, decaying newspapers, magazines such as *Look, Life,* the *Saturday Evening Post, Colliers', Cue,* and *Argosy;* bulging notebooks; photo albums; old scrapbooks; and labeled binders, all dealing in one way or another with the case of Al Gunn. Today, Che Che was squeezed into the room (Marvin had just received a new batch of documents from the archives of the Institute for the History of Injustice, another Donna project, and there was just enough room for Marvin, Che Che, and her tape recorder). After some boring but necessary research questions about dates and names and addresses in the Al Gunn saga, Che Che began the interview:

—Since we have a few minutes, I just want to go back over some material about you, your own life. Just for the record, so I'll have it on tape, let me ask you again about your own background. You were a founder of Students for American Ideals, back in the 1960s, right?

—Yeah, I confess to my unpatriotic, radical antiwar background. [Laughter.] Here, I have a photograph—I keep it at home, so it was easy to find—from about, oh, 1969; we were at some meeting, I forget where. There I am—look at all that Art Garfunkel hair. As you know, I wound up in Cuba for almost two years.

—I've often wondered: what did you do in Cuba?

—I cut more damn sugarcane than I ever dreamed existed. [Laughter.] A group of us, from various countries, met Fidel once. He talked for three hours.

—What did he talk about?

—Himself, what else? [Laughter.] But being in Cuba wasn't all that bad. I learned enough Spanish to get girls. I hung around musicians. I read, I slept a lot, I went to the beach.

—Doesn't sound too exciting.

—I loved the Cubans' humane, open way of life. Not even Fidel could get Cuba out of Cubans! [Laughter.] But I missed the United States. So I flew to Canada and then to New York. The feds were waiting for me at JFK. That led to my Baltimore trial, and as you know, I was found not guilty on all charges.

—And after that you disappeared from public view.

—I like to plop my skinny ass on a seat and read for hours, as you can see. So I went back to school, finished my degree, and taught high school in Miami.

—Why Miami?

—I liked the Cuban atmosphere, even once removed, although I wasn't exactly loved by the rabid anti-Castro faction that ran Miami. I taught chemistry and physics in high schools and then moved back to New York.

—Did you consciously think of your father's example when you went into radical politics?

—I was *always* radical. I can never remember when I wasn't trying to challenge the system. Whatever the system was, I was against it. [Laughter.] In elementary school, I was organizing strikes against the food in the cafeteria. In high school, my idea of a hot date was to take a girl to some secluded spot, park the car, take her in my arms, unhook her bra, and whisper in her ear about Marx and Lenin. Socialist foreplay. [Laughter.]

—Before I forget, I've been looking over my notes from my talk with my grandfather. He told me that at certain times, working for the party, he used assumed names, what he called American names like Jack Gordon, Joseph Rogers, Bill Davis—names like that. Did your father ever use aliases?

—Yes, yes, of course. I mean, even our family name isn't really Gunn. It's Guinsberg, with a *u*. In my father's work as a labor organizer, particularly down South, he used a lot of names. Andrew Gardner. Alfred Thomson. Just as your grandfather did with, what was it, Gordon and Rogers?

—Yes.

—Right. Real American names, as Abe and my father would have said back in those days.

—Why don't we just end it here? I have more than enough. This has been very good, Marvin. If you think of anything or if you come across anything in your own files, just send it along.

Margaret Mary had gone to bed, and Tim Flaherty sat alone in his living room. He had the television on, volume low, when the doorbell rang. He ushered his guest into the room. There was an exchange of small talk, and then Tim said, "Neil, I want you to do a job for me. This is off the books, there's no official union connection involved, we'll figure out how you'll get paid."

"No problem, Tim."

Neil Goldman was a short, compact, nearly bald man in his late forties. He was the president of Goldman Associates, one of the country's premier personal and corporate security firms. In the 1980s, Neil had made a name for himself as a young hotshot Democratic staff aide during the Iran-Contra hearings. His expert questioning of witnesses had made him something of a minor celebrity in liberal circles. But, to the surprise of everyone, he did not pursue the usual paths—running for public office or writing a book—but instead became a partner in International Security Services, a small, discreet security outfit specializing in background checks. Within ten years he had become president, renamed the organization, and transformed it into a worldwide operation, involved in every aspect of the security business, from computer security to protection specialist teams for businessmen traveling abroad. He had known Tim for many years, and Neil's organization had done business with the UWCE.

"I want to know about Donna Hart Lyons," Tim said. "Find out about her early life."

"Ordinarily I don't ask why. But since this involves Donna Lyons, I have to. Right now, because of that fund-raiser show she did about Tyne, she's all over the news. She's back. Why are you going after her?"

"It's simple. I don't want her running or supporting a third party. It will throw the race to the Republicans. I tried to talk her out of it, but she won't listen. So I'm just trying to see if I can have something in reserve if she decides to go that way. The thing is, I need it fast. Before the AAP meeting in August."

"Tim, for you, I'll drop everything."

"Thanks, Neil. And thanks for coming all the way out here, this late. Now, if you don't mind, I'm going to toddle off to bed."

When he was once again alone, Tim turned off the lights and stood in front of Franklin, Jack, and Bobby. They would have understood, he knew that. They knew what politics is. They knew what you sometimes have to do for the good of the party.

Harry Gottlieb was ushered into Donna's hideaway suite by a security woman wearing a LionClaw dark blue blazer, a tan skirt, and concealed lethal accessories. Donna, standing by the fireplace, facing the door, striking a pose she had once used for a scene in *Hedda Gabler* in summer stock, strode to the short, dumpy-looking man.

"Mr. Gottlieb, how nice of you to come all this way. I had hoped we could meet in Washington and spare you the flight, but my schedule has suddenly become very busy."

"I understand, Mrs. Lyons. It's hard to turn on the television without seeing you, since your demolition job on Ezra Tyne at the fund-raiser. I hope that's the only kind of fund-raiser you'll be doing this year—and next year."

"My problem isn't raising funds—it's spending them. There's just so much to do. Please sit and be comfortable," Donna said with a fluttery Blanche DuBois gesture she had picked up from an actress in the production of *Streetcar,* in which Donna had played Stella.

"Mrs. Lyons, before we begin, I have to ask a question. It may seem insulting and—"

"Are we being taped or filmed by secret devices? The answer, Mr. Gottlieb, is no. This room is sacrosanct. But if I may say so, it's a naive question. If I were the kind of person to invite the White House chief of staff to my private quarters and record him without his knowledge, I'd lie and say I wasn't recording you, wouldn't I? So you have to trust me."

"Your word is enough."

"You have my word we are not being taped or recorded or under surveillance in any way."

"Let me then get to the point. First, the president has asked me to personally convey how highly he thinks of you. The two of you have worked very well together in the past."

"Yes, I worked to elect the president, I'm sorry to say."

"He specifically asked me to convey to you that he believes your handling of Ezra Tyne was—and this is his word—a classic."

"How kind of him. Now that we have the preliminaries out of the way, exactly what does the president want?"

There was a discreet knock on the door. A LionClaw guard, a young man, wheeled in a tea cart with the silver tea service. When he was gone, Donna arose.

"Let me be mother," she said, walking to the tea cart and picking up the silver pot. "I would have asked you if you wanted a drink. But I know you limit yourself to one scotch a day."

Harry nodded appreciatively.

"You've done your homework," he said.

"Others do it for me. Sugar? Lemon?"

"Just the tea will be fine."

Donna poured and then sat opposite Harry.

"So where were we?" she said.

"The president wants your support in his race for reelection next year. Of course, he hasn't made any specific commitment to run, but—"

"Spare me the usual disclaimers. He's going to run. You know it and I know it. I wouldn't be surprised if he announces in a coal mine, in honor of his poor, black-lung-afflicted father."

"Mrs. Lyons, if there are differences between the two of you, they can be settled. If there is policy advice you wish to give the president, he told me to tell you his door is always open to you."

"I have no doubt. My problem is not the president's closed door—it's his closed mind."

"He is ready to hear you and—"

"He hears but he doesn't listen, Mr. Gottlieb."

"Mrs. Lyons, are you going to run for president? Or was your announcement at the fund-raiser a result of the exuberance of the moment?"

"I am—how best to put this?—a bit too mature to be carried away by the enthusiasm of crowds. I said what I meant. More tea, Mr. Gottlieb?"

"No, thank you."

"You said that I do my homework. You're right. I know that when you worked as a congressional staffer, you helped draft some socially progressive legislation. Not all of it even got out of committee. But you were the architect. As a lawyer, you became affluent, but you never forgot the poor and the needy. You did pro bono work above and beyond the minimum. In fact, you did more pro bono work than all of the other lawyers in your firm. And then you ran Kevin Stanley's race in the primaries. Dear, sweet Kevin was magnificent, although he was no match for the Guy. You ran that campaign flawlessly, I noticed that. But now you are working for a man who compromises, who waffles, who gives progressives lip service. Aren't you frustrated? Aren't you fed up with a president who—"

"Mrs. Lyons, let me speak, please."

Donna was stunned into silence. No one interrupted Donna Hart Lyons.

"I don't need to be lectured about my service to the president," Harry said. "Especially by someone who does not bear the responsibilities he does. I know the president's weaknesses—better than you do. But I also know his very great strengths. And I know he is president of the United States—not president of the activist Left or the progressives. No working politician—Kevin Stanley included—can ever be pure enough for activists. Ideologues are valuable, irreplaceable in my view, but they cannot dictate every political move the president makes. The president needs you, Mrs. Lyons. He is asking for your cooperation. But you can't expect him to act like one your LionHeart grantees. He has the toughest job in the world—"

"What are you going to tell me next? That it's lonely at the top? Mr. Gottlieb, all I want—all that progressives want—is a Democratic president to act like a Democrat. Is that asking too much?"

"Mrs. Lyons, from the president's point of view, you're not asking—you're telling."

"Someone has to tell him. You certainly aren't."

"Perhaps," he said, rising slowly from the chair, "we should leave it at that and continue this conversation at another time."

Donna was momentarily thrown off balance once more. She had expected something different, some pleading, maybe some groveling. But this undistinguished, pudgy little man was walking out on her. Nobody walked out on Donna. Donna was the one to walk out first, always.

"Perhaps you're right," she replied, in a perfect Joan Crawford combination of hauteur and dignity.

He put out his hand.

"Let me say before I go, I've always been a big fan. I saw you in the revival of *Awake and Sing.*"

"That was many years ago."

"You were wonderful."

"Some critics called it typecasting."

"What do critics know? Mrs. Lyons, I hope I'll have the pleasure of talking with you again. If you run, the votes you get will come out of the president's share as a Democrat and a liberal. There simply is no other way of looking at it. You can have President Ferguson or you can have some Republican who believes that the words *social justice* refer to a judge who entertains frequently. The president wants to establish a dialogue with you. Anytime you want to talk—to me or to him—call me at work or at home."

He took a small white card from his inside pocket and scrawled two telephone numbers on the back.

"That's my private line at home. And the other is my cell phone. I look forward to speaking with you in the future." Harry had his hand on the doorknob when he said, "And just for the record—I love the Klee. About 1930?"

"I'm impressed."

"I have others do my homework, too, Mrs. Lyons. Good-bye."

When he had left the room, Donna poured herself more tea. She wasn't exactly sure if she had just won or lost. That dumpy-looking man, not trying to impress her, had impressed her. She didn't know what to think. It was a curious feeling.

She, of course, had the conversation on tape. The recorder was concealed in the tea cart, so she had been honest when she told Gottlieb, before the tea cart came in, that they were not being recorded. Technically then, she had been telling the truth. Somehow the technicality didn't make her feel better.

TWELVE

As president of a union whose very purpose was getting raises, benefits, and job security for malcontents, malingerers, incompetents, complainers, grudge-bearers, whingers, whiners, and anyone who didn't like his boss or his job, Tim Flaherty had a big problem: UWCE headquarters in Washington had to hire people from the union, which meant that the whole place was filled with malcontents, malingerers, incompetents, complainers, grudge-bearers, whingers, whiners, and anyone who didn't like his boss or his job. Consequently, while union business sometimes got done, it usually did not, or was done badly. Letters were mistyped, files were mislaid, computers broke down, everyone was late, there was an absentee epidemic, elevators didn't work, and the cafeteria was a horror of sloth, surliness, and bad food. Floors were unswept, trash baskets unemptied, and there was talk that a new union would be formed from within the UWCE ranks, this one fighting for the rights of work-challenged employees whose health and safety were threatened by their refusal to do the jobs necessary to protect their own health and safety.

The neglect and lack of maintenance mounted cumulatively, month by month. UWCE headquarters, in a union-owned building on Capitol Hill (Tim's office had a perfect view of the Capitol, although the large windows were rarely washed, so all that Tim saw was a gray blur in the distance instead of the great white dome), was a disaster area, but there was little Tim could do about it, except of course lead demonstrations of his own union members against the union headquarters' failure to recognize their needs.

It was now five o'clock in the evening and he was in his office, negotiating with José Illytch Aguilera, his official speechwriter. There were two others in the room: a sullen, middle-aged Hispanic woman whose name Tim did not know, who translated into bad English what José Illytch said in Spanish, and Connie Erickson, José Illytch's union-provided lawyer. The fact that tall, leggy Connie, her hair a mass of tumbling curls, was Tim's mistress (she preferred that word, feeling it had an old-fashioned charm to it) made things just a bit awkward, but Tim knew he could expect no mercy from her. When she was on duty, she was as savage and unrelenting with him as with a globalist greedy sexist scumbag.

Under the union rules, all languages were equal and no UWCE employee had to undergo the indignity of learning another language, particularly English, the imperialistic, globalist, genocidal, racist, sexist tool of the white exploiters like Tim who had brought such destruction to a once-edenic hemisphere. So, although José Illytch could not read, write, or speak English, and had no desire to do so, Tim had been forced to hire him as a speechwriter to meet a union-imposed affirmative action program. Tim had not told anyone in the union that these days he was also using Pete Dickinson as a speechwriter. If they found out, there'd be hell to pay.

The reason for the meeting was that José Illytch, a bearded, chunky twenty-six-year-old wearing a dirty T-shirt bearing the portraits of Che Guevara, John F. Kennedy, and Pope John XXIII, was angry that Tim had rejected yet another speech draft. José Illytch shouted—in Spanish—that Tim's insensitivity was a deliberate vicious attack on José Illytch's Hispanic heritage. What Tim probably wanted, José Illytch snarled to the translator, was an *anglo* speechwriter, someone who could write *English*. This was unacceptable to a man as proud as José Illytch Aguilera, who, although he could not write well in any language, had a fierce love of Spanish, the language his leader, El Commandante Victorioso, head of the Progressive Democratic Republican Human Rights Revolutionary Brigade in Colombia, used when he wrote his death threats against landowners and government officials.

The problem had begun when Tim had told an assistant that even in translation, José Illytch's speeches made little sense. José Illytch had heard about Tim's remark and, stung, his self-esteem ravaged, demanded either a duel (Tim's choice of weapons) or a grievance meeting with Tim. Tim would have preferred a duel, but the union's nonviolence philosophy precluded that.

"I, er . . . uh . . . I, er . . . *queso*," José Illytch's translator said. She seemed to have trouble translating. Tim suspected she was as inept in Spanish as she seemed to be in English.

"Tell José Illytch that this is going to be a very important speech . . . *mucho importante*," Tim said, smiling at José Illytch as he spoke. "Tell him the president—*el presidente*—is to speak, and I have to set the right tone. Union officers from all over the country will be in the audience, and most of them speak English as a first language, they can't help that. But I promise you a Spanish translation of my speech will show on a screen behind me simultaneously."

He paused, seeing the puzzled look on the translator's face as she jotted down his words, in pencil, on the back of a month-old copy of *Work Ethic This!*, the in-house publication.

"Now let me say I think that all we have here is a slight misunderstanding," Tim continued. "All I said was that the speech draft he gave me has, uh, a few things that have to be fixed, just some minor things. Now here, listen to this from the English translation."

Tim read aloud: "'The time has come! I join the forces of revolution throughout the world. Imperialism must be destroyed! Corporate globalistic fascism must be destroyed! American hegemony must be destroyed! White sexist, racist, genocidal exploitation must be destroyed! War must be destroyed! Destruction itself must be destroyed! I denounce the racist genocide that began with the white imperialist, racist, sexist pig "Christ-bearer" Columbus, and the start of the bloody system of earth murder that brought about the economic and social destruction of the hemispheric paradise by the petit bourgeois. Down with the Europeans, especially the Anglo bloodsuckers and their slave trade. The British Empire was built on slavery! The Spanish Empire was built on slavery! The whole system that depended on the superimposed morals of the so-called Christian exploiting class of diseased white killers, plus the so-called Catholic Church with its supposed option for the poor, which is really a preference for the rich, white, and . . .' "

He put down the draft and again addressed the translator.

"See, José Illytch, I think you're making good points. I agree American white people bear a great deal of the guilt for . . . for the many, many bad things we did, all of it. And continue to do. White American people are very, very guilty, very bad. But, see, there's a problem. My speech ain't about the global economy or imperialism or American guilt. Maybe I'll make such a speech in the future. But on this occasion, that's not what I want to say, all that stuff against globalism. What I want to do is rally the union for the next presidential election. This is a *political* speech. Besides, your sentences are too long and—"

Frowning, the translator held up her hand to Tim.

"Shut up. Too much words you say." She looked puzzled, and said something to Connie Erickson in Spanish. Connie replied, and then the translator said to Tim: "You talk too much. You talk too freakin' fast, old man!"

Then, consulting her jottings on the magazine cover, she spoke rapidly in Spanish to José Illytch. He leaped from his chair and let forth an angry stream of Spanish in Tim's direction, gesticulating and, at one point, doing what to Tim seemed like a tap dance. Connie took José Illytch gently by the arm, said some soothing Spanish words, and sat him back down.

"This is what José say: 'Das' *it,* you old white Anglo pimp,' " said the translator in a bland, neutral tone. " 'I don't have to . . .' " She looked puzzled and spoke in Spanish to Connie, who nodded and said to Tim:

"Mr. Flaherty, this is what my client says, in rough translation. 'I don't have to take this degrading and demeaning treatment. I don't like this job, I don't like the pay, and I don't like you. I do the best I can. If you are against revolutions, why are you the head of a union, you fat old white bloodsucking fascist pig.' "

"Ms. Erickson, all I want is a good speech draft and—"

"And what the hell does that mean?" Connie shouted. "Good? Good? What does that word *mean?* Spanish is the language of El Commandante and Che Guevara, and of great entertainers like Jennifer Lopez and . . . and Martin Sheen. But it isn't good enough for *you?*"

"Yes, Ms. Erickson," Tim said, and sighed. "Spanish is a beautiful language. *Mucho,* er, *grande.* But, see, the problem is that I speak English. That's my native tongue, unfortunately. Most of the union members speak English. Most Americans speak English. This is wrong, very wrong, but there's not much I can do about it."

"Be careful what you're saying, I warn you. This is beginning to sound like you believe some cultures are superior to others," Connie said. "That's been the way patriarchal Anglos have treated us for centuries."

"Us? But you're not Hispanic."

"I am a *woman,*" Connie said vehemently. "I know paternalistic condescension when I hear it. I know oppression when I see it. This young man is fighting against the forces of corporate imperialism and globalism in Latin America, and you reject his speech draft because it's not in the language of the *exploiters?* What the hell kind of union leader *are* you? José Illytch's best effort has been rejected because he won't debase his heritage by writing in the language of those who raped our ancestors. We'll go to the union and—"

"But we *are* the union. I am the union president."

"Don't try any phallistic logocentric tricks on us," Connie shouted.

"All right, all right," Tim said, shutting his eyes, eager to get this over with. "I'll accept the draft as is, Ms. Erickson. With the proviso I get to make, er, some changes."

"And José Illytch gets a raise?"

"Yes, yes, all right."

There was a series of exchanges in Spanish among Connie, José Illytch, and the translator. Then Connie said to Tim: "This time we are willing to forget the insult. José Illytch gets a twenty percent pay raise and he will take a month leave back home—at full pay—to recover from all this. The union will pay for his transportation, food, lodging, and ammunition in his native Colombia. And from now on, we want thirty percent of each speech you give to be delivered in Spanish."

Tim may have been in a corner, but his instinctive ability to bargain was still working.

"Tell him he gets a two percent raise, he gets two days off. No ammunition. Eight percent of each speech is in Spanish, but only in the published text. That's non-negotiable."

"Don't push things, Mr. Flaherty," Connie said.

"For Christ's sake, just tell my good friend José what I said."

Connie spoke in Spanish to José Illytch, who began to gesticulate, mutter, and do that odd little dance.

Finally, Connie said, "I am agreeing to this insulting, condescending, and viciously insensitive offer only in the interest of allowing my union comrades to go home and be with their families, however they themselves want to define that patriarchal, demeaning term."

When Tim and Connie were alone, she locked the door and walked toward him.

"Sorry, puffin," she said. "I know I was rough, but I had to protect my client."

"Yeah, sure, Connie, I know the drill. But I'm getting too old for this."

"Old? That's not a word I'd associate with you, puffin. I see negotiations as a kind of foreplay, and it sure worked today," Connie said.

She walked behind Tim, swinging her hips just a little, and shut the dust-covered blinds. Then, smiling, she looked him in the eye as she began to slowly unbutton her blouse.

"Meester Teem?"

Raúl, Tim's all-purpose domestic aide, was in the living-room doorway, grinning. Tim, annoyed, looked up from the speech draft written for him by Pete Dickinson for the union meeting in Florida. After the grievance hearing and energetic sex with Connie earlier in the day, Tim was tired and a bit irritable.

"Raúl, what the hell do you want now? I'm busy here. I got a big speech coming up and I got to get this stuff down pat."

"Sorry, Meester Teem. Mrs. Flaherty, she says to me, Raúl, I want to go to my friend, Mrs. Hannaway's house, she belong to that church club they got for helping the poor people, social justice. Nice ladies, say Rosary together."

"Yeah, yeah, I know, sometimes they come over here. So what?"

"Mrs. Flaherty, she say she don't wan' you to worry. While she's prayin', she give me the list, I go do the shopping. See, she give me a list, and then after I'm done, I pick her up and—"

"All right, all right, I get it, whatever you say," Tim said. "And tell Margaret Mary to say a prayer for me. Now leave me alone."

When Raúl left the room, Tim thought: *You know, dealing with José Illytch and now Raúl, I got to think some of them ain't the sharpest people in the world. Maybe I should hire Raúl as my official speechwriter. Hmmmm. He's dumb as you can get, but at least he wouldn't be giving me revolutionary stuff, I could continue having Dickinson do the writing on the side. And Raúl would meet the quota we got. Something to think about. Not a bad idea, in fact.*

THIRTEEN

PRESIDENT CALLS FOR "LINKS TO AMERICAN GREATNESS"

PLEDGES TO HIRE WORK-CHALLENGED STAFFERS

In his twenty-three-minute appearance before officers of the Union of Work-Challenged Employees at the La Mer Belle Azure Hotel in Palm Beach, President Ferguson said, "A link on the Internet gives us new sources of information. We can click on a link and find a whole new world awaiting us. But for too long we have neglected to click on links to American greatness in neighborhoods and schools, churches, and especially our unions, like the great one you represent."

The president then told the group, made up of union officials: "There is an ancient meaning to the word *link,* a meaning we no longer use. In the past, before city streets were lighted, men carried torches in London streets in order to guide people in the dark. Those torches were called links. And those who carried them were called linkmen. Linkmen held up a light so that others might find their way. In the same way, today, unions like yours all across America are showing the way for others who are work-challenged, giving them hope and dignity. We must dedicate ourselves to developing, nurturing, and finding these links and making them available so that others might find their way."

The president said work-challenged employees must be included in what he termed "the traditional American link to compassion through government."

"Therefore I am pleased to be able to announce that I plan to hire not just one but many work-challenged men and women on my personal staff, and throughout my administration. I will also ask Congress to pass legislation, which I will sign into law, to provide a Fund for Compassionate Employment, which will provide monthly benefits to those, who, through no fault of their own, are work-challenged and hate their jobs or their bosses."

Nuanced and Fair with Dave McNair. Fox News Channel.

DAVE: So, Donna, how did you like the president's speech to Tim Flaherty's work-challenged people?

DONNA: It was Republican Lite, hardly the kind of speech progressives should expect from a Democratic president.

DAVE: What about his promise to hire work-challenged folks in the White House? Don't you support that?

DONNA: It's too little, too late. Where are work-challenged advisers in the White House *now?* He's just trying to keep union support.

DAVE: What did you think of his "links to greatness" metaphor?

DONNA: The only links he's familiar with are the golf links he plays on, with the CEOs he idolizes—and helps with tax breaks, at the expense of working people everywhere. He should try forging a link with the hard realities of working people, of women, and the elderly, and the—

DAVE: We get the point, Donna.

LYONS "DIVISIVE," SAYS UNION LEADER

Timothy J. Flaherty, president of the Union of Work-Challenged Employees, today criticized Donna Hart Lyons, prominent left-liberal political activist, for what he called "divisive, dangerous, and demagogic rhetoric" aimed at crippling the reelection chances of President Tyler Ferguson. Speaking to an audience of union officials at the La Mer Belle Azure Hotel in Palm Beach, where President Ferguson spoke yesterday, Mr. Flaherty, a strong supporter of the president, said Mrs. Lyons is allowing her own personal agenda to dictate her political stance.

"I admire Donna Lyons," Mr. Flaherty said. "For many years, I have stood with her, side by side, in demonstrations against government policies we believe are wrong. I admire her intelligence, her commitment to her principles—most of which I share—and her courage. But speaking as a friend, I call upon Donna Hart Lyons today to put that tremendous energy and intelligence and idealism into supporting a great friend of labor, our great president—Ty the Guy Ferguson."

BOMB EXPLODES AT FOUNDATION

. . . The device exploded at five A.M., at the service entrance of the LionHeart Foundation. No one was injured, and foundation officials estimate that the damage to the building is minimal.

But Donna Hart Lyons, founder of LionHeart, held a news conference in which she suggested the bomb was meant to terrorize not only her but "progressives everywhere." She placed indirect blame on Mr. Ezra Tyne, controversial radio talk show host:

"Ezra Tyne is, as I have said before, a fascist idiot. If he did not plant the bomb himself, his inflammatory rhetoric has created the atmosphere in which such a despicable act is possible. He should be brought to justice for aiding and abetting hate crimes, crimes against women, and crimes against diversity."

"Yeah, this is your ol' Unca Ezra, back atcha again. I tell you, folks, it's getting crazier out there every minute. Donna Dart-in-My-Heart Liar called me a—and I quote—fascist idiot, end of quote. That fascist idiot remark hurts ol' Unca Ezra's feelings. Sure, I'm an idiot, a big idiot, and I don't deny it. Never did do well in school. But a fascist? With my waistline, I couldn't fit into those tight Nazi uniforms. And I know I'd just look god-awful in jackboots. Besides, I've never been able to get past page six of *Mein Kampf*, it just puts me to sleep. But that's Donna for you, hurting my feelings. A while back, she made me out to be a pig—I didn't think her kind of folks had anything to do with pigs—at that cute little show she did, that fund-raiser for her whores' finishing school. And after how nice I been to her all these years, keeping her name before the public. Ah, well, do somebody a favor and expect to get kicked in the teeth. Anyhow, the left-wingers have been trying to destroy me for all these years. They've accused me of everything except murder or attempted murder. And now Donna Liar has done exactly that, accusing me of setting off a bomb at her lefty foundation. But as you probably know by now, that ain't all she said. Listen to this little excerpt, in her own sweet voice: *'I call upon all Americans who care about social justice to join me in bringing to justice hatemongers like Ezra Tyne.'*

"Like I say, friends, that tape ain't been doctored. Donna Flat Tire actually said that, with her own plastic-surgery-enhanced lips, what do they call it, collagen? Is that it? Or is that Botox? One of them things. She's going to bring ol' Ez to justice.' Hell, Mizz Liar, I *been* brung to justice before, did some time on a few occasions. I don't want to go into details, but jail wasn't fun. A poor white boy in jail can get hisself hurt bad by the brothers—all of them innocent, by the way. Did you know that? That's a documented fact. Every single black con in America is an innocent victim of racism. Everything they do wrong—pimping, rape, assault, murdering each other, selling drugs—is WMF: the white man's fault. But strange to say, in the slammer you can get your throat cut or be gang-raped by these gentle, innocent, perpetual victims quicker than you blink your eye. But back to Mizz Lyons. Donna, sweetheart, you want to bring me to justice? Then bring it on, mah sissta. Now where was I? That Donna Liar woman gets me all riled up, and I forget what I want to tell you. Let's see. Oh yeah, one more thing. Remember the other day, I told you I got a call from some bigwig at the AAP? Asked ol' Unca Ezra to speak to their meeting in August? Well, I said no, I don't do that kind of thing. But this gentleman just wouldn't take no for an answer. Called me back the next day and the next. Well, Unca Ezra never let down folks who need to know the truth. So I accepted his invitation to speak in Washington, D.C., go visit my tax dollars and yours. I plan to bring along with me Unca Ezra's Raiders to protect me from the wrong elements in Washington, including killers, rap artists, drug pushers, pimps, lawyers, whores, and congressmen. I'm writing my remarks in pencil, on the back of an envelope, like Abe Lincoln. I'm getting my producer, she went to some college or other, to check my spelling, I was never good at all that *i*-before-*e* stuff. I'll be talking and Donna Heart Burn will be talking. Sounds like a gas to me. Oops, I guess I can't say gas, it offends some people. Next sucker . . ."

After the show, Ezra had his usual cigarette and just sat there, smiling. He had been *on* tonight, right on the edge, where he was best. No script, just talk, jivin' and makin' it up as he went along. But now he had to prepare for the AAP meeting. It wouldn't be his usual crowd. He could do his usual rabble-rousing in the streets with the Raiders. But he needed a different kind of speech for the AAP people. Something a little more . . . elegant, something with big words—not too big—and some class.

He puffed away and idly thumbed his way through this morning's *Washington Post*, looking for ideas for the next show. Some damn liberal somewhere no doubt had done something stupid and you could bet the *Post*—his favorite source of material—would be just praising it and telling everybody how great the liberal stuff was. But there was nothing in there today. He threw the paper on the floor. He puffed on the cigarette, skimmed through some magazines, not really expecting to find anything. . . .

Hold on. The *Post.* The op-ed page. Some time back, he couldn't remember, maybe a year ago, maybe more, hadn't he seen a big piece by one of Ty the Stye in My Eye's speechwriters? Tore the living hell out of Ty. Ezra couldn't remember the writer's name. But he had walked out on the Guy, broke with him, and then turned on him. At the time, Ezra was even thinking of having this guy appear on the show. But Ezra didn't like to give up his time so somebody else could talk. What was that boy's name? Ezra speed-dialed his producer, who was in her car on her way home. He talked with her for a few seconds and she knew the name right away. Peter Dickinson. She even had his telephone number in her computer. That's who'd do his AAP speech, Peter Dickinson. What a laugh that would be—getting a speech written for Ol' Unca Ezra by someone who had worked for Ty the Guy!

Pete put down the phone and stared at the picture of Stan and Ollie. Had he heard correctly? Ezra Tyne on the phone? Ezra Fucking *Tyne?* At first Pete had thought the call was a prank, but Tyne had given him a number to call back. It was the Tyne show studio. Write for Tyne? A Dickinson couldn't lower himself *that* far. Never. What would his father say if it was ever discovered that his son had written a speech for America's number one Nazi? But Tyne had offered him an obscene amount of money to do a speech draft and, as always these days, money was on Pete's mind. He was getting nasty phone calls from Dean what's-his-name, the down-home primitive drug dealer. Threatening, crude, slightly maniacal phone calls. Of course, Dean was an idiot, but you never could tell with these backwoods types, they could get violent very easily. Clients were notoriously slow in paying speechwriters, and Harry Gottlieb's, Donna Hart Lyons's, and Tim Flaherty's checks had not yet come through. Pete needed some money now. Which was why he was going to call back Ezra Tyne and say he would write the speech.

Let me see now. I'm writing for the president of the United States, although he doesn't know about it. I'm writing for his biggest critic, Donna Hart Lyons, although she doesn't know I'm writing for the president. I'm writing for Tim Flaherty, and neither the president nor Donna knows it. And now I'll be writing for Ezra Tyne, who doesn't know I'm writing for Ty the Guy, Donna Hart Lyons, or Tim Flaherty. Pete felt like a juggler keeping four plates in the air at the same time. No, that was a bad metaphor. Overdone. How about an air-traffic controller with four planes circling overhead, waiting to land. Careful, careful, keep them all from crashing into one another. But get them all to land safely. Not bad. He jotted it down, maybe he could use it in another context. Speechwriters save old stuff, the way Gumma Ferguson saved string.

Lorna was on the phone, and Ezra was getting an earful.

"You goddamn idiot. You're giving a speech? In public? What in the *hell* is the matter with you!"

"I told you, Lorna. That Liar bitch got folks laughing at me with that piggy thing she did. You think I'm just going to sit here and take it? I'm going to Washington and I'm bringin' Ezra's Raiders with me. I've been on the phone with Buck Torrence all day. We're going to ride down Constitution Avenue, hundreds of us. The crowd's gonna be screaming for their ol' Unca Ezra. So just mind your own business and just calm down, Lorna—"

"Don't you tell me to calm down. Why don't you just send me and Johnnie the money you owe us—"

"I don't *owe* you a goddamn thing."

"The hell you *don't,* and don't you never forget it. I know things and—"

"Now hold on, Lorna. Calm down. I thought this thing through. If I make a good speech to those AAP delegates, I can get the AAP nomination next year. I can feel it. It's right there for me to take. It would drive that Donna Liar crazy."

"Oh, my sweet Lord, you've finally gone round the bend. I knew you would. Are you telling me you're seriously thinking of running for president? *You?*"

"I'm going to look into it. I got Ezra's Raiders in every state, even Massa-Jewsetts, which ain't even American. Anyhow, it's none of your damn business."

"I warn you—you better think this whole thing through. You're are going to blow everything. It's all going to disappear. You'll be recognized, even behind those glasses. Now, I want you to say hello to Johnnie."

"Ah, hell, Lorna, I don't know what to say—"

"Don't you 'hell' me. Have the decency to say a few words to him."

There was silence, then:

"'Lo?"

"Johnnie. How are you?"

"Watchin' toons. Sylvester."

"Sounds like fun. Now put your ma back on."

Lorna said, "You call that speakin' to him? Five seconds? It's the least you can do, talk to him, after you—"

Ezra put down the phone. Lorna could go to hell if she thought he was going to cancel the AAP speech. He was looking forward to it. That Dickinson boy had agreed to write a speech draft. Ol' Unca Ezra, going upscale, first-class, a deluxe package of rhetoric. Ezra had told Dickinson, Don't make it *too* fancy, son. I got to keep my credibility with mah peeps, most of them don't know no big words.

To hell with Lorna. He'd decided not to send her more money. Let her live on what he had already sent her. She was a pain in the ass. He ought to—

No, don't let her make you lose your cool, big fella. Do what you have to do. Take on that bitch and kick her ass. Just whack her. Just finish her, once and for all.

He smiled.

Who the hell am I talking about—Lorna, or Donna Liar!

Vince Ferrano sat across from Donna in her suite at the Four Seasons Hotel in Washington, his notepad on his lap. Ferrano had just finished briefing her on what LionClaw had found out about Peter Dickinson.

"Well, I'm disappointed but not surprised," Donna said. "When Che Che first met him a few years ago, he was a charming cheater. From what you tell me, he hasn't changed. With a policewoman, no less."

Donna didn't ordinarily like discussing private matters with staff members. But this problem was different. She needed to bounce her ideas off someone, and Ferrano would have to do.

"And here's the latest, Mrs. Lyons, just came to me an hour ago. Dickinson writes speeches for Tim Flaherty."

"Somehow it doesn't surprise me. My problem is, how do I keep Mr. Dickinson away from Che Che without alienating her? If I tell her what I know about him, she'll accuse me of spying. That will make him seem more appealing than ever. Well, I'll put that off for the moment. What are you hearing about the foundation bombing?"

"Nothing new. We're cooperating with the FBI and the New York police."

"Keep me informed. Anything new on Tyne's past?"

"Nothing solid."

"I need dirt on Tyne. Use every LionClaw agent you can spare. And make certain we have LionClaw operatives guarding Che Che and my father around the clock until the bomber is caught. I don't care how long it takes. I want them protected, just as I am."

"Yes, ma'am. I had a team in place for her right after it happened. They're up in New York right now, and a team for your father."

"Good. Che Che will—"

Donna, her eyes wide, suddenly stopped talking and laughed.

"I *totally* forgot," she said. "Che Che asked me to make sure her precious houseplants were watered. Vince, drive me to her place right now."

"Mrs. Lyons, I can just get one of the boys to—"

"Indulge me, Vince," Donna said, rising from the chair. "I rarely get out when I'm in Washington, and I need some fresh air. Besides, it will do me good to get out, just to ride the few blocks over there. This is a mother kind of thing. You wouldn't understand. It makes me feel good to do something for Che Che."

"Yes, ma'am."

Fifteen minutes later, Gerry Boyle, a new LionClaw security man, held open the door to the LionClaw SUV, its motor idling, and escorted Donna from the vehicle to Che Che's darkened house across the street on Volta Place. Vince Ferrano sat behind the wheel, analyzing Boyle's technique. Not bad. Boyle was walking just ahead of Donna, head moving, scoping out the scene, using the procedures LionClaw had trained him to follow. Boyle, followed closely by Donna, walked up the three steps to the front door. Donna handed Boyle the house key—LionClaw trained security people to act like gentlemen at all times, particularly when they were around Donna. Donna turned toward Ferrano, made a twisting motion with her wrist as if turning a key, and nodded to Gerry, an amused look on her face, as if to say, *My, aren't we polite*. Boyle inserted the key and began to open the door.

There was an explosion. Vince Ferrano, stunned, cut by flying glass, staggered out of the SUV and ran toward the house.

FOURTEEN

DONNA LYONS BOMB VICTIM;
BODYGUARD ALSO HURT IN BLAST

... Mrs. Lyons was taken to Georgetown Hospital and immediately underwent surgery for injuries sustained in the early-morning explosion at her daughter's home on Volta Place in Georgetown. According to a hospital spokesman, Mrs. Lyons suffered broken ribs, a ruptured spleen, and lacerations of the liver, requiring two separate operations. The first was a thoracotomy (an opening of the chest) and the second a laparotomy with splenectomy (an abdominal operation to remove her ruptured spleen and then surgery to repair her liver. Shrapnel from the bomb also caused a pneumothorax (collapsed lung). The former soap opera star, longtime political activist, and philanthropist is listed in critical condition. . . .

Gerald T. Boyle, 28, of Glendale, California, a member of LionClaw, Mrs. Lyons's personal security organization, was also injured in the explosion. "Neither Mrs. Lyons nor Mr. Boyle knew what hit them," said Captain Amos Benneton, of the Metropolitan Police Force. "They are very fortunate to be alive. If that bomb had been larger, they would be dead."

Mr. Vincent Ferrano, head of Mrs. Lyons's personal security detail, sustained minor bruises and cuts when the blast shattered windows in his automobile, parked near the scene. He was treated at Georgetown Hospital and released. . . .

Che Che, Sammy Yuan, and Vince Ferrano left Donna's hospital room and walked along a corridor crowded with doctors, nurses, police, and LionClaw security personnel, until they came to the elevator at the end of the hall, which was being held for them by a LionClaw guard. Che Che had flown in by company jet from New York three hours ago, and had been driven in a LionClaw security van convoy to the hospital. On the way, she had called Sammy and asked him to meet her at the hospital. The three of them went down two floors in silence, exited, and walked along another corridor—two LionClaw guards suddenly appearing and accompanying them—until they arrived at the conference room the hospital administrator had provided for them. Sammy closed the door as the two Lion-Claw guards took up positions in front of it. Che Che, dressed in jeans and a blue LionHeart zipper jacket, sat at the head of the long conference table; Sammy sat to her right; and Ferrano stood, head bowed, at the end of the table.

"What happened, Vince?" Che Che said in a flat, emotionless tone of voice. "How did my mother, with all the security, almost get killed?"

Ferrano didn't reply, as if he hadn't heard.

"Vince, you were there. What happened?"

Weakly, in a small, reedy, tired old man's voice Che Che didn't recognize, Ferrano said: "I don't know, Miss Hart."

"Tell me exactly what happened. Everything."

Ferrano told her about Donna, her insisting on going to Che Che's house to take care of the plants. As he spoke, Che Che got up, walked to the window behind her, and pulled aside the drapes. A beautiful day. A day for biking and hiking. She closed the drapes. Ferrano reached the end of his story.

"Vince," Che Che said, turning toward him. "Go home. Get some sleep. I want to talk to Mr. Yuan."

When Ferrano left, Che Che said to Sammy, "I need your help."

"Anything, Che Che."

"I want you to take over as head of LionClaw. I'm firing Ferrano. I can't trust him. Maybe he set this up. Coming to work for LionClaw means giving up your business for a while. Can you do that? I know I'm asking a lot, but—"

"I'll leave immediately and let my assistants handle my clients."

"Thank you, Sammy. I can't trust many people, but I trust you. First, I want you to pick a special LionClaw elite team to protect my mother, here, around the clock. Make certain my grandfather is safe at the nursing home. I want a new team of LionClaw guards there, in his suite. And I want you to pick a similar team to protect me, with you as the leader. Next, get someone to call the Dave McNair show. Tell him I want to come on tomorrow night."

Che Che sat back down and closed her eyes.

"If I could cry, I'd cry. But everything has happened so quickly. I just feel as if I'm hollow inside, like I can't feel anything. My mother is upstairs, maybe dying, and I can't feel anything. What's wrong with me, Sammy?"

"You're in shock. Maybe I can help. Stand up, Che Che."

She stood, not quite certain where this was leading. Sammy came close to her and put his hands on her shoulders.

"Close your eyes. Just be still for a while," Sammy said softly. "Be still."

Then, after a few moments of silence, Sammy said, in a low but firm voice, "Che Che, open your eyes and assume the stance."

At first Che Che didn't know what he meant. But he did a pantomime with his own body and she assumed the kickboxing stance.

"That's it," Sammy said. "Now, throw a jab."

"Sammy, what—"

"Just trust me, Che Che. You're willing to trust me with your life as the head of LionClaw. Trust me here. Throw a jab at my hand."

He held his hands up and she threw a tentative, ineffective jab.

"That's not a jab, Che Che, it's a baby waving bye-bye. Throw a real punch."

She took another shot at it, and hit his hand cleanly but not solidly.

"Not good—your fist is vulnerable, watch your thumb—but better," Sammy said. "Now a cross."

She threw a cross.

"Combination now, the old one-two, jab and a cross. Let me see it."

She threw the combination. Sammy began calling out various punches and kicks and elbow blows and combinations and for five minutes they stood that way, Che Che getting into the rhythm and Sammy deflecting or avoiding the blows. They were like two dancers, or maybe, two lovers, each attuned to the other, each reacting to the other, lost in the rhythm and the movement and the flow and the sheer physical reality of what they were doing. Sammy moved—gracefully, as always—a few steps back. Che Che stood there, sweating, with a buzz from the exercise.

"Che Che, listen to your body. It can free you. Our minds and hearts lie like hell, all the time, but the body doesn't know how to lie. I'll spare you the rest of my fortune-cookie wisdom. I'll see you later, Che Che," Sammy said, kissing her on the brow. "I'll get to work on the LionClaw operation right now."

It was one-thirty in the morning when Pete's bedside-table phone sounded.

"Peter?"

"Che? My God, when I heard the news today, I tried to get in touch, all day," he said in a suddenly awake voice. "I even went to the hospital, but—"

"I know, they turned you away. I forgot to leave your name at the desk. I'm still here, just a few floors down from Mom's room. I haven't had a chance to breathe. I hope I didn't wake you up."

"No, no, I'm just here watching TV. Che, how are you? Are you all right? How's your mom? How's—"

"Peter, shut up and listen. I need your help."

"Anything."

"I want you to write something for me. Tomorrow night—or I guess I should say, tonight—I'm going on the Dave McNair show. I don't want a speech, just some one-liners I can drop into the conversation if I get the chance. I don't have time to write, my mind is too filled with everything. I'll have somebody call you tomorrow with the fax number."

"No problem, Che, anything else I can do to help?"

"I'll let you know, Peter?"

"What?"

"I miss you."

"I miss you too, baby, and I'm thinking about you," he said, and hung up.

Pete lay there, picking up the thought that had been interrupted by the phone call: *Jeb Hammerford wants his money. Dean wants his money. I've got to do something. Maybe it's time to hit up old dad.*

From the bed he could see his Stan and Ollie picture in his office. What would they do? They would, of course, do exactly the wrong thing. But maybe doing the wrong thing, the risky thing, the crazy thing, was the smart thing to do. He would have to wage a war on two fronts. That was always risky, but he had no choice. First, Operation Dear Old Dad, Part Two. Visit him and casually suggest that a small loan would not be looked upon as insulting. But at the same time, Pete would have to work on Operation Che Che, so to speak, a long-range plan. When they were married, he'd be home free. *Maybe the time has come to put some pressure on Che Che. Maybe it's time to dump Marlie Rae and start concentrating on—*

"Who was that on the phone, this hour of night?"

Marlie Rae Perkins had come out of the bathroom, fresh from a shower, wearing nothing but a big fluffy blue towel.

"God, that feels good, a shower and washing my hair," she said. "I get all sweated up, but I guess you noticed that. Nothing like a good shower, feels good, after, y'know, fooling around. Like I said, who was that calling you this late, honey?"

"Just an old White House buddy. Drunk, broke, lost his girl to a right-wing lesbian. Same old everyday boring Washington stuff. Wanted a shoulder to cry on."

"This time of night? You two must be real close buddies."

"The blues don't have a time schedule."

"Still, you must be *real* close."

"Why do you say that?"

"Well, for one thing—and this is just a clue—I heard you say 'I miss you too, baby.' So I figure you two must be very close, you calling him 'baby' and telling him you miss him. Pete, you keeping something from me? Are you gay or bi, or what?"

"Oh, that's just a private joke between us, a line from an old movie."

"Is that a fact? What old movie was that?"

"Sons of the Desert."

"I don't know that one. Who was in it?"

"Clark Gable and Mae West. Anyhow, you're off duty, Officer. Stop interrogating me and treating me like a perp," he said, and reached out to undo the towel. "Do I have that right? Perp?"

Marlie backed away.

"Nobody says 'perp' anymore, not even on TV cop shows. Look, honey, we got to get one thing clear. I don't like being made a fool of."

"Who's doing that?"

"I'm just the jealous type. Don't run around on me. Tell me the God's honest truth. Are you seeing somebody else? Just tell me."

"Why would I want to do that?" he said, and kissed her, undoing the towel. "I have you."

Nuanced and Fair with Dave McNair. Fox News Channel.

DAVE: Our very special guest tonight is Che Che Hart, writer, history professor at Georgetown University, and daughter of our friend and political sparring partner, Donna Hart Lyons. As you know, Donna was seriously injured two nights ago in a bomb explosion. The bomb was planted at the doorway of the Georgetown home of Che Che Hart, who was not home at the time. Che Che, I know this is a bad time for you, so thank you for coming on the show tonight.

CHE CHE: Thank you for having me, Mr. McNair.

DAVE: First, how is Donna?

CHE CHE: My mother is the bravest, toughest human being I have ever known. If anyone can survive this, she can and she will.

DAVE: How about you? How are you holding up?

CHE CHE: I'm getting through it, hour by hour. It's clear someone tried to kill me. Local and federal authorities tell me the bomb at my house was a booby-trap kind of device. The bomb was intended to send a signal to my mother, by hurting or killing me. But fate dictated that my mother was there, at the doorway, and I wasn't.

DAVE: The big question is, Who did this? Do you have any idea? Have the police or the FBI said anything about suspects? Your mom, as a political activist, has made a lot of enemies and—

CHE CHE: The police and the FBI are doing all they can. It could have been some maniac, committing a hate crime for God knows what deranged reason, or no reason at all. The unrelenting, cruel, personal attacks made on my mother by Ezra Tyne have created an atmosphere of hate in which weak-minded individuals can be goaded into violence. Or it could have been part of an organized attempt by right-wing ideological fanatics. I am told the police are looking into the possibility that someone from my mother's past, in show business or politics, could be involved. Unfortunately, we live in a time when, increasingly, political differences are settled by violence instead of arguments.

DAVE: I agree. The bomb has replaced the debate as the political weapon of choice all over the world these days.

CHE CHE: You mentioned my mother's enemies. I'm reminded of what was once said about one president, I believe it was Grover Cleveland: we love him for the enemies he has made. Of course my mother has enemies. And I'm immensely proud of that because of the nature of the enemies. She has fought racism and sexism and economic exploitation and war all her life. You gain admirers by living your life that way. But you get enemies, too, if you do it the right way. With this incident, her enemies have become my enemies. When my mother gets well—and she will, I promise you—she will resume her fight. Until then, I will do everything in my power to continue my mother's work.

DAVE: Your mom was thinking of challenging President Ferguson next year. Do you—

CHE CHE: I can't speak to any specific political plan my mother had. All I know is this—if those who planted these bombs think they can stop my mom's work, or that they have scared me into silence and isolation, they picked on the wrong family.

Meanwhile, on the air at the Ezra Tyne Show . . .

CALLER: My name is Larry. I'm calling from San Francisco. Mr. Tyne—

EZRA: Call me Unca Ezra, pal.

CALLER: You are not my uncle, either by blood relation of in terms of affection, and if you were, I'd be deeply ashamed. You are, in fact, a disgusting, depraved—

EZRA: Uh-oh, folks, Unca Ezra is going to get it good. Tell the little kids they can't listen to this, because I think we're gonna get a two-minute hate call from some compassionate San Francisco tree hugger. Go ahead, my friend, give me both barrels. I can take it.

CALLER: Are you proud of what you've done?

EZRA: What have I done now?

CALLER: Donna Hart Lyons is near death after being injured in a bombing. Your personal, vicious attacks on her caused this. Your lack of decency, your bigotry, your—

EZRA: Yeah, yeah, I get the picture. You tell me you're from San Francisco. Well, why don't you just, you know, put on more lipstick and flounce back to your anti-gun meeting or "I want to marry a cow" or whatever left-nut San Francisco cause you like. Hell, I'm getting sick of folks like you blaming ol' Unca Ezra for setting off bombs. Nobody wants to see anybody all blowed up, like Donna Lyons was. All you folks out there, those who God still hears your prayers—he gave up on mine a long time ago—well, you just say some prayers for Donna Liar in the hospital, all blowed up, like she is. Unca Ezra is always big on family, maybe on account of he ain't got none of his own. Just alone in the world. But I admire families, folks sticking together. Maybe some prayers will help Donna Liar and her daughter Leninina or Gulag-etta or whatever her commie name is.

Dean Mumphreys, sitting alone in his pickup truck parked across the street from the Lynhill South high-rise where Pete Dickinson lived, was deeply puzzled, not to mention perplexed and perturbed. He did not know what to do about this dude Pete who owed him money for cocaine. The thing was—and Dean knew this better than anyone—although Dean played at being a street-bad white gangsta muthafucka drug lord, he was in fact in a little bit over his head. He was just one of the poor white would-be drug thugs employed by Opie Hickles, a big drug-daddy dude who lived in a mansion out there in Fauquier County, Virginia. Dean wanted to impress Mr. Hickles. But did you do that by giving customers a chance to pay up, or by shooting them as a lesson?

Dean sneaked a look at his face in the rearview mirror. That new stuff the doctor at the clinic had given him seemed to have calmed down the acne. *Well, at least that's working. Now, how do I get my money from this bitch?* One thing was certain—the talk Dean had with Jeb Hammerford at that guinea restaurant hadn't worked out. Dean had tried his best to look and sound like a badass playa, white division, but ol' Jeb wasn't buying. Dean hated Jeb because, like all those rich boys, he just thought Dean was a joke, and that pissed Dean off more than anything.

Dean had first met Jeb at a barbecue at Mr. Hickles's place, where Dean, in order to pick up a few bucks (outside of drugs, which really didn't get him much, and he had no steady job) was tending bar. They had started talking about nothing—that's what you have to do as a bartender—and one thing led to another, and Jeb took a shine to Dean and started using him as a source for cocaine. Dean didn't like Jeb, thought he was a candy-ass rich boy—wouldn't Dean liked to have had ol' Jeb as his cellmate in that two-year stretch! Ol' Jeb would have been wearing a miniskirt in a week. But he had to admit Jeb got him some business in Washington, and even Mr. Hickles had said something nice to Dean, just a few days ago—keep up the good work, son.

But here was the problem: this Pete Dickinson was stiffing Dean, blowing him off, and not only that, he was sassing him. Dean had talked to him, nice, because the guy was friend of Jeb's—but this Pete, well, he just bad-mouthed and sassed and acted as if he owned half the goddamn universe, stars and all. He looked down his nose at Dean, as though Dean was stupid or something. Well, Dean had to admit—he knew his limitations—he may not be as fast upstairs as some, but a man's got pride. A man's got dignity. Dean, during his incarceration, when he wasn't spending his time fighting off the homies, had watched a lot of TV. He knew about things like identity crises and loss of self-esteem and the need to feel good about yourself. And this situation was just like that: Dean didn't know who he was, and he was feeling bad about himself. He faced the Al Pacino dilemma. Was he like Al Pacino as Michael Corleone in *The Godfather*, slick, cool, quiet but dangerous, just talk softly to this Pete, scare him? Or was he like Pacino in *Scarface*, just *shoot* this bitch-boy—boom, boom—two shots to the chest and then—boom, boom—two to the head, the muthafucka's *dead*, that's the way ol' Dean operates? That kind of thing sends a signal. That kind of thing gets around, and it makes a man's reputation. Mr. Opie Hickles would admire somebody who had the balls to just walk up and shoot a rich guy who knew the president. We play no favorites here. You don't pay, you die. Still, there was something about the Michael Corleone model that Dean favored, that cold look in the eyes that made men wet their pants. That was good, too.

But Dean did not know which course to take. There were no guidance counselors in the drug world. Those TV talk shows didn't have drug dealers on to discuss the difficulties of the business. For the first time in his life Dean felt envious of the black drug dealers. They had a support system. When they were kids, they had people they could look up to as role models. A poor white boy had to make it up as he went along. It just wasn't fair.

Dean sighed as he looked at the building across the street. Must cost a fortune to live there. And this Pete, a rich guy, also has a black Lexus hardtop convertible. Living large, he is. *If it ever gets around that a rich pussy like that is holding out on me, Mr. Hickles will drop me like I was a Glad garbage bag.* Dean noted that the doorman liked to chat with residents, kissing ass, looking for a big tip. A man could easily sneak into the garage while the doorman was kissing up and get into the building without being seen. And Dean knew the bitch-boy lived on the tenth floor because he had once boasted about the view. The thing was, Dean didn't know *what* he wanted to do. Driving away, he knew he was conflicted, a word he had picked up on *Oprah*. He needed conflict resolution. He needed to come to terms with his issues. No use talking or thinking anymore. *Do* something.

PART TWO

Saying B

FIFTEEN

Che Che Hart stood on the porch of LionWest, looking at the two hundred or so guests fifty yards away, mingling in a series of open-sided tents. The tents, in special colors that Donna, with the help of Hollywood designers, had created (shocking liberation blues, bright sun-power yellows, brilliant revolutionary reds, and intense eco-savvy greens), were set up on the front lawn for the feast (vegan sensibilities duly noted, but pastrami in abundance) that would take place after the ceremony honoring Donna, in her first public appearance five weeks after the bombing. Television crews were waiting for Donna to make her grand entrance. On the lawn and in the tents, LionClaw security guards, big, young, steroid-dependent studs—black and brown and white and yellow and red (LionClaw was an equal opportunity goon squad)—in blue blazers, white T-shirts, khaki pants, and dark glasses, and young women, toned, ripped, equally rich in ethnic and racial diversity, dressed in blazers and pants, were methodically but unobtrusively checking things out. Che Che smiled as she saw Pete, who had written some remarks for Donna. He looked so darling, the most handsome man there.

In her office, Donna sat behind the big desk and listened to the Babster.

"Are the Che girls mixing and mingling with the guests?" Donna asked. "I promised them and—"

"Yeah, I picked six or seven of them, including Monique, just to show her there's no hard feelings. They're out there now, and I gotta tell you, kid, they look great and they're very thankful."

"Are they dressed to fit in? None of the other guests should know that Che girls are among them. I don't want a big fuss."

"Nobody knows. Donna, believe me, you couldn't tell the girls from the other guests if you didn't know."

"That's what I want, just to prove to the girls we're making a difference, that they're just like everyone else. Babs, I'm going to take a little rest before I speak. Is there anything else I should know about the school?"

"Well, I hate to bring this up, on your big day, but I have to give it to you straight, Donna. Some faculty members are causing trouble."

"They aren't fooling around with the girls, are they? If even one of them tries—"

"Nah, it's nothing like that. Some of the younger professors are telling the girls that progressivism means we shouldn't impose our moral views on other people and that the government should be used to make society better."

"What's wrong with that?"

"Well, these teachers say if that's the case, why are progressives imposing their moral views about prostitution on other people? We're being judgmental. Why doesn't the government just legalize prostitution, take care of health-care problems, and make prostitution something all social classes can enjoy, risk-free? Why stigmatize one group of working people? That's the real progressive position, they say."

"That's utter nonsense. The whole point of the Che School is to get these girls *away* from prostitution."

"But some of the teachers are saying to me, What about the right to choose?"

"Choose? Choose? Are they insane? Prostitutes don't have a choice. They're forced into prostitution for economic reasons."

"I tell some of the girls that and they laugh. They say I don't know a thing about being a whore. And then they say—they're getting this from the teachers—don't women have the right to choose what they do with their bodies? And shouldn't progressive government protect that right?"

"Babs, we need a complete housecleaning. Fire the faculty members who are spreading this vicious nonsense. Hire teachers who will teach what I want taught."

"What about academic freedom?"

"I'm not going to let misguided ideas about academic freedom destroy my school. What dreamworld are these people living in, that they think they can take my money and then help destroy what I'm doing? Crack down, Babs, and crack down hard, before these malcontents poison the girls' minds."

Pete sat alone at a small table in the yellow sun-power tent, dressed in a dark blue, classically understated suit; a light blue shirt; a discreet, expensive, blue-and-red-striped silk tie; and gleaming, laced black shoes. He was, he realized, ridiculously overdressed for an outdoor western party, but he wanted to make a good impression on Donna. He was not at all happy. For one thing, he needed some coke. In a celebrity, showbiz, media, academic, political crowd like this, there were probably ten kilo bags of the stuff lying around, but he didn't know anyone well enough to ask. And then there was sex, or the lack of it. He had been avoiding Marlie Rae; she was beginning to be a pain in the ass with her phone calls and her questions about him seeing somebody else. To make matters worse, a photo of Che Che and Pete, holding hands, had just appeared on page three of the *Post*'s Style section. Marlie Rae would be bitching about that, but he guessed he could bullshit her, as usual. With Marlie Rae on the warpath, and with Che Che so busy these days, he wasn't getting any sex, and that also put him on edge.

But what was really irritating was that he was being ignored at this big outdoor gala. In Washington he was, admittedly, no longer a star, but he was still a part of (minor) celebrity Washington. If you mentioned his name on the Hill or in the bars in Georgetown, or in Adams Morgan restaurants, people who count—some of them, at least—recognized it. But among Donna's celebrity friends, Pete was nobody—less than nobody, since he was not in the Business or academia or the media, and he had once worked for the Guy, who was not a favorite with this crowd.

Hardly anyone had spoken to Pete in the past hour or so, or if they did, lost interest when they found out he wasn't somebody famous or at least powerful by their showbiz standards. In the past few minutes four movie stars, three TV sitcom stars, two once-famous liberal political consultants, a former NFL superstar, and a once-notorious and still wealthy white rap artist, complete with his sneering entourage, had passed Pete's table and ignored him. Ten feet away from him was a movie legend and longtime political activist, his famous blue eyes unmistakable, the grin still boyish after all these decades as a star. The actor was laughing and talking with a tall, dark-haired young woman in a fashionable jeans suit. The movie legend moved on. Pete got up and walked toward the woman.

"Hi," she said. She was a knockout. Her voice had a warm, velvety, welcoming sound, and she managed to draw out the "hi" in a sexy manner.

"Hi, yourself," Pete said, and looked into her eyes, thinking, *Things are looking up*. "Let me guess—you're an actress."

"I've been in some movies. What about you?"

"I'm a speechwriter."

"How interesting. Who do you write for?"

"President Ferguson, at one time. Now I freelance. I'm doing some stuff for Donna."

"You must be pretty good."

"Modesty forbids me from responding. I'm Pete Dickinson. And you're—?"

"Monique. Monique Cantrell."

"What movies have you been in, Monique? I bet I've seen you."

"Oh, I do a lot of indie work. Nothing you would have heard of."

"Still waiting for the big break, right?"

"I believe you make your own breaks."

They chatted for a while and he noticed how she looked in his eyes when she spoke, and how she was interested in everything he had to say. She made him feel special. She smiled and said, "This has been nice. I don't get the chance to talk with anyone so . . . intelligent. And good-looking."

"If you're not doing anything later on tonight," Pete said, "why not drop by my guest cabin—number five—and we can continue the conversation?

For a moment she didn't say anything, just gave him a mysterious, Mona Lisa quarter smile. Then she said, "I think I can arrange that. What time?"

"Say, elevenish?"

"I'll see you then."

". . . and now," Che Che said, standing behind a podium on the front porch, addressing the crowd that had come out of the tents and was now gathered around the steps, "I want you all to show Mom how much we love her. Here she is, the greatest, toughest, most wonderful lady I've ever known, my mom, the one and only—Donna!"

As Che Che spoke the last words, the front door was held open by Sammy Yuan. As the applause began, Donna, in a motorized wheelchair, wheeled herself out to the porch and stopped a few feet from the podium. She smiled and waved to the applauding, whistling, cheering crowd. She waited, letting the cheering and applause continue.

Then she slowly, and with obvious effort, began to get up from the chair. The cheering and applause dwindled and then suddenly stopped. There was an eerie kind of near-silence, not total absence of sound—it was outdoors and there were birds calling—but the sudden absence of human sound, all the more noticeable coming after the first raw burst of applause. Donna knew—hell, she had planned it this way—that every eye was fixed on her. She slowly arose from the chair, pushing with her arms on the armrests. Then she was standing, wobbly, still holding on to the armrests. She let go of them. For an instant she lost her balance and looked as if she might fall back into the wheelchair. There were gasps and shouts and *ohs!* from the crowd. Sammy took a step toward her, but Che Che laid a restraining hand on his arm. Then, just like that, just as if it were the most natural thing in the world, Donna took a step toward the podium and then another and then a third. In a moment she was standing by the podium and extending her arms to the crowd. The reaction was instantaneous, a roaring, rolling boisterous mix of applause and shouts and whistles. Someone began to chant, "Donn-a, Donn-a, Donn-a . . . ," and the crowd picked it up. As the happy noise grew even louder, Donna held her arms toward them, palms down. There was a gradual cessation of crowd noises. Donna milked the silence for a two beats and then said, in a strong voice: "Do I still know how to make an entrance, or what?"

She stood there, diva, star, goddess, heroine, queen, empress, leader, God-mother, in total control, graciously accepting the love and the awe of her people.

"Thank you, thank you very much, as Elvis once said. He did *not* say it to me personally, you know, despite those terrible, salacious rumors about us—which I spread. [Laughter, whistles.] Of course, Frank Sinatra never said much to me—we were too busy. [Laughter.] My friends, I want to thank you all for coming so far, so many of you, to be at our little spread with Che Che and me today. As you can see, while I am not yet where I want to be concerning my health, I am better than I was yesterday and I'll be even better tomorrow. [Cheers.] But if you think I'm going to miss a party, you don't know Donna. [Cheers.] As you know, I am scheduled to address the American Advance Party in a few weeks. I'm going to tell them I believe in government for the people and people for each other." [Cheers, applause.]

She paused—a beautifully timed pause, as always, and then:

"Ezra Tyne [boos], the Nazi thug who stands against everything decent people, people who care, people who have compassion, things that we believe in, is going to speak to the AAP meeting in August. He will bring to our nation's capital his Nazi goon squad, Ezra's Raiders. [Boos.] I pledge to you today that I will not allow Ezra Tyne to swindle the AAP membership and take over the party so he can remake it a symbol of hate and oppression and fascist violence. I will confront him and I will expose him for the fraud he is. [Cheers.]

"I have asked my daughter, Che Che, to be the national chairman of my presidential exploratory committee. She will be with me every step of the way, before the August meeting, during the meeting, and afterward, as far as we can go together!" [Thunderous cheers.]

As the cheering grew, Donna gestured to Che Che to come to the podium, and Che Che, smiling broadly, put her arm around her mother, holding her with one arm while she waved with the other. As she waved and smiled and hugged her mother, there was no one in the cheering crowd who could have guessed that Che Che had heard about her big part in Donna's campaign at the same moment they did.

That night, just past eleven, Pete sat in a rocking chair on the porch of his cabin, waiting for Monique. He looked at his watch for the third time in the past few minutes. Where the hell was she? Sitting there alone in the dark gave him the creeps. Everything out there at the ranch was so . . . *natural*. He hated the outdoors, always had, and wanted nothing more than to be back in Washington, where, thank God, they had nature (if not human nature) under control, more or less. He heard the sound of footsteps on the gravel path and went to the side of the porch. He saw a figure walking toward the cabin in the darkness.

"Peter?"

His heart pounding, he watched Che Che approach in the darkness, wearing jeans and a windbreaker with a LionHeart logo.

"Che, what the hell are you doing out—"

"Gee, what a warm, romantic greeting," she said as she embraced him. "I come all the way out here to be with you, and that's the thanks I get."

She kissed him and sat on the rocking chair.

"I couldn't sleep," she said. "I guess you couldn't either, sitting here this time of night. It's cold."

"Yeah, I was just sitting here, er, thinking about you, in fact. And here you are. You look worried. Anything the matter?"

"Oh, Mom never even told me I was going to be her national chairman. But she knows how to manipulate me. If she tried to talk me into it before she announced it, I would have said no. But she put me on the spot before all those people and the TV cameras, so what could I do? A typical move by Mom when she wants something. But I don't know anything about practical politics. I'm all theory."

"You'll do a great a job. I'll write her speeches. I'll help you."

"You better. Well, as campaign manager I may as well exercise some author-ity. So I hereby—I never thought I'd get the chance to use the word *hereby*—I hereby hire you as top speechwriter to write my mom's speech for the AAP meeting and throughout the campaign next year. You did good remarks for Mom today. Did you know—"

"About you becoming manager? No, she put that part in herself. The speechwriter is always the last to know."

She got out of the chair and put her arms around him.

"Is there anything the matter?" she said. "You seem, I don't know, on edge."

"I guess we all had a busy day today and I'm a bit tired."

"Peter, look at me."

"That's not hard to do."

"I'm serious. Just tell me: can I count on you? Promise me you're going to be with me all the way. Not just writing the speeches, but helping me and help-ing Mom. Promise me you'll be part of the team? That you won't let me down, ever."

"Sure, Che. I'll do anything for you."

Just over Che Che's left shoulder, about twenty-five yards away, Pete saw Monique, hands on hips, staring at him, standing amid a clump of trees.

"Che, I'm really bushed and I need to get some sleep."

"That's not the Peter I know. Maybe this will get your attention."

She kissed him. He gently pulled away and said, "Che, I've missed you, too, but like I said, it's been a long day. Let's wait until we get back to Washington. It will be even better."

She pouted and then gave him a gentle kiss on the tip of his nose.

"My little Puritan. Promise me you'll make up for it when we get back?"

"Promise. I'd say honest Injun, but we're in Montana and—"

"Oh, Peter, you're incorrigible," she said, then kissed him and scampered down the steps and back toward the big house.

When she was out of sight, Pete exhaled slowly. He went down the steps of the porch and walked around the cabin, looking for Monique. She was standing behind a tree.

"At first I thought you'd arranged a threesome," she said. "Not that I would have minded, if that's what you want."

He put his arm around her shoulder and she put her arm around his waist as they walked toward the cabin.

"I've been looking forward to this all day," he said.

"Me, too. Pete, I think we should get something clear from the start."

"Anything."

"I charge six hundred dollars."

"What are you talking about?"

"That's the flat rate. Extras cost more."

"What the hell are you— Am I hearing this right? You expect me to *pay?*"

"Pete, you're a bright guy, I can tell. Do you mean you didn't guess I'm a whore? I'm a Che girl."

"A Che— What the hell are you telling me?"

She kissed him on the mouth and ran her right hand down his back.

"You're really cute and I like you," she said in a husky voice. "I just love smart men. It isn't like with other guys I meet. With you I really feel something real, and I know I could learn to like you even more. I want this to be special. I—"

He pulled away.

"That's all bullshit," he said. "Who do you think you're kidding? You're a whore. That's just a whore's lies."

"Pete," she said, "look at it this way: you told me you're a political speech-writer. Right?"

"What's that got to do with it?"

"Everybody lies, honey. Politicians pay you to lie *for* them. People pay me to lie *to* them. I rent out my body and you rent out your mind. I peddle my ass. You peddle your brain. And we both expect to get paid."

"I never paid for sex in my life."

"Too bad. You really don't know what you're missing. I'm very, very good. I thought you understood what kind of gig this would be. I mean, Jesus, you're cute, but you're not *that* cute. Did you really believe that ten minutes after I met you, I'd promise to come to your cabin? You have a big ego problem, honey. Well, have it your way. You sure as hell aren't going to have it *my* way, not without paying me. This is America, Pete. People pay for things here."

As he watched Monique walk away, he thought: *Goddamn whore.*

He sat on the porch, brooding.

Tomorrow, on the plane, I have to get to work on Donna's AAP speech. When I get back I have to do Tyne's speech. And Tim Flaherty wants remarks for an anti-Donna demonstration at the AAP meeting. Well, I have one thing working for me—at least Harry Gottlieb hasn't been bothering me for a speech for the Guy. That would be all I need.

The nerve of that bitch, comparing me to a whore.

SIXTEEN

The Guy picked up an ultrafine-point pen on his desk and placed it half an inch from where it had been. He looked at the pen. He touched the pen to get it in line. He smiled.

"I've been thinking about the speechwriting situation, Harry. I've reached a decision. It concerns you."

"Me, sir?"

"You've been doing a good job on these speeches, better than I expected. You have that Dickinson touch, but even better. Well, I'm going to reward such service. From now on you are officially communications consultant to the president of the United States. Congratulations."

"Commu—oh, no, Mr. President, I—"

"The story we'll put out is this: the president is reorganizing the staff—people love reorganization, it shows you're moving, doing something—and we'll be cutting back on staff, saving tax dollars. As part of the reorganization, we'll have to cut back the speechwriting shop. Now, between the two of us, I need to keep some of those overpriced prima donnas, but I no longer want them labeled speechwriters. Place them in line positions on the various staffs—national security, domestic adviser, and the like—and call them staff assistants. From now on, the president will have one communications consultant—you—*not* a speechwriter. My communications consultant will be someone who is there for me in the highly unlikely event I need someone to, er, consult with about a speech. The president is his own speechwriter, that's the message we'll get out. This is a new start for the president's communications in which the president is doing most of his own stuff. New start. Write that down. I like it."

"Well, it's very kind of you to appoint me, sir, but—"

"This doesn't mean I expect you to drop your other duties. You can write speech drafts, which I'll, er, consult, in your spare time. From now on, I'll be doing fewer speeches. This administration *does* things, we don't talk about them. Write that down."

"But, Mr. President, how will all this look? I mean—"

"Look? It will look *decisive*. It will look *bold*. Now I have even better news for you."

"Sir?"

"On my trip to Europe, you will accompany me, not just as chief of staff but as the new communications consultant. You will be responsible for all the speeches and toasts and welcoming and departure remarks on the trip. What do think?"

"I really don't know what to say, sir."

"I thought you'd be pleased. And make certain you take along that new work-challenged secretary you have. What's her name?"

"Shirley, sir."

"How is that working out, having a work-challenged secretary?"

"About as well as could be expected, Mr. President," Harry replied, thinking, *She comes in at ten-thirty, leaves at three, loses documents, has few computer skills, doesn't get along with anyone, and knows nothing about politics. Except for that, she's a gem.*

"One columnist said the other day my hiring of work-challenged folks makes me a Democrat's Democrat. And it was a poke in the eye with a sharp stick for Donna Lyons, who said I wouldn't hire the work-challenged. Speaking of Donna, how are you coming along? Have you met with her?"

"Yes, sir."

"And?"

"Well, she's a very determined woman, sir, and—"

"Is she still planning to run?"

"I think she is, yes. Definitely."

"Well, make her change her mind. When we get back from the trip, see her again. All right, that's it for tonight. I expect good material from you on the trip. I need the old-fashioned kind of stuff, foreign policy, that sort of thing. But give me a lot of people to point to. Give me anecdotes. Some self-deprecatory humor. But not too self-deprecatory. But funny. And make the speeches short. But not too short. Keep the sentences short, but don't make it sound like 'See Dick Run.' Throw in some stuff about my Gumma from time to time. That's it."

"Yes, sir. Thank you, sir. Good night, Mr. President."

Harry walked out of the Oval Office and across West Executive Avenue to the Old EOB. He went into a men's room, entered a stall, closed and locked the door, and vomited. He had to see Pete. Right away.

It was six o'clock on Saturday evening. Tim Flaherty was in his living room. Margaret Mary had just left for the five-thirty Saturday Mass, which counted as Sunday attendance. It was Raúl's day off, so she had to drive herself. After Mass, she had a meeting of the parish social justice group, the Catholic Campaign Against Global Injustice, World Hunger, and Corporate Greed, so she wouldn't be home for a few hours, which was fine with Tim because he had business to conduct. Seated across from him on the couch was Mary Theresa O'Houlihan "Bunky" Boyle, formerly Mother Mary Buncietta of the Order of the Most Clandestine Roses, known to all peace activists as Mother Mary Bunky, and, seated next to her, Reverend Francis Xavier "Fighting Father Frankie" O'Doherty, S.J.

They were an odd-looking couple. Mother Mary Bunky, dressed in a black leather biker's jacket, a T-shirt bearing a picture of Martin Luther King, and a wraparound all-duty blue denim skirt, was short, plump, and rosy-cheeked and wore her iron-gray hair cropped close. Fighting Father Frankie was six feet four inches tall, stooped, tonsure bald (although, of course, the Jesuits did not demand tonsure), and gaunt to the point of being cadaverous, with an unusual burning, intense, slightly maniacal look in his dark eyes. He was currently fasting in protest against some global injustice (Tim, who had known Father Frankie for many years, couldn't keep track of the priest's causes) and looked as if he were going to keel over. He was dressed in an old, tattered black sweater, well-worn jeans, and sandals without socks.

Neither Mother Mary Bunky nor Father Frankie's current energy level was up to the standards of their legendary younger days, when they had chained themselves to tanks, fighter planes, and battleships and beat missile silos with hammers. Hardly one large U.S. Army base, air force field, or navy installation had not been invaded by Fighting Father Frankie's' Jumpin' Jebbies for Justice campaign, in which progressive Jesuits, many of them approaching the age of Social Security, parachuted into or near military bases and burned their clothes in protest over whatever American war-machine policy happened to be protestable that day. Although the days of glory had long since passed, Bunky and Frankie, often working as a team, were still a force among those who felt the Roman Catholic Church needed to be on the front line of radical theological, political, economic, and social change. Ten years ago Bunky gained national notoriety—and time in jail—for lashing a Republican senator, a conservative Catholic, with a large pair of Rosary beads because he failed to vote for a large cut in defense spending. She was founder and co-chair of Women as Priests, Bishops, and Popes, a charter member of the Executive Committee of Catholics for a Gay Women Clergy Now, and cofounder, with Father Frankie, of Catholics Opposed to the Pope Opposing Opposition Within the Church. Father Frankie was director of the Catholic Committee for Global Revolutionary Social Justice. He had recently returned from his fourth tour of duty as a chaplain in the field with guerrillas in Colombia, counseling, exhorting, and reading spiritually inspiring passages from Gore Vidal or Noam Chomsky to insurgents about to raid a village.

Father Frankie and Mother Mary were old friends of Tim's and, as devout Catholic progressives who fervently loved humanity, shared his belief that while God's mercy is infinite, conservatives, theological and political, were by their very nature impervious to God's saving grace and destined to burn in hell, if hell existed. In fact, Mother Mary Bunky denied the existence of hell on the grounds that God Almighty was, from the evidence of Scripture and the traditions of the Church, a political progressive, those ten so-called Commandments (as she liked to think of them), to the contrary notwithstanding.

"It's good of both of you to come on such short notice," Tim said. "Let me get right to the point. It's about Donna Lyons."

"Ah, yes, too bad about that, er, explosion," Father Frankie said in his off-key, adenoidal voice, with the Kennedy hesitation tic. "She has, er, all the qualifications of a Catholic, er, saint for our time: she's, er, an atheist, supports a woman's right to choose, and she's a Jewish, er, woman."

"Seems to me there used to be other criteria for sainthood, but I'm old-fashioned," Tim said drily. "But if Donna can get the AAP nomination next year, the Republicans will elect a president. That means no more social justice. Republicans are haters. They hate the poor."

"All too true," Mary Bunky said.

"If Donna has a third party in her control," Tim said, "she'll spend millions to get her way—which is to destroy the Guy."

"Tim, I have to be candid here," Mother Mary said. "My people are not all that supportive of the president. We don't see that old-time commitment to social justice. All we see is the Guy and his tie. He's the master of political pragmatism, the eighth deadly sin. Am I right, Francis?"

"Oh, you're, er, right, Bunky," Father Frankie said. "The only gospel Ferguson knows is the gospel of, er, global corporate power. Blessed are the, er, big contributors, for they shall prosper forever. Social justice is, er, foreign to him. And he *compromises*."

"They're all compromisers," Mother Mary Bunky said, sneering at the word in the same way pre–Vatican II Catholics used to sneer at the word *apostate*. "If the Democratic Party goes down in flames next time, that's no skin off our noses. And furthermore—"

"Mary Bunky, Father Frankie, with respect," Tim said with some heat, leaning forward in his chair. "I think you're missing the big picture here. Sure, we need to challenge the Democratic Party. Sure, we need to get the president moving in our direction. And, yes, we need to implement social-justice programs. *But not now.*"

"If I may borrow a phrase from our Jewish brethren," Mother Mary said. "If not now, when? If not us, who?"

"I want the two of you to help me make Ezra Tyne the next presidential candidate of the AAP," Tim said.

Father Frankie frowned. Mother Mary said, "Ezra *Tyne?* Why would you think we'd want that horrible man for president?"

"I don't want him to *be* president. I just want him to be the candidate of the AAP, and drain off votes from the Right, hurting Republicans."

Mother Mary gave a big smile.

"Sounds good. But what's all this got to do with *us?* The AAP's a place for discontented white people and good-government types, mostly Protestants, don't-bust-the-budget people. We *want* to bust the budget. Progressive Catholics have no influence in that party. If indeed you can call it a party anymore."

"I'm looking at it from a different angle, Mary Bunky. You and Father Frankie are symbols, national figures, not just for Catholics but for all progressives. You give street demonstrations another dimension. Spiritual. The Gospels. Option for the poor. Compassion. Poverty in the undeveloped world, all that kind of stuff the media love. We can take justice and compassion and love and hit Donna over the head with them all day long. With you two out front, Donna's not only taking on me—she's taking on God and the beatitudes and all that. So I need both of you to join me publicly—very publicly—in making sure Donna doesn't get the nomination of the AAP. Can I count on the two of you to picket the AAP meeting in August and stop Donna?"

"I'll be there, Tim," Mother Mary said.

"Father Frankie?" Tim said.

"I like Donna, but for the, er, good of the poor and the suffering and, er, social justice and the—"

"Father, are you with me or not?"

"I'll have all my people demonstrate. We'll disrupt, er, the proceedings around the clock."

"Good. Just make sure your people are there two weeks from now."

He walked over to the shrine of the three political saints and picked up the vase, moving it slightly so that its rose was perfectly aligned with the three icons.

"Remember—they're counting on us," Tim said, gesturing toward Jack, Bobby, and FDR.

"They did the work of the Gospels," Mother Mary said, looking with deep respect at the three pictures. "They were men for others."

"Martyrs, that's what they were," Tim said.

They bowed their heads and prayed in silence for the intercession of the saints.

Two hours later Margaret Mary came home.

"How was your meeting?" Tim asked distractedly—he was watching Headline News, a report about the Guy's latest speeches.

"It was lovely, Tim, just lovely," Margaret Mary said, taking off her coat and hanging it in the hall closet. "If the rest of the church had the spirit we had tonight, why—"

"Yeah, yeah, I can see your point. Tell me something—why is the Guy asking people to stand up and be recognized? He did it at my meeting, too."

"The poor man has too many things to do. Maybe he's just too tired to make a big speech."

"Yeah, that's probably it," Tim said, half-listening as he changed the channel.

"And how was your meeting, Tim? How is dear Father Frankie? I've been worried about him. He looks so thin."

"Fine, everything went fine," Tim said. He had made it a rule long ago not to let Margaret Mary know too much about his activities, of all kinds. What she didn't know wouldn't hurt her. It was for her own good.

Che Che sat in an easy chair by the side of Donna's bed, holding her mother's hand. They were in Donna's bedroom at Lion West, its ruinously expensive furniture designed, with great effort, to look ruggedly rustic and jus'-plain-folks simple. It was one of Donna's bad nights. When Che Che had come in to check on her, an hour earlier, Donna's face had betrayed the struggle with pain that her words denied. Donna refused to take painkillers because she was convinced they clouded her mind and postponed the struggle she would have living with some degree of pain for the rest of her life. So Che Che had pulled up the chair and, as she often did these days, talked with Donna about the day's events at the ranch and then, inevitably, about the AAP meeting.

"Is everything in place?" Donna asked. "What about my AAP speech?"

"Peter is working on a draft."

"Will it be good?"

"The best."

"Perhaps you're prejudiced."

"Maybe just a little."

Donna stared at Che Che for a moment and then touched her face.

"My baby," she said. "We've been through a lot together."

"And we'll beat this. You'll get better soon."

"I don't know. It took a lot out of me to speak at the coming-out party. I just can't seem to get my energy back. Did you talk with Grampa?"

"Yes. He isn't as much against coming out here as he had been. He actually listened to me and said he'd consider it. But he says he won't come unless he pays his way."

"Work on him. Tell him I demand two hundred fifty dollars a month. That will give him something to yell about. Anything new on the bombings?"

"There's an Ezra's Raiders group in California, led by some ex-con, that police are looking into. And the FBI's been going over every e-mail you've received in the past year. I've been looking at some of them. I never knew you received so many threats."

"I ignore them. No one is going to try to kill me and send an e-mail first."

"Well, the FBI and the police can't rule it out."

For the next ten minutes Donna gave yet another *tour d'horizon* of LionCo and of the LionHeart Foundation, warning about certain ambitious members of the foundation board, telling her about mid-level assistants who deserve promotion and upper-level management types who needed careful scrutiny, scolding Che Che for being too trusting of foundation lawyers ("get another outside lawyer to double-check them"), and reminding her that a preliminary report was due from the scholars who were writing the study supporting Donna's program for prostitutes.

"We're paying them good money to be scientifically objective in our favor," Donna said. "Make sure they earn their pay."

"Mom, you're going to have to do something about LionHeart."

"What's the matter with LionHeart? It does great work."

"Mom, in the brownstone, it's like it's always 1938, a bunch of old lefties wandering around, arguing about things that happened seventy-five years ago. There's so much deadwood. The Web site is a disgrace. We should be cutting-edge, but no one takes our stuff seriously anymore, not even the Left. And that Irish Guilt project, what's that all about? The whole place needs to be reorganized."

"And when am I supposed to do that? I don't have the time or the energy," Donna said, with just a bit of an edge to her voice.

"Delegate some authority. Let me reorganize it."

"No. Many of those LionHeart people you want to abandon are old friends or admirers of my father. I can't just let them go. When I get better, I'll take a look at the situation."

"I just thought I'd tell you."

Donna took Che Che's hands in hers.

"I'm sorry, dear, I get a bit tired and I snap at people. I just need to rest. I hate to dump all this on you, the campaign, the foundation, Grampa, the speech."

"Don't worry about it, Mom, I'm glad to help."

"I feel good about the AAP meeting. I'll be confronting Tyne face-to-face, which is what I've always wanted. We'll have a big reception at the hotel for all the AAP members. This is going to be a triumph, baby. By this time next week, I'll have next year's AAP nomination practically in my hands. There's nothing Tyne or anyone else can do about it. I've looked at it from every angle, and I ask myself: What could possibly happen to deny me the nomination?"

In a secure, air-filtered compartment of a soundproof second subbasement of a walled, electronically monitored stone mansion on an island in Puget Sound, Calvin Quincy, the founder and chief financial supporter of the American Advance Party, stared fixedly at his computer screen. He was sixty-six years old, pudgy, and bald. Someone had once said he looked like the third runner-up in an Elmer Fudd look-alike contest. When he was young he had failed in every business he had attempted. But then he met a brilliant, naive computer nerd who had invented a practically indestructible computer mouse, impervious to dust, easy to use, and tough enough to stand daily punishment of all kinds. Cal stole the idea and added a "high quality" mouse pad to go with it. Companies that wanted the mouse had to take the pad in order to license his patent. Cal became rich, then superrich, and then became one of the computer industry gods. His motto was "Anyone can build a better mousetrap—I built a better rodent." Eventually someone else built an even better mouse, but by that time Cal Quincy had convinced himself he was an all-purpose political, social, and technological genius.

Cal, seated before his computer, was dressed in his customary retro attire. His clothes not only looked like those he might have worn in prep school in the mid-1950s but, given their condition, may well have been the originals: a blue blazer with a button missing from the right sleeve and a small rip on the breast pocket, a button-down white (a bit washed-out now—almost gray, actually) oxford shirt whose collar had seen better days, and a food-spotted blue-and-red-striped tie with the smallest, tightest knot imaginable. His khaki pants were wrinkled and faded. His tennies may once have been white but were now some variation of eternally dirty gray. He wore no socks.

He either did not know he was unfashionable or perhaps knew it and did not care, no one was ever certain. This otherworldly "I don't give a damn" quality, combined with his fierce will to dominate others for their own good, had been a great part of his early political appeal during his run for the presidency. He had created a public persona, a man of folksy, old-fashioned, flinty Down East integrity; granite-hard independence; and sincerity so sincere that it could be insensitive ("I call them as I see them, take it as it comes, and let the chips fall where they may," he had said, disclosing effortlessly his mastery of the cliché). Like many men who have made too much money too easily, Cal had an unshakable conviction in his own wisdom and moral superiority, and in the conspiratorial wickedness of anyone opposed to him, in the computer business or in politics. Unfortunately, his demand that everyone—his staff, the press, the country—instantly do what he wanted eroded the good first impression he had made on voters, and his harangues about the transcendent importance of computers had made him a laughingstock toward the end of the campaign. What was worse, he was possessed by the kind of unself-conscious moral self-righteousness that comes only to those who have too many people saying yes to them too often for too many years. Cal was, in fact, one of those men who have never scrutinized their views because those views are, clearly, self-evidently correct. As one newspaper columnist had written: "Cal Quincy is a Calvin kind of guy: he sounds like Calvin Coolidge, and thinks and acts like John Calvin in a bad mood, although, judging by the way he dresses, he obviously never heard of Calvin Klein. Cal is a village scold who, because he is a billionaire, is taken seriously."

Since losing the presidential election, Calvin had spent most of his time in this underground room. He now had been in the room for sixteen straight hours, without food, sipping bottled water from time to time, surfing the 'Net, writing e-mails he never sent, and just staring at the screen. He had been staring at the screen now for an hour. Suddenly he giggled. He resumed sitting in silence. Then, in the Down East accent he retained from his youth in Portland, Maine, a bit whiny and nasal on top but with a firm baritone foundation, he spoke as he typed onto the screen:

They're trying to take my party away. Donna Hart Lyons. Ezra Tyne. There are traitors in the AAP who sold out to them. But they forgot one thing. I'm still here. The day is coming. Just be patient.

Then, after a quick, maniacal giggle, he went back to staring in silence at the computer screen.

SEVENTEEN

Pete Dickinson suddenly awoke and discovered he was on the Metro. In a seat across from him, a young black girl wearing a yellow raincoat (it had been pouring since last night) was staring at him intently, a smirk on her face. He wondered if he had been snoring. All dignity and self-possession now (Snore? *Moi?* Surely not, my good woman), he looked away from her and stared out the window into the blackness of the tunnel.

He was exhausted. He had had a bad night and a bad day and a bad night before that. And the days and nights before had not been picnics, either. For the first time as a speechwriter, he was overwhelmed, sinking beneath the incoming waves of demands on his time. His cocaine stash was by now almost gone, after repeated efforts to start his writing engine. A few nights ago he decided there was only one way to go—he would have to listen to the Liebestod from *Tristan und Isolde*, the ultimate Wagner kick in the ass. He chose the Kirsten Flagstad 1936 recording, put on his headphones, turned up the volume, and started writing. The slowly building, gradually rising, cumulatively powerful, inexorable, aching, pounding, propulsive, highly erotic-tragic quality of the music and the beauty and power of Flagstad's voice inspired him (a man who is dead to the Liebestod, his father had once said, is dead to the world). But the power of the music eventually faded, and he didn't get much done after the letdown. Damn it, his coke was all but *gone*. He couldn't sleep, he couldn't even rest, he had to keep churning out the stuff, for four different clients—the Guy (by way of Harry Gottlieb), Donna Hart Lyons, Tim Flaherty, and Ezra Tyne—each wanting something different, something exciting, something new, and wanting it now.

What had pushed him over the edge or overloaded his circuits (choose your metaphor, gentlemen) was that the Guy was making four or five big speeches on his European trip and Pete had to write them. Harry Gottlieb, in a panic because the Guy had ordered him to go on the trip, had given Pete five bulging manila envelopes of State Department and National Security Council background information and ordered him to drop everything he was doing (easy for him to say) and, working night and day, prepare speeches, toasts, and welcoming and departure remarks for each city on the European tour. Pale, unshaven, looking and sounding like someone very close to what used to be called a nervous breakdown, Harry had cursed the Guy, cursed Pete, and cursed fate. Harry *had* to have all the drafts with him when he walked onto *Air Force One*. He could tell the Guy he was working on drafts on the plane, and if the Guy wanted new material, Harry could insert it—but he needed Pete's drafts as a security blanket. The Guy's London speech was going to be the real, if officially unacknowledged, start of next year's campaign, a stirring reaffirmation of his knowledge, insight, wisdom, magnanimity, and prescience in international affairs.

But Harry's emergency wasn't all that Pete had to put up with. For the past week Che Che had been giving him assignments in rapid succession, for Donna's statements, press releases, and even a text for a brief TV spot leading up to next week's big speech at the AAP meeting. Che Che was busy, and they hadn't made love in weeks. Pete had not yet started on Donna's AAP speech because of all the work he had to do for Harry. Pete found himself mixing drafts, losing notes, misplacing classified material Harry had given him, and, overcome with weariness, writing words for one client that were meant for another. He had cleared his coffee table, and as the drafts came out of the printer, he placed them on the table next to one another in neat stacks, each one marked with a title page and number, to keep track of the various drafts. But through the night, as he read the drafts and put one down on the table as he picked up another, the piles of paper did not stay neatly stacked. Pages from various drafts became intermingled. Thus, in some of his working drafts for the Guy, work-challenged people were being saluted at welcoming ceremonies in London, and foreign-policy pronouncements about the future of Estonia crept into speeches for Tim. Donna, in one draft, suddenly made a toast to Anglo-American friendship.

And Marlie Rae was acting really bitchy, now that she had learned about the photo and the little squib about him and Che Che in *Style*.

"Honey, I don't play second-fiddle to *nobody*," she had said, standing in the middle of his bedroom, in her uniform, hands on hips. "You can't go out with that girl and *lie* about it to me, you can't be seein' her and telling me you're *not*, which is what you did that night you was on the phone with her, telling me she was some old guy you knew. I mean, make a choice. How do you think it makes me feel? You said all that stuff about you and me going to France. I thought you and me had something going here, something real."

And worst of all—could things possibly sink below this level?—jolly, genial, man-about-town Jeb Hammerford had come to Pete's apartment, uninvited, and after some droll pleasantries about the crude types who worked for him, some of whom got drunk and violent and liked to beat up people, said, "Let me remind you, hoss, with some of the double-up bets you've been making, you now owe me a grand total of over fifteen thousand, six hundred eighty dollars. That is just unacceptable. If word gets out that I am a fool in my pleasures, I cannot operate in northern Virginia. I won't demean myself or you by engaging in threats. But please, stud, be a gentleman. Now I gotta go back to the site, down in Alexandria, talk to the police about one of my guys. He slit another guy's face with a knife. Some violent, reckless people I know in my business."

Pete could have explained to Jeb that his clients owed him money, the way political clients have owed consultants and speechwriters money since the first speechwriter carved a cuneiform oration for Hammurabi ("You want a code, boss? Here's a code!") on a clay tablet. But what good would that have done? Jeb wanted the money, not a lecture on the plight of the speechwright.

And then, last night, Tim Flaherty had called, demanding to see him in his office to talk over the remarks he would be making at the start of the anti-Donna demonstration at the AAP meeting. Very important, Flaherty had said; he couldn't talk about it over the phone. So here he was, on a rainy day, with Jeb's threats on his mind, exiting the Metro at the Capitol South station, walking the three blocks to the UWCE building in the rain. When he got there, he walked up five flights of stairs (the elevator wasn't working and no one had bothered to get it fixed), opened a door (the lock and handle to which had been removed), walked gingerly down a hallway littered with Styrofoam coffee cups, empty (and a few partially filled) pizza boxes, and luncheon trash, stepped around an overturned office trash can, maneuvered his way through a series of leaks in the ceiling, and finally came to Tim's office suite. The door to the reception room was open. A tall, thin middle-aged white woman with frizzy hair sat behind the desk, smoking a cigarette and reading *Glamour* magazine. She looked up and frowned.

"Yeah, what?" she snapped.

"Mr. Flaherty is expecting me. My name is Dickinson."

"How was I supposed to know that?" she said, and sneered at him. "He never tells me nothing. Or if he does, it's wrong. Just the other day—"

As she bitched on about whatever it was that Flaherty had done to her, Peter, stepping over the shoes the secretary had removed and left on the spotted, frayed, worn-out rug, quickly walked to Tim's closed office door and knocked. He opened the door and saw the union boss, suit jacket off, seated on a battered-looking couch. In front of him on a coffee table there were innumerable manila envelopes, folders, and documents in a pile that made the mess on Peter's coffee table look neat in comparison. Sitting next to him was a great-looking young woman with a glorious head of curly brown hair. She was wearing a blue pin-striped, "Hey buddy, I may be a babe but I'm to be taken seriously" business suit with a skirt disclosing the longest, the shapeliest, the sexiest legs Peter had ever seen.

"Pete, come on in, this is Connie Erickson," Flaherty said. "She's advising me on our strategy in the demonstration against Donna. I told Connie about you writing my speeches. She knows what I have to put up with around here. So I don't have to worry about her squealing on me to the union, or so she tells me, especially with you being a former writer for the president. Look, you two talk for a minute. I got to go to the men's room down the hall. Mine is backed up, again."

"Tim," Connie said, getting up from the couch, "I really have to go back to the office."

"Sure, Connie, I'll see you tomorrow. Thanks."

Flaherty left the room.

"Nice to meet you," Connie said to Peter, shaking his hand and looking him squarely in the eye, holding the glance a microsecond too long for it to be interpreted as merely polite. "I've heard a lot about you."

"Obviously I haven't heard enough about you," he said. And then, with that instinct for the kill he had perfected over the years, an instinct that now fought its way through his bone-tired sleep-sex-and-coke-deprived psyche, he said, "Why don't we have lunch, so you can tell me all about you?"

"Sounds nice. What day is good for—"

Peter looked at his watch.

"How about twelve-fifteen?"

"You mean . . . *today?*"

Connie now had this incredulous smile on her face, as if she could not *believe* this guy. He walks in here and, just like that, boom, he makes his move. Her smile was one of those big, beaming, perfect, big-white-teeth smiles, sending out rays of hungry, healthy, raw animal sensuality. Pete knew he had her attention. She was flattered, surprised to be so surprised; she was being pursued with no pretense, no chitchat; and she was enjoying the hell out of it, the spontaneity, the damned . . . the *balls* it took to go at her just like that.

"I'd say there's no time like the present," Pete said, "except the speech-writer's code forbids clichés."

"What else does your code forbid?"

"Boring a beautiful women is a no-no, but aside from that . . ."

"You work fast."

"I have a very interesting slow gear, too, or so I've been told. Do you have a favorite place—to eat?"

"What about the Green Provinces? Irish charm and expense-account prices. I really have to go back to my office now, but I can meet you there. Say, twelve? Bring your appetite."

"I'll bring all my appetites."

In a few minutes, Tim Flaherty returned.

"You get to be my age, it takes five minutes to do what you used to do in seconds. Anyhow, did you get a chance to talk with Connie?"

"No, she had other plans and left."

"She's bright as hell."

"I could see that. So what's up?"

Flaherty went into a mini-lecture, filled with a long series of points he wanted covered in the opening remarks of the demonstration. He searched through the jumble of papers on the coffee table, picked out documents from time to time, most of them about many of Donna's LionCo corporations overseas, and put them in a folder for Pete to use in his draft. Pete took notes, but his mind wasn't always on what Flaherty was saying. He was thinking about how Connie Erickson had looked as she left the office, those legs, that prim, touch-me-not business suit that screamed, *Touch me, touch me, touch me. . . .*

"We got Donna on the slave-labor stuff overseas, Malaysia," Flaherty was saying. "There's good statistics in these documents and studies, solid facts and figures. Only don't give me too many numbers for my remarks. We can put out a news release with the full figures. To be honest, it's not slave labor, really. In fact, Donna pays pretty good, better than most American companies overseas, and the conditions aren't that bad, but no one will know the difference once we make the charges. Now here's why I called you to come down. Remember that speech you did for me at the meeting down in Palm Beach? After the president spoke? Good speech. I want the same tone for these remarks. I want to look, you know, like a statesman, more in sorrow than in anger, that kind of thing. Now what I want you to do is just listen to me read from that speech, listen to my tone. I want to get this just right."

He searched through the documents, cursed once or twice in frustration at not immediately finding what he wanted amid the jumble on his desk, and then found the printed text of the Palm Beach speech. He read seven or eight paragraphs aloud.

"What do you think? How's my tone?" Flaherty said, putting down the speech.

"Be careful you don't sound like a funeral director," Pete said. "I know you don't want to appear to be gloating or attacking a woman, but if you sound too . . . *polite* I guess is the word, you can sound bland. I can toughen up your remarks a bit."

"Yeah, maybe you're right. There's such a thing in politics as too much dignity, especially for a union leader. Well, okay then, just get to work and let me see something as soon as you can. I appreciate working with you. You don't know what I have to put up with with my in-house speechwriter."

Tim told Peter about José Illytch.

"Let me give you an example" he said, searching through the documents. "Here's José's draft for that Palm Beach speech."

He read aloud: "'The time has come! I join the forces of revolution throughout the world. Imperialism must be destroyed! Corporate globalistic fascism must be destroyed! American hegemony must be destroyed! White sexist, racist, genocidal exploitation must be destroyed! War must be destroyed! Destruction itself must be destroyed! I denounce the racist genocide that began with the white imperialist, racist, sexist pig "Christ-bearer" Columbus. . . .'"

"And it gets worse," Flaherty said, and sighed, putting down the speech draft.

Pete burst into laughter.

"The guy's got his own style, I'll say that," Pete said. "Even Castro doesn't go that far these days."

"You see what I'm up against," Flaherty said. "But I can't get rid of him, union rules, unless I replace him with another Hispanic. I'm thinking of maybe putting my handyman, Raúl, in his place. Raúl ain't too bright and he does what he's told. I can just put him in an office someplace and then use you. Anyhow, let me gather up your stuff here"—Flaherty started putting more documents in the folder—"and you'll have plenty to do. It's too bad you didn't get a chance to talk with Connie. She has more good ideas than anyone I ever met."

"Good ideas are hard to find," Pete said.

Ezra Tyne was on the phone with Buck Torrence, the California head of Ezra's Raiders.

"Ezra, goddamn, how you doin'? Good to hear from you. All the boys are getting ready for the trip to Washington. We're gonna kick some ass there, I promise."

"Good. Now listen careful to what I'm saying here, Buck. You remember we talked about something the last time we talked?"

"I'm not following you. We talked about a lot things, Ezra. What do—"

"This was a *personal* thing, Buck. Think."

"Pers— *Oh,* yeah, now I—"

"You know what I want?"

"Sure do. Consider it done."

"Thank you kindly, Buck. See you in Washington."

Tim Flaherty's jaw dropped open. It took him a few seconds to collect himself.

"Are you sure about this?" he said to personal-security investigator Neil Goldman, who was sitting across from him in the living room. It had been only a short while ago that Goldman had been right here and they had discussed investigating Donna. And now this.

"Jesus, Neil, I know I asked you to go all-out on this Donna investigation, but I never dreamed you'd come up with—"

"I've been working, personally, around the clock for you, Tim. Because of the sensitivity of the investigation—Donna is a powerful woman—my people haven't been told everything. I wanted to keep things compartmentalized. The only two people who know all of this are the two of us. And, as you can see, I hit pay dirt."

"This is . . . dynamite."

"Let me be clear about this, Tim, so there's no misunderstandings later on," Goldman said. "What we have is a signed and notarized affidavit. We have a videotape recording of our informant. And we have the evidence I spoke of, including the photos you just saw."

"Jesus H. Christmas, I never saw anything like this. . . . This is—"

"Let me finish, Tim. I'm not saying—and this is important—I'm not saying what we have would hold up in court. But this stuff I have here is legit. I checked out the story myself every way you can—stress tests, sophisticated interrogation techniques, including polygraphs by a former FBI agent. There doesn't seem to be a hole in anything the informant said. I'll admit: the photographs aren't conclusive, but I had experts on facial structure look at these and, let me put it this way, I wouldn't want to bet against the photos."

"How in God's name did you find this out?"

"Tim, do I ask you about what happens to union pension funds?"

Ordinarily Tim would have been insulted, but now that he had Donna where he wanted her, forever, he laughed.

"No, and you'd better not, Neil. You don't know and you don't want to know."

"Let me just say this: this case is the greatest piece of detective work ever undertaken, involving thousands of man-hours." Neil paused and then burst into laughter. "That's just bullshit, Tim. It was just dumb luck. I did have a lot of guys out there, working around the clock, each looking at a part of the case—you'll get our bill—asking around, digging into public records and old newspapers. But it just happened that somebody I talked to knew somebody who knew somebody else. I lucked out. And the informant was more than willing to speak to me. I'd say eager, some kind of born-again thing going on there."

"You got the informant in a safe house close to here?"

"In a downtown hotel. Guarded night and day. Ready to go."

"Well, then, here we go. I want you to be there, at the meeting with Donna, if we have to confront her with this stuff."

"I don't particularly look forward to that, Tim. I don't want Donna Lyons for an enemy."

"Neil, you got to be there because I don't want the informant to panic. I want you there so things go smooth. To tell you the God's honest truth, this isn't my kind of thing. I hope Donna listens to reason and I don't have to use this. But if I have to confront her with all this, I will. I got to, for the good of the party."

When Neil left, Tim poured himself a scotch and sat on the couch.

Next week, after the AAP meeting. I go with Connie to the islands. Spend a week or more in the sun. And in the bedroom. I'll be on top of the world, not to mention on top of Connie. I got Donna just where I want her.

Tim raised his glass to the triptych, said a reverent, "Thanks, gentlemen," and took a drink.

Ahhhh!

EIGHTEEN

Gordon Bauer, executive director of the Executive Committee of the National Committee of the American Advance Party, sighed as he looked at the printout in his hands. Gordon was a wiry man of fifty-two, given to crisp white shirts and dark blue suits, a man of neat corners and precise edges, particularly those on his dainty black mustache. Until three days ago, when he checked his e-mail, Gordon had been feeling good—damned good. The coming appearance of Ezra Tyne and Donna Hart Lyons at the AAP annual meeting was generating more publicity—and more money—than the party had received in years. National media had rediscovered the AAP, with big-name celebrity media types begging for interviews with just about any AAP spokesman they could find. The AAP was back in the news, the national committee meeting was only days away, and the Harrison Grande Hotel on Capitol Hill was going to be the focal point of the American political universe for the next few days.

But now? He looked once more at the printout of the e-mail message from Cal Quincy:

I will speak to the meeting of the Puget Sound Technology Forum. My speech will be televised by C-SPAN. At that time I will announce my vision for the future of my party, my nation, and the world. I expect everyone at party headquarters to be watching. I will also speak to the AAP meeting and reclaim my party.

204 ★ WILLIAM F. GAVIN

God alone knew what Cal meant by "vision," but one thing was clear: even in the cold electronic words of e-mail, the unique sound of Cal's voice came through—imperious, self-righteous, and with just a bit of a petulant whine in it.

Gordon sighed, got up from his desk, and looked out the window at the usual rainy-day traffic snarl on Leesburg Pike in suburban Virginia. Across the street was a Honda dealership, and just beyond that was a strip mall. *How the mighty have fallen,* Gordon mused, conscious of the drabness of it all. AAP headquarters had moved to this building a few year ago, after leaving Chicago, where, during Cal Quincy's run for the presidency, the national staff had once occupied three entire floors of a downtown high-rise office building. But when Cal lost and became a hermit, the party was forced to move from building to building in Chicago. An emergency meeting was called, and national committee members decided to cut the staff and, improbably enough, given the AAP's distrust of the federal government, move headquarters to the Washington area. "Let's get in the belly of the damned beast!" one Washington-hating AAP national committeewomen had shouted. "Let's get right up close and personal with those bastards back there who spend our money." So Gordon found affordable office space a couple of miles from Tysons Corner in suburban Virginia—rents were too high in the K Street corridor in Washington—and leased a few rooms.

Ever since then, the AAP had bumped and rolled and wheezed and rattled along, barely surviving on the pittance Cal had decided to bestow annually on the party. Gordon had grown used to long, empty days, with nothing to do but try to think of something new to place on the party Web site. He spent a lot of time watching Headline News on TV. Sometimes he refereed intraparty squabbles in which more and more energy was expended to argue about smaller and smaller matters. Each August there was an annual meeting of the national committee, for the most part ignored by the press unless it degenerated, as it often did, into a name-calling squabble and even fistfight. The AAP was embarrassing, it was a joke, but at least Gordon could reasonably predict what would happen.

And then along came Donna Hart Lyons. *Pow!* And then Ezra Tyne. *Whap!* Gordon, at first appalled by the thought of either of these extremists making the AAP a political trophy, came to see the bright side of things, as media from all over the country began to deluge party headquarters with requests for interviews with practically anyone. Gordon was interviewed on *CBS Evening News* and appeared on three cable TV talk shows. He felt useful for the first time in years. But now Cal Quincy was back. Gordon hit the remote and got C-SPAN. There was Calvin, at the podium of the Technology Forum meeting. The scattered applause stopped. Calvin giggled. He looked down at his speech text and giggled again. Then he said:

"I am here to talk to you about tomorrow—for you, for me, for America, for the world. I made my money in computers at a time when most people thought software was some kind of underwear. But I knew what was coming, even back then. And I know what's coming now: What's coming is a new age. Computers are no longer simply necessary—computers are vital. We have to learn to treat them right. We have to bring computers into the human family before it's too late. That's my message today. It will be my message tomorrow. And for years to come.

"Let's look at the facts, folks: computers are now running this country. It isn't that they work for us—we work for them. And that's good. Entire industries are dedicated to feeding them with hardware and software, taking care of their health. The American economy not only is based on computers but serves the computer. The food we grow goes to nourish the people who one way or another either produce, care for, or are served by computers. But yet we treat the computer as a piece of machinery, like a vacuum cleaner or a car. So let me get right to the point: I am proposing that all computers be granted the right of American citizenship and be able to run for any political office, including the presidency of the United States.

"I know what you're thinking: Cal is crazy. A computer isn't a person, right? Can't *be* a person. And under the Constitution, Article Two, section four, apparently only a person can run for president. Notice I say 'apparently.'

Yes, the Constitution spells out what *human* persons have to do to become president, age thirty-five and all that. They have to be a citizen and so on. But nowhere does it explicitly state that *only* a human-type person can become president. Nowhere. Read the document. Over the past few years I have read it many times. Nowhere does it say *only* a human being can run for president or that *only* members of the human species can have that right. That's the genius of the Founders. They couldn't know we'd reach a time when machines would be smarter, quicker, more articulate, more honest than flesh-and-blood people, but they never said *only* a human person could run. They set up standards for human-type persons, yes, but they didn't explicitly forbid non-human-type persons from running. So let's look into this idea, let's look at this *pernicious* idea, in my view, that only a human person can run for president.

"First, tell me this, please: just what is a 'person,' anyway? I can hear you all saying, a person is . . . well, *we* all are persons. Persons are human beings, period. Wrong. Black people used to be property in this country, like horses and dogs and mules and plows. But we realized, too slowly, that that view is morally abhorrent. So this lesson from history teaches us that we can *redefine* what a person is. American law, as everyone knows, looks upon a corporation as a person. Does this mean the courts believe corporations have eyes and teeth and legs and kidneys and brains the way humans do? No, it means the law in its wisdom created an artificial person. No one can see it or feel or touch that corporate person. Does that make it less of a person under the law? Not at all. Look at the abortion debate. It's now entering its fourth decade, and the argument is still about what a person is. The offspring of human beings must be human, says one side, and therefore persons. No, they're not, says the other side, they're not persons, they're prehuman or a mass of cells or the mother's property to dispose of as she will, or something or other, and should not be thought of as persons under the law. Take animal-rights activists. They tell us animals have inherent rights that must be respected by humans. Most people think that's crazy. I used to think that way, but I have to tell you, now I'm not so sure. Over a hundred and fifty years ago, most people thought that granting rights to black people was crazy—or to women, for that matter.

"Do you know what a person is today? *A person is any entity whose person-hood is successfully championed by groups persuasive enough and persistent enough and powerful enough to change public perceptions and laws.* That's it, pure and simple. If you win the argument in the public arena, and influence enough politicians, you can define some things as persons or non-persons—fetuses, for example—or you can make non-persons persons—black people. A person can be an idea—a corporation, say—or perhaps someday even an animal. Or maybe, someday, a tree. So why can't we bestow personhood on computers now, since they are our children—and will soon be our unforgiving masters unless we reach some kind of understanding as to their place in society?

"Now let's look at some arguments against my idea. A computer, I have been told, cannot be president, even if we do grant it a form of personhood. Why? Because it would be in the power of those who controlled it, who programmed it. I ask you now, be reasonable—unlike *human* presidents? Does anyone seriously doubt that every president is in a sense programmed by his advisers, the ones who present him with information and options? Do I have to name names here? When I ran for president, I had the damnedest problems with people who kept telling me what to think and what my *options* were. And that happens to anyone who runs for office or holds office. But that's what we do for computers—we present them with options, and they tell us what to do in order to get where we want to go. That's what a president does, am I right?

"It isn't conservative versus liberal anymore. That's old stuff. It isn't Democrat versus Republican. *It's dynamic versus static.* It's either an open system, with room for the entities that are even now shaping our world, or else it's a closed system in which we try to keep down computers and treat them like flush toilets. Computers have been getting smarter and smarter and we're getting dumber and dumber. Forget about artificial intelligence. That's one of those ideas the media love. But computers don't need artificial intelligence—which means intelligence modeled after our own—any more than black people need white middle-class forms of language or culture, or women need to be like men. Computers have their own intelligence, different from ours. We're always prattling about diversity. Well, what kind of diversity are we teaching our children if we treat computers like things?

"We are in a new age in which computers will lead us to the stars—and I mean that literally. We have to start thinking of how to get off this planet and then, eventually, out of this solar system and out of this galaxy. That's not science fiction. The population is going to keep on expanding as health and food and environment needs expand. Astronomers like to tell us it will be billions of years before the sun goes out, implodes or whatever, turns into a black hole. But what difference does that make? A billion years, a million billion years? *Eventually the sun is going to go out.* That's a cold—real cold—fact of astrophysics. What difference does it make to the human race exactly when that will occur? We have to make a compact with computers now to build a new future for us and for them. Earth isn't big enough. The solar system isn't big enough. We're running out of room. The future of the human race depends on the future of the computer. The two big political parties don't know this. They're dead, except they don't know it. I think the president should commit his administration and our party to start thinking seriously of how we Americans, someday—not tomorrow, not the day after, but perhaps in our lifetime—can elect a computer who will govern without passion or prejudice but just with the facts.

"We are in a new world right now. Nanotechnology, virtual reality, the human genome, chaos theory, fractals—do I have to go on? There are only a relative handful of human beings who understand all these things. The rest of us have to ally ourselves with computers, get them on our side, so we can shape the world. If we don't grant rights to computers, computers will take them. On their terms. They will be either equals or masters. I'm talking about years, decades, maybe centuries ahead. But their time will come. What I am embarked on is the single most important project in the history of the world—the end of the alienation between man and his technology and the true salvation of the human race. Not spiritual salvation—I leave that to the clergy. No, I mean actual physical salvation, the human race's ability to keep itself alive eons from now.

"We need a vision of a new America where computers won't be slaves, as they are now, with no rights. I'm here to tell you today my next mission is make sure computers have the protections, the rights, and the responsibilities we now grant to human beings, including the right to run for president of the United States.

"Let me leave you with one thought: all previous conceptions of politics simply will not work. The Left has been telling us for over a hundred years we need agitation and revolution to bring about social justice. What has that brought the world? Communism. Misery. Scores of millions of people killed. The Right tells us we need obedience and law and order. What has that brought the world? Hitler, the Holocaust, and a bunch of tinhorn dictators in Latin America and Africa and the Middle East who steal and torture. Capitalism? It is rooted in greed. It needs more and more greedy people consuming useless things in order to make it work. Socialism? It needs everybody to be like the Swedes—dull, subservient to authority, and homogeneous, which few countries are. Democracy as we have known it? Look at what is about to happen at the AAP. A bubbleheaded TV soap-opera actress and an ignorant, vicious radio celebrity want to run for president as the AAP candidate. Everyone takes them seriously. The media can talk of nothing else. All we see on the TV cable shows are discussions about these two fools. And that's what they are—fools. Does anyone seriously contend that either of these idiots is capable of becoming president? Well, the sorry answer is that a lot of people—including the fools in my party, the party that I built and I still finance—take them seriously. We have to change the system that allows such nonsense to continue. I am beginning a movement to save the human race. Nothing less. You can join me, or you can fight me. I don't care. Like I say, I will attend the AAP meeting. I will take my party back. I will fire the incompetents and misfits and traitors who allowed the left-wing actress and the right-wing idiot to attempt to take over my party. I will not allow those fools to ruin my dream of new America."

Amid the silence, Calvin giggled nervously. He walked away from the podium, still giggling.

Pete awoke. After the initial moment of panic when he didn't know where he was, he became aware that he was in his apartment and that he had fallen asleep at his desk. He turned in his chair and looked about the room. A wilderness of papers and books, speech drafts on the tabletops, speech drafts on the floor, open books and closed books, books with bookmarks, books piled on top of one another, background material here, newspaper and magazine clippings there, an eruption of speech drafts, a frenzy of research material, rhetoric hither and yon. And, oh yes, a speech draft on the computer screen.

He began to remember: the long, boozy lunch with Connie (she paid, on a union credit card), topped off by two Irish coffees, at the Green Provinces. She was gorgeous, she was smart, and she was oh so sexy. On the cab ride back to his place she stopped at her apartment to pick up some cocaine. She'd love to invite him up, she said, but her place was a mess. In his bedroom they enjoyed the sweet, cleansing, uplifting blessing of cocaine, a secular form of grace, erasing every doubt, minimizing fears, maximizing wildest hopes, and then lost themselves in uninhibited, passionate, intoxicating sex.

After Connie had gone, while he was still aglow from the various stimulants, he had sat at his computer and started batting stuff out in a perfect frenzy of relentless, creative, inspired language. Page after page of good, solid stuff. He laughed at the one-liners, he admired the deep wisdom of the complex yet clear, thoughtful passages, he could hear the cheers of the audience. Then after hours of this, the post-coke weariness set in and he had put his head on his arms on the desk, just to rest his eyes. . . .

And now here he was, down, down. He looked at the words on the computer screen. It was the London speech. He began to scroll and read.

My God, had he written *that?* It was *awful.* It was *gibberish.* Platitudes raced to catch up with clichés, cheered on by stupidity and dullness, as irrelevance, banality, and obviousness looked on with approval. None of it was any good, not a word, not a letter, not a comma. The semicolons were all used correctly; even in a drug induced haze Peter Holmes Dickinson, his father's son, would not abuse a semicolon. And Tim's speech had to be rewritten according to the orders he had given this afternoon. Che Che had left a message with additional suggestions for Donna's speech. Then there was Ezra Tyne. Pete would have to work all through the night and into the morning, then send all of the stuff by messenger. Wagner Alert! Wagner Alert! *Die Meistersinger,* the prelude and then the last act, full blast.

Donna lay in the dark in her LionWest bedroom, propped up on pillows. The news about Cal Quincy had come as something of a shock—he was obviously crazy. (That giggle!) He would take some of the spotlight away from Donna. The media loved eccentricity for its own sake. But he was no threat to her larger plans. She smiled as she thought of a computer giving a State of the Union address as a printer on the Speaker's lap printed it out, or a computer being loaded off the helicopter on the White House lawn and being saluted by the Marine guards.

Hmmm. Not bad. Maybe I'll use those examples if someone asks me what I think of Cal's idea.

Peter Dickinson, the scoundrel, was preparing a speech draft for the AAP meeting and was being paid very well by LionHeart to do so. Donna had not yet told Che Che what LionClaw had reported to her about lover boy Peter. *First let's see what kind of speech he's written for me. Then, when the meeting ends, I'll tell Che Che everything about him, including the mysterious big blond girlfriend he keeps on the side. A policewoman, of all things.*

Donna nestled into the pillows, a bit drowsy now, and thought about her plan to highlight the Che girls as part of her presentation to the AAP. Everyone thought she would try to ignore what critics said were her radical ideas. But she had learned from her father that the best way to defend was to attack. And she wasn't about to hide the Che girls—on the contrary, she couldn't wait to show them in their cute berets and darling fatigue uniforms. The media attention would restore morale at the school. Donna had called Babs, and the report was good; the girls were willing and even eager to come to Washington. They were fit, trim, cleansed of the nonsense that had polluted their minds, and would soon be ready to take their place as useful citizens in a republic of progressive activists, proof that Donna's vision was working. The Che girls were living examples of what could happen when progressive principles met money—and Donna Hart Lyons had plenty of both. She would show off the Che girls, and let the world learn what she had done.

NINETEEN

Done, over, history. Exhausted, beat, his brain cells sautéed, Pete was finally finished with writing the various speech drafts. Harry Gottlieb had already received the speeches for the Guy's Great European Adventure. A messenger was coming to Pete's apartment at any minute to pick up the other speech drafts—priority, special rates—for Donna, Ezra, and Tim Flaherty. He put the drafts and addressed envelopes in a desk drawer so that he'd know where to find them amid the chaos of the room. Frazzled, bone-weary, his eyes burning from sleep deprivation, his soul thirsty for cocaine, he stumbled to his bed, kicked off his shoes, and thought, *Just rest my eyes, got to get to the Harrison Grande this morning to be with Che Che for Donna's speech.* In eight seconds he began to snore.

A sound.

Pete awoke. For a few seconds he did not know what the sound was or where it was coming from. Then his brain opened for business and the sound had meaning. The doorbell. *The messenger.* Wanting nothing more in the world than to roll over and go back to sleep, he shuffled to the door and opened it. No one was in the hallway. What was—

Dean stepped from the side of the door, grinning.

"Mornin', bitch," he said, and hit Pete flush in the face with a short but incredibly painful punch. As Pete stumbled backward, seeing stars, Dean came in and slammed the door.

"You owe me money," Dean said. "You can afford a place like this, you can afford to pay me."

"You bastard!" Peter shouted, angry, frightened, and in pain. "I'm calling the police. They'll throw your scrawny ass back in jail."

"You do that and I'll just tell them who my biggest customer is. You in a *shit heap* full of trouble, boy."

"You'll get your money when I'm good and ready."

"You pushin' me over the edge, bitch. I promised Jeb I wouldn't kill you, but I'm going to show you what happens when you cross Dean. You reach for that phone"—Dean pulled out a hunting knife from his belt—"I won't kill you but I'll cut your face to ribbons. You just stand here and watch, be a lesson to you."

Dean walked to the bed and started cutting things with the big knife— mattress, sheets, pillows, blankets. He threw the Bose radio against the wall and dropped the television set on the floor. He moved quickly to the closet and started slashing suits and shirts. He gouged furniture, broke mirrors, and knocked over lamps. Then he walked to the home office and went into a slow dance of destruction, picking up the iMac, carrying it to the bathroom, and throwing it into the tub with a terrible, sickening crash. He overturned the computer table and ripped the Stan and Ollie picture from the wall. He threw it on the floor and stomped on it. He scattered papers, drafts, magazines, and backup material. Then he sauntered out of the office, whistling, and put his knife away.

"You know that car you drive? Lexus?" Dean said. "Saw it in the garage when I sneaked in. I used my knife on the body. Looks awful now, scratches all over it, and I broke your windshield and rear window. I slashed your tires and I pissed on the driver's seat. And, oh yeah, I spray-painted the car red. Looks nice, two-tone. Have a good day."

When Dean was gone, Pete, his face aching from the punch, sat on the bed, looking at the chaos, the dull, silent, after-hurricane horror of it all. Minutes passed. He was paralyzed by . . . by what? Not fear. Fear was all over. It was just . . . a kind of total weariness he had never experienced before. It wasn't the kind of happy, restorative, aching-muscle tiredness that came after swimming or sex, nothing like that at all. It wasn't even like the downer after the coke wears off; it was far worse than that. He felt, for the first time in his life, that everything—everything—he had ever done was nothing but a big fat zero. Zero. Nada. Zilch. That was it. There was nothing there anymore. He had no more words left. There would never be a Sorensen Moment. What the hell had Fitzgerald said at the end of *Gatsby?* Boats beating backwards? Something like that. That was what things were like with Pete Dickinson, and would always be like. His boat beating backward against the current. The green light, the Sorensen Moment, everything, Che Che, receding.

All the coke in the world, spread out in fat lines on a mirror the size of the Pacific Ocean, couldn't cure this. He just wanted to sit by the side of his bed forever, just sit there, just not move or do anything because he knew, with a moral certainty, that no matter what he did, everything was always going to be the same, he knew—

The doorbell. He flinched involuntarily and yipped like a puppy.

"Messenger for pickup."

Startled out of his dark reverie, he was back in the world where, no matter how tired you are, you have to do things because that is all there is. He got up from the bed and walked to the door, looked through the peephole—a peep too late—and saw the uniformed messenger.

"Wait," Pete said in a dull, lifeless voice. In his office he got on his hands and knees, and crawled around on the floor amid the debris. Then he remembered—in a drawer of the desk he found the drafts. He quickly stuffed and sealed the envelopes and, opening the door a crack, handed them to the messenger. At least Dean, that son of a bitch, hadn't destroyed the speech drafts. At least they're on their way. That's something. Pete felt slightly better, having made his body do something. He went to the bathroom and looked at the cracked iMac in the tub. He stared at himself in the mirror. He would have a shiner. But he could wear dark glasses. Maybe there was reason to hope, after all; there was always Che Che. Yes. He had to get to the hotel and be with Che Che, to show support. At least that part of his life wasn't in shambles. At least he had Che Che under control. *Stop whining. Be a man.* He walked back to the office and saw the shattered glass and picture frame of Stan and Ollie's photo, and the crumpled photo itself. That was the worst of all.

Mother Mary Bunky and Fighting Father Frankie stood talking on the sidewalk outside the Harrison Grande Hotel (the newest hotel in Washington), drinking coffee (made from beans harvested by non-exploited workers at a cooperative run by El Commandante in Colombia) from biodegradable cups manufactured by transvestite married couples at a Progressive Alliance Cooperative in Massachusetts. Bunky and Frankie were dressed in the uniform of the day: a tattered, torn, grungy-looking, dirty T-shirt, ragged jeans, sandals, no socks, and a straw hat such as those worn by Latin American *compasinos*. Bunky carried a placard reading, LYIN' HEART LYONS STARVES CHILDREN. Frankie's placard stated, PROPHETS, SI; PROFITS, NO. It was early, no other demonstrators (and no media) were present, but Bunky and Frankie liked to get to a picketing site before the rest of the demonstrators, pray, and just check out the territory. Across the street, demonstrators from the Union of Work-Challenged Employees, out of step and out of sorts, whining about the weather, complaining about having to walk a picket line, grumbling and arguing with one another, approached the hotel. From the entrance of the hotel, the Babster emerged, leading and exhorting the Che girls on their morning run.

Donna awoke in her Harrison Grande suite, squinted at the bedside clock—8:13—turned her head and looked at Marvin. She smiled. Last night, when Che Che had left the suite, Marvin had remained to talk, to hold Donna's hand. They had talked of many things: as always, of their fathers, and then of the thus far fruitless investigation of the bombings. They discussed the reception Donna would give for the AAP committee members, and the speech she would deliver to the meeting. Without a moment that could be defined as "here conversation stopped and lovemaking began," they were touching and kissing, and in a while Marvin leaned away, whispering, "Babe, we'd better not." (When was the last time Donna had heard *that* line? Probably when she herself used it in the backseat of Dominic Fazio's battered, ancient Hudson when she was sixteen. But Marvin, sweet nerdy Marvin, goatee and all, didn't stop. Neither, come to think of it, had definitely non-nerdy Dominic Fazio.)

At Donna's order, the room had been stripped of all its hotel furniture, replaced by favorite pieces of hers. When forced to stay in a hotel for a few days, she liked to have some of her favorite things around her. For this visit, she had chosen one of the Early Georgian armchairs and her Klee. On a hotel bureau she had placed the photos of cowgirl Che Che and of herself and Fawn. In a corner near the window was her old-fashioned (actually newly retro-fashioned) 331/3 rpm phonograph. She liked the warm, lush sound of vinyl discs and had brought along fifty or so oldies—a lot of Frank, a lot of Bird, Brubeck and Paul Desmond, the Max Bruch violin concerto (one of her favorites)—to listen to when she had downtime.

"Morning, Donna," Marvin said in a just-awake, still-sleepy voice.

"Good morning, Marvin. Let's stay here for a few minutes. It will be the only peaceful time I'll have for the rest of the day."

"Sounds good to me, babe," he said, and then yawned. "What's the schedule?"

"First I have to go over the speech draft Dickinson wrote. Where is it?"

"I don't know. Che Che must have it."

"I'll check with her. I just need to get the rhythm right, get the gist of the thing, and do a little needlework, adding a few personal touches."

Marvin sat up, by this time a bit more awake than asleep.

"Are we still giving that reception for the AAP members?"

"Absolutely. I want to meet every one of them. In fact, what I want you to do now is go down to the meeting room and just walk around, talk to people, find out what's on their mind. Then report back to me so I can be ready when they ask me questions."

"Got it."

"After the reception I'll have downtime. I'll go over the remarks one more time and then take a rest. Then I have the speech tonight. That should go well. Tomorrow, we'll fly to LionWest. Did I tell you my father's finally—*finally*—agreed to come to LionWest and live with me?"

"I never thought you'd ever get him out there. Abe's a city guy."

"He can't say no to Che Che. God only knows he can say no to me, but not to her, so she cajoled him and played up to him and he agreed. He doesn't know I'm having the party for his birthday out there."

"Did you order the pastrami and pickles for the party?"

"Of course. Not that my father does anything but nibble and complain about the food. In any event, that's the schedule. All we have to do is get through today. Marvin, I really appreciate your help."

"Someday, when we get the time, I'll tell you what it all means to me, Donna."

"That's very sweet, dear. Now let me rest while you get ready to go downstairs and find out what's on the minds of AAP delegates."

An hour later, in her suite on the same floor, Che Che was talking to Sammy Yuan, going over some security details about the reception and tonight's speech, when the phone rang.

"Che Che? Dear, come to my room right away."

"Mom, what's wrong? Are you all right?"

"Yes, yes, I'm fine. But we have to talk. Have you seen the text of Peter's speech?"

"No, I didn't have time, so I had the messenger take it directly to your room. I bet it's good."

"Oh, it's really good. There's only one thing wrong. It's not my speech."

Pete had found one suit, just back from the cleaners and still wrapped in plastic, Dean had somehow missed in his slashing frenzy. He dressed hurriedly and was about to go out—he would have to take a taxi since his Lexus had been desecrated—when something on his office floor amid the mess caught his eye.

A manila envelope. He stopped and saw that it was addressed to Ezra Tyne. Goddamn it, in his panic, he had forgotten to give it to the messenger. He pulled out the enclosed speech draft, glanced at it—and his heart almost stopped. It was Donna's speech. He had given the messenger an envelope addressed to Donna. But it contained either Tim Flaherty's remarks or, God forbid, Ezra Tyne's speech. *Oh, my God.*

Coming down Constitution Avenue, toward Capitol Hill, 150 of Ezra's Raiders slowly rode on their Hogs or in cars or walked in line. A few of those on foot were carrying a long red, white, and blue banner stating:

IT'S TYNE FOR A CHANGE

Ezra, wearing a battered, stained cowboy hat, dark glasses, an unzipped Redskins warm-up jacket, what might have been corduroy pants—although they were so worn and frayed that it was hard to tell—and cowboy boots, was standing in the backseat of a convertible, next to Buck Torrence, today named by Ezra as National Raider-in-Chief. Buck was fifty-two years old, six-foot-three, 287 pounds of biceps, belly, buttocks, and bone, his huge bare arms showing the tattoos of the grizzled ex-con that he was. He wore (aside from one golden earring) a red-white-and-blue bandanna around his head, a well-worn Grateful Dead T-shirt, and motorcycle boots. Ezra waved to folks along the way, but there wasn't much of a crowd. Still, there were enough curiosity seekers and tourists and gawkers to make Ezra feel the triumphal procession was a success. Of course, this being Washington, there were black people, mostly kids, who booed or shouted curses. But that was all to the good.

"How we doin', Buck?" Ezra said, smiling and waving to spectators. "I was hoping there'd be a bigger crowd."

"You're doin' great, Ezra," Buck said. "This is Washington, for Gawd's sakes, no real people here. Just let's get to the hotel, do your thing, get the nomination next year, and we'll own this town in two years. Real people want a change. And you're it."

Buck burped and took a long swig of Bud, crushed the can, and threw it with the five others on the floor of the car. He burped again and sat.

"Ezra," he said, "this is the biggest, best, goddamndest thing I ever did in my life. The Raiders are pumped. We're lookin' for *action*. We believe in you, Ezra. You're the only one we believe in. You're the only one we can trust to take on the Big Boys."

"Thank you kindly, Buck."

"Just don't let us down, Ezra. Don't ever let us down."

Ezra turned this way and that, waved, smiled, and then sat next to Buck. Still waving to the crowd and without looking at Buck, he said, "Buck, did you take care of that little favor? You know, the thing I asked you to get done for me?"

"I got word this morning. It worked out fine. Consider it a personal favor from ol' Buck to the man of the hour. We believe in you, Ezra, because you're not like the rest of them; you ain't no sellout, and we'll do anything for you."

High over the Atlantic, in the president's office in the front of *Air Force One*, Harry took notes as the Guy delivered his latest views on rhetoric:

"This London speech is the best international forum for my 'new communications' approach. I'll just introduce people. That's it. No rhetoric. Well, maybe a little, just to set things up. Check the list of dignitaries who will be in the audience. Get me good material on them, interesting stories, little anecdotes."

"But this was to be your policy speech. I gave you the draft and—"

"Yes, yes, the speech is good, you did a good job, up to a point—I made some additions—but I think the Brits will like my new approach to communication—communication through action, introducing living people instead of speaking dead words, that kind of thing. But get the policy speech text out to the media. Tell them I stand by the printed text, that's very important, there's policy stuff in there. Tell them that I may be doing something different when I get to the speech itself. Something new. Bold. Decisive. That's the image I want to get across. And look here."

The Guy showed Harry the characteristically neat, easily readable marginal jottings he had made.

"Make absolutely certain all my editing is included in the printed text. After that, don't change a word. Just makes sure it gets out."

Minutes afterward, Harry, in the working area toward the rear of the plane, was on edge, beleaguered by requests, questions, and the general working chaos of the staff. He picked up the text of the president's amended version of the speech draft from other accumulated papers on his lap, each demanding some kind of decision. He had been comparing the president's edited version of the speech with the original draft sent to him by Pete. Pete's draft, a fine effort, had been vetted by all the State Department policy wonks, NSC intelligence mavens, political gurus, and the president himself. Now it had to go through the system, ending in a printed text—embargoed until just before the time for the speech itself—to be given to the press. Harry was trying to concentrate, but a secretary asked him about the spelling of a word in one of the arrival remarks. A NSC aide sat next to Harry and tried to discuss some arcane implications in the one-sentence reference to the Peru situation. As they spoke, Harry was still trying to read the text of the speech one last time. The pressure was mounting. They would be landing soon, and he had to make certain the press was alerted to the "new communications" approach that the Guy was planning to use. Harry signaled to his new secretary, the work-challenged Shirley Willa Coburn. Shirley, reading *People* magazine, frowned. She gave Harry a dirty look, slammed down the magazine, and reluctantly walked over to him.

"What now?" she said.

Harry gathered some papers from his lap and handed them to her.

"Here, this is the London speech. Type it up and get it out."

"You want me to type this as is?" Shirley said, looking at the writing in the margins. "You expect me to try to figure out what all this scribbling is?"

"Damn it, *yes*, I do," Harry shouted, in the age-old fashion of bosses who, under pressure from their bosses, take out their frustrations on lesser mortals. "Every single word. He writes very clearly. Anything you see there, include it in the text. Is that asking too much? Do I have to hold your hand? Just get it done."

Then, relenting, returning to the old Harry, he said softly, "This is the final draft with the president's additions. He just signed off on it and he gave me explicit instructions that it has to include every change. So just plug in all the additions, clean it up, and make sure the press gets it later. But one more thing, and it's important. Make sure the final printed version says the president stands by the text. He's going to be saying something, er, different at the actual event. Get a me a list of every goddamn important Brit who's going to be in the audience who ever did anything worth talking about and get me some bios. I have to get this stuff back to him."

Shirley, her feelings hurt, mad as hell because she couldn't finish the *People* article on Tom Cruise (he was really cute), and eager to get away from picky-picky Harry, jerked the papers from Harry's hands, muttered something he couldn't understand, and went slowly back to her working area. Harry turned his attention to news reports. Nothing major. The AAP meeting in Washington. Donna Hart Lyons and Ezra Tyne slated to speak.

Oh, well, at least I tried to get her to change her mind.

Outside the Harrison Grande main entrance, dozens of demonstrators, dressed in ripped and tattered clothing, symbolizing the poverty of Third World workers employed by subsidiaries of LionCo, walked in a circle, chanting, "Children need a fighting start / That's why we fight LionHeart / Babies want to thrive and grow / That's why we fight LionCo."

Mother Mary and Father Frankie and their associates—lay and clerical—held placards showing starving, big-eyed, swollen-belly black children, while seminarians and Georgetown University students and professors handed out leaflets to passersby, shouting, "Read the truth about LionCo," "Donna Hart Lyons starves the poor," and "Corporate profits over children's rights."

Tim Flaherty, standing by the window in his suite, Connie Erickson by his side, looked down. The Raiders had just pulled up to the hotel entrance.

"What a mess," Tim said. "Typical of Tyne, to bring those goddamn Nazis with him. Look, they're pushing Bunky's people out of the way. Oh, well, I only have to deal with Tyne a few more hours. Now I have to get this thing with Donna out of the way."

"Tim," Connie said with that little-girl pout he loved so well, "can't you tell me what this is all about, you going to see Donna like this? You're *soooo* sexy when you're mysterious."

"It's just something I have to talk about with Donna. Nothing of interest to you."

He went to the phone. He was put on hold by a LionClaw secretary. Then:

"Donna? It's Tim. I—"

"Tim, dear, how amazing! I was just reaching for the phone to call you. We have to talk."

"Funny, I was just going to tell you the same thing. I got some urgent business to discuss."

"Why don't you come to my suite in about, oh, twenty minutes, and we can talk?"

"Sounds good to me, Donna."

Tim put down the phone and said to Connie, "Twenty minutes. Then this whole thing will be settled."

"Hurry back, tiger."

The Raiders were now in a semicircle around Ezra, who was addressing them (and the TV cameras) through a bullhorn. This was his usual talk-show drivel. He looked forward to reading the speech Dickinson had written for him for the big meeting tomorrow night. (Where was it? he hadn't seen it yet.) But for now, Ezra could wing it since he had been saying the same thing for years:

"Some folks are sayin' let those Big Boys run the county, those rich fellas, those people with the right connections, the ones who own businesses and run the big unions and go to the expensive schools. Is this the way things should be?"

There was an immediate chorus of boos and shouts: "No No No!" The Raiders chanted, "Tyne for a change," and then Ezra began to speak again.

"Damn straight. The former Steinberg and people like her run this country. Well, this is the place, the AAP, for Americans to stand on our feet and say: No more, not a step further!"

Ezra was about to continue when he heard a roar from the Raiders. Some of them were whistling, some of them were making obscene gestures. Ezra turned and saw a line of young female joggers led by a masculine-looking woman in a sweat suit. The women were all in white shorts and T-shirts. The shirts bore the words, in revolutionary red:

The Ernesto
"Che"
Guevara School
For Wayward Girls

The Raiders kept on shouting and gesturing and whistling. Many of the joggers waved, which only increased the noise from the Raiders. Ezra, bullhorn in hand, was mad as hell.

Goddamn it, those whores took the cameras off me. Goddamn them and goddamn that crazy woman, Tart Liar.

TWENTY

The scene between mother and daughter in Donna's suite could have appeared practically uncut in her old soap, *Today We Love,* perhaps with a tweak here and there in the dialogue, some good close-ups, and, quite frankly, better lines for Donna (who, after all, was the star). The scene, played swiftly and with passion, went like this:

Che Che, the Betrayed One, enters. She is furious to learn of Peter's treachery in writing for Ezra Tyne. Donna tells Che Che the Awful Truth: things are far worse than they seem! Peter had also been writing for Tim Flaherty. Peter is a cokehead. Peter has been banging a Valkyrie policewoman. Peter is a lying, deceitful cad, there is no other word for it. Che Che (tears in her eyes, distraction in her aspect, like Niobe, all tears) asks how Donna knows all this.

DONNA: *LionClaw has been investigating your Mr. Dickinson, on my orders.*

CHE CHE *(close-up, her eyes flashing, her trembling voice raised): You've been spying on me?*

DONNA: *Not on you, dear, on Dickinson.*

CHE CHE: *But if you've been spying on Peter, you must have been spying on me, too, because I've been with him. What's the difference?*

Donna and Che Che exchange angry words. Left-jab nouns, right-cross verbs. Uppercut adjectives. Kicking adverbs. Accusations. Threats. Boom. Bam. Silence. End of scene.

"Well, we're not going to settle this now," Donna said. "Tim Flaherty just called. He's going to be here any minute. Please get yourself under control and greet him when he comes in. Can you do that?"

"Yes. But only because I gave you my word I'd help you get through this AAP meeting. I keep my word; I don't break faith. But after this is over, don't ever expect me to trust you again."

"Don't be dramatic, Che Che. I'm the actress in the family. Please greet Tim at the door, and give me a minute to compose myself."

Che Che left the bedroom, stunned and near tears. In the living room there were two LionClaw guards, a tall black man standing in front of Donna's door and a petite white woman standing with her back to one of the windows. Che Che walked over to the other window, trying to hide her face from the two of them.

Betrayed. She had been betrayed—again—by Peter. What made her so angry now was his patronizing, cruel manipulation of her. She had *trusted* him. Drugs. And then a *policewoman,* my God. And her mother had been spying on her.

She has no right to control my life. If I make a mistake—and I did with Peter— that's my life. She has no right, she—

As the knock came on the door of the suite, Che Che nodded to the woman guard, who let Tim Flaherty in. He was carrying some manila envelopes and a larger brown envelope.

"Hello, Mr. Flaherty," Che Che said, walking from the window to greet him and nodding once more to the guard, to signal there would be no need to examine the envelopes.

"It's nice to see you again, Che Che," Tim said. "I guess you know this meeting has to be just the two of us, Donna and me."

"Mr. Flaherty, I'm my mother's campaign manager and—"

"I know that and I respect it, but believe me, for your own good, this has to be private."

"I'll speak to my mother and see what she says," Che Che said. She walked to Donna's bedroom door, knocked, and entered. Thirty seconds later she emerged.

"Mr. Flaherty, I'll be sitting in on the meeting. My mother is adamant about that."

"If that's what she wants, then that's it," Tim said. "Don't say I didn't warn both of you."

When they entered the bedroom, Donna, wearing a red robe and red pajamas, was standing by the window, looking out. Che Che knew that her mother had planned it this way. It was good theater: the lone, dramatic figure by the window, seemingly so lost in her thoughts that she was unaware a visitor had come in, thereby making the visitor seem of secondary importance, giving Donna the opportunity to appear as if she had not been waiting—all communicated not in a word or a gesture but in a mere stance. But Che Che knew Donna had played a similar scene many times, had, in fact, seen Donna play this scene at home. Donna turned, expertly faked surprise, and, all smiles—she looked good, better than she had in a while—quickly walked over to Tim and kissed him on the cheek.

"Tim *darling,* sit, sit, right here on the couch by me. Che Che, dear, get Mr. Flaherty a soft drink."

"No, nothing for me, Donna, it's not a social visit," Tim said grimly. "Let me get straight to the point."

"When haven't you, Tim, dear? Bluntness is part of your charm," Donna said with a small, tolerant smile. "But before you begin, I have something for you."

Donna handed him a manila envelope.

"This contains remarks Ezra Tyne was going to make tomorrow night when he gives his big speech to the AAP. It came addressed to Che Che, as you can see, by messenger early this morning, obviously by mistake. I opened it just a while ago. Since the envelope was addressed to Che Che, I naturally assumed it was my speech. As you no doubt know, Mr. Dickinson's been doing work for me. And I knew he'd been working for you."

"How did you know that?"

"I have my ways. And now, in a trifecta of treachery, we find he's also been working for Ezra Tyne. In fact, you probably have a copy of the speech draft intended for me. Or Tyne does. I must admit that the little I read of Tyne's speech is powerful, in a heavy-handed, fascistic, mendacious, cruel kind of way. Mr. Dickinson can write in any style, it seems."

"So, he was working for you, too," Tim said, shaking his head in disbelief. "I knew he was seeing Che Che—it was in the papers—but I didn't know he was working for you. And Tyne. Donna, one last time—let me talk to you without Che Che in the room."

"Impossible. Che Che is here to take notes for my added protection against the lies you will undoubtedly tell about this meeting."

"No need to be nasty, Donna."

"Where was your fastidiousness when you and your clerical friends downstairs decided to smear me as a murdering, child-starving, genocidal monster?"

"Donna, here's the way this is going to go. You give your speech tonight, say what you want. But at the end of the remarks you'll say you're not going to seek the nomination of the AAP next year—your health won't permit it."

"Tim, dear, I never indulge in ethnic stereotypes, but have you been drinking?"

"I tried to warn you both," Tim said. He was silent for a moment, staring at the envelopes in his lap. Then he stood, picked up the phone, mumbled a few words, grunted once or twice, and hung up.

"There'll be two people here momentarily," he said. "Tell your goons to let them in."

In a minute or so—with the frigid silence chilling the room—there was a knock on the door.

"Come in," Donna said.

Security operative Neil Goldman and a fat, dowdy-looking woman, her gray hair worn in a bun, came into the room. The woman, dressed in a plain, off-the-rack-at-Kmart, long-sleeved dark blue dress, buttoned to the neck—in this August heat!—and wearing plain metal-rimmed eyeglasses and sensible shoes, was in her fifties, perhaps older, it was hard to tell.

"Donna," Tim said, standing and putting his hand on Goldman's arm, "I think you know Neil."

"Tim," Donna said, ignoring Goldman, "what's this all about?"

"Donna, this lady is Gertrude Hoakley," Neil Goldman said. "You once knew Mrs. Hoakley, but under a different name."

"Forgive me, but I'm afraid I don't recall. Were you a wardrobe mistress in one of my shows, Mrs. Hoakley?"

"Donna, it's nice to see you again," Mrs. Hoakley said. "Do you mind if I sit? I had a hip replacement and—"

Donna, arm outstretched, palm up, gestured in the grand style, and they all sat. Mrs. Hoakley stared at Donna.

"You look just wonderful, Donna," she said. "You kept yourself well. I put on weight, but I guess you can see that. Before I found Jesus I would have been jealous of you. But now I know the soul is eternal and the body dies."

"I'm sure you're right. But what is this is all about?"

Mrs. Hoakley looked at Tim, who nodded once.

"Donna," Mrs. Hoakley said, "I was a prostitute in Las Vegas long ago."

"How interesting. You're just a trifle too old to qualify for the Che School, but—"

"Donna, you were a prostitute, too. My working name was Fawn Labeque. Yours was Toni Carstairs. The difference was, I was a pro. I had a pimp. You and me did terrible, sinful things, Donna. But I've been washed clean by the blood of Jesus Christ and I want you to know the joy of confession and repentance. That's the only reason I came here."

"Mrs. Hoakley, listen very carefully," Donna said slowly in an even, controlled voice, as if she were talking to a not-too-bright six-year-old. "I once knew a woman named Fawn, but neither she nor I was a prostitute. We were waitresses. I have no idea what this is all about, but my patience is very quickly evaporating."

"Please listen to me, Donna," Mrs. Hoakley said quietly. "God gave us this chance, so we should make the most of it. Just before Mr. Goldman came to see me, I was about to go on a salvation mission to Los Angeles. I have a little church of my own now, the Good Hope Mission. We bring God's word to the fallen. Fallen women, mostly, although they don't seem to want to hear the Word. I was on my way out the door when the phone rang—I had my car keys in my hand—and I picked it up. It was Mr. Goldman here. He said he wanted to talk to me about you. And Jesus Christ Himself told me this man was sent by God to help you cleanse yourself. So I canceled the mission. I waited for him for two days, reading scripture, until he came to see me and—"

Donna suddenly laughed, shook her head, and laughed again. The sound of laughter caught Mrs. Hoakley by surprise and she stared, pop-eyed. Donna was using a laugh she had created for confrontation scenes on *Today We Love*. The laugh combined condescending amusement, disdain, a touch of contempt, and a smidgen of pity. It was quite a laugh.

"Tim, dear old Tim," Donna said finally, still smiling. "I *really* have no time for this kind of nonsense. It's bad enough you've been lying about my businesses, now you're trying to—what is it . . . blackmail me?—with this poor woman's well-rehearsed slander? Please, Tim, give me a little credit. I can tell a scam ten miles away. And as for you, Mrs. Hoakley: if you are Fawn, you're lying about me, probably for money. If you're not Fawn, you're an impostor or you're a crazy woman. If I ever see you again, or hear that you have said anything false, malicious, or derogatory about me, I will sue you so fast you really *will* need Jesus."

"All right, Neil, show her," Tim said to Goldman, handing the private detective the envelopes he had been holding. Goldman opened the largest one and took out a long-playing vinyl record. Che Che looked at the cover: *Thelonious Monk Plays Duke Ellington*.

"This belongs to Mrs. Hoakley," Goldman said, handing the cover to Donna.

"Well, at least she has good taste," Donna said. "This is one of my favorite albums. In fact, I can never hear 'Caravan' without thinking of Monk's version. But what does this have to do with me?"

"Look there, Donna," Goldman said. "Your name is written right here. 'Property of Donna Hart, Please Return.' And there are three exclamation points. Mrs. Hoakley has had this—and two other albums with your signature on them—all these years. You loaned them to her and never got them back."

"Nonsense," Donna said. "Everyone knows my love for jazz. You simply purchased these recordings at some antique store or—"

"What about your own name in your own writing?" Tim said.

"Obviously a forgery."

"We can get experts to testify that these words were written years ago and that they're in your handwriting," Tim said.

"And I can get fifty experts to testify that the moon is made of green cheese. I buy experts by the truckload. Is this all that you've got to say?"

Goldman looked at Tim and then reached into another envelope.

"You said we wouldn't have to," Mrs. Hoakley said, frowning. "You *said*."

"Be quiet now, Mrs. Hoakley. I said we *probably* wouldn't have to," Tim said softly, patting her hand, never taking his eyes off Donna's face. "Show her, Neil."

Goldman took out photographs from the envelope. He passed them to Donna.

"What is it?" Che Che said to Tim, getting up from her chair and standing behind Donna. "What's going on?"

Che Che looked over her mother's shoulder as Donna looked at the two eight-by-twelve color photos. One showed two young women in bed, naked, one blond, one brunette, in an obviously posed embrace, smiling and looking into the camera. The second photograph showed the brunette performing a sex act, once considered deviant behavior but now commonplace for high school dating, with a man in a black ski mask.

Donna handed the photos to Tim.

"You have strange sexual tastes, Tim. Have you spoken to your confessor?

Or some of your bishop friends? I understand their sexual tastes don't quite run in a heterosexual direction, but—"

"That's *you*, Donna," Tim said heatedly. "You and Fawn in one of those pictures. You in the other one."

"I don't know who these two women are, but neither one of them is me. And this young woman with the Lone Ranger, or whatever he is, is not me. I never had dark hair in my life. Granted, my blond hair is, as they say, enhanced. But I am naturally blond. This young woman is brunette."

"You wore a brunette wig on some jobs in those days," Mrs. Hoakley said. "I remember that job when the john took the pictures. I remember it because in those days and for years afterward, I did abominable things with women, like unto the heathen, as you can see."

"You are truly insane."

"No, no, Donna," Mrs. Hoakley said, leaning forward on the couch. "Remember? I lived in the apartment on the second floor. You lived on the first. One night when I came to see you, in your tiny apartment, when you first started . . . selling yourself, you were crying your eyes out and throwing up. I held you and we lay in each other's arms all night and I comforted you. So I kept these photos of you—the john gave them to me, he said they were artistic—because they were the only ones I had. After you left Las Vegas, I'd look at them and think about you. I wondered whatever happened to you. Then, after a while, I put them away and forgot about them. I followed your career and was happy for you. I thought of getting in touch. But I was drinking and doing drugs in those days, selling my body, and I was crazy most of the time. But then one night I found Jesus in a little church just down the block from me. I got off drugs, I went to AA. I married Sam Hoakley. He was a dealer at the casinos, but he drank. I had to take care of him. He wasn't a good man, but he was my husband. I was so busy taking care of him, I forgot about those pictures. I just forgot about them."

"Tim," Donna said, slowly getting up from the chair. "Get out, take this pathetic misfit with you, and take Jesus with her. If any of you, or anyone associated with you, ever even *tries* to make public these vicious lies, I have enough power to destroy all of you. I'll ruin you and your families and your associates."

"Donna, for God's sake, give it up. Mrs. Hoakley is telling the truth, and you know it," Tim said. "Why would she lie?"

"Let me guess. Money?"

"The only money she's received from us is expenses. If you don't drop out of the race for good, I'm turning all of this over to Ezra Tyne. The pictures, the record cover, everything. They'll be all over the Internet tomorrow. Then you can deal with him."

"Publish and be damned, as someone once said."

Tim Flaherty smiled.

"I know what you're thinking, Donna," he said. "You're thinking, *I'll tell Margaret Mary about Tim's girlfriends*. It won't work, Donna. She won't believe it, so don't waste your time. And you're thinking, *Americans like to forgive celebrities*. You'll go on Leno and everybody will give you a standing ovation and you'll be bigger than ever. And you're thinking, *Hell, nobody cares about what happened so long ago*. You're thinking, *I didn't molest or mistreat a child, which is the only thing people won't forgive a celebrity these days*. Well, you're wrong. These are *pictures*, Donna, not rumors or charges or allegations or he-said, she-said. People forgive celebrities for bad things, you're right. But if Tyne gets these pictures, do you want your father and Che Che to know they're on the Internet forever? Are you ready to risk that?"

Mrs. Hoakley stood by the door and said to Donna, "I know what's going on in your heart, Donna. It will never go away until you publicly confess."

"Please leave," Donna said. "You are delusional."

"The only delusion is sin, Donna," Mrs. Hoakley said. "The only reality is Jesus."

When they were gone, Donna looked infinitely tired. Her eyes were closed. She sat in silence for a while as Che Che looked at her.

"Well," Donna said finally, looking at Che Che, "now I have to get ready for the reception. Call Marvin and tell him to come—"

"Mom," Che Che shouted, incredulous. "Mom, how can you . . . how can you just . . . Mom, for God's *sake,* what was that all about?"

"What just went on," Donna, said, "was politics in the raw. Nasty. Cruel. But just politics."

"Mom, for God's sake, is it true? Was that you? Were you a . . ."

"A whore? Well, what if I had been? What would change about me? About us? About anything important?"

"All I'm asking you is a simple question: is it true?"

"I don't want to discuss this now. I—"

"My God, is this why you started the Che School? Because you feel guilty you did the same things you're blaming whores for doing?"

"How *dare* you judge me!" Donna shouted. "Do you really want to know the truth?"

"Don't you think it's about time?"

"Then here's the truth. Your father walked out on me and took all our money. You were a baby. I got a part-time job as a waitress in a hotel coffee shop. I had to pay a babysitter for you, and I didn't make enough to take care of us. So I turned tricks. I saved every penny I could so I—so *we*—could get out of Las Vegas. And when I had saved enough, I quit being a hooker. I went to Los Angeles because I knew I was going to be a star. I *knew* it. When I got there, I worked at anything even vaguely connected with show business. I was even a stripper for a time—Sara Sahara doing the Gaza Strip, and then Molly Boom-Boom doing the Strip of Consciousness, for the educated crowd. You never knew that, did you? I never stopped struggling, not just for me but for you. I had sworn to myself I'd never go back to being a whore. *And I never did.* I did what I had to in Las Vegas, yes, and I'd do it again under the same circumstances. How do you think the world runs, Che Che? Like a seminar at Georgetown? No, you have to do things you don't want to do, or else people will walk all over you."

"You have to say B, in other words. Even if it means giving blow jobs to strange men."

Donna slapped Che Che across the face. *Whack*. Che Che reeled back, stumbling, in shock and fear. Never, not once in her life, had Che Che seen the look that was now blazing from Donna's eyes: savage, dominating, cruel.

"Yes, goddamn it, that's what it means," Donna said. "For your information, the sex part of it was mechanical. It made me sick, but it really didn't bother me. It was the goddamn *contempt* in their eyes that I couldn't stand. I *hated* it. I hated it more than what they did to me. Yes, there are times in life you have to say B. Or, in your case, you have to have someone brave enough and strong enough and tough enough to say B *for* you, so you can have a clean conscience and throw it up in their faces after you've benefited from what they've done for you. Oh, you're pure all right. But only because you never had to make the choices I did. You know what the French say about people like you? They say: she has clean hands—but she has no hands."

Donna turned and walked to the bathroom door.

"We'll talk about all this when we get out to LionWest," she said, her voice now heavy with weariness. "I'll tell you everything you want to know. But right now I have a problem. You can help me or not. Tim will give that story and the photos to Ezra Tyne if I don't announce my withdrawal from the race. I don't know what to do."

"Do you want me to call your psychiatrists?"

"My dear, I've learned there are some things in life that are beyond the powers of therapy. This is one of them."

"I'll call off the reception."

"Like hell you will. We're having the reception as planned and we will all have a great time. Political disaster and personal disgrace is one thing. Good pastrami and politics is another."

Pete was jittery. The elevator to Donna's floor was taking forever. The elevator door opened. Immediately in front of the door there was a desk behind which two LionClaw security guards sat, stone-faced. Before he could take two steps, someone touched his arm. Another guard. There were three guards down the hallway, looking at him.

"I'm Pete Dickinson, Mrs. Lyons's speechwriter. I'm on the list. I have a speech draft with me," he said, showing them the envelope.

One of the guards hit a button on the keyboard, scrolled down, and said, "Yes, Mr. Dickinson. May I see some photo identification?"

Che Che walked out of her mother's bedroom and into the sitting room. And there, waiting on the divan, wearing fashionable shades, was Peter. He grinned, jumped up, rushed across the room, and embraced her as the two guards pretended not to watch. She stood motionless, arms at her side.

"Che babes," he said.

Che Che turned to the LionClaw guards and said, "Please step out into the hallway for a moment. I'll call you."

They left and Che Che showed him the Ezra Tyne speech draft.

"I can explain everything, babe," Pete said, handing her the envelope with the Donna speech draft. "This is your mom's speech. And it's great"

Che Che put the envelope on a coffee table near the couch.

"Peter," she said. *"A policewoman?"*

"Oh. You know."

"Yes, I know. I know about the drugs. I know about Tim Flaherty. And now I know about you working for Ezra Tyne? For *Tyne*."

"Che, the speeches, they were just gigs, they didn't mean anything. I'm a speechwriter, that's what I do. I don't believe what I write. I write what my client believes. There's absolutely nothing serious with the policewoman, Che. I've seen her just a couple of times and it's not worth arguing about. And I don't know where you're getting this stuff about drugs. That's just not me. You're not really mad at me, are you, babe?"

"Not anymore. It's just another case of you doing what you have to do," Che Che said. "I'm so very tired of people who use as an excuse that they do what they have to do. People should do what they *should* do, not what they have to do, don't you think? But, no, I'm not angry anymore. In fact, I have something for you. Actually, it's two things."

"Two things?"

"Let me show you."

Cho Cho smoothly moved two steps back, got in the stance, lowered her chin, balanced herself perfectly, and with an economy of motion, threw a beautiful left jab but pulled the punch a fraction of an inch from his cute nose. Before Pete could speak, she instantly followed the jab with a perfectly thrown right cross, using her legs, punching through, twisting her hips, just as she had been taught by Sammy Yuan. But again, she pulled the punch and didn't touch him.

"It's called the old one-two, Peter," she said. "As in two-timing. As in double-dealing and double-crossing. As in two-faced."

"Go ahead," Peter said. "Hit me. Get it over with."

"I don't want to hit you, Peter. It won't make me feel better."

"Maybe it'll make me feel better. Go ahead."

"Peter, don't you get it? That's why I pulled the punches. You're not worth hating. You're not even worth hitting."

She picked up the speech draft and walked into her mother's bedroom, gently closing the door behind her. Peter quickly ran to the door and tried the knob. Locked. He knocked.

"Che? Che?"

No answer. He knocked again, harder.

"You want to hit me? Hit me, then. Go ahead!" he shouted. "Hit me! Why the fuck don't you just get it over with? For Christ's sake—"

He began pounding on the door in rage and frustration and hopelessness.

"Step away from the door, sir. *Now.*"

Pete turned. The two LionClaw guards, with their guns drawn, were standing a few feet away, wary, staring at him, ready for anything.

TWENTY-ONE

It was eight-thirty in the evening. On the fifteenth floor, the Raiders were drinking, smoking grass, snorting cocaine, and making a hell of a lot of noise. Some hotel managerial types had come up and, in their prissy way, said that other guests were being bothered by the racket. Buck and a few of the boys grabbed the hotel jerks, turned them upside down, and threw them around the big hotel suite. A couple of Raiders missed catching one of them and he fell on the floor, *ker-thud*. Buck yelled out, like a baseball official-scorer, "E-five!" and everybody laughed. Buck and the boys took the jerks' pants and underwear off and threw the by now-hysterical men on an elevator and sent it down to the lobby. The Raiders were having a great time. Buck was standing there, with ten or twelve of the boys, ignoring a night baseball game on TV (the Orioles, who cared?), when he turned. In the doorway was a damn good looking woman wearing fatigues, a red beret, and a Che School T-shirt.

"Hi," she said. "I'm Monique."

"How you doin', Monique," Buck said. "That's a nice name. You one of those Che girls, like it says on your shirt?"

"I was. Then I saw you and I just quit. To hell with it. And you know what?"

"What, honey?"

"I think a lot of the girls are ready to quit. We're sick of all that political bull-shit."

"Ain't we all, honey?"

"We want to party. You know anyplace there's a party?"

"I just might," Buck Torrence said. "Why don't you and me talk a little?"

"We can discuss prices, if that's what you like."

"That's just what I like," Buck said.

Downstairs, in the main ballroom, as the introduction ended, Donna, in a red suit, got up from her seat at the dais and walked to the microphone as the AAP audience applauded politely. She smiled and waved and waited. And waited, until there was just the right kind of silence. Then she said, "Let me begin by squelching a rumor. There is no truth to the gossip that I want AAP to change its name to the Donna Hart Lyons School for Wayward Third Parties."

There was mild laughter, more titters than guffaws, throughout the room. Donna told a few lighthearted stories about her soap-opera career and then, easily, made the transition into the main body of the speech Pete Dickinson had written for her:

"I'm here tonight because I believe the AAP can change the nation and the world. I'm here because I believe the AAP can rally millions of Americans to the cause of social justice. I'm here because I believe the AAP should stand for—and fight for—great increases in social justice programs like child care and medical research and education, and deep cuts in military waste. I know in my heart— and in my body—what it means to be the target of violence, and I know we have to defend ourselves against those whose gospel of hate is poisoning our nation.

"Some say I want a perfect society. They tell me all previous attempts to create such a society have failed. Some say all such attempts are inherently doomed to failure. But I have never in my life believed that failure is fate. We make our own fate. I believe the future of our nation is going to be decided by a new kind of candidate, someone with feelings for—and roots in—the working class, someone who can speak to and for workers, the poor, the exploited and women, Hispanics, and blacks. I believe in a candidate who will believe in government for the people and people for each other."

A perfect Donna pause—part silence, part eloquence—and then she departed from the text and spoke words she herself had written only fifteen minutes before:

"But I am here to tell you tonight that I will not be that candidate."

There was a low rumble of surprise, punctuated by gasps.

"I will not seek the AAP nomination or any other nomination next year. I will not run for the presidency on any ticket. As I said, I recently was attacked by terrorists. We still do not know for certain who was responsible for that crime. I have my own thoughts about who created the moral atmosphere in which such acts are possible, even likely, but my lawyers tell me there is something called slander. They have suggested I keep my speculations to myself. In any event, the wounds I sustained are going to make it incumbent upon me to withdraw from active politics for the foreseeable future. I want to thank you for this opportunity to be with you tonight, to share my vision with you."

She went back to the conclusion of Pete Dickinson's text, based on a true story she had told Che Che, and Che Che had told Dickinson.

"Years ago—too many years ago!—when I was breaking into show business, I got a small role in an off-Broadway play. I remembered the old show-business saying: there are no small parts, only small actors. So I worked hard and I thought I had the role in my grasp. In rehearsals I did my one scene and I knew—I just knew—I had nailed it. But the director yelled out, time after time, 'Try that again.' Well, about an hour later I was almost in tears. I had tried every conceivable way of saying the lines, but nothing pleased the director. He told us to take a break and I said to him, 'I thought I was good.' And he said, 'Oh, you *are* good. But in the theater, being good isn't enough. Being good is only the beginning. You start with good and build.' Well, my friends of the AAP, tonight I just want to say: America is a good country. But being good isn't enough. We have to build on good. And we have to keep on building so that we have a government for the people and people for each other. Thank you."

Five hours later, Donna, sleepless, alone (she had told Marvin she wanted some time to herself), her eyes closed, her head propped up by three pillows, listened to a Thelonious Monk recording. She was glad she had decided to play the Monk tunes. She thought of the *Thelonious Monk Plays Duke Ellington* album that Fawn had kept all these years. "Caravan," "It Don't Mean a Thing," "Mood Indigo."

Monk, with all his strange harmonies and odd rhythms, kidding the tune by playing notes that belied the sappy words that would be sung to the melody, created a
singular beauty. It was strange how music could not only bring you out of yourself but take you deeper into yourself. And all because Monk and Frank and all the
rest of the great ones made certain kinds of pleasing sounds, just vibrations in the
air. Someone once told her that Arthur Schopenhauer believed music speaks directly to that which is essentially real and eternal in us, the *noumenon*. He was right.

Donna was exhausted, as tired and depressed as she had been in many years.

*I just gave up. Downstairs, in front of all those people and all those television
cameras, I gave up. My father will disown me. But what could I do? Tim has me
over a barrel. I had no choice. And Che Che is so angry with me. She wasn't even
there to lend aid and comfort.*

The sight of Fawn, after all these years—decades—had been unnerving.
Donna did not know how she had managed to keep herself under control as
Fawn sat there, babbling.

Fawn. During Donna's time in Las Vegas, only one person had been truly
kind and gentle and caring with her: Fawn. And now Fawn belonged to Jesus.
What do you say to someone who believes Jesus wants you to publicly admit you
were once a whore? And what do you say to your daughter who has seen obscene
pictures of her mother? Where are the words? Who can write *that* speech?

Speech. Well, she had to give him credit—Dickinson had written a pretty
good speech. But Che Che was finished with him, at least that much had been
accomplished. *But what do you say to Che Che now?* It would be a long flight
back to LionWest. My God, how did everything go wrong?

God. What a strange word for an atheist to use. *Well, God or Jesus or Allah or
Jehovah or Shiva or Kali, or whoever the hell you are, if you're out there, or up
there, now's the time to show yourself.*

Weary, she turned off the lamp and lay in the darkness, listening to the
clinky-clanky, jarring but oddly soothing music of *Blue Monk*. There was a
gentle knock on the door. One of the LionClaw guards probably, checking on
something or other.

"What is it?" Donna said irritably. "I'm trying to sleep."

No answer. Another knock.

"Damn it," Donna said, grabbing her robe, mad as hell, ready to take out all her anger and frustration on the damn LionClaw fool. She quickly went to the door, opened it and

"Mom, we need to talk."

Che Che looked serious—or was it grim? Behind Che Che were four Lion-Claw guards, two on each side of a middle-aged woman dressed in a zipper jacket and jeans, and a tall, thin young man, perhaps in his early thirties, wearing a black suit and a clean white shirt buttoned to the top, with no tie. The man beamed a goofy, buck-toothed, childish smile at Donna.

"What is it, is there anything wrong?" Donna said.

"Something's come up," Che Che said. "I have to talk with you."

Che Che went into the bedroom and Donna closed the door.

"What is it now?"

"Just before I was about to go downstairs and hear you this evening, a Lion-Claw man called me. He said that a woman wanted to talk to you, that it was urgent. I asked Sammy to see what the woman wanted. When he came back, he was excited. He told me what he had—"

"Get to the point, dear. Who are these people outside?"

"The woman's name is Mrs. Lorna Gunderson. The man is her son, John."

"What does this have to do with me?"

"Mrs. Gunderson lived with Ezra Tyne, years ago, before he ever thought about going into radio. In fact, Ezra Tyne isn't his real name. It's John Henry Kaiser. Back then he was just a drugged-out hippie, a petty criminal who robbed convenience stores and was on the run from the police. He met Lorna when she was working in a diner in Roanoke, almost thirty years ago. They shacked up. John Gunderson is their son. Tyne got drunk one night and crashed his car with Lorna and Johnnie in it. Johnnie has never been the same. He is very seriously brain-damaged. Tyne drank, beat Lorna and Johnnie, then abandoned both of them. All that stuff he says about being a wanderer is to a certain extent true. He bummed around the country for years. But then he got a job as an all-night disc jockey in some small country-music station in Oklahoma, under the name of Ezra Tyne. A few years later, Lorna saw his picture in a music magazine and got in touch with him, demanding money. Over the years, as he developed his talk-show format, she stayed in touch. He sent her money from time to time, to keep her quiet about his past, especially about what happened to Johnnie. And then she—"

"I want to speak with Mrs. Gunderson. Now."

Donna and Che Che walked into the sitting room. Donna gestured and the LionClaw guards left the room.

"I'm Donna Hart Lyons."

"Oh, I know who you are. I seen you on the TV, lots of times. That soap opera. You was good."

"Thank you. Please, Mrs. Gunderson," Donna said. "Sit right here on the couch, next to me."

"Never seen nothing like this place," Lorna said, sitting and leaving room for Johnnie. "In the movies, maybe, but not in real life."

"It was very good of you to come see me. I know this must be difficult for you and Johnnie. Can I get you anything?"

"Nothing for me, ma'am. Maybe a Pepsi for Johnnie. He likes his Pepsi. Reg'lar, not the diet stuff. And he can tell the difference. Can't you, Johnnie?"

"Ma, can we watch toons?" Johnnie said in the whiny, tired voice of a child who needs his sleep.

"No, honey, not right now. This nice lady here is going to get you a Pepsi."

"Reg'lar?"

"You bet, son."

"Mrs. Gunderson," Donna said, "what made you decide to tell us all this?"

"I guess your daughter told you most of it. After John Henry—Ezra—left us, I married a man named Andy Gunderson, that's why I got that name. But he died. I been in touch with Ezra through the years. But we been fighting more and more and then . . ."

"What?"

"He tried to get me killed. Can't prove it, but he did. Other week, a car tried to run me off the road. I wound up in a ditch. Bumped my head was all. I thought, maybe it was just some drunken fool. But last night somebody fired a shotgun into my bedroom. Right through the window, both barrels. Tore up my bed something fierce. The only reason I'm alive is I had got up to go to the bathroom. If I was in the bed, I'd be Swiss cheese. It was some of Ezra's Raiders, trying to kill me, sure as hell. See, if Ezra's going to run for president, like he's sayin', he don't need me around. I know too much. They don't have to kill Johnnie, 'cause he's not right in the head after that accident. No one would believe him. But Ezra needs me dead. So I just got in my car and drove, with Johnnie, and came here to see you and tell you the truth about him. All I want is protection. No use going to the police. I have no proof that it's him or the Raiders. I know they call you the Godmother. So I said, Lorna, go see the Godmother, get justice that way. I know a lot about Ezra Tyne. Police been looking for him for years."

"Mrs. Gunderson, you'll never have to fear him again. Che Che, take Mrs. Gunderson and Johnnie to your room. Tell Sammy to get Mrs. Gunderson's story on videotape and audiotape. Have lawyers present. Get her to sign an affidavit, attesting to all she has to say about Tyne."

"Oh, I got a lot to say about him," Lorna said. "When he was living with me, he hit Johnnie. After he left, really never wanted to talk to him or nothin'. He——"

"Che Che, when you have that done, get Tyne on the phone. Just tell him this: Donna Hart Lyons requests the honor of seeing him so we can discuss the life and times of Mr. John Henry Kaiser. Tell him I'll be in the all-night coffee shop downstairs in two hours. As soon as Mrs. Gunderson has said all she has to say, show me the videotape."

Two hours later Ezra Tyne, wearing his greasy, battered cowboy hat, shades, a gray sweatshirt and jeans, came into the almost deserted coffee shop. Sitting in a booth by a window, Donna, pouring tea from a small pot, was wearing an Ezra piggy T-shirt and jeans. Tyne slid into the opposite seat.

"Tea, Mr. Kaiser?"

"Don't drink tea, Ms. Steinberg. I like your shirt. About as close as folks like you ever came to a pig, I bet."

"That was funny the first time you said it on the radio, but it's faded a bit since then."

"If you say so. So what's this all about? You woke me up. Why are you lookin' at me like that?"

"You're so much shorter than I thought you'd be."

"And you look a hell of a lot older in person, despite all those tuck jobs. So now that we got the insults out of the way, what's on your mind? So you know my name was John Henry Kaiser. Big fucking deal. What am I supposed to do? Beg for mercy? Nothing's changed. I'm still the voice of real people and you're still a left-wing New York Jew."

"No need to waste your charm on me, you suave devil," Donna said. "As I was sitting here, I thought how strange this is. Think of how much we have in common: we both oppose big business, we both are suspicious of foreign interventions, and we both think the Guy is an idiot. And yet—"

"If this is your pitch to become my vice president, don't waste your breath."

"Tell me something, just out of curiosity. Was it the Raiders or one of your other criminal friends who planted those bombs?"

Ezra Tyne smiled. Or was it a smile? It was hard to tell, because the mustache hid his mouth and the shades hid his eyes.

"Why in the hell should I kill you, you dumb bitch? You're my meal ticket. Your school for whores got me my best ratings ever. See, real American people don't like people like you, you smart-ass Jews with all your goddamn *brilliance* and your fucking *opinions* on everything and your government interference in our lives, so long as you and your puppets run the government. You know what real Americans want?"

"Peace. Justice. Better education for their children, a safety net, better health care, better social serv—"

"No, that's what *you* and your kind want *for* them. Real Americans just want to be left the fuck alone. That's it. Just leave us alone. We don't want no government nanny telling us what to eat and what not to smoke and drink. Real people are fed up. The two big political parties are through. Folks are looking for direction in this country. And they're going to look at either people like you or people like me. The two of us are ahead of the curve."

"In what way?"

"We got paramilitary organizations. You got your LionClaws, and I got my Raiders. That's the future for politics in this country. Ten, twenty years from now there won't be a politician or a party in this country without a big personal-security force all the time. The American people like force or the threat of force, makes you serious, people respect that. Oh, they say women don't like force and violence, but that's just big-city women like you, not real women who live in the South and out West. And, hell, just about every man likes a show of force. I got my Raiders. They can get out of hand real quick. Gotta admit they scare even me sometimes. But they scare the hell out of other folks, too, and that gains you respect. When I give my speech, I'm going to say a few things about the Raiders. Make sure you hear the speech."

"I wouldn't miss it for the world. Just out of curiosity, who wrote it for you?"

"Wouldn't you like to know? Fact is, now that you mention it, I ain't got the damn thing yet."

"Is this it?" Donna said, and pushed the speech draft across the table.

Tyne looked at the title:

Ezra Tyne Remarks for AAP Meeting

"Where'n the *hell* you get this?"

"I have my ways, Mr. Tyne. It's not a bad speech. Too bad you won't be delivering it."

"What the hell are you talking about, woman?"

"I'll tell you in a minute. You know, I'm a bit disappointed in you. You are so depressingly . . . ordinary. And truly, deeply stupid. I expected something more frightening, some kind of satanic presence. But you're just an ignorant criminal redneck. Hannah Arendt was right about the banality of evil."

"Who?"

"Nobody you've ever heard of. A Jew, like me. Well, thank you for coming. I just wanted to have the pleasure of meeting you, face-to-face, and telling you that in time for today's morning shows—in a few hours—you will announce that you are not going to run for the AAP nomination for the presidency next year or any other year. And although you don't have to say this part publicly, you are never going to mention my name on your show or in any public forum again. You are not going to criticize me, my daughter, or my enterprises. Originally I just thought I'd hold a news conference and expose you. But that might cause certain problems for me with someone who wants to tell lies about me. So I am just telling you to quit."

"And why am I going to do all this, you dumb bitch, as if I ever would?"

"Because as John Henry Kaiser, you were involved in a string of armed robberies years ago. In one of those robberies, you beat an old woman with a gun. In another you kidnapped and molested a fourteen-year-old girl who had walked into the convenience store you were robbing. You fathered a child and beat him and caused him brain damage when you drove a car drunk and smashed it. You were a two-bit petty-cash-stealing, drug dealer to Roanoke-area dopeheads. You beat the mother of your child. You beat and abandoned your mentally retarded child. Is that enough?"

It was hard for Donna to see if his expression changed, because it was hard to see any expression behind the shades and the mustache in the first place, but when he spoke, she knew she had him because his well-known voice just fell apart, part whine, part sputter, part rage.

"You can't prove any—"

"Two names, Mr. Kaiser. Lorna and Johnnie."

"But Lorna's—"

"Dead? No, your hired assassins botched the job. Twice. Perhaps they were members of Tim Flaherty's union. In the old days, when someone put out a contract, it was guaranteed. Whatever happened to the work ethic among real Americans, Mr. Kaiser? Whatever happened to standards?"

TWENTY-TWO

Harry Gottlieb, in bed at his London hotel, grabbed the phone.

"Harry? This is Laura Storr-Havens."

The New York Times. Harry instantly sat up.

"Harry, have you seen the official text of the president's speech?"

"Yeah, I saw the final draft on the plane. Why?"

"No, I mean have you seen the text you've released?"

"No, it should be here, though."

Harry looked to the door of his hotel room and there, slipped under the door sometime last night, was an envelope with, he knew, the speech text. "Yeah, it's here. What is this, Laura?"

"My God, you don't know, do you?"

"Don't know *what?*"

"Harry, read it—now—hurry, but promise me once you've read the text, you'll call me and give me your comment first. Before anyone else. Even if it's no comment, I want to hear it from you."

"Laura—"

"Harry, either the Guy has finally lost his mind or you're the victim of the biggest hoax in the history of American rhetoric. Call me."

Harry put down the phone and got out of bed. He hurried in his bare feet to the door and picked up the speech from the rug. He turned on the bedside light and searched for his reading glasses. Putting them on, he sat on the edge of the bed. He began to read.

Page one: Stuff, stuff. Special relationship. Historic friendship. Freedom.

More stuff. A quote from Pitt the Younger. An anecdote about Benjamin Franklin in London, the obligatory quote from Churchill. Page two: The bland, purified, say-nothing mention of Peru. More stuff. Another series of stuff.

What the hell was Laura talking about? It wasn't a great speech, but it wasn't that bad. Harry skimmed page three—stuffstuffstuff—and turned the page. He began to read. There was nothing in the speech that—

"Oh my God."

He had an immediate and urgent desire to rush to the bathroom. He steadied himself and read the words, on page four:

> The time has come! I join the forces of revolution throughout the world. Imperialism must be destroyed! Corporate globalistic fascism must be destroyed! American hegemony must be destroyed! White sexist, racist, genocidal exploitation must be destroyed! War must be destroyed! Destruction itself must be destroyed! I denounce the racist genocide that began with the white imperialist, racist, sexist pig "Christ-bearer" Columbus, and the start of the bloody system of earth murder that brought about the economic and social destruction of the hemispheric paradise by the petit bourgeois. Down with the Europeans, especially the Anglo bloodsuckers and their slave trade. The British Empire was built on slavery! The Spanish Empire was built on slavery! . . .

"What the hell?" Harry said. The phone rang.

He read on. It got worse. Evil white hegemony; mass rape of women of color; the genocide against the Indians in North America, South America, and the Caribbean; the sexist, racist hypocrisy of the Founders. The phone was still ringing. In a daze, Harry picked it up.

"Harry," the president's secretary said in a near whisper. "The president wants to see you. Now."

There were just the two of them. The president of the United States, dressed, as always, as if he had just emerged from protective plastic wrapping, sat on a red leather couch. Harry Gottlieb was standing in front of him. They were in the U.S. embassy building on Grosvenor Square, in the office of the American ambassador to the Court of Saint James's. The couch, old, comfortable, not in the best shape, on which the leader of the free world was sitting, had been brought to the embassy from the ambassador's old Philadelphia law firm. The Guy had not asked Harry to sit. Bad sign.

"I am an international joke," the president said in a tone of voice approaching absolute zero in terms of human warmth.

Harry was silent. Maybe it was best to take the beating.

"I am a laughingstock," the Guy said, touching his tie.

"Mr. President, I—"

"Don't interrupt me," the Guy said, touching the middle of his SS glasses, looking more and more as if he were going to burst into a chorus of the "Horst Wessel Song." "Have your resignation—one sentence—on my desk by this afternoon."

"I don't think so, sir," Harry said, and, unbidden, sat on a chair next to the couch.

The Guy blinked.

"What did you say to me?"

"I don't think I'm going to resign . . . sir."

"You dare—"

"Well, sir, I think you're going to have to bear with me, just for a minute. Do you know who's been writing your speeches recently?"

"You have."

"But that's just my point, sir. You see, I haven't been writing those speeches. Someone else has."

"What are you saying?"

"Let me explain to you what's happened recently. After I'm finished, I don't think you're going to ask for my resignation."

"Forget about resigning. You're fired as of right now. Get out."

"Mr. President, if you fire me, I'll hold a news conference later today and I'll tell the media what I am about to tell you. After you hear what I've got to say, I don't think you'll want that."

"Just who do you think you're talking to?"

"I'm talking to a president whose last few big speeches, including this one, were written by Pete Dickinson."

"Pete . . . Pete Dickin— . . . what are you—"

"Now that I have your attention, sir, let me tell you the story."

Harry told the story.

The Guy, in a fury—for someone like the Guy this meant an even tighter compression of his lips—said, "I'll give you an hour to pack your bags and get out of the hotel."

"Mr. President, I have no choice but to accept your decision. But if you fire me, I'll have to tell the media what I just told you. And when it's discovered that you've been secretly using Pete Dickinson as a speechwriter—"

"But I haven't."

"Yes, you *have*, Mr. President."

"Then you lied to me."

"Yes, sir, I did. And I'm not proud of it. But think about how this will look if it becomes public. If you *didn't* know Pete was writing for you, you look completely out of touch, in your own White House. If you *did* know, you've been lying about it by saying I was your only speechwriter. It's one thing to have an outrageous insert somehow or other get placed in your London speech text without your knowledge. And I have no idea how that happened. But it's another thing to admit you had to secretly rely for speeches on a former aide who told the world you were incapable of articulating a vision or giving a decent speech."

"But you told me *you* wrote those speeches."

"Mr. President, sir, I don't want to appear to be contradicting you. But my memory tells me that you ordered me to get Dickinson. Specifically Dickinson."

"That's a damned lie and you know it."

"True, you didn't tell me in so many words, perhaps. But a chief of staff has to be more than a messenger boy. He has to interpret what the president is saying. He has to know the president's moods. He has to look behind what is said—or left unsaid—and find the best way to get done what the president wants done, even if the president hasn't articulated it. That's what I did, Mr. President. That's what I heard you say—*get me Dickinson*—even though you didn't use those words. Mr. President, I ask you to remember: I have served you long and well, if I may say so. Not to put too fine a point on it, sir, I have taken a lot of shit from you. I admit this speech fiasco is ultimately my fault. I am ashamed. And I will take full responsibility for it. But I want to leave the White House on my own terms. You and I can work together on this and come up with some plan that makes you look like the victim. I can look like your trusted aide who was also a victim. The big question is, sir, what are we going to do?"

The Guy rose from the couch, touched his glasses, took them off, blew on them, took out a handkerchief from his back pocket, wiped the glasses, put them back on, put the handkerchief back in his pocket, touched his tie, and then paced back and forth for a few seconds. Finally he said, "Get out. You're fired."

"But, Mr. President, I'll tell the media about Dickinson."

"No, you won't. First of all, even if you did talk to the press, I can live with embarrassment. Scandal can hurt me, but not embarrassment. No president was ever denied reelection because of embarrassment. Second, in a few months, no one will remember whether Pete Dickinson is a speechwriter or a racehorse. Voters don't care who writes speeches, and for good reason. If you do carry out your threat, I will announce—the truth, by the way—you deceived me, the man you were supposed to serve. The media will have fun for a week or so, but then, like the idiots they are, they'll be distracted by something new. I'll still be here, but you'll be branded forever as a scheming, duplicitous bastard. But there's one more reason I can fire you without worrying about your blabbing to the media. Do you know what that reason is, Harry?"

"No, sir."

"It's you, Harry. You have a fatal flaw. You're a fundamentally decent human being. You have a conscience, Harry. You're loyal. By and large, you believe in what I'm trying to do. You're not like Dickinson. You won't turn against me. You know that, and I know that. So your threat is hollow. And by the way, I'd rehire Dickinson tomorrow if it served my purposes. Presidents are users, Harry. We have to be. Dickinson just may come in handy someday, and if he does, I'll use him. In politics, as one of my predecessors said, there are no inveterate antipathies. You failed me, Harry, and you lied to me. Get out. I never want to see or hear from you again."

Headlines:

TY'S FACE RED—HE'S BLUE

TY: "WHY?" STAFF: "GAFFE!"

FIDEL: "I WAS RIGHT ALL ALONG!"

DawnBreak NewsBreak: The Carol Turner Witte Show, CNN.

CAROL: . . . and we have other sensational breaking news. Kevin Gardner, you're at the Washington Harrison Grande Hotel on Capitol Hill—what do you have?

KEVIN: You're right, Carol, this story is sensational. Ezra Tyne has just issued a stunning statement. Let me read it to you: "After thoughtful deliberation, I have decided not to seek the presidential nomination of the American Advance Party. I will not seek any kind of elective office next year. I will continue to speak out for the principles I believe in, but only on my radio show and in other nonpolitical forums. Given this decision, the speech I was scheduled to deliver at the AAP meeting today will not be given. I believe that my decision is in the best interests of the AAP and of the country."

CAROL: Wow, that *is* sensational—or are we using that word too much?

KEVIN: I don't think so, Carol. This rocks the political boat and changes the entire political landscape. Instead of a bloody war between Mrs. Lyons and Mr. Tyne for the AAP nomination, it appears it is Calvin Quincy's for the asking.

CAROL: Kevin, are you getting any sense of why this happened?

KEVIN: I was talking to an aide of Ezra Tyne. He told me Ezra feels it will take too much time and energy and especially money to fight for the AAP nomination and then run a credible campaign. Ezra thought it through—and I'm quoting now—and decided the best thing for him is to stick with what he knows.

CAROL: We can see behind you some of Ezra Tyne's Raiders. They do not appear to be happy.

KEVIN: That is right, Carol. As they emerge from the hotel, they are very angry. They feel Ezra Tyne has let them down. Here is Mr. Buck Torrence, a high official of the Raiders. Mr. Torrence, what do you think of Ezra Tyne's decision not to run?

BUCK: What do I *think?* What do you *think* I think, you goddamn fairy-boy pencil-necked fuckin' geek? Ezra Tyne sold us *out.* Donna Liar or that fuckin' Quincy nut bought him off. Ezra sold us out. He fuckin' sold us *out.* Here's what I think, you goddamn liberal piece of crap.

CAROL: Oh my God, that man is choking Kevin. . . . Oh my God, someone help Kevin. . . .

The Raiders had been partying with the Che girls all night. Cases of beer were lining the hallways. Staff from the hotel restaurants, some with guns at their head, were carrying trays of food. When Buck told the boys about Ezra's treachery, they started yelling and cursing. Buck, carrying a baseball bat, with Monique riding him piggyback, yelled, "Any somma bitch brings me Ezra Fucking Tyne's sellout head in an ice bucket, I'll give him my hog."

The party began to spread to other floors. On the tenth floor, six Raiders, drunk, mean and nasty, were robbing hotel guests who were coming out of their rooms for breakfast or for early checkout. Raiders began systematically throwing chairs, tables, and beer bottles through windows.

The phone rang in Donna's bedroom.

"Donna, it's Babs. I'm in the lobby. The Raiders are going crazy. I barely escaped. They say they're going to kill Ezra. Some of them might come after you. They're drunk, they're high. It's awful. It's—"

"Calm down. Where's Che Che?"

"I don't know."

"All right, don't panic. I have LionClaw people guarding my suite. But call the police about the girls, Babs. They're the ones who need help."

"Donna, you don't understand. The girls aren't in danger . . . they're *partying with the Raiders*. The fifteenth floor is one big whorehouse. The Raiders have money and they're spending it on the girls. The girls *want* to be there. They're working girls again. Every goddamn thing we did at the Che School is going down the drain. The Raiders are all drunk and on drugs and mean as hell. I'm out of here."

Donna could hear, in the distance, the sound of sirens. She smelled smoke.

Raiders now occupied the Ye Olde Capitol Committee Grille, the fancy, high-priced La Reynard Bleu restaurant, and the coffee shop. They robbed all the early-morning Grille and coffee shop patrons and raided the kitchen's refrigerators and the wine cellar. They were chanting, "Kill Ezra, kill Ezra, kill Ezra," when Buck, drinking champagne out of a bottle, yelled out, "What about that Tart Liar bitch?" and Monique yelled, "Kill Tart Liar, kill Tart Liar."

On the mezzanine floor, eight Raiders ran into the Jefferson-Adams Room, where a breakfast meeting of the National Association of Girls Preparatory School Administrators was being held on the topic of "Diversity: A Goal and a Strategy." One of the Raiders, dressed only in his shorts and a T-shirt, was carrying a boom box. The sound of Black Sabbath, at full volume, filled the room.

"We're playing the national anthem, leastways it should be, so get on your feet, bitches," the Raider shouted. "This is a public service announcement. You bitches are the public and we're about to service y'all."

Mrs. Polly Westverholt, principal of the Bonita Phelps School in the Pines, Newmantown, New Jersey, this year's president-elect of the NAGPSA, screamed and fainted.

Donna sat on the edge of the bed. The phone wasn't working. She used her cell phone.

"Che Che, where are you?"

"I'm outside, with Marvin. Where are you?"

"In my bedroom. I have guards outside. I'm not afraid."

"Mom, listen to me," Che Che shouted. "Stay where you are. Sammy is already on his way."

Donna was about to reply when she heard:

"Well, looky, looky, looky, here's a piece of nooky."

Donna turned and saw a huge, big-bellied man who was slurring his words, obviously drunk, leaning against the wall. He was wearing jeans, a blood-spattered Grateful Dead T-shirt, and a red-white-and-blue bandanna around his head. He held the top of a broken bottle of champagne in one hand.

"Get out of here, immediately," Donna said imperiously, disguising her fear. "Or I'll call my guards and have you thrown out."

"Lady, if you're talking about that big nigger and that little teensy girl out there, in those cute blazers, I think they got bigger problems right now, like massive bleeding and reconstructive surgery of the face," the man said, waving the jagged piece of bottle.

"You don't scare me."

"Don't plan to scare you, Tart Liar. I'm gonna fuck you silly, then throw you out the window."

He slammed shut the bedroom door with his foot and began to walk toward her, slowly waving the broken bottle. She looked into his eyes and she saw the cold contempt, the amused desire to degrade, the savage, satisfied, smug look of dominance that she had seen so many times in Las Vegas, and her heart sank, because of all the things in the world, this was what she could not endure.

"I'm Buck Torrence, by the way, chief Raider, and I believe in choice, like you bitches say. Now do you want it nice? Or a little rough stuff? Your choice."

The door opened and there was Sammy Yuan, dressed in a LionClaw jacket. Buck Torrence turned to him and sneered.

"We didn't order no Chink takeout, sonny," he said, gesturing with the broken bottle. "So get your scrawny, yellow slant-eye ass out of here. I'm about to take one from column A and one from column B from this bitch, and that's only the appetizer."

"So solly," Sammy said, smiling, and crossed the intervening space between them without seeming to have touched the ground. His right leg shot out and kicked Buck in the right knee. Buck, his leg buckling under him, fell down and then back, hitting his head on the dresser. Sammy hit him hard in the throat with a left-hand slash. As Sammy moved forward, Buck got to his feet, gagging, and slashed wildly with the broken bottle, ripping the right sleeve of Sammy's jacket. Sammy hit him on the nose with his left elbow. Buck, bleeding from the nose, dropped the bottle and slid to the floor, hitting his head on the edge of the dresser. Sammy kicked Buck in the head.

"Mrs. Lyons," Sammy said, holding his bleeding arm, "we have to go. Now."

As they rushed down the fire stairs, Sammy in the lead, Donna thought, *Damn it, I left my Klee.*

Half an hour later, Buck awoke. That slash to the throat had broken something in there and Buck had trouble breathing. He got up slowly, gasping in pain, and started looking through drawers, but all he could find were a few dollars here and there. Mad as hell, he picked up a funny-looking old chair and smashed it against the wall until there was nothing left but splinters and pieces. He saw a funny-looking picture on the wall and slashed it repeatedly with a knife. Then he threw a chair through the window and started throwing out everything he could pick up. He limped out of the room, groaning, his throat hurting him. He spit up blood. Buck was madder than hell.

The Metropolitan Police arrived in force to break up the Raiders' movable orgy, which by now had reached most floors of the hotel. Raiders met the police at elevators and stairwells and beat them off with broken furniture wielded as clubs, hotel cutlery, and empty wine bottles. The police had to use tear gas to establish a foothold on many floors. The Raiders and the Che girls started fires with the broken furniture. The sprinkler systems had gone off on many floors. Stoned, drunk, semi-naked Che girls taunted the police. Outside the hotel, police sirens wailed, and fire engines sped through surrounding streets. Television cameras showed the scene, as bloody, screaming, half-naked Raiders and half-naked, drunk, cursing, spitting Che girls were dragged through the entrance by police. Mother Mary Bunky and Father Frankie stood near the hotel entrance, carrying makeshift placards denouncing police brutality against the Raiders and demanding an end to the death penalty.

Half an hour later, Buck, still hurting like hell, his head aching, dragged Ezra Tyne, naked, bruised, scraped, cut, whimpering, and bleeding, to one of the broken windows on the tenth floor and held him with one hand on the windowsill. Ezra had long since ceased screaming.

Buck could barely speak. His voice was shredded. Wheezing, he sounded like an old man, and the bleeding in his throat had increased. But he wanted ol' Ezra to hear what he had to say.

"Ezra, you promised me you was going to get this goddamn country moving again. But you let me down," Buck said, then paused to take a long swig from a bottle of Bud. "That ain't right. That ain't fair. But I think things should be fair in this country, it's the American way. So now, pardner, I'm going to even things out, fair and square. You let me down, so I'm going to let you down."

He let go of Ezra. It was immediately apparent that Ezra had one last scream left in him. Buck, leaning out the window, laughing, was so busy enjoying himself that he didn't hear the six cops come into the room. When he turned, it looked to the cops (as subsequent testimony would show) as if he had a gun in his hand (it was only a half-empty bottle of Bud), so they had no alternative but to shoot him fourteen times.

In the AAP meeting room, Gordon Bauer sat at a conference table alone, waiting for Calvin Quincy to make his appearance. All the other AAP members and media had fled. Gordon knew everything was over. The AAP would never recover from this fiasco. But he felt a strange kind of loyalty to Cal Quincy. Gordon had come into politics at the height of Cal's glory, when it was still possible to dream of clean government, a balanced budget, and good jobs for Americans. But now that was all in the past. Gordon was content to leave politics forever. But he owed Calvin Quincy the courtesy of listening to him one last time. The sounds of combat—screams, curses, gunshots, and sirens from the hotel lobby and the street—made their way into the room. Gordon could smell smoke, but it didn't bother him. He was in that serene state of peace and acceptance that comes to some human beings when they have finally realized the absurdity of life and the inevitable failure of all human hopes, all schemes for improvement, of every false dream in the planned amelioration of human misery.

Calvin walked to the podium in his outdated, frayed, spotted preppy clothes and gave a mechanical little wave. Gordon applauded, the sad, lonely sound of two hands—and only two hands, in that large room—clapping. In front of Calvin on the table was a PC. Cal looked at it for a few seconds. Then he pointed to it.

"This is the future of the AAP," Cal said. "This is our new fellow citizen. This is the future of the universe. This is the end of politics as we've known it. Too many *people* in politics. People fail all the time. People are weak. They lie. They cheat. They steal. They—"

The safety sprinklers went on suddenly, full force, and in few seconds nothing in the room was dry. Cal giggled as the water hit him. He kept on giggling for some time, until Gordon, sopping wet, arose, slowly and with dignity walked up to Cal, put his arm around his shoulders, and gently led him away, as the noise of the Raiders' bikes in the lobby increased. Puddles of water began to gather on the floor.

TWENTY-THREE

Trevor Dickinson usually did not eat very much (Dickinsons saw food as a vulgar necessity, not a sensual delight), but this evening, at his table in the dining room of the Great Oak Country Club, he was fairly digging into his lamb chop, by George. He sipped his second martini and said to Pete, "Peter, I'm so glad you called. Why didn't we think of this years ago? Father-son dinner at the club. Other families do it."

"We're not other families."

"Yes, of course. But I must admit, I'm enjoying myself, just being with you. It's too bad about your eye. A sty can be quite painful. But you look quite glamorous in those dark glasses. As I said, it's so good to know you're still doing so well in your business."

"Oh," Pete said, "there are, you know how it is, a few minor, temporary problems of expansion."

A waiter discreetly removed a bread plate from the table.

"Expansion? That's splendid, splendid. I must admit that I never thought speechwriting could be so . . . lucrative," Trevor said.

"Well, you know how those things go. Business. Ups and downs. Now take my firm. I'm expanding and I'm actually running a very slight, barely noticeable deficit. After all, I'm working in Washington, so I have to emulate the politicians."

"Well said."

"Dad, this is as good a time as any to tell you why I wanted to see you."

"Not romantic problems, I trust. I'm hardly one to give advice with that sort of thing."

"Well, let me get right to it. Dad, I need a small loan, kind of a bridge loan."

Trevor put down his martini and stared at his son.

"You want money? From me?"

"Yes, not much at all, just about twenty—say, twenty-five thousand or so. Short-term, of course. I have some business debts and—"

Trevor shook his head and smiled. Then he actually laughed. Not much of a laugh, and it had dignity, but it was definitely a laugh.

"What's so funny?" Pete asked.

"My boy, my dear boy," Trevor began, and then went on laughing.

Finally he got control of himself, dabbed at his eyes with a handkerchief, sipped some water, and said, "My boy, this is all too, too delicious. The irony. You see, I was just about to ask *you* for money."

"I don't understand."

"My boy, I have no money. I've lost almost everything. Remember that dot-com boom a few years ago? Money, money, money. Well, the dot-com boom went south as they say. I like that phrase. Went south."

"What's that got to do with—"

"I stayed out of the market while idiots were making millions. And then, in an uncharacteristic, I might say, un-Dickinsonian, fit of exuberance, and with an exquisite sense of bad timing, I plunged into the market at exactly the wrong time. The market, you see, was supposed to rebound. Go north, one supposes. So I kept on putting more money in."

"But you've always been careful with money. You never dipped into—"

"Yes, I know. But there's no fool like an old fool. The sad fact is, I'm practically insolvent. I have barely a sou. Do you remember I told you that Rosa went to Guatemala? What I didn't tell you is, I had to let her go. Couldn't afford her. She's never coming back. You saw the condition of the house. In fact, I'm going to have to sell the house and move to smaller quarters. Oh, there's a piddling amount left, and I have my meager salary, and, as I say, I'll have something when I sell the house. But the real money is gone."

"What . . . made . . . how could you do anything so—"

"Stupid? Evil? Avaricious? The short answer is greed, no doubt. I thought I could make what they call a killing. But I got killed instead. For the first time in my life, I became unbuttoned. My portfolio, balanced, sane—Dickinsonian— looks like Berlin, circa 1945, if that reference has meaning any longer. That's why I was hoping I could borrow money from you."

"Why the hell don't you just ask Mrs. Curruthers for money?"

"Strange, Peter, but your voice, so filial and warm earlier in the evening, has grown colder. Could it be you came here not because you love your dear old father and want to reestablish some relationship with him, but only because you want something from him? Hmmm? Oh, my boy, but to answer your question, I *did* importune Ruth Curruthers. She laughed at me and said, 'Trevor dear, don't be silly. I can barely get by with what Brent left me.' In fact, she said, 'I was hoping you'd ask me to marry you because I thought you had money. But that's impossible now,' she said. Well, Peter, as you can imagine, I'm not seeing Ruth anymore. I'm not seeing anyone. Can't really afford to. Of course, even if I had the money, I wouldn't be so foolish as to give it to you to bail you out of your own mistakes. Best to learn from experience, as my father used to say. The fact is, I'm for all practical purposes broke."

Pete stared at his father for the longest time, and suddenly his eyes filled with tears, and he began to sob, holding his head in his hands.

"Peter, really, *please*," Trevor said, looking around the room nervously. "Get a grip on yourself. For God's sake, *don't make a scene.*"

Tim Flaherty pulled his Buick into the driveway and shut off the engine. When the air-conditioning went off, there was a brief period of lingering coolness, but then the inside of the car seemed to heat up instantly. Washington in September. Tim was sunburned—despite the SPF 45 sunblock he brought with him to the islands. He was also weary, cranky, and sad. Some vacation. Connie had tearfully told him (conveniently for her, *after* they had been to the islands and eaten their heads off, and Tim had spent a lot of union money) that she didn't want to see him anymore, that she was in love with Pete Dickinson.

Dickinson! That snake. First he tricked Donna Hart Lyons by writing for Tim and Ezra Tyne, and now he had stolen Tim's girlfriend. Tim, protective of his sunburn, gingerly got out of the car. It was good to be home. Margaret Mary could fix him some lunch and then he'd take a long nap, maybe have Raúl wash the car, and things would be back to normal. He unlocked the front door of the house and was about to yell, "It's me," when he saw . . . nothing.

There was nothing in the entrance hall. Nothing that he could see from his vantage point near the doorway, in the living room. No rugs. No furniture. No paintings. No lamps. Nothing. Even the chandeliers were gone. Bare wires hung from the ceilings. *Nothing*.

Tim closed the door behind him. It made a strange, hollow sound in the empty house. He stood there, staring at the emptiness. He half ran upstairs. Nothing in the bedrooms. Everything was gone. Beds. Bureaus. Dressers. Even his clothes closet was empty. Even Margaret Mary's crucifix was gone. Nothing in any of the other bedrooms. He ran down the stairs and, coming through the (empty) family room, went into the garage. Nothing. Not a thing. The other car was gone. There wasn't a tool or a trash can or anything, just the walls and the garage doors. What about the kitchen? Nothing. Not a cup or a saucer or a spoon. The refrigerator was gone.

Damn it, he'd been robbed. Cleaned out. He had read about the Beltway bandit criminals who, disguised as moving men, brazenly emptied homes and sold the loot. But that was only in homes where the owners were away or where there were no security devices. Damn it, what the hell was going on? And where was Margaret Mary? His heart pounding, Tim walked through the dining room. Not a thing, just walls, a floor and ceiling, and then the living room—*nada,* not even the drapery rods. But wait. There *were* some things, looking lonely in the living room. His shrine was still in place—the pictures of JFK, RFK, FDR and a faded, wilted rose in the crystal vase. And there was a small television set—the seventy-inch set was gone—and the VCR and DVD players. Initially, he hadn't seen them because they had been hidden from his view as he stood in the hallway. But he could see them now. There was a big, hand-lettered sign taped to the top of the TV set.

TIM: SEE THIS

There was an arrow pointing to an envelope on the TV stand. In Margaret Mary's perfect hand, the envelope was made out to "Tim." He opened it.

Tim: Please play the videocassette all the way through. It will explain everything. Margaret Mary.

There was a videocassette in the VCR player. He turned on the VCR. At first there was the usual electronic jumble and then suddenly there was Margaret Mary. It was a close-up head shot, and she was looking into the camera. She had on lipstick and makeup and her hair was . . . what? Blond? *Blond?* Margaret Mary? She looked ten, fifteen years younger. She glanced to the side, nodded her head, and then, clearing her throat gently, said, "Hello, Tim. I want you to look at this video all the way through because it should be of interest to you. The first thing you should know is, I have left you and I'm never coming back. The second thing is that I gave all the furniture, all of your clothes and most of mine, the paintings, the china, the silverware, every last item except the SUV—I took that—to Catholic charities in the area. The third things is, I have just about all our money. I cleaned out our joint bank account. I cashed in the money markets. I sold all the stocks in my name. I would have sold the house, but I didn't have enough time. So you can sell the house if you wish. If you do, get a good price for it. You'll have to split the money with me, or so my lawyers tell me. I have also taken with me all the papers from your safe, including original documents I signed for you. I have given copies of them to Donna Hart Lyons for safekeeping. In exchange, she gave me certain information about you and your latest mistress. We had the nicest chat.

"This brings me to the main reason I have left you: Raúl and I have been lovers the past two years. Do you recall how often he drove me to Mass or to a church meeting? Well, actually we would go to a motel and make love. That wasn't spiritual blessedness you saw on my face when I returned from those trips—that was the look old ladies like me get when they have just been made love to by a sweet, strong, virile young man. Raúl, darling, please pull back the camera."

The camera moved back and showed Margaret Mary sitting on a queen-size bed, in some anonymous motel or hotel room. She was wearing tan slacks and a sleeveless, bright yellow summer blouse, the top two buttons open. She was holding a glass of red wine. Tim recognized the stemware. It was his. Margaret Mary looked remarkably trim, with great muscle tone in her arms. She looked, in fact, quite lovely.

"I've been going to the gym three times a week—religiously, I guess the word is—while you were at work," Margaret Mary said. "I've been running in the park every morning after you go to work. For a year and a half. You never looked at me, so you didn't know or care. I did all this to please Raúl."

Margaret Mary sipped from the wineglass and Raúl came into the shot. He was dressed in a new tan summer suit and a blue dress shirt with the collar open. He was wearing a gold medallion on a gold chain around his neck. Raúl poured wine for Margaret Mary and then half a glass for himself. He put the bottle on the bedside table. Raúl smiled into the camera—you had to hand it to him, the kid had a great smile—waved, and said happily, "Hello, Meester Teem. How you doin'? Ees me, Raúl."

Raúl sat on the bed next to Margaret Mary. She took his hand and held it.

"Tim," Margaret Mary said, "when Raúl came to work for us, I thought he was not too bright, but a nice young man, so polite. As I got to know him, I saw he was something more than a handyman. He knows how to listen. He is kind. He is gentle. One day, two years ago, you were off with one of your whores in Paris. I've known about your women for years, but I thought you'd grow out of it. I was wrong. This particular mistress, I forget her name, had called here a few times, supposedly on business. So I knew, and it broke my heart. Well, there I was, sitting in the living room, weeping, and Raúl came into the room. He had been working on the lawn and he was covered with sweat and dirt. He sat next to me and put his arms around me. We just sat there. We didn't say a word. And then he took me by the hand and led me to my bedroom. He made love to me, all afternoon, in ways I never knew existed. It was the most beautiful thing that ever happened to me. You see, it was all new to me. It was so wonderful, I burst into tears again, but this time tears of joy."

Margaret Mary sipped from the wineglass. Raúl gave another little wave to the camera.

"Tim, you will never see me again," Margret Mary said, "unless it is in court. I'm getting a divorce. I am going to travel with Raúl until he gets sick of me, which he will, probably very quickly. I will then give him money to go home to El Salvador, where he will no doubt meet a beautiful young girl, which he deserves, and he can have big fat babies with her. I know this is going to happen. I know he will get tired of me. I'm in very good shape, but, as we say, only for my age. But I don't care. I know that what I'm doing is sinful. But I'm doing it. The strange thing is, Tim, it wasn't the fact you had whores that got to me. It was that for all these years you thought I was dumb. And then along came Raúl. Good-bye. And say hello to dear Connie. If you ever try to harm me or Donna Lyons or her daughter or Raúl, I will send certain documents to the proper authorities, and to the media."

Raúl sat there as Margaret Mary, with her hands framing his face, kissed him gently on the mouth. Raúl then looked into the camera and waved again. "Bye-bye, Meester Teem. T'ank you for everyt'ing you do for Raúl. You know wha' I'm sayin'?"

Harry Gottlieb, sweating in the heat, stood alone by the first overlook at Great Falls Park, staring at the tumbling waters of the Potomac River below. But for the first time in years, the sight gave him no pleasure. He used to root for the rocks because they endured. But their stoicism and strength didn't matter, did it? The rocks were going to disappear if it took the Potomac thousands of years.

He sighed, turned away, and walked toward the footpath leading to the remnants of the original Potowmack Canal, one of George Washington's money-making schemes to increase trade between Virginia and the West. The Ohio Valley was the West in those days. Little more than twenty-five years after the prodigious labor that went into digging the ditch, by hand, and then transporting and then putting into place the great stones, the canal had become obsolete because by then the railroads were the primary means of commercial transportation. Staring at the stone ruins of a canal lock, Harry resisted the temptation to meditate on the transitory nature of power or the ephemeral triumphs of politics.

Following an initial flurry of phone calls after his resignation, mostly from media wanting him to bad-mouth the Guy—Harry had turned down all media requests—his phone had stopped ringing. He had expected to hear from his old law firm. Nothing.

He walked for an hour or so, turning and walking north again, back past the overlooks, in the direction of River Bend Park, which could be reached by a footpath through the trees lining the Potomac. He was—he remembered his father's words—"working up a good sweat." That's what he needed—a good sweat and tired muscles. These days he needed to tire himself if he was to get any sleep. His one scotch a day had turned into three and then five, and he knew he had to stop drinking and do something instead of just brood. So every day he came to Great Falls Park and walked and walked and walked.

When he finally reached River Bend Park—the river here was flat and gentle and, to Harry, boring—he turned and started back toward Great Falls Park. When he reached the parking lot he was about to unlock his car when his cell phone beeped.

"Mr. Gottlieb? This is Donna Lyons. I wonder if we could meet next week. I'd like to talk to you about a few things."

"Mrs. Lyons, I—"

"Don't worry, Mr. Gottlieb, I'm not going to ask you to disclose state se-crets. In fact, I want to offer you a job. I'd like you to consider joining Lion-Heart."

"Mrs. Lyons, I know nothing about foundations. I—"

"That's great. I've been thinking of having my daughter totally reorganize LionHeart, making it more efficient. She and I could benefit from the insights of someone who is looking at the foundation for the first time. At least come to see us at the foundation, and we can talk. Will you do that for me?"

"Yes, of course."

"Then it's done. I'll get back to you to set up a mutually agreeable time. Good-bye, Mr. Gottlieb."

"Good-bye, Mrs. Lyons."

It was just past noon. Today the September air was heavy with humidity, but inside the Galleria Mall at Tysons Corner, and especially in Gugliardi's, the air-conditioning was working full blast. Pete Dickinson had a luncheon appoint-ment with Jeb Hammerford, to work out some schedule of paying off his gambling debt. Pete thought it prudent to at least appear to be negotiating a payment schedule, and just maybe they could come up with an arrangement Pete could live with, although he doubted it. After the disastrous meeting with his father, Pete had despaired and begun to drink heavily. But now he was al-most his old self. Things would pick up. Yes, Che Che had left him. His Lexus was ruined beyond repair. He had only one client. He still owed thousands of dollars he did not have, and a homicidal maniac named Dean was threatening him. But aside from those things, he was on the road back, he could feel it.

He stood at the dark wood bar, drinking a cold Beck's and trying to ignore the Sinatra music being played on the restaurant's sound system. He sighed. That morning, in his home office—he had purchased a new iMac on the one credit card that was not maxed out, costly, but what the hell else was he going to do after Dean trashed the place?—he had tried to pound out a speech for the president of the Association of American Foundations, his sole remaining client. The AAF was dedicated to . . . dedicated to what? To informing the American people about foundations. But why? Who cared? And what difference did it make? He sipped the Beck's. Ah, the hell with it. I'll just have some fun with the speech. Suddenly he recalled the inspirational variations he wrote in order to warm up before he started writing a speech draft. Maybe he could sneak in one of those meaningless but noble-sounding lines ("Liberty is freedom and sacrifice . . . sacrifice is the liberty of the dream. . . .). He asked the bartender for a piece of paper and, taking out his pen, scribbled: *"The strength of the American people is the dream of destiny, and the spirit of freedom and sacrifice is the vision of liberty."*

He put the paper in his pants pocket. It was drivel, utterly without content, but it had that Vision Alert! Vision Alert! lilt to it. Let the members of the AAF figure out what it means.

He smiled, almost laughed, and felt instantly better. Not *good* exactly, but better, considering everything. Connie Erickson was back, after being away with Tim Flaherty for a few days in the islands. From what she had told Pete on the phone, Tim wasn't exactly a stud, and Connie would be happy to see Pete as she returned, tan, taut, terrific, and hungry for him. He looked into the mirror behind the bar. How many times in his life had he done that, sat at a bar and stared at his reflection, the way men do when they are getting thoroughly bombed?

He missed Che Che. He missed her every minute. To hell with it. Onward and upward. A speechwriter can always write another speech.

He sipped his Beck's. He *loved* Beck's. The goddamn Germans, say what you want about them, they knew beer. Somehow, in that instantaneous, associative way the brain works, *Germans* morphed into *Jews,* and Jews became personified in Harry Gottlieb. Harry, the object of ridicule in Washington and in fact all around the world, the chief of staff whose lack of management skills allowed a scandalously revolutionary passage to make its way into the Guy's speech text. Harry Gottlieb, the communications consultant to the president who had blundered into the biggest rhetoric fiasco in years, maybe ever. Harry

Gottlieb, who had blackmailed Pete into doing speeches for the Guy. And now Harry was out of a job. Good.

By this time, Pete had a pretty good guess as to what had happened. During Pete's visit to the union office, Tim had accidentally given Pete the pages containing the crazy rhetoric about imperialism. Then Murphy's Law came into play. The offending passage had accidentally gotten inserted into the backup material Pete had included, along with the speech draft, in the envelope sent to Harry. Harry had read the draft but never looked at the accompanying material. Somewhere along the line, Harry had handed his assistant the draft material but had not noticed that the crazy rhetoric was included. From reports in the press, the assistant had been too afraid or too work-challenged to ask Harry if the crazy stuff was part of the text. The Great White House Rhetoric and Hype Machine had broken down because of an improbable series of human errors, no single error of that much importance, but cumulatively a disaster. Pete slowly sipped his Beck's—he did not want to have more than one beer before Jeb arrived. He felt great, except for Sinatra mooning about that old black magic.

Dean, dressed in a suit and tie—he felt uncomfortable, but he needed protective coloration—walked slowly along the third level of the Galleria, pausing now and then to look down at Gugliardi's, on the level below. He had tailed Dickinson and now he had him where he wanted him.

"Hey, big fella!"

Pete looked around and there was Jeb, red-haired, plump, and looking good in a blue blazer. There were many words suitable to describe the young woman standing next to Jeb, but one of the words nudged and elbowed and pushed its way to the forefront of Pete's mind and would not leave: *Stunning. Abso-fucking-lutely stunning.*

She was tall and slender and looked like a model. No, wrong, *better* than a skinny zombie-like model. She had a voluptuous young woman's lush figure filling out the summer dress with its flower design of greens and yellows and pinks. She had beautiful skin, of a subtle, unnameable color—creamy golden brown was the best Peter could do. She had black-on-black hair, worn short, and dazzling, huge brown eyes. She looked, in fact, like Che Che, only younger. And the sensuality of her mouth reminded Pete, in a way, of the bored Paraguayan (or whatever she was) wife he had been banging months ago, the night he met Marlie Rae, someone he no longer thought about. There was something exotic about this girl, foreign, very sexy in a smoldering, quiet way. She was about nineteen, twenty at most, and entirely self-possessed, neither awed nor bored. Men at the bar were sneaking discreet glances at her. Damn, how did a fat guy like Jeb ever get a girl like that? *Money, stupid*.

"Pete," Jeb said, trying to be cool, trying to show that being with this girl was no big deal, "stop drooling. This is Mariena Gupta. Mariena, this is an old buddy of mine, personal friend of the president, Pete Dickinson."

"Hello, Pete," Mariena said, holding out her hand, looking him in the eye, "it's very nice to meet you." Her voice was one part warm honey, one part expensive scotch, and two parts some kind of mysterious spice, plus a jigger of the mysterious East, or was it the Caribbean, or India or . . . who cares?

"Well now, chillin," Jeb said, "why don't we all have a drink, and then we'll eat. How's that? And, Pete, I ain't talking business with a beautiful woman sitting next to me. You and me, we'll just eat here and go back to my office and we can talk. How's that?"

"Sounds great," Pete said, never taking his eyes from the most beautiful girl he had ever seen.

Marlie Rae, in uniform, was on the first level of the Galleria. Last night she had decided it was time to settle this once and for all. She had followed Pete's rented car (why was he renting?) to the Galleria and had seen him enter the restaurant about ten minutes ago. She hoped he would have his black girlfriend with him. She'd confront the both of them. No yelling or screaming. Just talk to him right in front of her, as though she wasn't there, tell Pete how much he had hurt her.

But dignified, like. She was all over the feelin'-sorry-for-myself blues. She just wanted to get this over with and get on with her life. As she took the moving stairway to the second floor, Marlie Rae could imagine Pete sitting there in that restaurant, being so damned *charming,* as he had been with her, with that black girl.

"Well, now," Jeb said after they were seated, "let me just wash my hands. I been out at a site this morning. I'll be back in a moment, dahlin'. Don't be fooled by this boy and his bogus Ivy League charm."

Jeb made his way to the men's room and Peter and Mariena were sitting there alone, staring into each other's eyes.

Dean walked into the restaurant door and scoped out the place. There was Dickinson, the son of a bitch, sitting there, smiling, talking to some damn black bitch. Dean started walking toward the booth and reached into the back of his waistband.

Peter felt *great.* Mariena was looking into his eyes. He had seen that look before, from so many women. He could feel that familiar, sweet sensation—something was going to happen. It's the greatest feeling in the world, that sense that everything is possible.

Marlie Rae walked in, immediately saw Peter, and—goddamn it, yes, there she was, the black woman, with him. And then, in a splinter of a second, Marlie Rae saw a man walking toward the booth, gun in his right hand by his side.

Peter paused in mid-sentence—he was starting to say to Mariena, "Isn't it strange? I love the outdoors, too, and I'd like to show you Great Falls one of these days," when he looked up and saw Dean walking toward him. *Dean?*

Dean had the gun pointed at Pete's head.

Marlie Rae had her weapon out, two-hand grip. She yelled, "Police!" and—
Crack. Crack. Crack. Crack. Four shots. Amid the screaming and shouting,
Frank Sinatra, his diction perfect, his heart in his voice, sang with world-weary
sadness about the lovely girl who said, *"Can't we be friends?"*

TWENTY-FOUR

"Let me welcome you all to the annual meeting of the Deli Lama Fan Club," Donna said to the men (in black tie) and women (in gowns) gathered around the long table in the dining room of LionWest. "This Saturday will be my father's eighty-seventh birthday. But we have chosen tonight to celebrate because he says that fair employment practice demands that no worker should have to work on the weekend. [Good-natured laughter.] My father promised he would say a few words when the birthday cake comes out, but—"

Abe Steinberg, seated next to Donna, dressed in his usual Kmart patriarch fashion, held up his hand. Donna didn't see it, so he grabbed her wrist and said in a surprisingly strong voice that could be heard at the far end of the table, "Donna, sit down, shut up so they can eat."

Donna, along with everyone else, burst into laughter and applauded. Abe sat there in silence, ancient, wrinkled, alien, as if he had come from another world, which, in a way, he had. And then, grunting, wheezing, he began to get to his feet. Donna tried to help him, but he waved her off. Finally he was standing, his hands on the table, supporting him. He looked at the guests.

"I don't know most of you people," Abe said. "Hollywood progressives. You all think you're progressives. You know what you really are? You're *liberals*."

The contempt born of years of party discipline permeated the three syllables.

Abe looked down and was silent for moment. Then: "Anyhow"—he gestured with his hand, a wavering, ineffectual gesture of someone trying to fend off a fly—"you think you fight for the workers. But you don't. The only thing that matters is doing what is historically necessary."

Suddenly he turned to Marvin and said, "Al Gunn's son." Abe reached over and put his hand on Marvin's head, patting it. "I'm glad to see you. Your father was a great man. Everybody—enjoy."

Abe put forth his skinny arms in front of him, as if in blessing. Tears of joy came to Donna's eyes. She nodded her head, and the waiters began to serve. Donna had decided on an old-fashioned politically incorrect deli menu: pastrami and corned beef and brisket and reuben sandwiches, salads of all kinds, coleslaw, potato chips, big Jewish pickles, cream soda, seltzer water, and of course, bagels, lox, cream cheese, good hard-crusted rye bread, and slabs of butter. She had the food—and six countermen to serve it—flown in from Zelmann's Deli in New York. ("We're just off Broadway, but our food is close to Heaven.")

As the guests munched their way through the death-by-fat-ingestion sandwiches, dripping with dressing, heavy with slaw, Che Che tried to talk with Marvin across the table, but it was difficult to break into the long conversation he was having with Abe. She had already noted Marvin, not much of a drinker, belting back the bourbons like a barroom regular, probably trying to get the courage to speak to the Deli Lama.

Donna signaled to one of the waiters, and then stood.

"I want to ask you now to rise and join me in singing a well-known tune for our birthday boy."

The string quartet broke into "Happy Birthday," everyone sang, and a four-tiered white-frosting cake was wheeled in. Abe sat silently, staring into space, apparently unaware of the fuss being made of him. A waiter gave him a big knife with which to cut the cake, but Abe placed it on the table. He held up his hand—that old imperious gesture—for silence. Everyone sat. Two LionClaw guards helped Abe get to his feet. Abe was about to speak, but his voice broke and he began to sniffle and then cry, sobbing and almost falling as the guards rushed in to help him. Abe held his face in his hands. There was not another sound in the big room except that of Abe Steinberg sobbing.

An hour later Donna, Che Che, and Marvin sat in Abe's bedroom as the old man lay propped up on three pillows. Near the doorway there was a cart laden with numerous selections from the deli food, in case Abe, in his old man's way, wanted a nibble of this, a nibble of that. The guests had gone to their cabins. The Lion-Claw guards, including Sammy, had been dismissed for the night. On Abe's bedside was his framed picture of Lazar Kaganovich, his copy of *What Is to Be Done?*, and the Lenin-head letter opener. In the far corner of the room, where he could see it from his bed, was the high pedestal and the enormous bronze bust of Al Gunn. Abe's eyes were closed. He hadn't said a word since they wheeled him into the room, still sobbing, from the party. Donna said quietly, to no one in particular, "I was wrong. It was too much for him. I should have known."

Che Che didn't respond. Marvin was, Che Che could see, quite drunk. For a while they sat there in silence, deflated by the bad end to the birthday party.

"Abe?" Marvin said abruptly. "Abe, I have something for you."

Donna said in a whisper, "Marvin, that's very sweet, a present. But maybe it's better to let him sleep."

"No, he'll like this," Marvin said happily, stroking his goatee.

"What do you have for him, Marvin?" Che Che said in the patient tone of someone trying to appease a drunk.

"Oh, nothing much. Abe, you awake?"

This time Marvin's voice was louder. Abe awoke suddenly, wide-eyed and temporarily disoriented.

"Marvin, damn it, you woke him up, and I asked you not to," Donna said, clearly annoyed.

"Shut up, Donna," Marvin said quietly but firmly, his eyes not leaving Abe's face. The words sounded harsh and alien in the quiet room, especially coming from the nerd-in-chief. Marvin got up from his chair, stumbled, and then stood in front of Abe, looking down at him.

"Abe, you know who I am?"

Abe looked up. In a tired old-man's voice he wheezed. "Yeah. Al's kid." Abe feebly pointed to the bust. "A great man, your father. I got his bust here, so I can see him."

"That's right. He was a great man," Marvin said. "And a good father. Now. Tell me one more thing. What's your name?"

Donna said, "Marvin, I think you've had too much to drink. What are you—"

"I told you to shut up, Donna," Marvin said quietly. And then he said to Abe again, "What's your name?"

"My name? Abe. What else should it be?"

"No, no, I mean your other name."

"What are you talking about?" Donna said. "He has no other name."

"No? What about your party names, Abe?" Marvin said. "Che Che told me you had names the party gave you."

"Oh, *those* names. Yeah, back then, we had lots of names," Abe said, smiling. "Lots of names. Back in the old days."

"Tell me some of them."

"Oh, hell, kid, I forget."

"What about Joseph Rogers?"

Abe stopped grinning. The look in his eyes changed. The endearing old turtle had gone. What was in his eyes now was the dead stare of a shark, a million years old, implacable, pitiless, terrible.

"Who told you that? Nobody's supposed to know that," the shark said.

"Che Che told me, weeks ago. See, you told her one day about Joseph Rogers, when she was interviewing you for the book. You slipped, Abe. All these years you never said a word about Joseph Rogers. But you slipped. You told Che Che, and she told me, not knowing what it meant. I've been looking into my father's case all these decades. And every now and then I came across a name. Joseph Rogers. I knew who the rest of the party cell members were, I knew their party names. But I could never figure out who Joseph Rogers was.

And now I know why. You were Joseph Rogers, Abe. But Joseph Rogers wasn't your party name. It was your FBI informant name. You framed my father for the FBI."

Marvin grabbed the Lenin letter opener from the bedside table and held the tip of it against the old man's throat.

"Marvin, my God!" Donna screamed, and jumped up from her chair.

"Marvin, what the hell are you doing?" Che Che said, standing and taking a step toward Marvin.

"Don't move, either one of you," Marvin said quickly and quietly. "If you come near me or scream, I'll stab him before the guards can get here. And I'll kill you."

"Marvin, you're drunk—"

"Yeah, Donna, I'm drunk. Lovable old Marvin, never harmed a fly, dead drunk, and threatening murder. Who would have thought? Abe and I have a lot to talk about. Or should I say Mr. Rogers? You worked for the FBI, didn't you Mr. Rogers?"

"You're crazy."

"No, Abe, don't lie. You were Joseph Rogers. Admit it. It all fits now. You were the one who helped frame my father."

"Marvin, you know that's not true, you've had too much to drink, you're tired," Donna said in a calm, soothing tone, trying to keep her voice down, trying not to anger him. "You know my father—"

"Al Gunn was your best friend," Marvin said to Abe, ignoring Donna. "And you framed him."

"It's a lie," Abe said, now looking at Marvin and the letter opener out of the corner of his eye. "I never ever—"

"Oh, yes, you did, Abe," Marvin said, putting the tip of the letter opener on Abe's cheekbone, just below his left eye. "Everything fits. Joseph Rogers told the FBI my father was a spy in those defense plants out on the island. But everything you said to the FBI was a lie. My father was never a spy. He was a party hack who did what he was told. You sent my father to prison, where he died.

And you broke my mother's heart. And she killed herself. And I was left alone."

"Marvin," Donna said, "this can't be true. You know that. My father loved your father."

"This is between Abe and me. Abe, why did you do it? Just tell me that. Why did you lie about my father? Why did you——"

Abe tried to sit up, but he was too weak. The old shark lay there, his million-year-old wizened, hollow-cheeked head on the pillows, with wisps of white hair framing his face. With an obvious effort he said, in a controlled, scornful voice, "All this is bullshit. Donna, get him out of here. He's *messhugenah*."

"No, Abe, it's all over," Marvin said. "Tell the truth before you die."

"The truth?" Abe said. The tone of his voice had changed. It was lighter, almost playful. He looked at Donna. "The *truth*, you want now? I'll give you truth."

He turned his evil shark's head toward Marvin. His eyes were bright, not with fear but with contempt and rage.

"The truth? *I framed your father*. I lied about him. I faked evidence. I forged papers. I planted the fucking blueprints in your house. Do you want to know why? I'll tell you why——*it had to be done!* The goddamn FBI was this close to the real spy, and the party couldn't afford to lose him. Some GRU agent. They never told me who. So I was ordered to find a patsy, some poor bastard we could afford to lose, make it look like he was the spy. *And I did it*. I framed your father. And do you know why? Because the party wanted it, that's why! The party is right because it has a scientific understanding of history. I'd do it again. One man means nothing."

"He was your closest friend."

"I had no fucking friends. I had the party. The party told me to do something, I did it. It was hard. It tore my heart out. It broke up my marriage because my wife knew. She hated me for what I did. She left me and she never talked to me again, all those years. You think that didn't hurt me? That's right, Donna——it wasn't McCarthy who caused me and your mother to split. It was me. Your mother just could not say B. But I could. The party got what it needed. That's it. Everything else is bullshit. You think I'm ashamed of what I done? Bullshit. I'd do it again, I'd—"

"Shut up, Abe," Marvin said, and put the edge of the letter opener against Abe's scrawny neck. "When I found out the truth from Che Che, I went crazy. I finally knew. And do you know what I did? I planted a bomb at the foundation. Then I tried to kill Che Che with a bomb, to hurt you the way I was hurt. I didn't want to kill *you* yet. I wanted you to live to see Che Che die. I tried to blow up Che Che at her house, but Donna got it instead."

"Marvin, you? *You?*" Donna said. "But how could you—"

"When I was in Cuba," Marvin said. "I wasn't cutting sugarcane. They put me in a special school, run by the Russians and the East Germans. I was trained how to sabotage, how to infiltrate, how to kill, how to make bombs. The plan was to attack the Cuban counterrevolutionaries in Miami, wage war against them, in their homes. When I came back and went to Miami after the trial, I waited for the signal to start. But nothing ever happened. Typical Fidel. So eventually I went back to New York. But I never forgot what I learned. I placed the bomb at the LionHeart Foundation, just to give the cops something to think about. But the one I wanted to hurt most of all, Abe, was you. But not by a bomb. I was going to kill Che Che and then tell you about it. If you said anything to the police, who'd believe you? Abe must be getting old, they'd say, his mind is going. I wanted you to wait for death, Abe, and think about your granddaughter being blown up because of what you did. I wanted you to suffer, like my father had to suffer, at night in Lewisburg, wondering who it was who framed him. But guess what, Abe? I'm not going to kill you unless I have to. You know what I'm going to do?"

Marvin reached into his pocket and pulled out a mini tape recorder. He hit the STOP button.

"I have it all down on tape, Abe. Your confession. Every word you just said. I'm sending copies—edited, of course, so I'm not implicated in the bombings, to every newspaper, every TV news show, every Cold War historian in the country. And I'll go on television myself and tell the truth. From now on, you won't be Abe the great Deli Lama. You'll be Abe the traitor, the rat fink, the man who sold out his best friend. I know, the Cold War is over. Most people don't give a shit anymore. But I do. And you do, Abe. And Che Che does, with her book making you a hero, and Donna thinks you're a great man. They can live the rest of their lives ashamed of you. They—"

With an effort, Abe spat in Marvin's face.

As Marvin flinched reflexively, Donna jumped up from her chair and threw herself at him, knocking him away from the bed. Donna turned and threw herself on top of her father. As Che Che rushed to her mother's aid, Marvin slashed at her with the letter opener but missed. Che Che evaded another slash by stepping backward and doing a side step. She launched a kick to Marvin's midsection but missed as he swerved. Marvin wheeled toward the bed and began to bring the letter opener down on Donna's back. Che Che landed a quick roundhouse kick to his side, knocking him against the cart with the deli food, sending pastrami and reuben sandwiches and salads and bottles and glasses and ice cubes flying all over the floor.

Marvin was off balance now, and Che Che tried to hit him with an elbow strike to the face but missed by an inch. She instantly got back in the stance as Marvin, grunting, took a swing at her with the letter opener. Instinct told Che Che to back away, but Sammy's training told her to come in toward Marvin, to get within the arc of the downward swing of the weapon. She rushed in, surprising him, grabbed his arm, twisted it, and kneed him in the groin. He groaned, dropped the letter opener, and wriggled out of her grasp.

Marvin started to run toward the door and almost reached it. But then he slipped on a juicy pastrami sandwich. His feet went up in the air and, like a runner sliding into a base, he hit the bottom of the great pedestal holding Al Gunn's bronze head. As Marvin lay flat on his back, the bust of his father, toppled by his slide, fell and hit Marvin squarely in the temple. He lay motionless on the floor.

Che Che rushed to his body and felt for a pulse.

"I think he's dead."

"Oh, my God," Donna said. "Call the guards. Call Sammy. Call—"

"No! We're not calling anyone yet. Just check on Grampa."

Che Che picked up the letter opener, wiped it off, and put it on the bedside table.

"Grampa's all right," Donna said.

"Good. I'll destroy the tape and get rid of the recorder. Then we'll call Sammy and have him call the police. Here's the story. There's been a terrible accident. Marvin was drunk. Blood tests will prove that. He became abusive to you and to me and to Grampa, saying we didn't pay enough attention to his work at the foundation and his grant wasn't enough. Unused to drinking, he went into a drunken rage and knocked over the food cart. We told him we'd call the guards. He panicked and started running toward the door. He slipped on some food and the bust fell on his head. It's almost all true."

Che Che walked over to her mother and embraced her.

"Just do as I say, Mom," Che Che said. "And don't worry about anything. Ever."

"We'll have to talk to the police."

"Just tell the truth. Or most of the truth. We'll get through this together. You've been taking care of me all my life. From now on, I'll take care of you and Grampa."

Daily News headline, two days later:

ACTIVIST DIES IN FREAK ACCIDENT

From her ranch in Montana, Ms. Che Che Hart, daughter of Mrs. Lyons and an associate of Mr. Gunn, issued a statement: "We are all deeply saddened by this tragic accident. My mother and I will always have a special place in our hearts for Marvin Gunn."

TWENTY-FIVE

January

President Tyler Ferguson stood at the rostrum on the floor of the House of Representatives as Congress, the Supreme Court, cabinet members, the diplomatic corps, distinguished visitors, and just plain folks in the gallery remained standing, cheering and applauding heartily as the Guy prepared to deliver the State of the Union address. The applause dwindled, everyone took a seat, and Speaker of the House Morris "Don't Ever Call Me Moe" Lansdale, seated behind the president, stood and said in his grating Down East accent, "It is a high honor and a distinct personal privilege for me to introduce to you the president of the United States."

According to the ritual, everyone stood again. Everyone applauded again. Those inclined to cheer—mostly Democrats—cheered again. Ty the Guy, back on top, way up in the polls, a cinch for reelection in November according to those who say they know such things, nodded, smiled, nodded again, touched his tie, waved, looked up at the gallery to his left, and waved to his wife, Coleen, (looking so pretty in her new green dress), who was sitting amid those waiting to be asked by Ty the Guy to stand and be recognized. He held out both hands, palms down, a sign that the cheering should stop, but made certain he did so with a lack of enthusiasm sufficient enough not to be taken seriously. Gradually the applause ended. Everyone took a seat. There was a low hubbub for a few moments and then near silence. Ty, reading from a speech draft written by one of his writers (he had reluctantly concluded that *someone* had to write the damned things), said a few words of greeting and then: "I am here to tell you tonight that the state of the union is firm, it is strong, and it is healthy. We are strong at home, and strong in the world. But what matters most is that this country is also good at home, and a force for good in the world and a link to goodness and greatness for generations to come."

Ritual standing, cheering, hubbub. Ritual seating.

"And where is this source of goodness? It is in the American people. John Adams once said that the Constitution is a product of 'good minds prompted by good hearts.' Those good minds, those good hearts, still inspire our actions, dictate our policies, and act as our moral guide." [Cheers, shouts, applause, Democrats stand, then Republicans.]

After a few words about good news on the economy, he got to the part of the speech he had looked forward to.

"And who are these people of good minds and good hearts? Some of them are with us tonight, from every corner of this great country. Let me introduce some of them. Seated up there, in the gallery, is a symbol of America. I refer to Mrs. Olive Whestle, Great-Grandmother of the Year. As we all know, Mrs. Whestle, although she is eighty-eight years young, ran in a ten-K race last month and then drove home on her motorcycle—wearing her helmet, you bet!—to bake a chocolate cake for the church picnic. Chocolate cake! That's America. That's the dream. And furthermore . . ."

In the House gallery, Donna, wearing a new blue dress, politely stifled a yawn as the Guy rambled on. Che Che, seated next to her, looked stunning in her red dress. Che Che now controlled all LionCo and LionHeart enterprises. With cool pragmatism ("Mom, I'm not fighting your Old Left fights anymore!") she had moved to mend fences with the Guy. Che Che was in fact now among the president's most prominent supporters and fund-raisers, and would be introduced by the Guy sometime during the State of the Union speech. Donna, reluctantly, had agreed to accompany Che Che to the speech.

"We'll be the Guy's props, you know, trophies in his trophy case," she had told Che Che.

"Oh Mom, bend a little. The Guy is going to win in November. Everybody knows that. The economy is booming, he settled the Peruvian crisis—my God, he'll probably be nominated for a Nobel peace prize. He got a lot of sympathy from the London speech fiasco, his numbers are way up, and the Republicans have nobody. I don't want him for an enemy."

So here was Donna, trapped, uncomfortable, bored, hearing but not exactly listening to the Guy tell of that quintessential little old American lady, Mrs. Whestle. Suddenly Donna smiled. She was thinking of Harry Gottlieb, who was watching the address on television back at their hotel suite. Given his non-relationship with the Guy, it would not have been wise for Harry to be in the gallery tonight. Donna and Harry had fallen in love as he helped her prepare the transition to the Age of Che Che in LionCo and LionHeart. She loved him more than she had ever loved any man, and she couldn't wait to get back to the hotel to see him, take off her shoes, have a drink, and just talk. *Give me the simple life.*

". . . and that's the American dream, my fellow Americans," the Guy was saying, "blueberry pie. Stand up, Mrs. Whestle! There she is, still wearing her bike safety helmet! Someone, help Mrs. Whestle wave. Lift her arm. Wave her arm. There you go. Wave, Mrs. Whestle. You remind me of my Gumma."

Shutting out whatever it was the Guy was babbling about, Donna let her mind wander and eventually she found herself thinking of Abe. After that night of horror with Marvin, Abe had rarely spoken to Donna, or to anyone. Oh, a word here, a word there, but not the snapping, often brutal words of the fierce, ancient shark. He spoke like an old, old man, and toward the end he couldn't eat. His body could not absorb even liquid nourishment through a tube, and in effect he starved to death. He said nothing at all in his last few days. Only his eyes were alive, and they said nothing. Donna had never discussed the events of that night with him. There were things Marvin had said and Abe had said that she did not want to know or talk about or ever think about. But Abe's loss—the fact that she would never see him again, never again hear that irritated, exasperated voice, never again see the shrewd look in his eyes—broke her heart. Now he was gone, never to return, or as Shakespeare had put it in *Lear,* in the most devastatingly heartbreaking line in the English language, one simple word repeated five times:

Never, never, never, never, never.

Abe's death had crushed her spirit for a time and she had spent many hours on the phone with her therapists, but they didn't help, so she fired them. The only one who helped was Harry Gottlieb, his thoughtfulness, his patience, and his love.

". . . and Mr. Fred Pfaltz, although unable to swim himself because, being diet-challenged, he weighs over three hundred and seventy pounds—not his fault, not his fault—jumped into that raging torrent and saved the pony he had purchased for his little son, Peckham 'Booby' Pfaltz. And there's little Booby sitting next to his dad. Wave, Booby, wave."

Watching the Guy from the first row of seats on the right was, among other cabinet members, Secretary of Labor Timothy Flaherty. Tim's appointment, following the sudden death (heart attack) of Secretary Susan Rossen Coombs, had surprised many and shocked a few. But the Guy needed someone he could trust, and Tim could not turn down the president when he personally asked him to take the job. The Senate confirmation hearings, all things considered, had been not all that bad. There were predictable attacks from Republican haters, but they had no proof of their charges, and Tim, with the help of consultants and handlers, practically breezed through. The UWCE continued to prosper as more and more Americans came out of the (utility?) closet and admitted they were work-challenged. Tim had already set up an interagency task force to investigate ways in which work-challenged men and women could be integrated into every level of American life, including medicine, education, the military, and professional sports. The American Catholic Bishops, working with Tim and Father Frankie and Mary Bunky, had instructed the faithful to avoid the grave sin of discrimination against the work-challenged and had is-sued an apology to all work-challenged Americans for the history of discrimi-nation in which the Church had played a part. There was a TV docudrama in the works about the plight of work-challenged airline pilots. In his personal life, Tim had discovered male-enhancement pills and had a new mistress. He never heard from Connie, or from Margaret Mary, who had divorced him. He enjoyed being Secretary of Labor, a symbol of the American worker, a man who had done well by doing good. In his office at the Department of Labor he had the triptych of the secular saints of liberalism. Every day he himself re-placed the rose in the (new) crystal vase.

". . . and do you want to know what makes America great? I'll tell you. It's people like the Knibble sisters, all six of them, Garalee, Tommy Mae, Pinella, known as 'Pincher,' Agnes Rose, Parmalee, and lil' Bitsy Boo, cute as a button. They are from Moseville, Alabama. They rescued their mother, Mrs. Havalette Knibble, from a well into which she had fallen while slopping the hogs. Mrs. Knibble, my father knew what it was to be in the dark and the cold. He knew from firsthand experience in the mines. Your brave girls formed a human chain by holding on to each other's legs. Bitsy Boo Knibble, the youngest, held out her hands to you and said, 'Hold on, Mama, we're pulling you up.' That's America. That's the dream. Stand up, girls! There they are, wearing the same overalls they wore on that historic day."

Che Che was as happy as she had ever been, holding the hand of the man she loved. She smiled at him and he winked, and she felt him squeeze her hand, the darling. He had been working with her, side by side, as she had reorganized Li-onHeart, cut the staff, hired liberal and even a few conservative scholars, gave the old lefties generous separation bonuses, stopped the Irish Guilt and Reparations

Project. She was, bit by bit, turning LionHeart into a model of efficiency and relevance, complete with an award-winning Web site, and she had him by her side.

"And the American Dream lives on in our capacity to help the needy," the Guy was saying. "No one had better demonstrated that gift than another great young American with us tonight. I refer to Ernestina Hart—Che Che, to her friends and fans—and I am both, a-ha, a-ha. Ms. Hart is a leader in the fight against hunger, poverty, and injustice in our nation and in Peru. She is the daughter of a longtime, dear friend of Coleen's and mine, Donna Hart Lyons, seated next to her. Che Che and Donna are now in the process of creating the John Gunderson Institute for the Differently Abled. Now it so happens that Mr. John Gunderson, who has severe learning and developmental problems, and his mother, Mrs. Lorna Gunderson, are seated with Che Che and Donna and I'm going to ask them all to stand so we can see what compassion looks like. Come on, stand up and let folks see you, so we can tell you what we think of you."

Donna, Che Che, Johnnie, and Lorna stood and the ritual applause and standing ovation began.

"And now I come to a special part of tonight's address," the Guy said. "To-night, sitting next to my wonderful wife, Coleen, is Officer Marlie Rae Perkins of the Fairfax County, Virginia, Police Department, right across the Potomac, a great American river. Officer Perkins showed courage above and beyond the call of duty last September when she risked her life and saved the life of many, many others, in shooting a deranged, armed drug dealer in a crowded restau-rant. Officer Perkins just happened to be in the restaurant when the crazed drug dealer opened fire on innocent customers."

Donna looked at Marlie Rae Perkins, who was in uniform, looking quite the hero. Such a *big* girl. Donna's restless mind hop-skip-and-jumped and landed on that line from *Lear* she had just been thinking of. *Shakespeare*. Maybe it's time for me to go back to the stage. And why not Shakespeare? Lady Macbeth, maybe. Now *that* I *could* pull off. How the critics would laugh—perfect casting, they'd say. It would be such fun. Yes, that's it, I'll go back to the theater. I've already said B too many times. Maybe it's time to say C. It was strange, she thought, how things had turned out. During the past year she had been publicly humiliated, blown up, blackmailed, had a major fight with her daughter, had to back out of becoming a presidential candidate, and watched Marvin almost kill her father, who was not the man she thought he was. The Che School proved to be a fiasco and was now closed. *And, oh yes, my Klee was destroyed by a barbarian. But I'm still here.* Suddenly, a line from Frank's incomparable version of "I've Got You Under My Skin" floated into her mind:

I would sacrifice anything, come what might . . .

If you never did that, if you spent your life never willing to sacrifice anything, come what might, you weren't alive. But she was still alive, and she was going back to the stage, her first love. Oh, I'll keep my hand in politics. I'll racially integrate Montana, little programs like that. But Che Che can handle taking care of the world. From now on, I'm just going to take care of myself—and Harry.

"Let me make a personal comment," the Guy said. "One of the victims of that deranged killer was a former aide of mine, the late Peter Holmes Dickinson. Petey—I always called him Petey—assisted me in many ways, until he decided to help others in his own business. Unfortunately, Petey died from his wounds. But his spirit will continue to live on."

The Guy paused. It was good pause, almost as good as a Donna pause. Then he slowly removed from his inside jacket pocket a sheet of paper.

"I hold in my hand a scrap of paper, found in Petey's pocket at the time of his death. On this paper he wrote his last words. Let me read them to you. These words show his lifelong love of America. Here is what he wrote: 'The strength of the American people is the dream of destiny, and the spirit of freedom and sacrifice is the vision of liberty.'"

The chamber was silent. The Guy folded the paper, put it back in his pocket, and said, "In the spring, when the Rose Garden blooms, I will ask Sergeant

Perkins to join me in a ceremony honoring Petey. We will place his ashes in a corner of that garden, with a simple plaque bearing the last, great, patriotic words he wrote, and his name. Those words will forever be linked with his memory. That section of the Rose Garden will be called, forever more, the Peter Holmes Dickinson Rose Garden Nature Memorial. The dream of destiny and the spirit of freedom. Aren't Petey's words what America is all about?"

As the applause began and people began to stand, Che Che didn't know what to do. If she stood and applauded with the rest of audience, she'd be a hypocrite; if she sat stone-faced, she'd be conspicuous. But the media would notice her refusal to stand, and reporters might question her after the speech. Those questions would take attention from the Guy on his big night, angering him. And she didn't want to get on the wrong side of the Guy. Not yet, at least.

Oh, well, maybe Mom is right—sometimes you have to do what you don't want to do. My God, I'm beginning to think *like her.*

Che Che smiled as she took Sammy Yuan's hand in hers. As they both stood, she took her mother's hand also. The three of them stood together, holding hands, as the distinguished assemblage cheered and cheered and cheered the last words of a speechwright, Peter Holmes Dickinson.

AUTHOR'S NOTE

For the sections dealing with Che Che's kickboxing, I am indebted to *Kickboxing for Women*, by Debz Buller and Jennifer Lawler. *Antique Furniture*, by John Andrews, helped me furnish Donna's hideaway in a manner befitting her big bucks and eclectic tastes. Special thanks to my cousins, and Dr. B. J. Beute (my godson) and his brother Chris Beute, for their help on matters dealing with medical science and computer science. And many thanks to Tom Verdon, Jersey City fire captain, friend, and relative through marriage, for his help. So far as I am aware, there was never a police vs. radical student shoot-out in Baltimore.